XKARNATION

REBORN AS A DEMONIC TREE
BOOK 4

aethonbooks.com

REBORN AS A DEMONIC TREE 4
©2024 XKARNATION

This book is protected under the copyright laws of the United States of America. No part of this publication may be reproduced, stored in a retrieval system, or transmitted, in any form or by any means, without the prior permission in writing of the publisher, nor be otherwise circulated in any form of binding or cover other than that in which it is published and without a similar condition including this condition being imposed on the subsequent purchaser. Any reproduction or unauthorized use of the material or artwork contained herein is prohibited without the express written permission of the authors.

Aethon Books supports the right to free expression and the value of copyright. The purpose of copyright is to encourage writers and artists to produce the creative works that enrich our culture.

The scanning, uploading, and distribution of this book without permission is a theft of the author's intellectual property. If you would like to use material from the book (other than for review purposes), please contact editor@aethonbooks.com. Thank you for your support of the author's rights.

Aethon Books
www.aethonbooks.com

Print and eBook formatting and design by Josh Hayes.

Published by Aethon Books LLC.

Aethon Books is not responsible for websites (or their content) that are not owned by the publisher.

This book is a work of fiction. Names, characters, places, and incidents are the product of the author's imagination or are used fictitiously. Any resemblance to actual events, locales, or persons, living or dead is coincidental.

All rights reserved.

ALSO IN SERIES

Reborn as a Demonic Tree
Reborn as a Demonic Tree 2
Reborn as a Demonic Tree 3
Reborn as a Demonic Tree 4
Reborn as a Demonic Tree 5

Check out the series here! *(tap or scan)*

1
ETHEREAL ROOTS

Ashlock had never been a morning person. Even when he had been a human back on Earth, the morning sunlight filled him with more dread and sleepiness. Rather than waking up to the constant chirping of birds, he would roll over, bury his head deeper in his pillow, and pray for a few more minutes of rest.

Ever since becoming a demonic tree, his slothful nature had only worsened. It was partially the fault of his personality that had followed him through death to this new world, but it was also due to his new biology.

Time passed at a different rate to him, and even with the marvels of Qi, he was still a giant tree with a body that spanned a thousand miles in every direction and spread throughout the eight-thousand-meter-tall mountain he called home.

Whatever the reasons and excuses, the point was he sucked at mornings, and the only thing worse than the mornings was a very eventful one that was sprung upon Ashlock before he could even bathe in the sunlight for a while.

He had a headache, and it was not because of Dante Voidmind blowing himself up supernova-style inside his soul.

[Warning: Foreign Qi Detected]
[High Risk of Soul Corruption]

Ashlock looked at the messages he had seen before and, unlike last time, didn't feel a hint of panic. Soul corruption used to terrify him, but with his latest S-grade skill, {Nocturnal Genesis}, which slowly healed soul damage, such a risk didn't bother him.

[Generating solutions…]
[Convert foreign Qi into spatial Qi]
[Merge void Qi with a system skill to upgrade it]
[Dispel void Qi into the nearby atmosphere]

Just like last time, he was given a list of options.

"If only I was immune to all types of Qi and not just void Qi." Ashlock sighed as he picked the second option. "Having someone go supernova inside my soul would undoubtedly kill me, but wouldn't it be cool if I could merge my skills with other affinities?"

The system messages drifted away, and his all-too-familiar status screen appeared.

[Demonic Demi-Divine Tree (Age: 9)]
[Star Core: 9th Stage]
[Soul Type: Amethyst (Spatial)]
[Mutations…]
{Demonic Eye [B]}
{Blood Sap [C]}
[Summons…]
{Ashen King: Larry [A]}
{Midnight Ink Lindwyrm: Kaida [B]}
[Skills…]
{Skyborne Bastion [SSS]}
{Necroflora Sovereign [SS]}
{Mystic Realm [S] [Locked until day: 3626]
{Progeny Dominion [S]}
{Dimensional Overlap [S]}
{Nocturnal Genesis [S]}
{Eye of the Tree God [A]}
{Abyssal Whispers [A]}
{Deep Roots [A]}
{Magic Mushroom Production [A]}

{Lightning Qi Barrier [A]}
{Qi Fruit Production [A]}
{Consuming Abyss [B]}
{Blooming Root Flower Production [B]}
{Language of the World [B]}
{Fire Qi Protection [B]}
{Transpiration of Heaven and Chaos [B]}
{Superior Poison Resistance [C]}

"Compared to last time, I have so many more options to choose from," Ashlock lamented. It was too early in the morning to make such an important decision, and he was also pressed for time.

Beyond his trunk were literally thousands of people and monsters that had emerged from the Mystic Realm, awaiting his direction, and he also wanted to see how they had progressed.

[Select the skill you wish to merge with the void Qi]

As if sensing his wandering attention, the system reminded him to choose. The void Qi could harm him if left unused and floating around his soul.

"Let's think this through. Assuming it works the same as last time, whatever skill I choose will go up a grade and be changed due to the addition of the void element. {Devour [C]} became {Consuming Abyss [B]}, and without it, I would likely be dead by now. The void tendrils have been invaluable for disposing of stronger opponents that got past or defeated my allies."

So, ideally, he would pick one of his attack skills to upgrade...

"I don't have any attack skills other than {Consuming Abyss}." Ashlock scanned down the list. "And other than {Skyborne Bastion [SSS]} or perhaps {Dimension Overlap [S]}, which are sort of attack skills but not really."

The more he thought about it, the more he realized these two would be interesting options. {Skyborne Bastion} because it was an SSS-grade skill, and he was curious if there was a grade higher than the SSS grade. Whereas if he upgraded {Dimension Overlap}, he might gain access to the void where Maple's siblings live.

But these two skills already had a big issue. They were expensive.

Sacrificial credits were getting harder to come by, and as Ashlock progressed, more skills relied on SC to function.

"Skyborne Bastion is one of my strongest skills right now, but the thousand credit cost is already far too steep. If I upgraded it now and the cost jumped up to create void bastions, I would never be able to afford it. Dimension Overlap is the same. Even if it unlocked a feature where I could go and visit Maple's siblings, I bet it won't be cheap."

Ashlock didn't dismiss these skills, but he hunted for something better.

"Mhm, I don't see how my production skills could benefit from the void element much. My protection and resistance skills would greatly help me, but they feel like a waste. If I need to use those skills in a fight, it means all else failed, and I am in great danger. So I would rather pick a skill that lets me avoid that."

Ashlock then noticed {Transpiration of Heaven and Chaos [B]}. "There isn't much point in upgrading my cultivation technique as I believe it was listed as one of the system rewards for reaching Nascent Soul Realm, right?"

[Rewards upon formation of the Inner World:
You will ascend to the Nascent Soul Realm.
The System will be upgraded with new features.
{Transpiration of Heaven and Chaos [B]} will be upgraded.
Your attacks will carry the weight of your Inner World behind them, and your rate of cultivation will increase the more you develop your Inner World.]

"Oh yeah, there it is. Of course, there could be an argument for upgrading it to an A grade with void affinity and then upgrading again to an S once I reached Nascent Soul Realm, but I want to pick something that will help me both now and in the future." Ashlock dismissed it. He had no idea how long it would take him to gather those ten thousand credits and different star cores to reach the next realm, and in that time, a better cultivation technique wouldn't help as it wouldn't advance him past the bottleneck.

Progeny Dominion, Nocturnal Genesis, and Abyssal Whispers were also ticked off his list as he didn't want the void affinity affecting his connection to his offspring, warping the dreamscape before he figured out the purpose of those moons, or buffing his telepathy skill to the point it obliterated any mind he used it on.

"So what does that leave me with?" Ashlock mulled over the list, and then a skill that he used every day in the background that was in desperate need of an upgrade caught his eye. "{Deep Roots [A]}, now that is an old skill. It constantly empowers my roots with Qi, allowing them to burrow deeper and grow far faster than a normal tree. The distance I can cover that would take another tree years takes me a few days due to this A-grade skill. I can also hollow out my roots to turn them into tunnels, which Stella used to travel through the mountain before we both got better at using portals."

It sounded like a simple skill, but its importance in his life should not be underestimated. Spreading his roots was integral to expanding his power and influence upon the realm. Anywhere within Ashlock's roots was his domain. He could flood areas with Qi and open portals to transport people across vast distances. Connect with faraway forests and hunt monsters and people before they get closer. Not to mention, his Bastions moved faster over land under his control.

All of this happened because of his roots.

His agency depended on the spreading of his roots. The further he reached, the more powerful and safer he was. In a way, his roots were his ultimate attack skill, as they enabled everything else.

"I can also see how void affinity would greatly empower my roots. Maybe I can burrow deep enough to latch onto that ley line that causes the beast tides to follow set paths," Ashlock mused. He had not forgotten about the ley lines. They were basically the Qi arteries of the realm, and the area along them had higher concentrations of Qi, which caused sects to be built upon them, but it also attracted the monsters.

[Choose system skill: {Deep Roots [A]}?]

Ashlock was a little hesitant. He was spoiled for choice, and there had been so many good options. No matter what he picked, there would be some regret, but overall, he felt this was the best choice for his current objectives.

"There could always be a next time if I get my hands on some of the Voidmind family and force them to go supernova inside my soul."

Mentally accepting the system prompt, he watched as the skill vanished from his list, and information began to flood his mind as something took its place.

[Skill upgrading...1%]
[Skill upgrading...27%]
[Skill upgrading...53%]

A short while passed, and as the information settled in his mind, he knew he had made a good choice.

[Skill upgrading...100%]
[Void Qi corruption eradicated]
[Skill upgrade successful]
[Upgraded {Deep Roots [A]} -> {Ethereal Roots [S]}]

A wave of power surged through the entire mountain and across the land as his roots slowly changed from simple fleshy roots coated in a layer of Qi to something more.

It wasn't until now that Ashlock realized how weighed down he had been. Much like burying his foot in wet sand at the beach when he had been human, Ashlock's roots had tons of rock and earth pressing down and restricting their movement. He just hadn't noticed since it had been like that since his rebirth as a tree.

Until now, he had spent a lot of Qi and nutrients trying to force his roots through the rock, which grew more challenging and costly the further from his trunk he ventured. But now he felt reborn as his roots began to take on an ethereal nature, much like the ones that phased through reality to connect him to his Bastion, and he was freed from the pressure.

"God, that feels so good." Ashlock relished in the relief washing through his vast body. It was impossible to describe, but it was as if the weight of the world unknowingly suffocating him had been lifted.

Ashlock closely inspected his nearest root right below his trunk, as it had been the first to complete the transformation. It looked similar to before but was ever so slightly transparent. He could see his cursed sap flowing through it and the hollowed-out center, which had served as a tunnel before.

"Before, my roots could only burrow deeper; I couldn't move them around freely due to the rock restricting them, but if the information regarding the skill is correct, then…" Ashlock tried to raise his root upward, and to his astonishment, it worked. As the root rose to the surface, the rock above vanished as if eaten by the void. Ashlock felt Qi being drained from his Star Core, but to his relief, no sacrificial credits were spent.

"So, at the cost of Qi, I can move my roots around freely as if they were tentacles underwater. Well, it is more like viscous mud; there is still some resistance, but it's way less than before. Am I like a rock octopus now? No…more like an octotree." Ashlock wiggled around for a bit and wanted to experiment more, but at the rate of change, it would take a few days for all of his roots to transition to their new ethereal form.

Which was a shame since he was looking forward to the other effects of the skill.

Turning his roots from fleshy sap to ones that were more ethereal in nature came with many advantages. Worrying about the distance from his trunk was a thing of the past. Because his roots were now ethereal, the transfer of Qi down them offered no resistance, so he lost no Qi to the surroundings during the transfer.

Which was a massive boon to everything he did. He could exchange Qi and nutrients with his offspring with the same efficiency no matter how far they were from him, and he could fight distant battles without wasting as much Qi.

"The fact I don't leak Qi into the surroundings as much also helps me spread my roots closer to my enemies without them noticing, perhaps even under their very feet," Ashlock concluded because one of the most significant advantages of the void element that had turned his roots ethereal was its ability to remain undetected.

It was what made Khaos an apex predator that could appear beside and rip apart cultivators before they even knew how they died. Other aspects of the void also carried over to his new roots, such as their capabilities to go through anything. Defensive arrays? Runically enhanced walls? Dimensions? The void itself? There was nothing to block or stop his roots from spreading.

"Space also seems compressed in my roots, considering how fast my cursed sap appears to flow," Ashlock muttered as he examined his own root a little closer. Deciding to quickly test it for curiosity's sake, he had the hollowed-out root rise out of the ground beside him and then, under everyone's curious gazes, used telekinesis to drop fruit into it.

The fruit blinked in and out of existence, traveling through the root as if the distance was near zero and arriving at the tunnel exit down in the cavern a second later. Eight thousand meters had been crossed in an instant. The fruit didn't gain any velocity, so rather than splatting hard on the ground, it simply plopped onto the stone.

"I am glad I tested that beforehand with a fruit. It would have been a disaster if Stella or someone went through and got slammed into the ground as if they had been shot via a railgun." Ashlock already had many ideas for this aspect of his new ethereal roots, as it seemed safe for even mortals and weak cultivators to use it.

"Basically, it's like a portal, but I don't have to manually keep opening and closing it. The possibilities really are endless. I could use this to connect Red Vine Peak to Ashfallen City, create a way for the Redclaws to venture deep into the wilderness in seconds, or use it for our pill empire…which is still in the process of selling a single pill, but let's ignore that small detail."

Ashlock had felt some spatial Qi being spent to send that fruit down, so his roots were definitely using his spatial Qi to shorten the distance.

"Oh shit. If I spend my Qi, will the system take away my ability to reach Nascent Soul Realm?" Ashlock dug through his system screens and pulled up the notification.

[Requirements to turn Chaos Nebula into an Inner World:
2565 / 10000 Sacrificial Credits
0 / 1 Absorbed Fire Star Cores
0 / 1 Absorbed Water Star Cores
0 / 1 Absorbed Earth Star Cores
0 / 1 Absorbed Wind Star Cores
0 / 1 Absorbed Metal Star Cores]

He couldn't see anywhere that mentioned or suggested that he couldn't spend as much Qi as he wanted, which was a relief. As usual, the system only really cared for the precious sacrificial credits and left him and his cultivation alone.

"Master, please excuse my interruption."

Ashlock was pulled out of his consciousness by a gruff voice he recognized immediately. Since his {Demonic Eye} was still open, he gazed down at Larry standing before him. In the red hue that showed Ashlock the flow of Qi, Larry looked like a blazing sun of power on par with Nox, who had died moments earlier and been turned into a tree and planted in Ashfallen City.

"Larry, my loyal summon. How can I help?" Ashlock asked, but he suspected the answer.

"I was hoping the honorable master would bless my evolution."

[Larry has accumulated enough Qi to evolve to S grade]
[New evolution option(s) have been added due to consumption of divine flesh]
[Ashen King {Larry} wishes to evolve]
[Yes/No]

Was that even a question?

"Yes, of course, I approve of your evolution," Ashlock replied to Larry, and the system also seemed to hear his words as the words faded and new ones took their place.

The divine evolution options for the Ashen King filled his mind.

2
DIVINE ASH

Ashlock looked down the short list of options, and as with Kaida's evolution, there was a very obvious one at the top that glowed with a sense of grandeur and divinity.

But he skipped it to check out the others to satisfy his curiosity, as this was the first ever S-grade evolution that would put Larry firmly into the Nascent Soul Realm power level. So what would the system have offered Larry if he hadn't eaten the eggs of a Midnight Inkwing?

[Ashen Emperor]
Larry's royal bloodline progresses, and his control over ash becomes absolute. He can now create constructs or creatures from ash, and his tactical prowess is heightened. Larry's horns will turn silver, signifying his royal status, and the halo of ash orbiting his crown of horns becomes more pronounced and controlled. His mere presence will be enough to inspire awe in allies and crush enemies.

"So the first option would have been a natural upgrade to the Ashen King evolution path he was already going down," Ashlock pondered. "This evolution appears to turn Larry into a summoner-style control mage. Which makes sense for an emperor. He would go into battle by crushing his enemies under his royal presence and then unleashing an army of creations made from ash to kill them."

It was a good option, and he was curious about what else the system would offer.

|Ashen Stormbringer|

Larry becomes the wielder of mass destruction. Gaining immense insight into many Daos, this evolution allows Larry to summon not just ash storms, but also thunderstorms, blizzards, and windstorms. His fur becomes stormy gray, swirling with mini-storms, and his horns crackle with lightning.

"If the Ashen Emperor was a control mage class, this is more of a destruction mage." Ashlock thought back to how the Winterwrath Grand Elder had attacked the Ravenbornes while riding a titan of ice flanked by a blizzard that engulfed the valley. "Large-scale storms sure are destructive…to mortals and weaklings. But to stronger opponents, they are nothing but a hindrance to their spiritual sense and Qi regeneration rather than a life-threatening attack."

There was a reason so many of his sect members were better at single-target fighting: it was the best way to win in this world. Battles weren't won by defeating an army but rather by taking out the strongest member of the opposition. This is where people like Khaos, Diana, and Stella came in, as they could reach and kill anyone they needed through movement techniques.

It also mentioned that Larry would command these storms due to heightened Dao understanding rather than gaining more affinities. So Larry could only summon a blizzard in an area of dense ice Qi, for example.

"I would prefer that Larry had the capabilities to fight someone in the Nascent Soul Realm by himself rather than be a support style mage by summoning storms because until I reach Nascent Soul myself, Larry will be the strongest sect member beside Maple."

|Venomous Overlord|

Specializing in toxins, this evolution grants Larry the ability to produce and control various deadly venoms that he can merge with his ash. His fur takes on a sickly green hue, and his horns drip with a potent poison.

Ashlock read over the description of the last offered evolution, and rather than thinking about its fighting capabilities since it could be countered by simple poison resistance pills, he focused on a different angle.

"Wouldn't this evolution be perfect for the poison pills that Stella was working on?"

Even if it were useful, Ashlock definitely wouldn't pick this option as he could already imagine how sad Larry would be to learn his S-grade evolution had reduced him to a poison-making lab rat. The spider would do it if ordered, but Ashlock knew Larry preferred to serve the protector and hunter role for him.

"It seems the S-grade evolutions for Larry were less about changing his body or form to something like an Arachne and more focusing his fighting style," Ashlock concluded. "Out of these three, I would have chosen to progress Larry's royal bloodline and control over ash with the Ashen Emperor evolution path, but I think it's obvious which one I will be picking…"

Ashlock looked back at the top of the list to the option that had been so hard to overlook and not peek at while he went over the other options.

[Herald of the Divine Ash: Larry (???+)]

Having eaten the flesh of a divine being from an upper realm, Larry has unlocked a new path to power. As a Herald of the Divine Ash, he will begin his path to become a deity. Alongside unlimited cultivation potential, Larry will gain divine authority over ash and decay. He will be able to decay any matter at will within his realm of influence. Also, as a divine being with governance over an affinity, Larry's body will be reformed entirely from divine ash, allowing him to reincarnate from ash and gain immortality.

"His body will be reformed from divine ash?" Ashlock felt that was familiar and was starting to see a pattern. "When Kaida had his divine evolution, his body turned from flesh and blood to one made entirely from divine ink. Are all divine beings made from their affinity, or is this something unique to my summons? No, wait…the Midnight Inkwing had been entirely made from ink, too, so maybe it is common for divine beings to be made from their affinity."

That aside, there was a lot of information hidden within the text describing the evolution.

"Since this evolution puts Larry on the path to godhood, will he become a deity at the SSS grade, or will he need to go higher than that to achieve true godhood?" Ashlock wondered but knew the only way to get a hint of the answer would have been upgrading his {Skyborne Bastion [SSS]} skill, which he hadn't done.

"Divine authority over ash and decay is interesting. Ash is easy enough to imagine as Larry already uses it, and having divine authority should mean that Larry won't need to consult Heaven as much to use techniques and can simply do things with ash. But decay is a state of matter rather than an affinity…right? How can he have divine authority over a state of matter? Can he simply command something to disintegrate into ash before him?"

That certainly sounded like something a deity would be capable of, and that wasn't all. Apparently, as a Herald of the Divine Ash, Larry could also reincarnate from the ash, technically making him immortal.

"I suppose that's the same for Kaida as well. Since they both have bodies made from the condensing of their affinities rather than one of flesh and blood, so long as there is enough of their affinity nearby, they can endlessly reform," Ashlock contemplated. "So, with all the information I was given, would Larry's fighting style with this evolution be an immortal drain tank? So long as he fights an opponent within a storm of divine ash, he can keep reforming his body even if destroyed, and he would deplete the opponent's Qi pool until they cannot resist the decay and disintegrate into a pile of ash."

It was terrifying, and as expected, the divine option was far better than the basic ones provided by the system.

"System, I choose the Herald of the Divine Ash."

[Evolution path {Herald of the Divine Ash} chosen, evolution initiating…]

"Thank you, Master," Larry said gruffly as a tear in reality opened above him. Silver flakes of ash poured down like divine glitter and began to swirl around Larry, forming a cocoon. Even as the tear in reality vanished, there was still a divine presence weighing down on the mountain from Larry's cocoon.

Ashlock used telekinesis to float the divine ash cocoon up into his branches and nestled it close to his trunk, where he could protect and watch over him while he evolved.

With his new void skill picked and Larry's evolution out of the way, Ashlock could finally focus on his sect members who had left the Mystic Realm. Glancing over them with his {Demonic Eye}, he would be able to quickly assess their progress by the amount of Qi stored within their souls.

But first, he gazed up at the behemoth of twisted dark red wood that loomed over the entire mountain peak, casting a shadow. It was the Titan Tortoise that Ashlock had turned into an Ent and named Geb. It felt like he was looking up at the canopy of a four-poster bed, with the underside of the Ent creating a ceiling overhead with its four legs taller than even him.

Geb wasn't *quite* mountain-sized, but he was darn close to the size of a smaller one. Perhaps a large hill was a better descriptor, just with legs, a maw that could swallow a Bastion whole, and a small forest of red bark trees adorned with golden brown leaves that matched the color of its fifth-stage Star Core soul fire.

Ashlock needed Geb to move for a very tree-specific reason. The darn thing was so big it shrouded him and his offspring from the glorious morning sunlight.

"Geb, can you move to the south side of the mountain range? There should be a space near there that you can settle down, and you won't look too out of place," Ashlock told the Titan Tortoise. "You're blocking my precious sunlight."

The behemoth let out a low roar that shook the whole peak before it turned its enormous body and descended the mountain. Since its legs weren't solid and were more a collection of twisted red roots, it could step around Ashlock's offspring without flattening them as it moved, which he appreciated.

As Geb left, Ashlock got a clear view of its turtle shell-like back. Nestled among the golden brown–leaved trees were many huts built from stone, and he saw *thousands* of Mudcloaks scurrying around and looking back at Red Vine Peak with their glowing blue eyes.

"Wait…there were more of them?" Ashlock looked before him. Gathered around the hole to the citadel were orders of magnitude more Mudcloaks than before. He had been worried that they wouldn't all be able to fit in the citadel, which was a hole spanning a hundred meters wide and eight thousand meters down. But there were even more living on Geb's back?

"Douglas," Ashlock said through {Abyssal Whispers}, **"just how many Mudcloaks did you manage to save in a single month?"**

The man wearing a beige suit and casually leaning on his walking stick met the gaze of his demonic eye, and judging from the earth Qi flowing through his body, he had broken through to the ninth stage of the Soul Fire Realm. It made sense he hadn't managed to leap into the Star Core Realm as he had been too busy commanding a war.

"Many are still left, but I believe we saved at least half of them," Douglas said respectfully as he stepped forward. *"With the help of Geb, we saved six large settlements of Mudcloaks and wiped out eight kobold strongholds."*

That was impressive progress. Perhaps all of the Mudcloaks would be saved within the next Mystic Realm visit, but then he would need to think about where to put them all.

Douglas glanced to the side at the departing back of Geb. *"Immortal, would it be possible to make a portal or tunnel between the citadel and Geb so the Mudcloaks aren't separated? During our war, many Mudcloaks made Geb's back their new homes, and I don't believe they will all fit inside the citadel."*

"I can handle that, so don't worry," Ashlock replied. He would have one of his hollowed-out {Ethereal Roots} connect Geb with the citadel so the Mudcloaks could move between the two places. **"Could you show the rest of the Mudcloaks the citadel and have them settle in? They are crowding the peak."**

Douglas chuckled as he glanced around at the thousands of Mudcloaks, staring at the sky or the ground to avoid Ashlock's demonic gaze. *"Okay, everyone, follow me to your new home. Don't get too comfortable, though, as I am sure the Immortal will have some very reasonable work for us soon, like building an entire city in a single night."*

"I deserved that." Ashlock sighed, ignoring Douglas's smirk as he led the Mudcloaks into the citadel's depths. It took a while for all the little monsters to vacate the peak, but once they did, Ashlock could let out another sigh of relief. He didn't usually get claustrophobic, but having the entire peak being a sea of little monsters had unnerved him.

With that out of the way, he swept his gaze over the remaining sect members. Since he wanted to have a more private chat with the core group, he focused on the Redclaws, who happened to be standing next to one another.

"**Excuse my gaze. I am just checking everyone's progress,**" Ashlock told them through {Abyssal Whispers}. Most of them had to gobble down Mind Fortress pills upon him, forcing his presence into their minds. From the looks of things, everyone had experienced a single stage of growth. This was solid progress for some, but it showed signs of a lack of talent or focus on others.

The Redclaw Grand Elder had gone from the sixth to the seventh stage in the Star Core Realm, meaning he was getting closer to the bottleneck of the Nascent Soul Realm that Ashlock was now stuck at. Meanwhile, Elder Margret and Elder Mo had both gone from the first to the second stage of the Star Core Realm.

"Good growth but not very impressive considering what the more talented younger generation can do," Ashlock thought. He knew this world had a different view of the word "talent" as they deemed people with poor spirit roots or drowning in heart demons as talentless, which he could cure with his truffles.

In his eyes, talent was something else. He had started to notice that just like studying in school or practicing martial arts, some people simply don't like or have a talent for cultivation. Even if given a path to a longer and safer life, not everyone was willing to sit in a dark cave for sometimes years to contemplate Heaven's whispers.

Elder Brent was a good example. He willingly remained behind to supervise a new city of mortals rather than delve into the Mystic Realm and try to reach the Star Core Realm.

"Something about being blasted by heavenly lightning that has the chance to obliterate his soul must not have appealed to him." Ashlock chuckled as he finished his inspection of the Redclaw Elders, and then his gaze landed on a young woman with a bright smile and the same crimson-red hair as the rest of her family.

Amber was the most talented of the Redclaws' younger generation, and it looked like she would hold onto that title.

Humming within her chest was a freshly formed Star Core, and Ashlock started to suspect the reason why all the Elders hadn't made as much progress as he had hoped.

"Amber, you reached the Star Core Realm. At such a young age as well, I am impressed," Ashlock praised her and enjoyed how excited she looked despite trembling a little under his demonic gaze. Her Elders also wore proud expressions. They must have worked hard in the Mystic Realm to help her ascend. "**You should return to your peak and celebrate your ascension with the others. And to the Elders, you have all made good and steady progress.**"

The Grand Elder stepped forward and bowed. *"It is only due to the Immortal's generosity and guidance that we have come this far. For decades, maybe even centuries, I have been the only Star Core cultivator holding our family together. Yet in a few short months, not only have a few of my fellow Elders joined me in this realm of power but so has a member of the younger generation. Such progress is unheard of and, if continued, would put us on par with the other major families of the Blood Lotus Sect."*

"**Then my investment and trust in you will not have been wasted,**" Ashlock responded as he saw resolve in the Grand Elder's eyes. "**With a war brewing nearby and the beast tide on the horizon, I will need all the firepower we can muster.**"

All the Elders and Amber followed their Grand Elder's lead, paid their respects with a bow, and said in unison, *"We will do our best to serve and repay the Immortal."*

"Did they have that speech practiced?" Ashlock thought with some amusement. The more he interacted with the Redclaws, the more he liked them. "Next Mystic Realm, I should give them all the skin improvement truffles and have some more of the younger generation join."

The Grand Elder clearing his throat drew Ashlock's attention. *"If that is all, we will be on our way."*

"**Yes, that is all. Check on Elder Brent when you return. I hear he has been having some headaches due to the mortals of Ashfallen City.**"

The Grand Elder nodded while taking to the skies on his flying sword. Elder Margret, Elder Mo, and even Amber, with less grace than her Elders, followed closely behind, drawing streaks of crimson flame through the air.

With them gone, Ashlock looked down at the bench below his

demonic eye where the others had gathered. Elaine sat on the bench, tending to Stella's wounds, while Diana played with Kaida nearby.

It didn't take more than a glance with his demonic eye to notice how shockingly far all his inner circle members had progressed. Especially Diana and Kaida. There was also something hard to miss...

"Was Kaida always that big?" Ashlock wondered as the ink Lindwyrm towered over Diana and licked her forehead.

3
DUEL

Ashlock inspected Kaida and discovered the reason for his explosive growth in size.

"My summons and monsters generally don't follow the same cultivation system as humans, but if I had to guess, Kaida has gone up around three stages in the Star Core Realm," Ashlock muttered with a hint of surprise. Just how much ink Qi had this greedy snake absorbed? "If he experiences this much growth in the next Mystic Realm visit, he might be closing in on his evolution to A grade."

Since Kaida's entire body was made from heavenly ink, the more he absorbed, the more he would grow.

"Kaida, you are too big now to act like this," Diana protested as Kaida wrapped his body around her. The poor woman looked like she would drown in ink as she gasped for air.

The Lindwyrm, now easily thirty meters long, frowned at his favorite human's words.

Through his demonic eye, Ashlock saw how the heavenly ink Qi that made up Kaida's body began to condense, and his body started to shrink. It continued until he reduced his length from thirty meters to only three.

Diana gasped in relief as she stopped being coiled around and looked down at Kaida, who was now wrapped around her feet and clearly asking to be picked up like old times with his big golden eyes.

"Okay, fine, come here." Diana tried to pick Kaida up but strug-

gled. He may have reduced his size, but he was now far more dense. Kaida let out a sad hiss as Diana failed to lift him.

She put some Qi into her arms, and the stone below her feet cracked as she picked up the Lindwyrm with a grunt. *"There. Are you happy now?"*

Kaida licked her face, leaving an ink stain across her cheek, as if someone had taken a paintbrush and slapped her with it.

"Can you stop licking me?" Diana grumbled as demonic mist carried the ink stain away.

Ashlock noticed her muscles were tensed, and if she didn't keep cycling her Qi through her body, lifting Kaida would be impossible. "Even with her partial demonic form due to her bloodline, which gives her immense strength, she still struggles to pick up Kaida. Though if she was to fully transform, I am sure lifting him would be a piece of cake."

"How did you even get so big in such a short amount of time?" Diana asked Kaida a question Ashlock was also curious about, but Kaida simply smirked and refused to answer.

Stella laughed from the bench. *"He's a glutton, just like Tree. I bet he found more of those eggs to eat or swam around an ink sea for a month!"*

Kaida hissed in annoyance from Diana's arms.

"What? Am I wrong? Don't act so mysterious. It's not like you did something heroic or insane, such as robbing the Azure Clan or fighting a fire titan. Or did you—" Stella stopped speaking and winced from the pain. *"Ow, ow, ow…"*

"Stop squirming around and give the healing pills a minute to fuse your spine back in place." Elaine gently pushed Stella back on the bench. *"The fact you are still in one piece is baffling."*

"I'm fine, really." Stella waved her off. *"I still have Sol's healing light running through my body. Just give me a minute, and I will be as good as new…"*

Stella did, in fact, not look fine at all. Her white clothes were soaked with blood and were shredded in places. It was as if she had crawled out from a warzone. But through his demonic eye, he could verify that Stella wasn't lying. Even with Sol's healing light and the pills working in harmony, the rate at which her bones and organs were healing was horrifying. Cultivators really were a league above humans, as what Stella was treating as nothing to be concerned about would have killed a mortal person a hundred times over.

"**Sorry, Stella, I got distracted by other pointless things. I should have repaired Sol first and had him heal you again,**" Ashlock said through {Abyssal Whispers}.

"Oh, Tree, I thought I felt your gaze on my back but wasn't sure." Stella looked over her shoulder and stared into his demonic eye with a smile. *"This really is nothing. I am just glad you are okay... You are fine, right?"*

"**Nothing a long sleep can't fix,**" Ashlock reassured her. His system had offered to repair him for thousands of credits, but he had no interest in that. A few long sleeps under the nine moons and he would be as good as new.

"Thank the heavens. I got worried when you suddenly went silent after eating Dante." Stella sighed. *"Even with the curse weakening her, Nox was stronger than I thought a fresh Nascent Soul Realm would be. Her presence was enough to flatten me to the floor, and every hit she landed obliterated my defenses as if they were mere parchment, and I felt her attacks down to my bones."*

"**Next time will be different,**" Ashlock said. "**I am on the cusp of ascending to Nascent Soul Realm, and you have all grown considerably since I last saw you. Stella, to block Nox's attacks and survive, you must have had a very productive session in the Mystic Realm.**"

"I went from the fourth to the sixth stage of the Star Core Realm," Stella said proudly. *"It was hard, but due to your fruits and the Qi-gathering array, I managed to make such progress."*

"**Very impressive,**" Ashlock agreed. "**You are a step behind the Redclaw Grand Elder while being only sixteen.**"

"That is great progress, Stella. You should be proud," Diana agreed. *"To be on the way to Nascent Soul Realm while so young... At your age, I was stuck in the Soul Fire Realm yet was hailed as a prodigy until the heart demons formed."*

"Thank you." Stella beamed. *"How about you, Diana? How was your progress?"*

Diana grinned, showing her fangs. *"I went from the first to the fourth stage of the Star Core Realm."*

Stella's smile faltered. *"What?"*

"Don't get jealous now." Diana gave Stella a knowing look. *"Keep things in perspective. I am five years older than you. It's easier to progress through lower stages, and I found a realm specifically designed to help people of my bloodline progress in their cultivation. Not to mention the usual downside of my affinity, which is a risk of heart demons, is nullified by the truffles so generously grown by Ashlock."*

As Diana spoke, Ashlock saw Stella's gaze slowly grow more tranquil.

"Yes, that is all reasonable, but progressing three stages in a single month is not," Stella grumbled. *"Elaine, what about you? How much have you grown?"*

Under Stella's tranquil gaze, Elaine shuffled to the edge of the bench. *"Errr, nothing as impressive as you two."*

Ashlock would have to disagree. If what he saw through his demonic eye was to be believed, she had grown in leaps and bounds.

Stella squinted at her. *"I killed your brother for you because you didn't want to do it. The least you could tell me is this, right?"*

"I suppose so…" Elaine pushed her glasses up and smiled awkwardly. *"I went up three stages in the Soul Fire Realm, so I am at the ninth stage now."*

"So you also grew more than me," Stella looked at her feet and muttered. Her shoulders sagged, and she looked like she had just received terrible exam results.

"I am the one who should be feeling bad," Elaine protested. *"I am a decade older than you and still stuck in the Soul Fire Realm and lacking the thing that matters most: combat experience. If anything, I am playing catchup even more than Diana."*

Stella's eyes widened, and she glanced up at Diana. *"Combat experience…"*

"I don't like how you are looking at me with that overly calm gaze." Diana shuddered. *"Just spit it out."*

Stella stood up and drew her sword from her spatial ring. *"It's been a while since we had a duel. Do you remember when you first arrived here, and we would spar day and night?"*

"Yes, I remember you wouldn't stop demanding combat practice until you consistently started beating me, and then you weren't interested anymore."

"Well, so much has changed since then." Stella grinned, which was unnerving when paired with her bloodied clothes and calm gaze. *"We have both awakened bloodlines and progressed into the Star Core Realm. Wouldn't now be a good time to see the difference in power between us?"*

"Aren't you injured?" Diana raised a brow.

Stella cracked her neck and rolled her shoulders. *"In good enough condition to beat you."*

"Arrogant as always." Diana clicked her tongue. *"Fine. If it will sate your envy, then I don't see why not. We can duel."*

"Is this really a good idea?" Ashlock asked. **"Back then, the most you two could do was cause some damage to buildings, but now you could kill one another in a single well-placed attack."**

"I survived being stamped on by Lucius while he was empowered, did I not? And Stella was smacked around by Nox and is now pointing a sword at me minutes later," Diana said to his canopy. *"So long as neither of us aims for the head, it should be fine. We have Sol to heal us..."*

"No, you don't," Ashlock reminded them. **"Dante struck Sol with a void attack, so he will take a while to repair."**

Ashlock had no interest in spending many of the hard-earned sacrificial credits he needed for his ascension on repairing Sol just so Stella and Diana could compare their egos. Cultivators really were unruly sometimes.

"Well, if I die, have Kaida revive me with some long-forgotten revival technique." Diana chuckled, setting Kaida down with a grunt. She then gestured with her chin for Stella to follow her over to the central area of the mountain peak, where they would have space to duel.

While they took up their positions a hundred meters apart, Ashlock had to wonder when Diana had changed. She used to be the more cautious member of the group but was now more arrogant and up for fighting.

"She became more emotional and impulsive ever since awakening her bloodline and transitioning into a demoness," Ashlock muttered. "Is this the fabled demon's pride?"

"Are those two really best friends?" Elaine asked as she sat alone

on the bench with Maple on her lap and Kaida having returned to his full size coiled nearby.

Ashlock chuckled. **"Yes, though I suppose they act more like competitive sisters. Stella has a bit of a habit of getting jealous and paranoid when others progress faster than her."**

"I see, that makes sense." Elaine nodded. *"Who do you think will win?"*

That was a good question. **"Hard to say. It all depends on how serious Stella is about winning, and if her tranquil gaze is anything to go by, she is taking this duel seriously, so Diana may be in trouble if she isn't careful. But Stella is also injured, and Diana did experience some explosive growth in the Mystic Realm, so it's hard to say."**

"Her gaze did seem odd. It was almost inhumanly calm. Is that related to her bloodline?" Elaine asked.

"Yes, though her bloodline is far more mysterious than Diana's. We are still learning more about it every day…" Ashlock said and realized something. Why had her bloodline activated during a duel with Diana?

"From the top of my head, her bloodline activated during the alchemy tournament, fighting Nox near me and the bounty hunters on the Bastion," Ashlock mused. "But it didn't activate when she tried to chase down Nox or trespassed the Azure Clan library. I was starting to think it activated when she felt threatened or if my life was in danger, but why wouldn't it activate when being stared down by an Elder from an upper realm?"

Ashlock looked at Stella. She stood with her sword tip pointed at Diana on the other side of the mountain peak with an utterly calm expression as the wind messed with her hair.

"Time to see who of us is the strongest," Stella said without a hint of emotion. Purple soul fire erupted around her body and down her sword, making the air ripple and warp as if bending to her will.

Ashlock felt this situation further cemented his hypothesis that Stella's bloodline was that of a ruler. "Perhaps Diana hadn't been far off. Stella really is the sin of pride and envy, for better or worse. If she feels her authority or pride is at risk, her bloodline will activate to help bridge the gap."

It was still a hypothesis, but it seemed to fit when compared to all previous examples of her bloodline activating. Ashlock had noticed how Stella's pride turned to envy when Diana mentioned how much she had grown in the Mystic Realm despite all the good reasons for their differing growth.

Ashlock had thought that Stella was simply too immature and seeking praise to understand that just because Diana and Elaine grew by three stages did not diminish the fact she was one of the strongest in the whole sect at only sixteen.

But perhaps it was less about her personality and something ingrained into her, just like how Diana would enter a berserk state when fully unleashing her demon form.

"Stella, I hope you don't make any excuses when you lose," Diana said as she began her transformation. Majestic wings of feathered darkness thrice her size sprouted from her shoulders, her fangs grew, and her nails elongated into claws. Finally, her eyes transitioned from gray to black. She opened her mouth and breathed out a cloud of mist that began to surround and conceal her form. Shadows manifested and started moving around the mist, letting out wails of misery that echoed across the mountain peak.

If not for his demonic gaze, Ashlock would be unable to tell Diana apart from the shadows inhabiting the mist. The difference between this mist made from her new affinity and the one made from water Qi in the past was like night and day. Due to the addition of the demonic Qi, this haunted mist was far harder to penetrate with spiritual sight and seemed to empower Diana.

"Now I am not so sure who will win…" Ashlock mused as he watched Stella fearlessly walk toward the encroaching mist. "I suppose whoever strikes first will be the winner; the question is does Stella have an answer to Diana's mist?"

As it turned out, she had more than just an answer.

4
I AM A MONSTER

Diana crept through the dense demonic mist, flexing her wings and fingers in anticipation. Having taken on her demonic form and surrendered to her bloodline, she had a primal urge to charge at Stella, who stood on the other side of the mountain peak with an annoyingly unfazed look despite the encroaching demonic mist.

But then she would lose without a doubt. Stella, despite her flaws and young age, was talented. It was like she had been born for combat and fought life-and-death battles since childhood. If that wasn't bad enough, Diana had seen her fighting once her bloodline was active. It turned her from a talented but experience-lacking fighter to a ruthless being devoid of openings and weakness. It was as if she had a third eye in the back of her head and could foresee the future.

"Be patient," Diana hissed to herself as she kept her eyes and spiritual sense peeled for the first sign of movement from Stella. Even the slightest twitch or ripple in spatial Qi would not escape her notice.

As a spatial cultivator, distance was a non-factor for Stella in this fight. If not for the demonic mist concealing her location, she could appear behind Diana in the blink of an eye.

Diana watched from the shadows of the mist as Stella took in a deep breath and tilted her sword horizontally. Purple soul fire flowed down the blade's edge, making the air shudder. It looked like she was preparing to attack but was looking at the wrong part of the mist.

What is she doing? Diana wondered. *I have never seen her open an attack like that. Is this a new technique she learned during the Mystic Realm? How did she manage that and increase her cultivation by two stages?*

Diana believed she had a very fortuitous encounter in the Mystic Realm. She had stumbled upon another training ground of the Ravena Clan floating among the thousands of pocket dimensions. The demonic mist there was dense and of peak Star Core quality. A large Qi-gathering formation had been constructed on the island, and she could cultivate it without worries. She had even retrieved some flowers she planned to give to Ashlock later. Yet somehow Stella had still inched ahead?

Unaware of Diana's bafflement, Stella closed her eyes and crouched with her sword outstretched horizontally. She then rapidly spun around on her heel as her soul fire shot down her blade. Her sword cleaved through reality, sending tears that streaked to the other side across the mountain peak. She didn't stop there and kept spinning and cutting reality as she slowly stood up to her full height.

Diana saw it all in slow motion due to her heightened demon senses as the attacks approached.

If Stella had unleashed a single dimension slash horizontally or vertically, Diana could have simply avoided it and had her mist refill the gap. However, since Stella sent multiple horizontal waves of dimension tears her way, there was nowhere to run or hide.

So you want to force me out. Clever girl. Let's take this fight to the air.

Diana pushed Qi into her artifact boots that they had looted from the dead bounty hunters. They took on a ghostly form in reaction to her Qi, and she felt her body lurched up in a blur as she leaped into the sky and spread out her wings.

From above, she watched in real time as the dimension tears tore through her mist, and anything that was left lingering was sucked to the other side as the rips in reality snapped closed with a thunderclap and a rush of air.

Stella finished her attack by calmly opening her eyes and looking straight up at Diana as if she had known her exact location all along.

It must be some kind of spatial perception, Diana mused. Knowledge of spatial cultivators wasn't as widespread as other affinity types, but she had still endured lectures from tutors when she was young and spent a lot of time watching Stella fight, so she knew the basics. *The first lesson had been that distance when facing a spatial cultivator is meaningless, and the second lesson was always to watch your back—*

Stella vanished as if she had been an illusion. Diana relied on her heightened perception and reaction time to spin around and grab Stella's blade with her claws in a shower of sparks and ringing steel.

"Surprised?" Diana smirked as Stella's eyes widened ever so slightly. "You know I don't only have ridiculous strength as a demon, right?" With Stella's sword locked in place, Diana used her other arm to push down on Stella's shoulder with all the force she could muster, sending the girl plummeting to the ground and impacting the stone with a loud crash followed by hairline cracks spreading out from the impact site.

Flapping her wings to gain height as she had the advantage in the air, Diana looked down with a fang-filled grin. In that short exchange, she had confirmed a drastic difference in strength and speed from before entering the Mystic Realm.

Diana felt Ashlock's eye shift its focus to her, and she shuddered.

"Hey, you know she asked for it, right? This duel was her idea, and she almost cut me in half if I didn't jump up in time," Diana muttered and rolled her eyes. "It's not my fault she's arrogant and needed a lesson. Stop being so protective. She is fine."

Diana knew that the tree cared for her and enjoyed her company, but it was clear who his favorite was. Ashlock was far too protective of Stella, and there was definitely a hint of disapproval in the tree's gaze at her actions of hurling his adopted daughter into the ground.

The dust from the thrown-up rock blew away in the fierce mountain winds, and as Diana suspected, Stella arose from the destruction and was totally fine. A simple throw like that wouldn't even leave a scratch on a Star Core cultivator.

If I had been going for the kill, I would have infused my claws with my demonic mist rather than using raw strength. And instead of throwing Stella to the ground, I would have snapped her neck or torn her arm off.

"You know, Diana, this is why I love to practice with you," Stella said as she stood there looking up, still wreathed in spatial flames. Her gaze was tranquil, but a light smile tugged at the edge of her lips.

"Oh?" Diana raised a brow. "And why is that?"

"Every time we fight, I learn something new." Stella rolled her shoulders, likely to rid herself of the stiffness from being hurled into solid stone. "I just realized that I have come to rely on my bloodline too much. From my understanding of it so far, it gives me heightened reaction times and helps me focus on the flow of battle. Perfect for swordfights where I can react and copy an opponent's fighting style, not so much when the opponent can just grab my sword and lock me in place."

Diana smiled and was glad Stella was still as focused on self-improvement as before.

"So? How do you plan to beat me, then?" Diana asked.

"Well, with your demonic mist gone," Stella brought out a thin strip of black cloth and began wrapping it around her eyes and head, "I think a different fighting style that Tree inspired me to try someday would be better."

"Oh, a new fighting style, inspired by Ashlock of all people... ahem, I mean trees." Diana spread her wings and flexed her claws in excitement at the thrill of battle as something seemed to arise within her. "This should be interesting."

Stella suggested this fighting style would only work without my demonic mist obscuring me, and judging how she couldn't locate me and opened with a large-scale attack to get rid of it before, it must have been a serious hindrance to her.

This short duel had already showcased the strengths of her newly improved demonic mist. The addition of demonic Qi made it far superior to the water Qi mist she could make before.

Satisfied, Diana decided to hold back on flooding the area with her demonic mist again to allow Stella to try this new fighting style and also to not waste precious Qi on a duel with a dear friend.

Come on Stella, show me what you got. Diana watched in anticipation as Stella's spatial ring flashed with silver light. A second sword appeared in her other hand while a dozen daggers manifested and orbited her with telekinesis. They all lit up with purple soul-fire-like candles as their blade tips pointed toward her.

With her eyes covered, Stella didn't even look at Diana as a dozen aflame daggers shot toward her. Perhaps for a mortal or weaker cultivator, these high-speed daggers may seem like a threat, but to Diana, they were like toothpicks the richer mortals liked to use after a crude meal.

Bringing one of her feathered wings of darkness before her, she easily slapped them away but then felt a searing pain in her back.

Ow, what the fuck was that? I blocked them…

Diana didn't even have to look behind her to realize what had pierced her back. Looking down, she saw that Stella had stabbed one of her swords through a portal near her feet. The attack hadn't gone too deep and had skillfully missed anything important, but it still made Diana grit her teeth in pain as Stella withdrew the blade and flicked off *her blood* onto the stone as the portal to her side snapped closed.

"Pay attention," Stella said as she snapped her fingers.

Diana felt a ripple of spatial Qi near her leg as a rift opened, and those same daggers she had just so easily slapped away before re-emerged. Pushing Qi into her boots, her body blurred as she floated backward to dodge them.

"Above."

Diana shrouded her fist in demonic mist Qi, punched upward without looking, and shattered a freshly forming rift. It was well known that spatial rifts would become unstable and collapse when interacting with other Qi types, especially demonic or void Qi. It was why spatial cultivators couldn't simply redirect every attack that came at them through portals.

Phew, if Stella hadn't told me in time, that would have hurt—

"Left, right—"

"What?!" Diana said as two portals opened on either side of her. Flexing her wings, she slapped both portals out of existence, causing them to snap closed with a gust of wind.

"Front, back—"

Diana twisted her body to destroy one and block a flurry of daggers from the other with her wings, but her eyes widened as she felt a ripple of spatial Qi from…

"Above," Stella said simply as Diana howled out in pain. Two swords from separate portals overhead had struck down and dug into her shoulders. Her vision began to take on a red hue, and it felt like her brain was pulsating in her skull as blood rushed around her ears. She was…enraged.

"Run, Stella," Diana hissed out as demonic mist poured out her mouth and wings, which devoured the portals. Her control over the primal urge to tear Stella limb from limb brought on by surrendering to her demon bloodline for power was loosening.

Stella didn't hear her warning as she remained on the ground with the blindfold on, directing the many portals opening and controlling the flying daggers.

Diana felt her vision tunnel onto Stella as everything else faded into a haze. Qi surged through her body and into her artifact boots, and she *rushed* at Stella. The ground came faster than even Diana could process what was happening, and before she knew it, she punched a crater into the ground and shook the mountain peak.

"Missed me."

Diana felt **rage** consume her as she rocketed up from the crater and turned to face Stella in the air. The blond girl stood a bit away with a slight carefree smile as if everything was under her control.

"You know, if my bloodline wasn't active and I hadn't covered my eyes to heighten my perception of the spatial plane, you might have killed me with that—"

Diana wasn't listening—she *couldn't* listen—her body was moving on instinct and was far more focused on slashing Stella's neck so she would stop speaking than whatever she said.

"Run," Diana begged as the world once again blurred forward, and she briefly caught Stella's carefree smile turn to one of surprise before she vanished in a pop of spatial Qi.

Diana hated how she felt even more enraged because her prey had escaped. With empty claws, her head snapped in the direction Stella had teleported off to, and her body was already moving to complete its one and only task: slaughter.

"Diana, stop," Stella said as she vanished again with Spatial Step.

I wish I could. Diana cursed inwardly. *That's like telling a starving person to stop eating mid-bite or a drowning person not to breathe. I am not me anymore... I am something else.*

"Please stop. I don't want to hurt you!" Stella shouted from behind her.

Diana twisted around to follow her prey, and she blurred forward like an unstoppable phantom through the demonic mist that began to fill the mountain peak. Her speed and reaction times increased while Stella grew slower.

"I don't want to hurt you, either, so get serious, Stella. I know you can stop me if you try!" Diana yelled as she tried to wrestle back control of her body. "I am not in control right now. I need you to knock me out!"

Diana hadn't felt this out of control in a long time and suspected it had something to do with her recent drastic leap in power. She hadn't given herself time to readjust and get used to feeding her bloodline the correct amount of demonic mist Qi to have it awaken but not consume her very sense of self.

"Your bloodline is better than mine!" Stella shouted back. "It always has been. Even with the difference in our cultivation, I can't win!"

That filled Diana with a different kind of rage.

"Is this the bloodline you are so jealous of, Stella?" Diana roared out as her claws blurred for Stella's throat and once again barely missed. "Look at me. I am a fucking monster bound by my primal urges. Is this truly something to envy? To feel threatened by? I am trying to rip off my best friend's head against my will right now, and all she feels is jealousy?"

Stella reappeared a few meters away with a gasp. Sweat dampened the cloth over her eyes, and her hands were trembling. The fast-paced spatial steps within an inch of her life must have been getting to her as she felt genuinely threatened yet didn't wish to fight back with the necessary force. The demonic mist swirling around, dampening her senses, likely wasn't helping.

Surely, if it got too dangerous, Ashlock or Maple would step in to stop me. So why haven't they yet? Diana wondered. She felt Ashlock's gaze follow her every move and knew of his capabilities, yet he wasn't even trying to suppress her with his presence, let alone sending one of his Ents to deal with her.

There's no way Ashlock can't see I am out of control and in a berserk state, so the only other option is he wants me to keep going. To keep hunting Stella like a monster. But why?

"Just surrender," Diana snarled. "If you surrender the duel, I may regain control and stop being a monster. I don't want to hurt you—"

"You think Nox would have stopped killing Tree if I fucking surrendered?" Stella snapped back. "Would the assassins sent to kill me in childhood have retreated if I begged? No. They would not. I stand by what I said. Despite the cost, your bloodline is better than mine, and I can't win. Whether you are sane or not, does that matter? Monster or human, I face an opponent I can't defeat in my current state. I am not jealous of you. I *fear* you."

Diana surged forward, and Stella disappeared once again.

"What I need is to improve—we both do," Stella said calmly across the peak. "That is why the duel will not end. Not until we have reached our limits and surpassed our current selves."

"But it's not me you are fighting," Diana hissed as she turned and stood at full height with her wings stretched. "I am moving with nothing but the instinct to kill."

"I wouldn't want it any other way," Stella said with that infuriatingly calm smile as she tore off the headband and stared at her with those tranquil eyes. "Let's both become monsters together."

A strange aura of pressure seemed to come from Stella as the tips of her hair turned white, and she began to walk forward. The air around her cracked and warped with every step, and the purple soul fire took on a lighter hue.

Diana didn't rush forward at the opportunity to kill. Rather, she felt the red hue plaguing her vision and the rage consuming her mind slowly retreat, and she instinctually took a step back.

Yet despite her retreat, she still wasn't in complete control. Her body that was hellbent on slaughter knew when to take a step back if death was assured.

The hunter instinctually knew it had become the prey.

5
A COSMIC TRUTH

Despite Ashlock's protests in her mind, Stella refused to let the duel end.

She knew it had deviated from its original purpose—Diana had become consumed by her bloodline and entered a berserk state where all she saw was red—but Stella felt like she was on the cusp of something. Now wasn't the time to pull back but rather push against her limits.

It was hard to describe, but down to her bones, she knew something more was locked away inside. Some untapped potential she had yet to unleash for reasons not yet known. She had spent months toiling away on ways to even use her bloodline's potential only to feel a hint of this dormant power when facing down Nox and protecting Tree, but she had the daylights beaten out of her before it could manifest.

This time, however, was different. Diana was still a few stages below Stella, even in her bloodline form. So logically, victory was possible, perhaps even assured. Still, there was a gap in the fighting experience, and Diana's demon form gave her unmatched speed and strength that helped her easily bridge the gap and even surpass Stella to the point she felt *fear*.

Fear of death, but also fear of being outdone. Diana was not only a demon in reality but also a mental one for Stella to overcome. Diana showed what was possible, the heights that could be achieved from a bloodline's power, which Stella desperately craved.

It wasn't until Diana tried to call off the duel because she claimed she was *a monster acting on nothing but instincts* that something clicked within Stella's mind. If Diana could surrender herself to instincts, why couldn't she? Her bloodline had already activated without her direct control until now, so why was she trying to have complete control over it?

Just trust in the process, Stella assured herself as she removed her bandage and returned to reality from the spatial plane. Her bloodline was active already, that much she knew, as that hallmark tranquil calmness that spread from her mind to her fingertips was present alongside the feeling of being zoned in.

Information of her surroundings flowed through her mind at a nearly limitless rate alongside an encroaching headache. The many portals, the dozen daggers being manipulated with telekinesis, her own position in relation to Diana, and pockets of safety away from the demonic mist were all under her control simultaneously. Focus never wavered or deviated from one thing to another.

This was the bloodline experience she had grown used to, but something nagging at the back of her mind knew this was not the limit. It was as if there was so much more to explore just beyond the curtain, and Diana had driven her to the point of discovering what could be possible.

Stella stopped thinking so much and surrendered herself to her instincts. Whatever felt right in her gut was what she would do, even if it would cost her losing her head to Diana's claws.

Bizarrely, she felt the urge to step forward—toward Diana, the overpowered demoness that had spent the last few minutes trying to swipe at her throat with razor-sharp claws shrouded in demonic mist.

As she walked, in the silence of her mind where she kept her thoughts empty to be in tune with her instincts, she heard what could only be described as a whisper. It was like that voice in the back of one's mind that warns of danger or opportunity, a sixth sense perhaps. The whispers gradually got louder to the point they filled the silent void of her mind.

Refusing to ruin this moment by having thoughts, Stella let the whispers in without questioning their origin or intent. *Just trust in the process.* It was terrifying to surrender oneself to their most primal form and to continue walking to what she believed was certain death.

But the death never came. Stella wasn't sure when it happened, but the air around her had started warping and cracking without her intent, and to her surprise, Diana didn't rush forward at the opportunity to kill her. No, she *stepped back* in what Stella saw as fear.

The whispers got louder and louder as they seemed to reach a zenith. Stella's ears started ringing, and her head felt pressured as if her skull was struggling to contain the chorus. She wanted nothing more than to scream at them to be silent and to nurse her head, but she pressed on.

Just trust in the process.

It was like a mantra she repeated over and over. She was doing everything against what she felt was right, but she knew being stubborn was not the way to change and improve.

But then the sky vanished.

The blue sky filled with fluffy white clouds that lazily went by—it was always there, a constant in anyone's life and therefore pushed into the background—was gone. Diana didn't seem as distressed as someone should be at the sudden disappearance of the sky, so it must be something only she could see...

Stella stopped to look up, and what could only be described as the inside of a giant golden tree carved out into a spiraling library of celestial origin that spread upward into infinity loomed overhead in the nonexistent sky. Despite its incomprehensible nature, Stella felt a strange attachment and familiarity to the place, as if it had always been there, just out of reach and understanding.

Between the millions of bookshelves, ethereal streams of condensed knowledge flowed, and simply focusing on one for a single second made Stella's head pulse and the ringing grow louder. Still, even from such a brief interaction with the celestial library, Stella became confident of one thing.

I always felt like learning new things came easily to me. Rather than resistance to learning like others, for me, it felt like training an old muscle. Whether it be learning an ancient runic language to the point of fluency in a year from nothing but dusty old books or mastering alchemy in a matter of weeks to the level I could nearly win a tournament. People called me talented, but I never felt that way as that retracted from the work I thought I had put in, which didn't make any sense. But now it is all so clear...

Stella smiled. "All of this…is me. My past lives—"

"Arrogant as always," a voice boomed down from above, and to Stella's horror, she saw a humanoid cosmos floating within the vast library and glaring down at her with stars for eyes. Just gazing upon this celestial being made her body begin to falter and her consciousness waver.

"What do you mean?" Stella squeaked out as she felt incredibly small and pathetic. Ashlock's gaze contained this same otherworldliness but nothing to this extent.

"As the carrier of an ancient bloodline and to tap into its latent power, it's understandable for you to be arrogant. You are what the heavens would call…special," the cosmos said, shaking the world. **"However, this knowledge has been meticulously collected over the eons by your ancestors, not you. Instead of past lives, it would be more correct to say their knowledge lives on through you. I digress. There is much for you to learn, but you are far too weak as of now."**

Stella screamed in agony. Every word the cosmos spoke felt like the world falling upon her, shaking her soul to its core. It was painful, so, so painful, but she gritted her teeth and glared up at the cosmos.

"I have already learned and suffered enough. Tell me more. I can handle it!" Stella half begged and demanded. She hated nothing more than being kept in the dark and dismissed when she was so close!

"Foolish child, knowledge is power," the cosmos thundered. **"Those of our bloodline have ruled the realms since time immemorial, but knowledge without strength is as helpful as giving a sword to an ant."**

"But I am not an ant!" Stella protested. "I am almost at the peak of the Star Core Realm. I have mastered ancient runic languages and alchemy. I even know how to make runic formations, and my skills with the sword are far above those of my age! I seek knowledge… anything. So please…"

"Knowledge without strength to act upon it is nothing but a curse," the cosmos bellowed. **"You will wish to change the world yet be powerless to do so."**

Stella felt like coughing up blood at this point, but she refused to back down. Call it greed, stupidity, stubbornness, or even arrogance; she didn't care. She was determined to get something of value from this exchange rather than more questions, even if this cosmos did nothing but look down on her and disregard her achievements.

"I don't believe you," Stella insisted. "How could knowing be worse than being kept in the dark?"

To her surprise, the cosmos didn't berate her and call her a foolish child. Instead, it had an impossibly wide grin and leaned closer. **"How, indeed? Do you dare to find out?"**

Stella had to admit the cosmos's drastic tone change and unsettling smile made her second guess her provocation. But what could it possibly say to make her take back her words?

"I do dare," Stella replied, shuddering down to her soul when the cosmos smiled even wider.

"Very well, then, I will give you a hint at the truth—or so I claim. Without power, how can you differentiate reality from fiction?" The cosmos laughed, and Stella felt her consciousness start to escape her.

"Stella Crestfallen, have you ever wondered who your mother is? Do you remember her face or voice?"

My mother? Stella thought hard as the ringing in her ears worsened, and she felt ready to pass out. *I was so young when she left me… How could I possibly remember her? But now that I think about it, Father never mentioned much about her, either.*

"Do you not find it strange that you lack many brothers, sisters, and cousins as a noble family in this backwater sect that you are a part of? Having a large extended family is the norm in a world where people can live for centuries. So where is yours?"

"I…" Stella wracked her brain for an answer. Why had she never found that strange? Diana was the last of her family, but that was because the rest were wiped out, and there were still likely a few cultivators with the Ravenborne blood out there. But she had come into this world with basically only a father and whispers of a mother she had no memory of.

There was the story about her family sacrificing themselves for the Patriarch. But she had later learned that the Patriarch was simply keeping her around to use her as a pill furnace, so that story lost its validity in her eyes. For all she knew, they had been made up as there was no evidence of their legacy. No artifacts or personal items were left from their supposedly long lives.

"I don't know," Stella admitted. Her family history had always been a bit of a mystery, and with them all gone and leaving her alone on this mountain peak with nothing but murderous servants as a child, it was not like she had anybody to ask. "Could you tell me?"

The cosmos beamed as it leaned even closer, its starlike eyes twinkling with a mixture of malice and excitement. **"Ever wondered why you formed such an attachment to Ashlock? Or how can you understand the thoughts and focus of the other trees around you? Your dear mother is not human; she is, in fact, the World Tree. The very thing Ashlock will have to destroy to fulfill his destiny."**

Stella froze as she failed to comprehend the absurdity she had just been told. Her mother was the World Tree? How was that even possible? How could that even work— Stella dropped to one knee and felt the vast celestial library carved within a golden tree overhead begin to fade away as her mind shut down.

My mother is the World Tree? Stella couldn't believe it. *Then what of my father? Not Ashlock, but the bastard who abandoned me here in death?*

Having read her thoughts, the cosmos answered, **"He lives."**

Stella coughed up blood as the sky flickered back into existence.

The peaceful blue sky that had served as nothing but a background now seemed far more sinister. What other secrets could it be concealing?

Stella flopped onto the ground as her body gave up. Her vision was blurry, and the ringing had yet to cease. Every thought she had followed with a spike of pain, she wanted to cry. So she did. Warm tears streaked down her cheeks, and she wanted nothing more than a hug now. This was all too much.

Diana paused from taking steps back as the air around Stella stopped crackling from her mere presence. Yet she did not charge forth. That insanity and bloodlust had gone from her eyes. It seemed she had been shocked into control.

"You…win, Diana," Stella croaked with a light smile. It felt oddly insignificant to admit defeat compared to the world-shaking thing she had just experienced.

"What nonsense are you sprouting?" Diana said as she retracted her wings and claws. "Are you okay?! What happened?"

"No, I'm not okay at all…" Stella said as the ground beneath her began to rumble, and she felt something emerge and wrap around her waist. Glancing down with all the effort she could muster, her eyes widened as she saw it was Ashlock's root. Which was strange since it felt nowhere near as solid as she had expected.

"Calm down, Stella, don't cry. I got you." The thousand voices she was so used to rang in her mind as she felt her body lifted from the ground, and she was carried over to Ash. She was gently brought into his canopy and laid against his trunk on one of the thickest branches. The root remained wrapped around her to stop her exhausted body from falling, and to her surprise, it reached up and...patted her on the head.

"There, there," Ash said. *"Everything is all right. Rest here for a while, and tell me what happened when you have recovered."*

Stella reached up and held onto the root resting on her head. "Don't ever let go."

"Wouldn't dream of it."

I want to stay like this forever. Stella smiled as she felt the exhaustion catch up to her, and she fell asleep in Ashlock's embrace.

6
ANCIENT BLOODLINE

Ashlock had seen Stella distraught, scared, and angry in recent years, but she had almost only ever cried when she feared his demise. She was usually quite a strong girl when it came to her own problems, so something drastic must have occurred for her to go from battle maniac to crying within seconds.

"I wonder what happened." Ashlock used the tip of his ethereal root to wipe away the tears streaking down Stella's sleeping face. She had passed out and fallen into a deep sleep within a second, so it was likely backlash for whatever she had done at the end of the duel.

"For a moment, I felt the pressure of a being on the same level as Senior Lee coming from Stella," Ashlock mused as he continued patting her head as she peacefully slept. "She then looked to the sky and collapsed, coughing blood a moment later."

It was all bizarre, and all he could hope was that Stella would fully recover and fill him in on the details. He may have dulled emotions as a tree, but he knew when to put his curiosity aside and give her some space to recover before firing off questions.

"See, I can be a caring dad sometimes." Ashlock chuckled as he enjoyed this unintended feature of his new {Ethereal Roots} skill. It effectively turned his roots into limbs he could move freely so he could finally give a sort of hug. "Even if you are a rascal. I told you so many times to stop the duel because Diana was out of control, but you stubbornly pressed forward, so I can only hope whatever you saw in the sky was worth it."

"I can give her sweet dreams if you will allow it."

Ashlock looked down with his demonic eye at Elaine, who was still sitting on the bench with a deep look of concern on her face.

"With your illusions?" Ashlock asked.

Elaine nodded. *"She looks very distressed, so it might help her sleep peacefully."*

Ashlock glanced back at Stella. Her hands that had been gripping the root patting her head had fallen to her sides, and she had a look of unease on her sleeping face. Maple was curled up in her lap and looking up at her.

"If you are sure it will work, that would be nice."

"Sure, it's a simple illusion shaped by the happy thoughts in her mind, no matter how dormant they are." Elaine stood up and effortlessly jumped to Ashlock's lowest branch. Sometimes, he forgot that cultivators were superhuman, but seeing Elaine, who looked like a nerdy researcher, easily jumping three meters at a time up to where Stella was situated reminded him that looks could be deceiving.

Elaine gently tapped her finger on Stella's head, and within seconds, Stella's face transitioned from one of unsettled terror to a light smile. Her breathing also became less erratic and more relaxed.

"Thank you," Ashlock said.

"No worries, it's the least I could do." Elaine moved Stella's hair from her nose and put it behind her ear with a sigh. *"Almost hard to remember how scary she can be when I see her sleeping like this."*

Ashlock still vividly remembered the debate where Stella ordered Elaine's death; now, here Elaine was, wishing her sweet dreams.

"She has been getting better," Ashlock said. **"As she gains more life experience and interacts with a wide variety of people, her dark view of the world has slowly shifted. Or at least I like to think so."**

"I can only imagine what she has been through." Elaine stepped back with a frown. *"I have been told things here and there, but they paint a very vague picture."*

"Yeah…it's been complicated, to say the least."

Diana appeared in a blur next to Elaine, making her almost lose her balance on the branch.

"Ah! You scared me." Elaine readjusted her glasses. *"Are you…"*

"Sane? Yes, I am," Diana said as her eyes, which were black like ink, transitioned to her usual dull gray. They flickered between Elaine, Stella, and Ashlock's demonic eye. *"So? How is she?"*

"We don't know," Ashlock admitted. **"But Elaine used her illusion Qi to help her sleep peacefully, so I suppose we will see when she wakes up. What about you?"**

"Oh, me?" Diana blinked, surprised by the question. *"Not great, honestly. I fed my bloodline too much power and lost myself to its rage when Stella managed to land those hits on me. I'm sorry…"*

If not for Stella constantly telling him to stay out of it, Ashlock would have stopped the duel then and there.

"No need to be sorry. I take responsibility for whatever happens next," Ashlock reassured her. **"Stella told me to stay out of it, so I did. I trust her, but in hindsight, maybe listening to her was a bad idea. We will have to see if I made the wrong decision when she wakes up."**

Diana nodded as she massaged her temples. *"Yeah, that sounds like something she would do. Crazy…if not for that sudden pressure that shocked me out of my berserk state, I really would have taken her head off. I need to go rest. The backlash is killing my head."*

"Go for it. I need to rest, too." Ashlock sighed. What a fucking insane morning it had been. The sun had hardly risen, but he already wanted not just today to be over but this entire week. He had reached the bottleneck for Nascent Soul, upgraded one of his abilities with void Qi, turned Nox into a tree, and watched Diana and Stella almost kill each other in a duel that went way too far. All the while, he was still heavily injured with a large cut in his trunk that was leaking Qi.

Diana spread her majestic feathered wings but paused. *"Before I go, I wanted to give you this."*

"Oh? A present?"

"It's a bundle of demonic mist Qi flowers I managed to bring back from the Mystic Realm." Diana placed the bundle of black-and-blue flowers on the branch. *"Not sure if you can do anything with them, though a grove of them would be nice. Only if you want to, of course…"*

"Diana, you are like family to me." Ashlock picked up the flowers with telekinesis and brought them before his eye for inspection. **"Forget just a grove. I will give you a bastion of demonic mist Qi someday. Just give me some time, though. I must divert my resources to reach the Nascent Soul Realm for now."**

"Thank you, Ashlock. That means a lot." Diana gave a fang-filled smile as she turned to leave. *"Call me when Stella wakes up."*

"I suppose I will head out as well, then, and cultivate at the illusion Qi grove." Elaine jumped down. *"If you need anything, you know where to find me."*

"Sure thing. See you both soon," Ashlock told them.

Diana glided into the distance while Elaine walked through the mist wall and vanished from sight as she headed toward the mountain ridge of groves.

Now, it was just him and a sleeping Stella. Making sure she was secured in place with his root so she wouldn't fall during her sleep, he focused on the new flower Diana had just given him. He twirled it around for a while with telekinesis before his eye until a system prompt appeared.

[SINISTER FOG BELLFLOWER ANALYZED]

Opening his {Blooming Root Flower Production} skill menu, sure enough, this flower had joined his list of possible flowers he could grow.

"Might as well get a grove for Diana going before I sleep," Ashlock said, searching for a nice area with {Eye of the Tree God}. Since he also wanted some of his offspring to take on the demonic mist affinity, he decided to head to the east to the demonic tree forest.

He selected a large area among the newly growing trees and spawned hundreds of Sinister Fog Bellflowers. Qi flowed from his Star Core through his roots, and a field of black-and-blue flowers bloomed into existence, and a demonic mist soon started forming.

Ashlock let out a long yawn as he returned to Red Vine Peak. He was beyond exhausted.

Since it was still daytime, he retreated into his mind and fell into a state similar to daydreaming, focusing all his nutrients and Qi into repairing himself. He had earned a long rest…

Idletree Daily Sign-In System

Day: 3598
Daily Credit: 35
Sacrifice Credit: 2565
[Sign in?]

"Huh?" Ashlock stirred awake and wondered if he was miscounting. "I swear I had thirty-three daily credits last time I checked…"

Had two days really passed? Swiftly leaving his mind with more energy than usual, he glanced around. The sun was once again peeking over the mountains in the distance as if he had gone back in time by an hour. Stella was still peacefully asleep in his roots, and there was no sign of the others.

"Did I really sleep for two days?" Ashlock wondered if there was a quick way to check. Looking around, he eventually looked down at himself and saw that the large cut in his side made by Nox was half healed, and the cracks that had spread throughout his body were gone.

[Damage calculated at 17%]
[Repair body with credits? Yes/No]

"No way," Ashlock dismissed the prompt. With how high his cultivation was now, the cost of such an instant repair would be steep, and he needed to save every credit he could to form his Inner World and reach Nascent Soul Realm.

That aside, this amount of healing should be impossible in a single day, so maybe two days really had passed. Which made the fact Stella was still asleep so concerning. Had using her bloodline or whatever she saw in the sky inflicted such a backlash?

Larry was also still in his cocoon of silver ash, so it was quiet…

"I wonder how Nox is readjusting to her life as a tree?" Ashlock would grin if he could. He hadn't heard anything from the Redclaws regarding her yet, so it should be going well.

"Morning, Tree." A sheepish voice drew his attention to Stella, rubbing her eyes and yawning. *"I had the most pleasant dream. All the terrible things I'd been told went away like a spring breeze."*

"You can thank Elaine for that," Ashlock said as softly as he could as he loosened his hold on her waist now that she was awake.

"**She used illusions to help you sleep because you seemed deeply troubled.**"

"*Oh, that was nice of her,*" Stella said absentmindedly as she stared into the distance through a gap in his canopy. A long silence followed as the morning breeze rustled Ashlock's leaves and played with Stella's hair.

"**Do you want to talk about it?**" Ashlock eventually said. Talk about what, he wasn't exactly sure. Stella had mentioned something about being told terrible things.

"*I…don't know,*" Stella muttered as she tore her eyes away from the horizon and looked down at Maple in her lap. "*There's just so much to unpack that I don't even know where or how to start.*"

"**Diana asked me to get her when you woke up. Should I? Maybe she can help you work through it.**"

Stella slowly nodded. "*Okay, some of it will be interesting to her, I suppose.*"

Ashlock went and got Diana, who had been resting under the water Qi trees at the edge of the mountain peak.

"*Stella, you slept a long time,*" Diana said as she landed on the branch and gave her a warm smile. "*It's been a few days since our duel. Are you fine?*"

"*Physically? Sure I am.*" Stella cracked her neck and rolled her shoulders. "*I feel quite well rested, actually. Or at least as well as I could after what happened.*"

Diana's smile faltered. "*Look, if I caused whatever that was, I am sorry—*"

Stella waved her off. "*No. If anything, you helped me reach the 'ultimate' state of my bloodline. I should be thanking you.*"

"**Ultimate state? You learned more about bloodlines?**" Ashlock asked, unable to hold back his curiosity anymore.

"*Yes, I did, alongside some…other things,*" Stella said mysteriously. It seemed like a lot was going on in her mind as her gaze kept growing distant, and she kept opening her lips as if about to say something but then holding back.

"*Was this ultimate version you speak of the source of that presence I felt?*" Diana asked as she sat on Ashlock's branch and let her legs and wings hang off the sides.

"Sort of?" Stella looked at Diana. *"Though I was suffering under it just as much as you were, if not more."*

"That explains why you coughed up blood and fainted for two days." Diana shook her head in disbelief. *"That pressure from a few meters away was enough to scare my bloodline to where it came from. What was it that has such a presence?"*

Stella breathed out a long sigh. *"That's the thing, I don't know. It never gave me its name. Just called me arrogant because of my ancient bloodline."*

"Ancient bloodline?" Ashlock was growing more confused.

"Let me start from the top; otherwise, even I will get confused." Stella spent a minute organizing her thoughts before continuing. *"Let's start with the topic that caused this mess. Bloodlines, to my understanding, have three stages. Let's call them passive, active, and ultimate. Now, I don't know if all bloodlines have all three, nor do I know if everyone has a bloodline or only a certain few. All I know is I have an ancient bloodline, and I was able to tap into all three states."*

"Larry did say there was something ancient smelling about you and Diana," Ashlock chimed in. **"I suppose it was this ancient bloodline he smelled."**

Stella glanced up at the silver ash cocoon overhead. *"Yeah, looks like he was right."*

"So what is up with these three states of bloodlines?" Diana asked.

"Passive is the easiest one to explain, but bear in mind that I am working off many assumptions here, so this could all be wrong. However, I believe everyone with a bloodline will have some degree of this passive effect," Stella explained. *"In my case, the passive effect of my bloodline was the ability to learn things faster than usual from a young age. Learning was never hard. It always felt like warming up an old muscle rather than training up a new one, if that makes sense. You could almost call it my talent, if you will."*

Ashlock found that made a lot of sense. **"You always were quick on the uptake. So it was your bloodline that helped you progress so quickly in so many different areas?"**

"Yeah," Stella nodded, *"though it didn't hand those achievements to me on a silver platter. For example, as Diana knows well, I still had to spend every waking hour for a year straight to learn the ancient*

runic language to speak to you. A level of effort was still required on my part. It just came easier to me than it would to others."

Diana nodded. *"She worked so hard it was amazing to watch."*

"Calling in a talent sounds about right, then," Ashlock agreed. **"You are one of the hardest-working people I know, so I didn't say that to diminish your achievements. But it does help explain how you reached such mastery in many fields."**

"Yeah, and that brings me onto the second stage of a bloodline, the active one," Stella continued. *"Diana's transformation into a demoness is the best example of this. But for me, it was being able to enter the zone and hyper-focus on a task at the cost of a nasty headache for a bit afterward. This active part of my bloodline helped me win the alchemy tournament, and also, in many fights, it helped me manage the flow of battle. Yet the conditions to activate it are still rather vague compared to Diana, who simply feeds her bloodline power to manifest it."*

"Are you getting jealous again?" Diana teased. *"Even after seeing what happens when I let it run amok?"*

Stella shrugged. *"I see now that you have a more straightforward way of using the active part of your bloodline because the cost to use it is higher. My bloodline often activates when I need it, and the cost is nothing but a headache and exhaustion, whereas you trade your sanity for power. It took a lot for me to realize that. I focused far more on the result than the cost, which led to my...jealousy."*

"At least you can see that now." Diana sighed and leaned back, looking up into Ashlock's canopy. *"So what's this about an ultimate state you mentioned?"*

Once again, Stella became hesitant. She tried and failed to speak for a long time, with only the rustling leaves, chirps of birds, and streaks of sunlight accompanying the awkwardness.

"I surrendered to my instincts," Stella eventually muttered. *"I got the idea after seeing you embrace your demon form. In doing so, the whispers grew louder and louder, and then the sky was gone."*

Ashlock's demonic eye swiveled to gaze up at the vast blue sky. It looked the same as always, with clouds lazily floating by. Streams of various Qi types went by, as always. Nothing seemed amiss.

"In its place, a vast celestial library appeared carved from the inside of a golden tree that spread up to infinity." Stella raised her

arms as if trying to paint a picture. *"I didn't realize until it appeared, but it had always been there, feeding me knowledge. And upon witnessing this library of knowledge, I thought I had gathered it all from past lives until **it** told me otherwise."*

At the mention of a golden tree, Ashlock's thoughts instantly drifted to his many dreams and visions of the past World Trees that he sometimes saw after unlocking S-grade skills. This felt like too much of a coincidence. He dreamed of world trees, while Stella had access to a library made within one?

"Crazy celestial libraries appearing out of nowhere aside," Diana cocked a brow, *"past lives?"*

Ashlock wanted to pause on the whole library made from a world tree, but clearly, there were even more things Stella had to share, considering she passed over it so quickly.

Stella nodded. *"I felt a faint connection to all the information contained in that library that loomed overhead. Almost like a fragmented memory of a distant past, but in the moment, I was convinced that it was all knowledge I had collected in past lives."*

Ashlock found it interesting that Stella had a concept of past lives. Was the cycle of reincarnation known in this world?

"So what happened next?" Ashlock asked.

"A humanoid cosmos formed within the library and glared down at me with stars for eyes. It was the source of that pressure that made Diana step back and me to cough blood." Stella shuddered. *"If I had to guess, it was the ego of the library or perhaps one of my ancestors. It informed me with words that shook my soul that this was all the knowledge my ancestors acquired throughout the eons. That I was 'arrogant as always' and a carrier of an ancient bloodline."*

"Arrogant as always. That makes it sound like this cosmos has been watching you or has met you before," Ashlock said.

Diana added, *"Or there have been others with your bloodline in the past that were also arrogant."*

"Could be either, honestly. Its way with words was so confusing, and it didn't help that listening to it hurt so bad."

"So your bloodline's ultimate state is to peel back the veil of reality to expose a library that has always been there and to be shouted at by a cosmos?" Ashlock asked.

Stella shook her head. *"Simply focusing on a single stream of knowledge between the books gave me deeper insights into bloodlines. If I could have stayed there longer and explored more, I am sure I would have learned more than everything contained in that Azure Clan library."* Her face scrunched up in disgust and rage. *"But that cosmos ensured that was not the case. It called me a foolish child who didn't understand that knowledge is a curse—that knowledge is power, and without the capabilities to act upon knowledge, it's as useful as giving an ant a sword."*

Ashlock actually agreed with those words, but now wasn't the time to voice those thoughts. **"So what did you say in response?"**

"I called it out on its bullshit," Stella said bluntly, *"or at least I thought I did. I really believed knowing was better than being kept in the dark…"*

Stella trailed off at the end; the edges of her eyes started getting red, and her bottom lip quivered.

"What did it tell you, Stella?" Ashlock asked. **"You don't have to tell me if you don't want to, of course, but I can see you are hurting."**

Stella curled up into a ball, and while sniffling, she said something unbelievable.

"My Mother is the World Tree."

7
WORLD TREE'S DAUGHTER

Stella's mother was the World Tree? How the fuck was that even possible?

Ashlock had…questions. *Many* questions. Even with his system's vast powers, he wasn't yet capable of making a human-looking child and doubted he ever would.

The image of Stella's Father turned to a treehugger in his mind, and he felt his bark shudder at the thought—what horrible, unspeakable acts had occurred for this to happen?

Ashlock's mind was freed from its spiraling thoughts as he heard the silence broken by sniffling. Stella was still curled up in a ball to hide her face, and the more he looked at her, the more implausible her mother being the World Tree seemed. No matter how you looked at it, she was human through and through.

"Senior Lee has made it very clear that looks can be deceiving," Ashlock mused, but it still seemed impossible. Stella wasn't some godly being from a higher realm of creation but just a girl abandoned by her family…right?

Diana seemed stunned by Stella's words and unable to form a response as her mouth opened and closed like a fish out of water, so to fill the silence, Ashlock spoke to his daughter.

"What do you think about it?"

Stella raised her head, her eyes red. *"What do you mean?"*

"**Do you even believe that your mother is the World Tree? Are the words of the cosmos to be trusted?**"

Stella stared off into the distance with a look of realization. *"No... it kept insisting that knowledge without the power to act upon it was nothing but a curse. When I pressed on for answers, it laughed at me as if I was a fool and told me: 'Very well, then, I will give you a hint at the truth—or so I claim. Without power, how can you differentiate reality from fiction?'"*

"**So this cosmos thing could be lying?**" Ashlock said. "**Did it provide any evidence that your mother is the World Tree?**"

Stella frowned. *"No hard evidence, but it did make some good points. I have no memory of my mother, and my father hardly ever mentioned her. My family backstory is suspicious at best, with my family apparently dying in the last beast tide protecting the Patriarch."*

"Was that all this cosmic being provided as evidence?" Diana said while tilting her head. *"Those are some weak points."*

Stella shook her head. *"The cosmos also pointed out that I formed an unusual connection with Ashlock at a young age and that I can understand the thoughts and focus of trees around me."*

"Huh?" Diana said. *"You can do that?"*

Stella smiled weakly. *"Strange, right? When I was young, if I touched Ash's bark, I could tell if he was sleeping. As I've grown older, I can now feel if his focus is on me, and I can feel the emotions of his offspring like Willow."*

"Okay, that is weird." Diana bit her nail in thought. *"Do you have a dual core with nature affinity or maybe nature dao comprehension?"*

Stella shook her head.

"Is it a technique? Perhaps one taught when you were a child, so you forgot about learning it?"

Stella shook her head again. *"I don't need to use Qi or even think about it. Actually, until the cosmos mentioned it as a reason my mother is the World Tree, I never thought about why I could sense the emotions and focus of trees."* She shrugged. *"It felt normal to me, like breathing or blinking."*

"Maybe you really are part tree..." Diana squinted at Stella as if she was about to grow twigs out of her ears.

"**I still don't buy it,**" Ashlock said. "**Stella isn't the only one who has noticed my spiritual gaze, and my offspring emit their** emotions through Qi fluctuations. Considering we grew up together and how much Stella depended on my presence, I wouldn't be surprised if she grew more attuned to my spiritual gaze and the fluctuations."

Diana tapped her chin. *"That also sounds reasonable..."*

Stella gripped her head and pulled at her hair in frustration. *"Ugh, I have no idea what to believe! That stupid cosmos was right. Knowledge really is a curse. Today would have been like any other, and I would have lived on in blissful ignorance if I had kept my mouth shut, but noooo, I just had to demand answers."*

"I believe the cosmos is trying to teach you a lesson here," Ashlock said, "which it seems to have succeeded in doing. Unless it told you anything else we can use to verify its words? The World Tree isn't exactly close by to ask."

Stella froze at his words. *"There was something equally as shocking, which is made worse because it feels far more possible to be true."*

"What is it?"

"My father..." Stella's eyes widened as if she had just remembered. *"The cosmos said he is still alive."*

"Alive? I thought he died trying to force his way to the Star Core Realm?"

"That's what I was told through word of mouth," Stella agreed. *"I never actually saw his dead body for myself, though. But I assumed it was true because I was still young."*

"Assuming he is alive and we found him, what would you—"

"I don't care. That man is dead to me," Stella grumbled as she buried her head back into her knees. *"I grieved for him. I cried myself to sleep, wishing he would come back. But he never did. He left me here on this mountain all alone with murderous servants."* She leaned against his trunk and muttered, *"You are a better father than he ever was. Much better at sticking around."*

Ashlock had to admit that he felt some relief hearing Stella's opinions on her father. "Thank you, Stella. That means a lot," he said as he moved his root to pat her head.

"Ash...what should I do?" Stella asked after a while, looking up at his canopy. *"Should I believe the cosmos?"*

"Well, let's think. Verifying if your mother is truly the World

Tree would be difficult. Senior Lee told me the World Tree is capable of something close to speech through complex emotions, so we could ask her, but she is far away in the center of the Celestial Empire." Ashlock sighed. "There is also the issue that Senior Lee gave me the divine fragment that was supposed to be for the World Tree, and there's a chance she will try to kill me for it."

Stella bit her lip. *"The cosmos did say that the World Tree was the very thing you would have to destroy to fulfill your destiny."*

"That's a rather dramatic way of phrasing it, but that's not far from the truth. Nine divine fragments are spread throughout the realms, and one needs to acquire all nine to become a God. I hold one, and the World Tree needs it to initiate the Era of Ascension and rise to the next layer of creation."

Diana raised her hand. *"Question. Couldn't we bring the World Tree another of these divine fragments?"*

"We could," Ashlock agreed. "But then neither of us could become Gods as one fragment would be held by the other. It's complicated… There's a whole cycle that the World Tree doesn't know it's a part of, so it will never reach true divinity even if it had my fragment, but I have a chance of ascending to Godhood and ending this accursed cycle. With the help of you two and the others, of course."

"I don't really get it." Diana leaned back on her arms and gazed up into his canopy. *"But it sounds like this World Tree is going to be bad news to try and get answers from."*

"Yes, as a Monarch Realm being, I am not in a position to defend myself if I catch its ire," Ashlock said. "Or at least I think so. Monarch Realm is an incomprehensible level of power to me. Also, I do not know about the World Tree's combat capabilities other than Senior Lee saying the World Tree's presence was the reason the Celestial Empire could fend off the beast tides."

Diana whistled. *"Who knew your mother was so scary, Stella?"*

"Don't even joke about that." Stella glared at Diana. *"If she really is my mother, it opens up far too many questions that I fear the answers to. How was I born? Is my father human? What am I? Why am I out here in a demonic sect rather than living near her in the Celestial Empire? Will I turn into a tree and become as lazy as Ash—"*

"Oi," Ashlock interjected, **"when you experience time like I do** and have a body the size of a continent, you are allowed to be lazy. I could check on my roots in the far west and then head to the east, and I will be in a different time zone."

"Still lazy." Stella crossed her arms.

"With winter coming up, I am looking forward to being even lazier," Ashlock replied with amusement. Since the nights would be longer, he could spend even more time under the nine vertical moons, bathing in their lunar energies. To him, it was as pleasant as a visit to the spa had been, and he enjoyed the faster growth of himself and his offspring.

"If I do turn into a tree, I am going to grow right over there," Stella said, pointing at the ground near the bench. *"I will speak to you all day and night whether you like it or not. So you better hope it doesn't happen…"*

"So not much different from now?" Ashlock laughed. **"You know, for someone with legs, you sure like being rooted in place."**

"I have portals." Stella pouted. *"If I am needed somewhere or I want to visit someone, I can be there in seconds."*

"Wait…are all spatial cultivators this lazy? Is this the personality trait of spatial cultivators? Our sample size isn't the best. Willow and I are both trees. Titus is a walking tree, and Stella might be part tree."

"I am not part tree, darn it," Stella muttered, but it fell on deaf ears.

Diana hummed. *"I remember my father ranting about Grand Elder Valandor from the disciplinary committee, who is known to use strange white flame spatial techniques and is often late and lazy."*

"Wait, Grand Elder Valandor?!" Stella said. *"That name sounds super familiar, I think it was one of my father's friends. Oh yeah, I think he visited here when I was nine, and I tried to introduce him to Tree, but he wouldn't give him any fruit."*

A decision Ashlock was still glad about to this day. That guy was bad news.

"Wasn't he the person who said you had to pass that Grand Elder exam to stay as the sole heir to Red Vine Peak?" Ashlock asked as he pictured the white-robed man with a presence that made the whole building creak as it tried to bow to him.

"Oh yeah, I forgot about that." Stella snorted in amusement. *"I

believed it was impossible to reach Star Core Realm within five years, yet I still have a year left, and I am nearing the bottleneck for the Nascent Soul Realm. Hey, wouldn't it be rather funny to turn up to the exam stronger than the disciplinary committee members overseeing the test?"

"Not to mention your pure spirit roots and ancient bloodline." Diana shook her head with a smile. *"It's all so ridiculous. Those old farts would either faint in rage or accuse you of being someone from a higher realm wearing your skin. They would kill you on the spot."*

"Do you think Larry would let that happen?" Ashlock said. **"With his evolution, he will be stepping into a level of power on par with the Nascent Soul Realm. He might even be able to threaten the Patriarch."**

"That's true…" Diana muttered as she gazed up at the cocoon of silver ash nestled among Ashlock's branches overhead.

Stella giggled. *"If I summoned the bloodline library again and scared them with the cosmos' presence with Larry at my side, maybe they would bow down and call me Patriarch?"*

"You would like that, wouldn't you?" Diana smirked. *"I still haven't forgotten how you had hundreds of illusionary Elaines bow down to you."*

"Shut up." Stella glanced away, her face going red.

"Okay, we are getting off-topic." Ashlock paused as he gained the girls' attention. **"Asking the World Tree if it's Stella's mother is far too risky, so the better person to ask would be Stella's father, who is apparently still alive. If he is found alive, that gives more validity to the cosmos's ridiculous claim about the World Tree. Are we in agreement?"**

Both nodded.

"But how are we supposed to find him?" Stella asked. *"I haven't heard about him since he supposedly died. I don't even know his real name or remember his appearance."*

Ashlock had anticipated this issue. Stella hadn't seen her father in a long time and had still been a child back then when he supposedly died.

"Luckily, we have some leads. Grand Elder Valandor, for example, should know more about his whereabouts or at least his name and appearance as they were friends, right?" Ashlock suggested. "Another option would be buying information through the Eternal Pursuit Pavilion."

Diana grinned, showing her fangs. *"Is it finally time for me to begin my life as a bounty hunter and pill dealer?"*

"You both can. We still have those jade masks we looted from those foolish bounty hunters that hide your face and distort your voice, right?"

Diana's spatial ring flashed, and two masks appeared. *"Sure do."*

"Perfect, you can both use those and climb through the ranks, and maybe we can finally sell some fucking pills." Ashlock couldn't believe how they managed to do everything *except* sell pills. "I also need to eat Star Core cultivators of each basic affinity to ascend to Nascent Soul Realm, so you could use some of the earnings from the pills to place bounties on each other and the Ashfallen Trading Company."

Stella and Diana exchanged a grin.

"On that topic, I have evolved my roots to become more ethereal," Ashlock added as he patted Stella's head again. "It lets me do things like this, which is neat. But more importantly, the space within them is also now compressed, so the tunnels you once slid down to get into the cavern will act more like portals. Once I finish evolving all my roots and expand to reach the Tainted Cloud Sect, you two can freely move between the two sects."

Stella smiled as her hair was ruffled. *"I like this part of it more."*

Diana reacted differently as she shook her head again. *"That's absurd. Forget pills. Do you know how much you could make creating permanent portals between sects? Hell, even roots between cities in the same sect would boost trade."*

"I know," Ashlock assured her. He had seen the effects of globalization back on Earth and couldn't even imagine how absurd it would be if portals were involved.

"So what should we do for a few days while we wait for your roots to evolve?" Stella asked as she leaned against his bark.

Ashlock was about to suggest they rest or continue studying their bloodlines, but then he remembered there was someone he wanted to introduce them to…again.

"Talking of becoming a tree, how would you two like to meet Nox again?"

Stella's happy expression immediately soured. *"Ash, what did you do?"*

"Nothing much," Ashlock said innocently. **"I needed a guardian tree for Ashfallen City and thought a Nascent Soul Realm shadow tree would be a perfect fit, so I planted Nox's cursed-filled infant soul near the city…"**

Stella shrugged off his root and stood up with a grim expression. *"Where the hell is my axe?"*

8
SHADOW TREE

Nox had never liked the sun. She had kept to the shadows for centuries, drawing on the darkness to fuel her power and expand her Soul Core. She had felt exposed in the sunlight, like a fish out of water. Not only because her powers were heavily restricted and weakened under the intense light Qi, but also because people had sought her out. She may have put that 30,000 Yinxi Coins bounty to the back of her mind, but it had still hung over her head like death itself for many years.

The Celestial Warden may have an iron fist over the region as the figurehead of the Eternal Pursuit Pavilion, meaning most knew the bounty placed on her by the Lunarshade family was a joke, but upstarts clueless of the internal politics still tried their luck. Not to mention the other enemies she had made over the centuries would love to shove a sword through her chest.

It was weird to think out of that long list of enemies, the one that ended up succeeding was Stella from an upstart pill sect and a demonic tree.

But none of that mattered anymore. For all intents and purposes, Nox Duskwalker, the famed and despised merchant from the Tainted Cloud Sect and a Jade Sentinel of the Pavilion, died two days ago. She had watched on as her body and soul were torn up and fed to a demonic tree. What remained was a fleeting part of her, a fragment of her soul that had been twisted by a curse into something inhuman.

A tree.

The sun she had been so afraid of in the past now warmed her leaves that rustled in a peaceful breeze. She now rose to a height of around twenty meters, letting her lord over the other scarlet-leaved trees and having a clear view of the sprawling city of mortals she had been entrusted to defend. Ashfallen City.

"This is nice," Nox muttered in the confines of her mind. She had no mouth to speak, so talking to herself and watching the world pass by was all she could do.

She also spent much time coming to terms with her new existence.

Becoming a tree aside, she wasn't quite herself. A lot of things were…missing. She only realized the full extent of how much she had lost when she and all the other demonic trees slept under these nine vertical moons in a dreamscape. Under their lunar energy, her cultivation slowly recovered, and so did her memories and emotions as her soul healed from being ripped in half.

It was a strange experience being drip-fed fragments of her memories alongside small surges in emotions as she judged them without the full context.

Many things she had done in the past seemed so stupid and selfish in hindsight until she gained more context the next night, but by then, she had already changed her view and deemed it a poor decision, so the context carried less weight. It was almost like watching her life in reverse. She saw the consequences of her actions first and then the inciting incidents that caused them all with the damped emotions she now had as a tree.

It sufficed to say her life had been a joke—or at least that was the conclusion she had reached in two short days. It had been nothing but one wrong decision after another in the endless pursuit of power. In fact, it was almost torture at this point, having to regain her memories so slowly. She would rather remain blissfully ignorant of her past grievances if she could.

Talking of power, she still had some, even as a tree. Yet it was far below what she had at her peak as a human. Since she now only had half a soul, her presence had diminished to what she had wielded before her ascension. Furthermore, her fragmented soul, which had been fine for a human, was now stretched to fit the form of a still-growing trunk.

"Luckily, my connection to Heaven has remained strong, so I can still use the techniques I learned as a human," Nox said as she flexed her meager amount of stored shadow Qi, making shadows dance on her branches. "But now the question is how can I expand my power? I can't learn techniques like before, as I don't have arms. Even my breathing cultivation technique doesn't work anymore, so all I can do is sit here and hope I absorb some Qi."

It didn't help that the demonic tree that cursed her into this new existence ensured she paid her debts.

Strange ghostly roots that ran throughout the mountain had merged with her own roots during her first night—turning her from a lone tree into a part of a vast, interconnected forest that felt very much *alive*. Emotions ebbed and flowed through the roots of the many trees, and trying to comprehend them all drove Nox to insanity. Qi was pulled from her into the network against her will, but in return, she received water and nutrients that kept her alive.

Despite her relative strength compared to the demonic trees around her, she had no interest in trying to fight back at having her Qi taken. Spreading her spiritual sense and following the flow of Qi had drawn her focus to the demonic tree atop Red Vine Peak. It was a beacon of blinding and concentrated power worshiped by the other trees through the network as nothing short of a god.

Yet she wanted power, but not for the same reason as in the past.

That godly existence had entrusted her to watch over this city of mortals. Since Nox lacked purpose and very much wished to turn over a new leaf from her past, this seemed like a suitable goal. It was not like she had much choice, and it was hard to look down on mortals as lesser beings when they had legs...and could walk around freely.

"Shadow tree spirit, are you here?" A distorted voice brought Nox out of her thoughts. She heard the outside world as if someone was shouting through a wall if she didn't spread her spiritual senses. Once she did, the world sounded almost as good as when she had been human with ears. Looking around, she noticed a father and mother with their daughter walking up stone steps to where Nox grew on a raised ledge.

"Don't shout like that, Jasmine. You might anger the spirit," the mother scolded the girl who was skipping beside her.

Nox thought these three were particularly amusing. "So they are back again today?" Rather than drive them away with her presence that could easily squash a mortal, Nox welcomed anyone who would come and stop for a chat. Not that she could really reply. These two happened to live nearby, and the father had been among the first to notice her existence when returning from a shopping trip in Darklight City.

The other mortals mostly stayed away, never leaving their basic stone homes. But this Jasmine girl was a curious one and was probably more fearless because she was from the only family on this mountain apart from the Redclaws to have the talent for Qi.

"I never thought I would enjoy the company of mortals, though I suppose these three aren't mortals. They are just so weak they might as well be." Nox would have slaughtered these three for even looking in her direction in the past, but now she enticed them closer by leaking some Qi into the area. "If only I could do more than sit here in silence."

She had tried to use her Qi to communicate but thus far had little results.

"Look, Jasmine, I think it's recognizing our presence," the father said while ruffling his daughter's hair. *"Can you see those shadows dancing along the branches? Those don't match the morning sunlight, so it must be the spirit's presence."*

Nox tried to wrestle her shadows into words or something else, but her control over her Qi in this new form was fickle at best.

"Wow..." Jasmine muttered as she gazed up.

"There has to be something I can do," Nox muttered to herself. She didn't want to summon shadow fiends or use Night Beast Summoning because it would terrify these weak cultivators, and if she lost control of them, they could even die. "I need a body of some kind, a humanoid one to not scare them."

Nox thought for a while as the family wandered around, marveling at how tall she had grown in such a short time. Eventually, they sat down under her canopy cross-legged and began trying to cultivate from the instructions of a parchment. From a glance, it appeared to be the most basic breathing technique that those without an affinity used to cycle untamed Qi through their system.

It was a painful and inefficient technique used mainly by those outside the noble families with more specialized techniques for their affinities, such as rogue cultivators.

While they got to cultivating their abysmal techniques and gulping down pills, Nox continued thinking of a way to gain a body of some kind that was more humanoid.

"I know there are myths of tree spirits having a dryad form. Couldn't I make a shadow dryad?" Nox had a sudden realization. "My family's secret technique for making a second soul from our shadow, which I used to reach Nascent Soul Realm the first time. Couldn't I use that?"

Nox mentally activated the Shadow Soul technique and was relieved when the heavens understood her will. An intense pain followed as a tiny fragment of her soul was broken off and transported through her roots and into her vast shadow.

"Just as painful as the last few times," Nox hissed. It wasn't so bad if she kept reminding herself that tonight, she would have her soul healed under the nine moons. As the pain subsided a little, the feeling of control over her shadow heightened as if it were another limb.

Everything was going according to plan, except for the slight issue that her shadow was very much tree-shaped rather than humanoid. As the sun rose through the sky, her shadow was the area under her canopy. It hardly even looked like a tree and more of a hole-filled circle as streaks of sunlight snuck through her black-leaved canopy.

"Carving out a humanoid from this shouldn't be too hard," Nox muttered as she used her Qi to mold the shadows. Since her shadow was now part of her own soul, it was far easier to control than the surrounding shadow Qi since she didn't have arms or a voice to direct the heavens on carrying out her will.

"It definitely also helps that I lived as a human for centuries. Even though my soul has been altered by the curse to fit this new form, I still remember what it was like to be human."

It took until midday for Nox to wrestle her new Shadow Soul into submission and create something vaguely humanoid. It had everything a woman could need to put the mortals at ease. A striking figure with all the necessary limbs and a head with long flowing hair. The only problem was that it was nothing but shadows, so any finer detail than that would have to come with time and effort.

Nox sighed as she made her creation rise from the shadows and hide behind her trunk out of sight from the weak cultivators. "If I had a lot more shadow Qi, I could condense it down into a more liquid form or even remake it out of dark flames."

Sadly, it was the best she could do for now. Retreating from the confines of her mind, she inserted her consciousness into her Shadow Soul. It had a ghostly feel compared to her rooted-in-place body. She flexed her shadowy arms and fingers and had to admit it felt freeing to have limbs again.

Peeking past her trunk to see what the cultivators were up to, she froze as she locked eyes with Jasmine, who was taking a break from the brutal breathing technique. Her face was red, she was out of breath, and her hair was glued to her forehead.

"Ah! The spirit woke up!" Jasmine shouted as she pointed at Nox.

The mother was the first to respond, awakening from meditation and grabbing Jasmine by the hand. *"Julian, wake up."* She kicked him in the side, making the man blink in confusion. *"We need to run."*

"What the—" Julian stumbled to his feet and stood before his wife and daughter with his hands raised with whisps of untamed Qi enveloping his fists.

Nox didn't know whether to laugh or cry at this situation and then realized she could do neither. "I picked the least frightening form I could manage, yet they still backed away in fear. Are mortals really this skittish?"

Even with the Qi enveloping Julian's fist, it was hard to call him a cultivator.

With her hands raised to show she was not a threat, Nox floated around her trunk. What followed was an awkward standoff. Nox showed no signs of attacking while Julian stood there panting and burning his Qi to keep his feeble attack going.

Eventually, his arms dropped, and he kneeled over, gasping for air.

"Julian!"

"Dad!"

The mother and daughter went to help the man who had collapsed from surpassing his limits by…standing there. Discovering one's limits was one of the first things a cultivator learned. Just how had this man gotten to that age without knowing the basics?

"He's going to pass out if he isn't given some Qi." Nox floated closer, much to the mother's horror.

"Don't come any closer, spirit!" the woman shouted as she stood and tried to stop the shadow from approaching, but Nox simply phased through her body like a mist. Arriving before the man, who was thankfully still within her shade and not out in the sun, Nox placed her ghostly hand on his back and began transferring some untamed Qi.

The daughter, wielding Qi like a maniac, charged at her. *"Leave my dad alone! Don't eat him!"*

"Who said anything about eating? I'm trying to save him." Nox mentally sighed. Maybe she wasn't cut out to be a good person, and these mortals wore her patience thin.

The whole thing had turned into a mess. All Nox wanted was to guide them in cultivation and perhaps chat through hand signs. Instead, her reward for her efforts was one collapsed man on the verge of passing out that she was trying to *save* and two screaming people trying to slap her away as if she were an annoying swarm of flies.

"Just be patient," Nox convinced herself. "Once the father recovers, they will forgive me."

Her efforts paid off as Julian visibly recovered and managed to get his breathing under control. She was about to float away when she felt the tremendous presence that spread throughout the mountain focus on her.

"Nox, I am about to send Stella and Diana to meet you, so be nice— What in the hell is going on here?"

A voice that sounded like a thousand people speaking at once thundered in her mind and made her Shadow Soul tremble. It was barely formed, so it was not designed to handle such pressure.

"This is a misunderstanding," Nox said as she floated back toward her tree. "I was trying to help them…"

To be fair, she could see why the godlike tree would misunderstand. The scene didn't exactly paint a good picture.

A portal ripped open behind the mortals, and two people stepped through. One was likely the demoness that had impaled and rammed her into the ground, while the other was Stella…with an axe.

Stella took one look at the mortals before her presence came crashing down. "Nox, you bitch, do you have any idea how much effort I spent to save these three!" Stella teleported at her with the axe wreathed in spatial flames.

All Nox could do was raise her hands and pray her new life as a tree wasn't about to end.

9
SOUL DAMAGE

Ashlock surged his power through the mountain to create a portal before Stella.

She had been focusing on axing the shadowy humanoid floating before Nox's tree, so the sudden portal's appearance caught her off guard, and she let out a yelp as she tumbled through face first and ate the dirt nearby.

"Ugh," Stella groaned as the axe she had gotten from god knew where went flying. Such a dramatic redirect had not been his intention, and if Stella had been focusing, she could have easily avoided such a dramatic fall.

Ashlock was unsure of the situation despite Nox's insistence that it was a misunderstanding. Deciding it was better safe than sorry, Ashlock used {Progeny Dominion} on Nox. Since she was morphed into a tree from his curse and fused with his roots, she was now one of his many offspring and, therefore, under his control.

[Progeny selected: Initiating soul transfer…]

Ashlock felt a piece of his soul break off and travel through his roots. As it descended, the mountain glowed and trembled with power due to his presence. The spectacle of a mere fragment of his soul moving outside his body had grown more extreme as his power increased.

[Soul fragmented: Damage to soul mitigated]

A feature of the system he appreciated as anything to do with the soul was a scary process, even with the knowledge that he could heal. Moments later, his soul fragment had journeyed across two mountain peaks and forced its way inside Nox's soul within the tree.

[Connection complete: Time till sundown 5:10]

Ashlock dismissed the notification as something felt off compared to normal. The strange feeling could be chalked up to the fact that Nox was different from his other offspring, but something else was definitely bothering him.

Looking inward, his soul fragment was floating within Nox's soul, and his system skill {Progeny Dominion} gave him an iron-like control over it. Yet something felt like it had escaped his control…

"Please forgive me, oh great tree." Ashlock heard a distant-sounding voice in his head. Following its direction, he saw the humanoid shadow floating beyond the tree's bark with her hands raised. *"This really is a misunderstanding. I didn't want to scare the mortals, but I couldn't think of another way to communicate with them, so I tried to make a shadow in a humanoid shape—"*

"**Is it made from your Qi?**" Ashlock interrupted. If it was made from her Qi, why did it feel outside of his control?

This situation reminded Ashlock of how he used to control corpses with {Root Puppet} to write in blood on the walls in an attempt to communicate. It seemed that as an ex–Nascent Soul Realm cultivator, Nox could skip many of the steps he had struggled through as a tree on the quest for communication.

"What? No…well, sort of." Nox became flustered at his question.

"**For a tree, I have rather thin patience and expect obedience from my offspring.**" Ashlock tightened his hold on Nox's soul to prove his point. "**May I remind you why you still live? I would have devoured your infant soul for dessert if not for my benevolence. So just tell me what it is. How did you make it if not from Qi?**"

He hadn't been watching Nox over the last few days as he had been recovering from the terrible damage *she* caused to his trunk, so he didn't know if she was still the murderous merchant or had turned over a new leaf. Once he figured out how different she was now as a tree, he could treat her accordingly, but withholding information was not a good start.

"I'm sorry…your presence makes thinking hard; a thousand voices are ringing in my head, and I can't breathe under this pressure." Nox gasped, and Ashlock saw the human shadow flickering like a dying flame. *"I am not trying to defy you, so please…"*

Ashlock relaxed his presence as he realized he might have been too heavy-handed. Not only had Nox suffered, but the entirely black tree was now wreathed in lilac spatial flames, and everyone had stepped back to avoid being crushed by his pressure.

"Thank you." Nox's shadow regained shape, and her voice became clearer. *"To answer your question, my family has a secret shadow technique called Shadow Soul. It's a rare soul technique that lets us split a piece of our soul off and have it inhabit our shadow. Though it has many other uses, I used it to pre-prepare my infant soul for my Nascent Soul ascension and now to make this."*

Ashlock realized why it was outside his control since it was technically a second person, and only those fused with his roots and connected to his network were controllable with {Progeny Dominion}.

"So you used this technique to create a dryad out of shadows?" Ashlock remembered how he had devoured Nox's Shadow Soul before and gained many credits. **"What are some of its disadvantages?"**

Since Nox didn't have the system to handle the process and prevent soul damage, he felt such a powerful and secret technique would come with some downsides.

"Same as all soul-based techniques. It takes trial and error to learn new techniques, and when the penalty for failure is soul death, few have the guts to try, and of those that do, most die on their first try. For this technique specifically, the main downside is that if the Shadow Soul dies, you lose that part of yourself forever. Which can cause a sharp change in personality and warped view of the world."

"Did that happen to you when I devoured your Shadow Soul when you were escaping?" Ashlock asked.

Nox's shadow shrugged. *"That's the worst part. I have no idea. Soul damage is far more sinister than losing an arm, as you don't know what is missing."*

That was something Ashlock knew all too well. Thankfully, the system kept him from changing too much when he used {Progeny Dominion}, but he did feel like a part of him returned once the skill ended at nightfall.

"So Nox was able to make this human form due to a secret shadow affinity technique," Ashlock mused. "I wonder if spatial Qi would let me do something similar? Not that I am too fussed about having a humanoid body anymore, as I am far more comfortable in my bark and can do anything I want."

More importantly, he could not fully restrain this Shadow Soul of Nox's, which was a concern. Not that he would tell her that.

"Best I keep siphoning most of her Qi to keep her from growing too strong before I turn her into a bastion." Ashlock's {Skyborne Bastion} skill meant he would gain more control over Nox as the Bastion Core she would draw power from would be directly linked to him through his {Ethereal Roots}. The only issue is he needed one thousand credits to use the skill, and he was saving toward the ten thousand credits he needed to ascend to form his Inner World.

"Why did you do that, Ash?" Stella grumbled as she finally got to her feet after eating the dirt and patted herself down. *"Nox was clearly hurting those mortals I went through so much effort to save, yet you are protecting her!"*

"Mistress Stella, if I may…" Julian, who had recovered, gave her a bow.

Stella crossed her arms and looked down at Julian despite the specks of dirt still on her face. *"What is it, Julian?"*

"We also thought the shadow spirit was trying to attack us, but we misunderstood its intentions. It simply hid behind the trunk, watching us cultivate, and when we discovered its existence, it made no effort to attack us." Julian clenched his fists at his side. *"I ended up nearly passing out by expending all my Qi on defending my family. Yet the shadow spirit gave me some of its Qi to stabilize my condition despite my family's attempts to ward it off."*

Stella raised a brow. *"So you're an idiot."*

Julian froze under Stella's glare.

"The word you're looking for is 'inexperienced,' Stella. Not idiot." Diana shook her head as she went to pick up the discarded axe. *"They only became cultivators recently, so it's natural that they didn't know about Qi deprivation. Give them a break."*

"I didn't need anyone to tell me that using Qi until you pass out is a bad idea—"

"Did you forget you have a bloodline library in your head?" Ashlock pointed out.

Stella paused mid-sentence and frowned. *"That's true."* She stopped looking at Julian and focused back on the shadow floating before the tree. *"So it was a misunderstanding. Nox was not attacking but trying to help instead?"*

"Yes, that is why I stopped you," Ashlock said. **"And as you can see, a fragment of Nox's soul may inhabit this tree, but she is now one of my many offspring. So chopping her down with an axe hurts me, too."**

Stella's lips rounded into an *O*, and panic appeared in her eyes. *"I would never hurt you! Never ever—"*

"I know, Stella. I don't blame you," Ashlock reassured her. **"The situation looked bad when we arrived, and I am sorry for making you eat the ground when you were just trying to save them."**

Stella scratched the back of her head awkwardly. *"Looks like I jumped to conclusions. So what is that shadow thing? Is it Nox? Can it speak?"*

The shadow shook her head. *"I only formed this Shadow Soul moments ago. Perhaps I could figure out a way to speak with my Qi in time, but I can only shout in my mind for now."*

Ashlock relayed Nox's words to Stella.

"Is this the same Nox we know?" Stella questioned as she walked around the floating shadow woman with a frown.

"Well? Are you?" Ashlock asked Nox.

"I couldn't be further from the Nox you knew if I tried. Not only was the majority of my soul taken from me, but I am forced to reflect on my past actions through fragmented memories at night under the nine moons."

"You are also taken to that dreamscape and have your soul healed during the night?"

"Yes, alongside the rest of the forest," Nox replied. *"Should I not?"*

"To enter there means you really have become one of my offspring. What do you think of the place? Any idea what the moons could mean?"

"My time under the moons is spent reflecting on my past, so I never thought too deeply about the moons themselves." Nox hummed in thought. *"I can take a closer look and think more about it for you tonight?"*

"That would be helpful. I hope you understand my hesitation to trust you, but if you help me, I will help you in return."

"I understand my position. I am to watch over Ashfallen City and repay my debts to you with Qi."

Ashlock felt it almost suspicious how reasonable Nox was being compared to his image of her in his mind, but as she mentioned, she is basically a new person under his domain now. Messing with the soul did that to a person.

"I am glad we have reached an understanding. Was there anything you wished to do that I could help you with?" Ashlock asked.

Having lived as a tree, he knew how lonely and frustrating the early years could be. The fact Nox was already adjusting so well was likely due to missing so much of her soul from when she had been human. Did she even remember what it was like to be human?

"Would it be fine if I teach these mortals how to cultivate?"

"Pardon?"

"Ah, sorry if that is stepping out of line," Nox said. *"I just wanted to help. Their techniques are too crude, and nobody seems to guide them."*

That was sort of on purpose. Ashlock had wanted to see how these mortals turned cultivators via his truffles would develop independently. If he had the Redclaws teach them, and all three ended up as fire cultivators, that would be a waste in his eyes.

"Wait...since I am stuck at my bottleneck and only have to gather the sacrificial credits and required Star Cores to form my Inner World, I can spend as much Qi as I want. So I can grow as many truffles, fruit, and flowers as I wish since my Qi regeneration nowadays is absurd due to {Nocturnal Genesis} and all the forests I am connected to."

If that were the case, Ashlock could grow truffles and have as many mortals turned into cultivators as he wanted. Weak cultivators, even without oaths, did not threaten him as they lacked the resources and techniques to rise in power. But with purer spirit roots to cycle Qi in their bodies, they become more productive and resistant to disease and the cold.

"Though I still need to give all the Redclaws a spirit root improvement truffle first, and even with maximum output, I will only be able to produce enough truffles to turn a few hundred mortals into cultivators." Ashlock grew excited but then soured on the idea when he realized he would need to distribute the truffles somehow. Should he sell them? If so, to whom? And how would the truffles get from Red Vine Peak to the mortals? What a headache…

His gaze drifted beyond the trunk, realizing he had forgotten the biggest advantage of running a sect. He could simply push the work onto someone else! He had the heavenly ink oath-bound Julian right here, who had been appointed as Head of Logistics' for the mortal branch of the Ashfallen Trading Company that was going to be used to sell pills to the mortals in the near future. The perfect man for the job!

"That just leaves distribution from Red Vine Peak." Ashlock pondered if he should send them via his {Ethereal Roots}. "Yeah, that could work."

"Is helping just these three really too much? I promise I won't go overboard…" Nox said with a sad sigh, and Ashlock realized he had been silent for a while, lost in his own thoughts.

"No, I was simply lost in thought as you gave me an interesting idea. You wanted to help teach people how to cultivate, right? That is fine by me… Actually, I have a way you could help them and others even more."

"Really?"

"Yes, you still have the power of at least a peak Star Core, right?"

"I do, in theory," Nox said. *"But I have limited Qi to work with, and my control over my Qi is far more fickle than when I was human."*

"That's good enough." Ashlock had never grown truffles anywhere except below his roots, as they were too dangerous to grow elsewhere without constant protection. However, Nox was almost on par with him in power, making her the perfect guardian tree for his idea.

"Nox, I will bless you with various truffles and fruits with profound effects. You experienced some of them during the negoti-

ations with Stella through weakened pills. I will handle the initial Qi cost."

"I don't understand..." Nox muttered.

"Just watch."

Ashlock opened his production menus. He selected one of each truffle type: Spirit Root Improvement, Heart Demon Expelling, and Skin Improvement. Qi was drained from his body through the root network, and they began to grow in the rock and dirt below Nox.

He also manifested a bundle of each fruit from her branches that he had planned to sell to mortals: Florist's Touch, Enlightenment, Neural Root, and Deep Meditation.

"What is all this?" Nox seemed baffled. *"How are these growing before my eyes?"*

"In your past life, you were selfish and only knew how to take from others," Ashlock said. **"Now, as a tree, you have an opportunity to learn the joy of giving. These truffles and fruits are a gift you can offer to anyone you wish, but you will have to handle the Qi cost of growing them back, so be frugal."**

Nox's shadow stared up at the branches that had been bare and now had stalks and the beginnings of fruits growing from them in awe. Yet Ashlock wasn't done.

"Do you have a favorite flower?"

"Not really. I never was one for gardening," Nox muttered absent-mindedly.

"Okay, then, what is the first flower that comes to mind?"

The shadow stopped gazing up and glanced at the little girl standing beside her parents and watching in amazement.

"Jasmine," Nox replied. *"A beautiful and delicate white flower."*

"Good choice." Ashlock summoned his {Blooming Root Flower Production} menu and decided to select the whole area around Nox. Qi filled the area, and the system fulfilled his order of a mountainside of jasmine.

Small white flowers bloomed from between the cracks in the rock, turning the dreary gray rock and dirt into a sea of white, like fresh snow. And in the middle of this field was Nox, the shadow tree who lorded over it all.

10

A CULTIVATOR'S PERSPECTIVE

Stella took her hand off of Nox's bark. She could tell Ash and Nox were talking to one another by the indescribable flow within the tree but could not comprehend their words. Maybe one day, she would figure out how to speak tree, but until then, she would have to rely on Ash projecting his presence into her consciousness and speaking to her there.

More importantly, Stella could feel no ill will from Nox. The merchant-turned-tree certainly wasn't as welcoming or cheerful as the rest of Ashlock's offspring when Stella got close, but she wasn't guarded nor hostile.

Nox is more curious than anything if her emotions are to be trusted, Stella thought as she stepped back. *I suppose it really was wrong of me to charge at her with an axe.*

Stella hated Nox with a passion, but if the tree version of her was like a new person, she wasn't one to hold grudges... Also, she liked trees. It would be a shame to cut one down, especially one capable of speech like Ash.

Willow is getting close to speech, and Quill can write on his bark, Stella mused as she turned to look at the shadow woman floating beside Nox's trunk. *But none of them are capable of this. Even Ash can only make Ents or control corpses.*

The humanoid shadow resembled a woman with long hair that floated down her back. It seemed quickly made, as other than some definition for her eyes and a mouth, there wasn't much else. Yet Stella could tell it was more than a bundle of shadow Qi forced into the shape of a human woman. It was far more than that—it felt alive.

It's as if it has a soul.

Suddenly, the surroundings became a torrent of power. Not the kind that hurt anyone or made them kneel. Rather, it let you know a miracle was occurring.

"Daddy, what is happening?" Jasmine asked Julian, who had recovered from earlier and was now holding his wife's and daughter's hands and staring up at the shadow tree with a lost expression.

"I…don't know."

"Don't worry, this is the power of the Immortal," Stella said casually. "My father."

Of course, not the deadbeat father who left me for dead on Red Vine Peak. I don't care if that bastard is alive or not, nor his reason for leaving me. Ash is the only family I have.

"This is the power of an immortal?" Catherine muttered in awe as she leaned against Julian.

Rustling overhead drew Stella's attention. Looking up into the dark canopy of black branches and leaves, splashes of color bloomed as bundles of fruits sprouted from stalks. From the reds, yellows, and greens, Stella could identify each fruit and their effects.

To think Ash could grow those godly fruits through his offspring. Does Nox even realize how much trust he has in her by this gesture? Stella wondered. *He has always kept those fruits as close to himself as possible in fear that others would find out and hunt him down or the Blood Lotus Sect would enslave him.*

Stella smiled. It was nice to see Ash being less cautious and more trusting of others, especially considering how powerful the Ashfallen Sect had become.

When will Larry awaken from his evolution? I hope it's soon, Stella pondered. *He was already so powerful before that after his evolution I wonder if I should be more worried for our enemies than us.*

"Wow!" Jasmine shouted as Stella felt power coil around her feet. "It's so pretty."

Looking down, Stella saw a field of small white flowers blooming from the cracks in the stone and soil. It continued until the entire area was blanketed in a white that swayed with the wind. It was breathtakingly beautiful.

"Cultivators really are gods in human skin to be capable of this," Julian muttered.

"No," Stella refuted, striding through the field of white flowers over to them. Just how *wrong* could they be to say only humans were cultivators?

"A cultivator is any being that can bend the world to their will. Be it a human, floating shadow, tree, demoness, or even a monster. Your skin and bones are nothing but a vessel for your soul—which is all that really matters. Do you understand?"

All three of the mortals kneeled before her with their heads bowed.

"I apologize for my ignorance, Mistress," Julian said with all his heart. "Please teach us the ways of cultivation. Despite following the parchments given to us and taking the pills, I find myself at a loss. The way of a cultivator remains a mystery to me."

Stella had been worried for a moment that the mortal's opinion of her had dropped because of her rash actions earlier, but it seemed her worries were unfounded. With her mood improved, she decided to impress these mortals with her insights and wisdom!

"Then let me teach you. First, you need to change your mindset and see the bigger picture. Mortals are much like these flowers here." Stella crouched down, plucked one of the white flowers, and twirled it between her fingers. She paused for a moment as she was unsure where she was going with this analogy.

"Flowers are plentiful and even beautiful for a time. But come winter, they wither and die. Their short lives come to an end, and another similar yet different flower will bloom in its place come spring. A constant cycle that cannot be escaped or defied. Those are the shackles of mortality that had bound you until recently."

Stella felt it a shame to toss the flower that had been grown by Ash, so she put it behind Jasmine's ear, making the girl smile. It was cute.

Focus, Stella. Now's not the time.

"Ahem. Now, in comparison to a flower, a cultivator would be a tree." Stella gestured to Nox, the black-barked tree that loomed over them. "Starting as nothing but a sapling, a tree faces the same threats as these flowers in its infancy. But it has far greater potential for *more*. As it grows and survives multiple winters, it rises toward the heavens as if to defy it. Eventually, the tree will tower over the mortal flowers and watch on unfazed as the life cycle continues and years turn into centuries."

Stella stood back up and looked down at the three mortals-turned-cultivators. "As you meditate on Heaven's whispers and learn more about our woven reality, you realize just how *insignificant* you really are. That's what drives cultivators to seek the peak—to reach immortality. A constant fear of the very thing they thought they had escaped: death. Or at least that is how I see things. Others may disagree."

A clapping came from across the clearing.

"That was well said, Stella." Diana grinned, showing her fangs. "Mortals beg for protection from cultivators, but to us, they are like ants. Clueless of the world, small and insignificant and far beneath us. We may often look the same as we all started as weak mortals, but can you really say mortals and cultivators are anything alike because of how they appear on the surface?"

As if to prove her point, Diana manifested and spread out her majestic wings of feathered darkness that were thrice her height—earning a gasp from the mortals.

"So that is why the Voidmind family abandoned us." Julian clenched his fists. "Even after being gifted the ability to cultivate by the Mistress, I still couldn't understand their cruelty. Why had they left us all to die? But the answer was that we were nothing but a field of flowers or a bunch of worthless ants to them?"

Catherine looked up and locked eyes with Stella. "What made us different? If we are nothing but ants to you, why did you save us?"

"The Immortal asked me to save the people of Slymere." Stella shrugged. "And because I wanted to. I am not so heartless as to watch people die in front of me if I can save them."

"Because you wanted to," Catherine muttered in disbelief. "I live because you saved me on a whim and nothing else…"

Diana sighed. "Cultivators are often seen as selfish because they have to spend the Qi they meticulously gathered over a long period to bend reality to their ideals. Julian, you passed out earlier while protecting your family, right? A valiant deed, but can you feel any Qi left in your body?"

Julian closed his eyes. After a moment, he let out an annoyed grunt. "No, it's all gone."

"Hours of meditation...wasted. That is the price of power, and sometimes we have to exchange more than just Qi, such as our souls or blood." Diana floated over the field of white flowers with a single flap of her wings; landing gracefully before them, she continued, "The Qi you spent all day gathering is now gone, and you will have to start again. Now imagine these two weren't your family but two random animals. Would you put yourself in harm's way to defend them with the same vigor and cost? Bear in mind, spending your Qi not only sets you back but also makes you weaker and possibly unable to protect those you love from threats."

"I see what you are saying." Julian gritted his teeth. "So the Voidminds didn't save us from the storm because our lives weren't worth the Qi. That still leaves a sour taste in my mouth. But the Immortal saved us. Does that mean he wasted his Qi and was weakened because of us?"

"When you wield power on this scale," Stella gestured to the field of flowers that had bloomed before their eyes, "saving mortals, even an entire city of them, is a simple affair. Few can threaten you when you are one of the strongest in the realm, and problems can be easily solved with a wave of one's hand."

"If I become powerful, I can save people, too!" Jasmine had stars in her eyes as she clenched her fists. "Just like Mistress Stella!"

Stella felt her eye twitch. *Does this girl think I spend my days going around and saving mortals? I couldn't think of anything more ridiculous.*

As if noticing her discomfort, Diana stepped before Stella. "You sure can, little miss. The best part about being a cultivator is that you get to decide how you use your power. The world is dark enough, so maybe a few mortal-turned-cultivators would help give the common people some light and hope. On that note, Julian, can you come with me?"

Julian rose to his feet with a serious expression. "May I ask what for?"

"The Immortal has requested that we work together on establishing the mortal branch of the Ashfallen Trading Company. The Mudcloaks will handle construction overnight, so we need to find a location and decide how it will look and be run." Diana held her hand as if asking for a handshake. "We will be working together from now on and have a lot to do. My name is Diana, and I handle the finances and business side of the Ashfallen Sect."

Julian shook her hand. "My name is Julian. I was appointed Head of Logistics, so it's a pleasure to meet you, too— Whoa!"

Stella looked up and held back a laugh as she watched Diana haul Julian into the sky by his arm, his legs uselessly kicking in the air. "See you later, Stella!" Diana shouted as she glided down the mountainside toward the center of Ashfallen City.

"Don't worry, he will be fine," Stella reassured Catherine and Jasmine, who peeked their heads over the mountain ledge. "I would be more impressed if he wrestled out of her grip and fell."

They didn't seem convinced as they kept watching until the pair became nothing but small dots. Stella shrugged and was about to return to Red Vine Peak to nap when she heard Jasmine call out to her.

"Wait, Mistress!"

Stella paused and turned back to face the girl. "Yes?"

"My dad told me if I wanted to become strong and join the Ashfallen Sect, I had to meet Kaida. Do you know where I could meet him?"

"Jasmine!" Catherine hissed as she crouched beside her daughter. "We talked about this…remember? We were going to wait a while to see if it's a good idea first."

What is she going on about? Stella wondered. *What did Kaida have to do with anything?*

"Lead them to Kaida and ask for the employment contract. He knows what to do," Ashlock spoke into her mind. **"Also, nice speech. Glad to hear you representing the spirit trees as cultivators."**

Stella felt her ears burning. Cleared of her confusion, she gave Jasmine a smile and said, "Sure, I can lead you to him. Are you coming as well, Catherine?"

The mother looked apprehensive, but her daughter's bubbling excitement was hard to say no to. Eventually, she sighed and nodded. "Yeah, I suppose it's for the best we join officially."

Stella's silver spatial ring flashed with power, and the largest sword she owned appeared levitating on the floor. Ashlock had given it to her a while ago. It was impractically large and heavy, so even with her strength, it was useless in combat, but its size made it useful for flying multiple people around.

I could just portal them over, but I think a ride on a flying sword will help them realize just how different cultivators are from regular mortals.

"Hop on, and let's go—" Stella froze as she felt Jasmine's hands wrap around her waist, and the rascal buried her head into her back. She then felt Catherine's hands grip her shoulders.

What in the nine realms are they doing! Maybe I should have taken the stupid portals. There is plenty of space on the sword to stand, so why are they hugging me? Oh wait, they don't know it's impossible to fall off.

Letting out a sigh and deciding it wasn't worth the effort to explain to them as they wouldn't believe her, Stella pushed Qi into the sword, and with a pulse of her Star Core, they shot into the sky.

Jasmine screamed into her clothes, and Catherine wasn't much better as she wrapped her arms tightly around Stella's neck and held on for dear life.

The whole time, Stella stood there rigidly with an annoyed expression tugging at her lips. She hoped they would calm down once she leveled out the sword and flew straight, yet the two didn't let go.

I am displeased.

Deciding enough was enough, Stella freed herself from the two sets of arms wrapped around her neck and waist and turned to glare at the two. "I have surrounded the sword with my Qi. It's *impossible* for you to fall off, and even if you did, I would catch you with a portal. So relax, stop screaming, and do not touch me."

The two didn't seem convinced, so Stella shoved more Qi into the sword to make it suddenly jerk forward, causing Catherine to fall backward, yet she was stopped by an invisible barrier with Jasmine in her arms. It took a moment for the woman to open her eyes that she had screwed shut and realize she hadn't fallen to her death.

"See? Why would I lie to you?" Stella clicked her tongue as she returned to looking forward. "Just listen to me. It's not hard."

"I apologize for doubting the Mistress." Catherine bowed slightly and calmed down.

"Wow, Mom, look at that beautiful palace," Jasmine said as she pointed behind them.

"That is the home to the Redclaws," Stella explained, "a noble family under the Ashfallen Sect that specializes in fire Qi. You likely saw some of their younger generation walking about Ashfallen City."

They had already passed over the White Stone Palace, and below them was the vast mountain range covered in demonic trees that were nothing but a red blur as they flew. Up ahead in the distance, Stella could see Ashlock towering over the mist wall that shrouded Red Vine Peak and felt his focus on her.

"Is that where Kaida lives? On that mountain peak?" Jasmine asked as she poked her head around her legs, and Stella appreciated how she avoided touching or holding onto her.

"That's right." Stella smiled. "It's also my home."

11
JASMINE'S MASTER

Stella approached the swirling wall of mist that obscured Red Vine Peak from the outside world.

From afar, all that was visible apart from the mist wall was Ashlock, who towered over the entire mountain peak. However, to most, his appearance was shrouded in mystery by a constant crackling of spatial Qi that warped his image. His true form was only visible to those attuned to spatial distortions and could see past his facade. To others, he just looked like…

"What is that massive tree?" Jasmine said in awe. "It's so big."

Jasmine couldn't see the thousands of brightly colored fruits hanging from his branches nor the cocoon of silver ash that would give birth to a nightmarish creature. If his otherworldly eye was open, it would also be hidden from the external world. Ash only showed his true self to people he trusted or those bound by oaths of loyalty.

Stella glanced down at Jasmine. She still had that little white flower nestled behind her ear and poking out of her pale green hair.

I wonder if Ash would kill them if they refused to sign the oath? Stella shook her head. It seemed unlikely, but life wouldn't be pretty for them.

"We are about to enter Red Vine Peak. The home of the Immortal," Stella said sternly. "To enter here is a privilege few receive. I hope you understand that once we cross this mist wall, you will be expected to devote yourselves to the Ashfallen Sect?"

Catherine, who had darker green hair than her daughter and a kind gaze, gave Stella a thin smile. "Forgive my earlier indecisiveness. It was just a lot to take in. We as a family are ready to give our all to the Ashfallen Sect."

"Good." Stella nodded as she directed the flying sword to crest the mist wall. She didn't want to see these two eaten alive today, so their devotion was appreciated. As they passed through a thin veil of spatial Qi, which made the world briefly wobble, the true colors of the mountain peak were revealed. "You asked what that massive tree was, right? The Immortal cultivates below its roots, and he planted it to look after me."

It was an easy-to-understand and hard-to-disprove lie, so Stella kept rolling with it. People would find it hard to respect or take orders from the spirit tree, but if they believed an Immortal was cultivating in a cave below for centuries at a time, they wouldn't question his words.

"Those fruits look familiar," Catherine said as she squinted at the many bundles of fruits growing from Ashlock's vast branches. "Didn't they appear on the shadow spirit's tree earlier?"

"Some of them did." Stella nodded as she steered the sword toward the giant hole that dominated the center of the mountain peak. "They have miraculous effects that make cultivation a breeze. If you become friends with the shadow spirit, I am sure she will share some of her fruit with you."

"We are already best friends." Jasmine grinned.

Stella wondered if she had found her soul mate. Who would have thought there was another person willing to become friends with a tree? "I'm sure you are." Stella ruffled her hair. "Trees love it when you speak to them as they get lonely, so make sure to visit her every day."

"Okay." Jasmine bobbed her head with determination.

Stella released her hand from the girl's head as the sword touched down at the hole's edge. After the mother and daughter also hesitantly hopped off, she absorbed the giant sword into her spatial ring and inserted Qi into the formation at her feet.

"We will take this floating platform across the citadel to reach Kaida."

Jasmine bounded on like an excited rabbit, while Catherine seemed less assured.

"Can we fall off this?" Catherine asked as the disc glowed and floated toward the monolith that rose through the citadel's core.

"I'm not actually sure." Stella tapped her chin. "Want to test it, Jasmine?"

Jasmine glanced over the edge and gulped. "Um."

"Do you trust me?" Stella crouched down to be at eye level with her.

Jasmine hesitantly nodded.

"Try running off the side. I promise that I will catch you."

"Promise?"

"Absolutely. Fall as far as you like. I will catch you."

"No, wait, Jaz—" Catherine tried to grab her daughter's shoulder, but the girl had already sprinted off the side.

Stella glanced over the side with her arms crossed as she watched Jasmine rapidly gain speed. The girl's screams drew the attention of the many Mudcloaks making their way up and down the spiral staircase between their abodes.

Catherine had a look of absolute horror on her face and seemed too stunned to utter a word.

Stella felt her lip curl up into a smile. *I know the Redclaws are loyal to me, but it's because of the oath they took. But for such a young girl, Jasmine trusted me enough to hurl herself off a floating platform into a hole that goes down for thousands of meters without a second thought. She put her life in my hands without being oath-bound to do so.*

This was what Stella had been looking for. Another sect member like Diana, who respected her and was loyal without an oath. A person she could have a genuine friendship with rather than one mandated and forced by the heavens. Catherine and Julian, on the other hand, seemed like respectable folks, but Stella didn't trust them without an oath.

Ash had pushed her to make friends and take on apprentices to share her knowledge with, such as Kane Azurecrest and the Redclaw twins Oliver and Olivia. But she disliked how one-sided and fake the relationship was, so she distanced herself from them. *Douglas was the same, though I have warmed up to him more. He's not such a bad guy; he just has a loud mouth and likes to argue. Elaine is also a nice person. She didn't have to spend her illusion Qi to give me pleasant dreams, yet she did it anyway.*

"Mistress Stella!" Catherine collapsed to her knees at her side and tugged on her trouser leg. "Please save Jaz. I will do anything…"

This woman is hopeless. She will never make a good cultivator if she's willing to throw herself to her knees and beg at every opportunity. Stella sighed as she spread her spiritual sense to lock onto Jasmine, who had fallen about halfway. Snapping her fingers, a portal formed, and a screaming Jasmine fell upon Catherine, who caught her daughter with a grunt. To be safe, Stella had slowed Jasmine down with telekinesis, so they were both being dramatic.

"See? She is fine." Stella didn't understand why this woman was so flustered all the time. It was just a little fun, that was all. And a secret test of trust that Jasmine passed with flying colors, but Catherine failed.

Catherine ignored Stella as she was busy hugging Jasmine a little too tight. "Oh, thank the realms you are safe, Jaz. I thought you were gone."

Stella clicked her tongue. *Are all mothers like this? Would my mother protect me nonsensically like this, too?* The image of a massive golden tree reaching for the heavens appeared in her mind, and Stella couldn't see how she would receive the same mothering.

Maybe I am the weird one?

"Stella, please don't tell children to jump off floating platforms." Ashlock's presence bloomed in her consciousness.

"Why not?" Stella mentally replied to the tree in her mind. "She trusted me to catch her, so she made the jump. I didn't force her to do anything."

"You knew the platform had no protective barrier around it," Ashlock refuted. **"Why did you even ask her to test it?"**

Stella smiled. "To test the loyalty of my future disciple, of course."

"You want to take Jasmine on as a disciple? Why? You're only sixteen. Can you really take care of such a young disciple? She's like eight or something and in the first stage of the Qi Realm."

"When has age ever held me back? If I can reach this realm of power at this age, then so can Jasmine, so long as we support her with truffles and fruit." Stella huffed in annoyance. "And that's not important. To be a good teacher, you need knowledge and strength, both of which I have. I am almost on par with the Redclaw Grand Elder, who rules over an entire family, and I have more knowledge than anyone due to my bloodline."

"*But you just told her to jump down an eight thousand-meter hole…*"

"Are you questioning my teaching methods?" Stella smirked. "How about we make a bet, Tree? I will have Jasmine reach the Star Core Realm before she is ten."

"*You want her to progress through eighteen stages and two entire realms in two years? When will you even have time to nurture her? Once my roots reach the Tainted Cloud Sect, you and Diana will spend a lot of time as bounty hunters, right? We need to sell pills so poor Ryker doesn't lose his inheritance, and we need to find more information about your father and the World Tree.*"

"She can join us," Stella said dismissively as the floating platform drew close to the monolith. "And why would that matter? Your roots make crossing vast distances instantaneous, right? I can teach her in between missions."

"*Fine. I will admit this does sound interesting, and I am curious what Jasmine would become under your tutelage. However, rushing to Star Core could lead to an unstable foundation. How about I admit you win if Jasmine can beat Amber in a duel?*"

"Amber? Is that the Redclaw girl that reached Star Core recently?"

"*Yes, she is considered the Redclaw family's prodigy and seems driven to improve. I don't care about the time limit, but if Jasmine can beat Amber in a duel, I accept that you could take on a disciple.*"

Stella glanced back at Ashlock, who towered over them in the distance. "Quite a steep demand, don't you think? Cultivation is one thing, but teaching such a young child how to fight is another thing altogether. Amber is impressive in her own right and a decade older."

"*Hey, you are the one who said age doesn't matter when it comes to cultivating. I set the standards so high because I believe you can meet them, and I want you to take this seriously.*" Ashlock replied "*You have a habit of picking up a new profession or idea and losing interest. If you are going to train Jasmine, I want you to train her to become the next pillar of the sect.*"

Stella turned to Jasmine, still being hugged tightly by her mother. The girl stared back with warm yellow eyes that contained no hate.

Only excitement. She was clearly trying to wiggle her way out of her mother's tight embrace but could not escape. They were both basically mortals, so the mother had more strength.

But that would change very soon if you become my disciple.

"Just one last thing before I agree. You know a disciple isn't a pet, right? You can't raise Jasmine just to use her to do your bidding while you lay around like a cat all day. That is the attitude of a bad and lazy master."

Stella froze. "Who do you take me for? I would never think that way."

How did he know? Agh, get out of my head.

"Fine, if she agrees to be your disciple, the bet is on. Train Jasmine to the Star Core Realm and have her win against Amber in a duel, and I will agree that you are the best master a disciple could wish for."

Stella grinned as she stared down at her future pet…err…disciple. For some reason, the idea of Ashlock admitting she was the best at something filled her with anticipation more than anything had before.

Now, I just have to convince Jasmine that I am the best master she could wish for.

Jasmine's heart, which had only slightly calmed down from the thrill of falling to her death, began pounding again as she was stared down by the Mistress. Although Stella looked younger than her mom, her gaze was far more frightening.

"Mistress Stella," Jasmine said as respectfully as she could. It was the tone of voice her dad had taught her to use when he had people from the Voidmind residence come to visit.

"Yes?"

Jasmine found it hard to tell what Stella was thinking, but she had a burning question. "What were all those little people that cheered me on as I fell?"

"Little people? Oh, you mean the ones living down in the citadel?" Stella crouched down to meet her height. "Those little guys are called the Mudcloaks. Do you want to meet them?"

The sunlight made Stella's blond hair glow like the heavens, but her pink eyes that seemed to curl up into a smile sent shudders down Jasmine's spine. Not even the feral dogs at the weekend market that tried to bite off her hand as she walked past were this scary!

"Are…are the Mudcloaks humans? Like me?" Jasmine stuttered. "They looked like children wearing black cloaks."

"No. The citadel is a city of monsters that live to serve the Ashfallen Sect. Your house was built by them." Stella stood up as the platform came to a stop. "You can meet them later, but for now, it's time to meet Kaida."

She told me to jump into a city of monsters? Jasmine's eyes widened. *That's so cool.*

"How horrible," Mom hissed into her ear as her hug tightened. "Are all cultivators so cruel? My poor Jaz almost died in a hole of monsters."

"Mom, I'm fine, really." Jasmine squirmed out of her mother's loving grip and offered her a hand. "Come on, Mom, aren't you excited to meet Kaida and become important to the sect like Dad?"

Jasmine saw pain in her mom's eyes as she hesitantly took her hand.

"Hurry up, you two. I don't have all day." Mistress Stella waved at them near the entrance to the black stone building.

Don't be sad, Mom, Jasmine thought as she squeezed her mother's hand and led her. *I know you two dislike cultivators. So when I get strong, I can protect you and Dad from the other mean cultivators and save others!*

Jasmine had seen the fate of mortals. Her exhausted dad would come home daily and rant at the dinner table about how cultivators treated him like trash. But the worst of all were apparently the mortal servants of the Voidmind residence. *They could boss Dad around because they served the cultivators even though they were also mortals. Dad sometimes went on for hours about how much he hated them until Mom eventually calmed him down.*

Lost in her thoughts, Jasmine walked over to Stella with her mom in tow. The large entrance led into a short hallway lined on either side by shockingly realistic statues. The two closest were two imposing men—one was dressed from head to toe in a beige suit and looked like a shady businessman, while the other was a dignified man with a stern expression and red hair.

"Mistress Stella, who are these people?" Jasmine asked and wondered if they would come to life and start moving.

"These are the core members of the Ashfallen Sect. The brown-haired man to your left is Douglas Terraforge, the ruler of the citadel and those Mudcloaks you met earlier, while on the right is the Redclaw Grand Elder." Stella's voice echoed through the hall because she was a few steps up ahead. She paused before a giant spider with a crown of horns. "This is Larry, the Immortal's pet that has been known to wipe out entire noble families."

Jasmine felt her mom freeze in place. "That thing…is real?"

"Yeah, you might even meet him one day, though this is how he looked when he was weaker." Stella shrugged. "If something like this scares you, you are not fit for this life. Cultivators fear monsters like these, but we fear each other more."

Can a spider really be that big? Jasmine felt her legs go wobbly at the thought. The largest spider she had ever seen was no more than the size of her palm, and she had a small hand—it had been dangling overhead when she woke up one morning, and she still had nightmares about it. Not that she would admit that to anyone. It was silly.

"The pink-haired woman is Elaine. She's great, and of course, you have Diana at the far end, who you met earlier, and then there's…" Stella paused before a statue of herself, and as Jasmine came to stand beside her, she saw a deep frown on her face. "I swear I don't look like that."

Jasmine looked between Stella and the statue and could see almost no difference. It was as if she were standing before a mirror.

"What do you think, Jasmine?" Stella asked her. "Do we look the same?"

Jasmine felt it down to her bones that there was a correct answer. Or was this a test? Should she lie? *No, Mom always told me to tell the truth.*

"Um," Jasmine gulped under Stella's glare, "I can't see a difference other than the squirrel you are holding in the statue."

"Is that so?" Stella reached down and roughly ruffled her hair. She smiled, but it did not put Jasmine at ease.

Mom was wrong. I think I should have lied. Was it because I mentioned the squirrel?

Jasmine combed her hair out of her eyes as Stella freed her from the ruffling and walked over to the grand doorway with a giant stone snake head above it with gemstone eyes that stared down at them as if judging. Stella seemed unfazed by the snake head as she effortlessly pushed the dark wood doors aside, revealing an expansive space beyond.

"Kaida! Where are you?" Stella shouted as she strode in like she owned the place. Jasmine took more cautious steps as this place felt important. Much like the tree outside, a beautiful tree grew from a lake of ink. Its scarlet canopy occupied a hole in the roof, casting the whole room in an eerie red hue.

And the sudden ripples on the ink lake weren't helping.

"Oh, there you are, Kaida." Stella scratched the back of her head. "Sorry if I woke you up. Diana was busy, so I brought these two here for employment contracts. Ash told me you would know what those were."

Why is she talking to the lake? Jasmine found Stella funny sometimes. That amusement faded as the lake parted, and *something* emerged. It was a snake as black as ink, only discernable from the darkness by two golden eyes that gleamed with keen intellect and curiosity.

The monster loomed overhead as its serpentine body coiled upward and almost reached the ceiling. Strange markings were carved into its hardened scales like a tapestry of a forgotten language that gleamed as if wet from the lake. But Jasmine soon realized the snake was *made* of ink, not simply drenched in it.

"Stop hissing at me and get down here." Stella crossed her arms and tapped her foot in annoyance. "The sooner you do your job, the faster I will be out of here. Fair deal?"

Jasmine tensed up as the giant ink snake that could swallow someone whole dipped its head closer to Stella. Yet, instead of doing anything, it simply let out a low hiss before passing the blond girl to the far wall covered in books.

With one of its short arms ending in three claws, the snake grabbed a stack of parchments nestled between a few books and a block of wood. It then dumped the parchments in Stella's hands and went to dip the block of wood in the lake.

"Kaida, if these blow up in my face, I am throwing you through a portal."

The snake let out what could only be described as an amused snort as it twisted its body back toward Stella with the block of wood now drenched in ink. Kaida gestured for Stella to put the parchments on the floor, and once she dropped them, the snake followed up by pressing the block down to print words on two of the parchments. Putting the block away, the snake's claw glowed with a heavenly gold as he wrote a sentence at the top of one of them. He was about to do the other when Stella tapped his arm.

"Wait a second." Stella strode over to Jasmine and crouched before her. Her gaze no longer had that hint of insanity that made Jasmine uncomfortable. It was calm and determined. "You can sign the contract written in heavenly ink and have your loyalty be bound by the heavens to the Ashfallen Sect like your mother and father, or you could take a different route."

Stella stretched out her hand as if wanting her to take it. "Become my disciple. It's a type of relationship that transcends oath-bound loyalty. I will become your master and teacher. As one of the Elders of this sect, I need a disciple, and you fit all the qualities I have been looking for. I will train you personally in the art of cultivation and war."

"Jaz!" Mom shouted and gripped her shoulders. "Think about this deeply. Swearing yourself as a disciple to a cultivator is a big deal. Do you really want this person as a master? Once you agree, there's no going back until death do you part."

"Is that even a question?" Jasmine reached out her hand, "The Mistress saved us, blessed us with cultivation, and is the daughter of an Immortal. If anyone should be my master, it should be her. Also…she's really cool."

Jasmine held Stella's hand and wasn't sure what else to do, so to confirm her intentions, she put on a big smile for her new master, as Dad always told her to do when meeting new people. "I would love to be your disciple."

A power washed over Jasmine as if the sky was watching. A

strange link formed between their hands, and even when they let go, Jasmine could feel a connection to her new master.

Through the connection, she could always tell where Stella was as the direction she stood in felt warm, and she could sense her mood. Her master was beyond thrilled about something.

"I'm cool?" Stella muttered in disbelief. She then looked to the sky. "Hey, Ash, did you hear that? Jasmine thinks I'm cool."

Jasmine gave a weary smile. *I have picked an odd master, haven't I?*

12

NO SECRETS

Stella felt an oddly warm connection to Jasmine, and it was not because she called her cool—though that did make her happier than it probably should have. Stella looked away from Jasmine, and the warm buzz turned cold; then, looking back at the little girl, the warmth returned.

"Well, that's strange…" Stella muttered as she stepped away and felt colder. It was a very subtle tingling, one she had to focus on, but it was ever-present.

"A giant golden eye briefly appeared in the sky when Jasmine accepted you as her master." Ashlock's voice rang in her mind. *"Perhaps taking on a disciple is a bigger deal than we thought."*

Stella honestly had no idea about disciples or masters. All she did was say profound-sounding words to make it seem like a bigger deal to Jasmine, like calling it "a type of relationship that transcends oath-bound loyalty."

I didn't mean that in a literal sense. I just didn't want Jasmine to obey me because the heavens forced her to do so via an oath. Stella bit her lip. *Catherine mentioned that once Jasmine agreed to become my disciple, there was no going back until death do us part. Is that also a literal thing? Am I stuck as Jasmine's master until one of us dies?*

Stella ran a hand through her hair as the seriousness of this fun little bet she had taken on with Tree became all too real. She had a disciple now, someone who depended greatly on her to learn more about cultivation and the world. *Who the hell thought this was a good idea?*

"Master, why do you feel distressed?" Jasmine asked, her eyes big. "Is something the matter?"

"Not at all. Why do you ask?" Stella put on a thin smile for her disciple while her mind was in turmoil. She already wanted to say this was all a mistake and go back to her life lacking responsibility.

Jasmine squinted at her as if she could see right through her facade. "Do you feel warmth toward me?"

"You can feel it, too?"

Jasmine nodded. "Yup."

"This must be the master-disciple connection." Stella crouched and held Jasmine's hands. They felt warm to the touch. "This will make finding you a breeze in the future. I can just fly on my sword or portal in the direction that feels the most warm."

Cathrine came to stand behind Jasmine and placed her hands on her daughter's shoulders. "I can't say I am not worried, but Jasmine has made her choice." The woman sighed. "It's said that the bond between master and disciple is greater than even that between family. So it would be pointless to say much more on the matter now that it has been done."

"Why does this feel like a marriage ceremony?" Ashlock chuckled in Stella's mind. ***"It's a good thing you didn't do this with Kane. That would have been rather awkward considering how cold you have been to him thus far."***

"Shut up. There's nothing weird about this unless you point it out," Stella mentally refuted. "And it was you who pushed Kane onto me, but this was my choice. I admit I didn't foresee Heaven's involvement in this and making it so official, but I am serious about this."

"I sure hope so."

Cathrine took a moment to calm down. The events of today must have been a bit overwhelming for her. "Mistress Stella, please take good care of my daughter… She is all Julian and I have. Remember, she is barely a step above a mortal, so she is still weak—what's this?"

Kaida had slithered over and handed Cathrine a parchment.

Stella smiled awkwardly at Cathrine. "It appears we have overstayed our welcome. Either insert some Qi or a drop of blood on the words at the top written in heavenly ink, and you will become an oath-bound member of the Ashfallen Sect."

Cathrine looked like she still had a lot to say but held it in with a sigh. "Fine. What about Jasmine, though? Does she still need to sign it?"

"No, as my disciple, she has no need for it." Stella smiled. For some reason, saying she had a disciple out loud made her feel a little proud, even if Jasmine was very weak as of now. "Don't worry. She will receive more cultivation resources than even the princes of the Celestial Empire could get their hands on. In my care, she will become a cultivator that surpasses others."

Whether that was true or not, Stella had no idea. *Are there even princes in the Celestial Empire? Maybe I should watch what I say while trying to sound aloof.*

"Then I am reassured." Cathrine closed her eyes, and after much effort, she managed to have her Qi appear on her fingertip. Tracing the words at the top of the contract that Kaida wrote in heavenly ink, the whole thing lit up with a golden glow.

"It feels like a cold chain is wrapped around my heart and soul." Cathrine frowned and placed a hand on her chest. "Does this not make me a slave to Ashfallen?"

Stella clicked her tongue. "That's the wrong way to look at it. Don't think of that chain as a shackle that binds you to Ashfallen but as protection for your daughter."

"How?" Cathrine raised a brow.

"If you betray the Ashfallen Sect by saying something either intentionally or unintentionally to the wrong person, you could put the entire sect at risk of annihilation. Including me and Jasmine here." Stella patted the girl on the head. "As a pillar of the sect, I would have to fight till the bitter end, and as my disciple, Jasmine would have to as well. But all of that is avoided with that chain. Heaven is always watching, and it will let you know and suffer if you are about to betray us."

Cathrine gave a slight bow. "I apologize. The fact you take the subject of loyalty so seriously should be commended, and you are right. This chain stops me from an accidental betrayal that could put Jasmine at risk."

A loud, angry hiss filled the room as Kaida slowly retreated into the ink lake.

"Send Cathrine back through this portal," Ashlock said as reality tore apart, revealing a view of Nox and the field of flowers on the other side. **"Before Kaida starts to hate you even more…"**

Stella groaned. "Stop being so grumpy, Kaida. We are going, all right?"

Kaida narrowed his golden eyes before vanishing into the lake.

"I suppose this is my cue to leave." Cathrine hugged her daughter tightly. "Jaz, you be a good disciple for Mistress Stella, okay? Don't do anything I would disapprove of."

Jasmine rolled her eyes. "You disapprove of anything fun, though."

"That's because you have a dangerous idea of fun," Catherine said, releasing her hug and walking toward the portal. She stepped halfway through before pausing and looking back. "Will Jaz be back in time for dinner?"

"Yes." Stella nodded. "Even I like my alone time. I will send her back this evening."

"Okay, be good, Jaz! Don't disappoint your new master, and come home safe."

"Geez, Mom, I get it. Just leave already." Jasmine pouted.

Cathrine waved from the other side of the portal as she stood near Nox. A moment later, the rift collapsed with a popping sound and a rush of air.

"We should go, too." Stella walked toward the exit, and Jasmine followed close behind, having to take two steps for every one Stella took.

Now, what should we do first? Stella pondered. *How did I learn cultivation? I vaguely remember that bastard father of mine teaching me how to cycle my Qi and the basics of a few techniques before he vanished. I should start by teaching her that, but I should have her eat all the truffles and fruits first. Wait, what affinity does she have?*

"Jasmine, do you know what affinity you have?" Stella asked as they walked through the hallway lined with statues.

"Affinity?"

"Yeah, there is untamed Qi that is all around us. It's chaotic and hard to control, so cultivators forge Soul Cores to absorb and manipulate a certain affinity." Stella willed for her hand to wreathe in spatial soul fire. "See, my affinity is spatial. So my soul fire is purple."

Jasmine looked down at her hand and focused hard. Colorless Qi coated her fingers, and it seemed like just this much was taking the breath out of Jasmine to keep it from dissipating.

"Okay, relax. That was untamed Qi, as you felt it's hard to control, right?"

"Mhm. Very hard."

"Was there any aspect of that untamed Qi that felt easier to hold on to? Imagine the untamed Qi as hundreds of different threads. Could you control one easier than the others?"

Jasmine paused beside Douglas's statue and closed her eyes. Qi gathered in her hand once more, and after a moment, she gasped and lost control.

"Master, I can't even feel these threads? Is that bad?"

We really do have to start at the absolute basics. Stella hummed as she tried to think of a shortcut. *Ash's truffles and fruits should help Jasmine discover her affinity.*

"Bring Jasmine to me." Ash's voice suddenly filled her mind.

Stella reached for Jasmine's hand. "Don't worry, I know someone who can help."

"Jasmine, as my disciple, you must know the truth." Stella sat beside Jasmine on the bench under Ashlock's canopy with a clear view of Red Vine Peak.

"The truth?" Jasmine asked, tilting her head.

"There should be no secrets between us, but make no mistake, what I tell you must always stay between us, okay? No sharing with your mom or dad what I teach and tell you," Stella said seriously. "We will be side by side for many years to come. So we must understand each other."

Jasmine seemed to pick up on Stella's tone because she nodded with resolve. "I promise."

"Okay, I don't want to get too much into my family as it's a complicated mess. But I never met my mother, and my father left me when I was a child. So the one who raised me and the person I consider my real father is Ashlock here." Stella patted the giant demonic tree that loomed over them.

"The tree?" Jasmine seemed understandably confused. "Not the Immortal under the tree?"

Stella shook her head. "There is no immortal. It's a lie we tell people because it's easier for them to understand. The true ruler of the Ashfallen Sect is Ashlock here, a demonic spirit tree. He was the one who raised me."

"You were raised by a tree?" Jasmine asked.

Stella nodded.

"That's so cool!" In awe, Jasmine looked up at Ash's canopy. "Can he talk?"

"Sure can, but we don't pretend he is an immortal for no reason." Stella laughed. "His voice alone would shatter your mind. Even the Grand Elder of the Redclaw family struggles to listen to it."

"Scary…" Jasmine muttered.

"Now I am going to need you to eat this." Stella passed Jasmine a Mind Fortress fruit. A pill would be far too weak, so Jasmine had to eat an entire fruit.

"All of it?"

"Yes, all of it."

Jasmine bit into the fruit. "It's so sweet." She kept munching on it for a while as it was nearly the size of her head. "I was getting hungry, so this is a good lunch."

I forgot Jasmine was a mortal who still needed to eat and drink all the time. How bothersome. Should I go hunt some tasty prey for her? She will stay small and weak if all she eats is fruit.

Jasmine finished the fruit and licked her lips. "That was tasty, and my mind feels so calm."

"What I fed you was a Mind Fortress fruit grown by Ashlock. It will help you withstand his gaze."

"Gaze?"

There was a loud cracking sound as the black bark above them began splitting open.

Jasmine went to look toward the noise.

"No, face forward." Stella placed a hand on her head to stop her from looking back. "Ashlock's words are one thing, but his gaze is even worse if you look straight at him. Despite the fruit's calming effect, this will be uncomfortable even if you look away."

Jasmine gulped, balling her fists in her lap. "Master, I'm scared."

"Don't be. Ashlock means you no harm, and I am here with you. Trust me."

"Okay…"

The cracking stopped, and Stella looked up with a smile. That otherworldly eye peeked out from the split trunk and glanced down at her.

"Tell Jasmine to cycle her Qi. I will try to see if her body is better attuned to any one type of Qi."

"Jasmine, can you try to cycle your Qi one last time? Ashlock will determine what Qi type you should focus on, as cultivating untamed Qi until you finally form your Soul Core will be inefficient."

The poor girl was trembling under Stella's hand. As expected, even after eating a whole Mind Fortress fruit and not looking, Ash's gaze on her back made her soul shudder.

"I will try…" Jasmine shut her eyes and manifested the meager amount of Qi in her hands. It was so little that Stella wondered if she could dissipate it with a simple Qi-filled sneeze.

"This is interesting," Ashlock said.

"What affinity suits her?" Stella eagerly asked. If it was spatial affinity, she could teach Jasmine many techniques. Even water, earth, or fire would be fine, as there would be experts within the sect to help. The following silence made Stella grow concerned. "It's not something rare like cosmic, is it?"

"No, it's actually something quite ordinary," Ashlock replied. *"She should be best attuned to the nature affinity."*

"Oh, that's good!" Stella was filled with relief. Nature affinity Qi was everywhere, so having Jasmine reach Star Core Realm should be a breeze. "Wait…why did you say it was interesting, then?"

"Well, it's obvious to me that she has a strong affinity to nature Qi, but she also seems to have the potential to cultivate numerous other affinity types. Which means she might have the ability to be a dual affinity."

"The potential…or she is one?"

"Potential. Jasmine's control over these threads of Qi is far less than nature. Without my insight, she would likely develop into a

nature-only cultivator. But if we focus her training in the presence of nature Qi and another Qi type, she will likely develop a dual-core."

Stella bit her lip as she looked down at Jasmine. Focusing on a single affinity would make the process faster and more manageable. *Should I even tell her? If she knows, she will want to have a second affinity while being clueless about how hard it is to cultivate one, let alone two. As her master, I should pick the best route forward, right?*

"Can I stop yet, Master?" Jasmine gasped out.

"Yes, yes." Stella relaxed her hand, and Ashlock closed his eye.

Jasmine glanced back at the bark that looked as if it had before with apprehension. "Did your father figure out what my affinity is?"

Stella grinned. "He sure did! You have an affinity for nature Qi."

"Wow!" Jasmine's eyes practically sparkled with excitement. "So I can control plants, right?"

Stella nodded. "That's right."

I shouldn't keep any secrets from Jasmine, even if it's for the best. Stella sighed. "There is also another thing. You have the potential to be a dual affinity…"

13
WORTHLESS MASTER

What followed were a lot of questions from Jasmine that Stella realized she didn't have good answers to. She may have a library of information in her head, but she could not access that latent knowledge if she didn't take the time to research something in depth.

I never had anyone to teach me how to cultivate correctly, and I never went to the academy or had tutors to learn about the different affinities. Maybe Tree was right, and I am not cut out to be a good master… No, that's not fair. This might not be my area of expertise, but I know someone who could answer all of Jasmine's questions far better than I ever could. Having connections with powerful people who can help guide my disciple makes me a good master, right?

"Jasmine, those are all great questions." Stella patted the girl on the head. "It's good that you are putting so much thought into this and are so inquisitive. Being interested in the world around us is key to becoming a great cultivator."

"So what do you think I should do, Master?" Jasmine asked.

Stella rose to her feet. "I think…we should ask someone who knows better than me!"

Jasmine frowned. "You don't know, Master?"

"Silly girl, let me give you a life lesson." Stella crossed her arms. "Nobody knows everything. We all have our strengths and weaknesses in every area of life. Would you judge a master alchemist for their poor swordsmanship? No, that would be unfair. The alchemist spent all their life studying rather than training to fight."

Jasmine nodded as she listened along. Despite her young age, she seemed good at listening and understanding.

"Remember what I said about my parents leaving? I didn't have anyone to teach me how to cultivate properly, and I never studied the advantages or disadvantages of each affinity and how dual cores work. Wouldn't it be better if we spoke to an expert than I pretend to know the answer and cause you to make a wrong choice?"

"That does sound like a good idea," Jasmine said. "May I ask what Master is an expert in?"

What am I an expert in? I'm not as bright as Elaine, as strong as Larry, or as caring as Ashlock. Douglas works far harder than me, and Diana has a better handle on her bloodline. Even after practicing swordsmanship as much as I have, I still lost to Nox. I am above average at making pills, I suppose, but that's not very remarkable to a child.

"I'm not impressive at all," Stella muttered. Realizing what she had said before her disciple, she coughed into her hand. "Anyway, we are talking about you right now, not me."

"Didn't you just say everyone has their strengths?" Jasmine tilted her head.

"That's the end of the life lesson. Let's go."

"Stella, don't sell yourself short, especially before your disciple who looks up to you," Ashlock said in her mind.

"I didn't lie, though," Stella mentally replied. "I'm not an expert in anything."

"You have a twisted view of what expert means. It must be because of how easy things come to you due to your bloodline. It devalues your achievements and takes away your confidence."

"If you say so." Stella frowned. "I don't think I have accomplished all that much."

"Anything you do will be amazing to Jasmine. Remember, she was a mortal until YOU changed her fate. To her, you are more than amazing. Think about it some more. Oh, and before you go, can you take these truffles I've been growing for a while to the Redclaws?"

"Sure."

The ground began rumbling as ethereal black roots rose from the stone.

"Master, what's happening?" Jasmine trembled beside Stella.

Stella rested a hand on Jasmine's head to calm her. "I know it's hard not to be scared of things, but so long as I am next to you, everything will be fine. Okay? Just relax."

Jasmine shifted her head to look up at Stella, and their eyes met. "Okay…" she said. "I trust you."

Stella smiled. "Good. This will be over soon."

The ground stopped shaking a moment later, and they were surrounded by dozens of roots poking out of the stone like a forest of bamboo.

Stella closed her eyes and entered the spatial plane. Her Star Core pulsed as she became wreathed in spatial flames and spread out her control. Targeting each truffle growing from the roots, she used telekinesis to free them and float toward her.

"Master is amazing," Jasmine whispered.

Stella waved her hand, which shone with a silver light as her spatial ring absorbed the truffles. It only took a few minutes to harvest around a hundred truffles.

"All right, let's see Elaine first and then head over to the White Stone Palace to see the Redclaws." Stella released her control over the area and set an anchor point near the illusion grove. She clicked her finger, and a rift tore itself into existence.

With her eyes still closed as she was in the spatial plane, Stella took Jasmine's hand and led them through. Her ears popped at the pressure change, and her hair and clothes rustled as the rift collapsed.

"It's warmer here," Jasmine noted as she glanced around.

"We are in the forest of fire affinity demonic trees. Do you see those crimson flowers growing along their trunks? Those are Blaze Serpent Roses. They release fire Qi into the air so it will be warmer near them." Stella pointed up at Red Vine Peak that loomed to the south. "We were up there a second ago."

Jasmine followed her finger and blinked in astonishment. "That's so far! Walking down to here must take hours, but we arrived in a second. You sure are amazing, Master."

"It's nothing, really." Stella waved Jasmine off as she walked down the mountain path. It forked down either side to various groves, and there were even signposts hanging from the branches of the trees near the forks.

"Wait up, Master!" Jasmine ran to keep up. "Where are we going? Is this where Elaine lives?"

"No, silly." Stella took a left. "We are going to where Elaine is cultivating."

"Who is this Elaine person? Are they Master's friend?"

"Something like that."

"Why are your eyes closed, Master?"

"You sure do ask a lot of questions." Stella grabbed Jasmine's hand. "My eyes are closed because I don't need them to see. The world has a habit of lying to you, especially when illusion Qi is involved. So stick close to me. I will lead the way."

Jasmine sealed her lips shut, but her self-enforced silence only lasted a minute. "Master, where did all the trees go?"

"Did you not listen to a word I said?" Stella sighed; inquisitive children sure were annoying. "This is a grove of trees that have the illusion affinity. They are also covered in Dreamweaver Orchids, which alter the environment's appearance. The trees aren't gone. It's illusion Qi playing tricks on your mind."

"Oh…" Jasmine wasn't convinced, so Stella led her to a nearby tree and planted her hand on its bark. That earned an utterly shocked expression as she met an invisible wall.

"Happy now?" Stella sighed as she continued guiding Jasmine down the path.

"Illusion Qi is scary," Jasmine said as she stuck closer than before.

Stella could see Elaine just up ahead in the spatial plane. She would have used a portal, but the dense illusion Qi made it difficult, and since it was a short walk, it wasn't worth wasting the spatial Qi to force a portal open.

"Elaine, sorry to bother you." Stella opened her eyes and left the spatial plane. Sure enough, it looked like she was in an empty clearing, but to her trained eye, she could see it wasn't quite right. The sound of rustling leaves in the wind was too close, and the sunlight on the ground was broken up as if sneaking through a canopy.

The illusion faded, revealing a pink-haired woman wearing glasses sitting cross-legged under a tree. The rest of the grove also materialized as the dense illusion Qi that had gathered here dispersed.

"Stella! It's rare that you come and visit me. I'm glad to see you recovered from your fight with Diana." Elaine got to her feet and flicked off the leaves that stuck to her robe. "Oh, who is this?"

"This is my disciple—"

"You took on a disciple?!" Elaine ran over and placed her hands on Jasmine's shoulders. "Dear, did she kidnap you? Threaten you with death? No…she must have tormented you by dangling you through a portal to become her disciple, right?"

Jasmine scrunched her face in thought. "I don't think so."

"Elaine, stop saying ridiculous things to my disciple. You're making me sound like some kind of monster."

"Ridiculous? I speak nothing but the truth." Elaine hugged Jasmine as if protecting her.

Stella rolled her eyes. "Okay, not ridiculous, but I don't do those things anymore."

Elaine squinted at her as if studying her expression before letting go of Jasmine, sighing. "Fine, I won't say anymore. Did you come here to introduce me to her?"

"That was part of it." Stella crossed her arms. "But we also came to you for advice. Ash had a good look at Jasmine and determined that she was best suited to the nature affinity. However, there were a variety of other affinities that she also seemed suited to, and as a dual-core who also got to pick their second affinity, I felt you would give us the best advice on what to do."

"Fascinating." Elaine pushed up her glasses. "I have never heard of such a thing before. Either Ashlock has discovered something unknown to the world thus far, or Jasmine here is very unique. Usually, dual cores result from horrific techniques like nocturnes, though some are born with an equal capability for two affinities."

Stella placed her hand on Jasmine's head. "She isn't a nocturne and wasn't born a cultivator, either. She was given the ability to cultivate by Ash's truffle."

"A mortal turned into a cultivator." Elaine tapped her chin. "That might explain it. Usually, being attuned to a particular affinity is passed down through a bloodline. But if you never had a bloodline to begin with, forcing you to pick a certain affinity, I suppose there's no reason you couldn't cultivate any affinity you wanted. Anyway, I am getting off-topic. What was your question?"

Stella nudged Jasmine.

"Um, Mistress Elaine," Jasmine seemed shy toward Elaine as she diverted her gaze, "Stella told me that cultivating two or more affinities would be bad. Is this true?"

"Great question!" Elaine's spatial ring flashed, and a bowl appeared in her palm. She crouched down and began piling leaves off the floor into the bowl. "Imagine this is your Soul Core. It's something you will form within your body in time, and these leaves represent nature Qi. The job of the Soul Core is to store Qi that you absorb during cultivation. It also forcefully converts untamed Qi into your affinity, but that's inefficient."

Elaine filled the bowl to the top with leaves. "When your Soul Core gets too full, it will grow bigger." She brought out a bigger bowl and dumped all the leaves into it. "This is what cultivation is. Not that complex, right?"

Jasmine shook her head. "I like how you explain things."

"I am a teacher, you know." Elaine winked. "It's my job. Now let's imagine you picked water as your second affinity."

Elaine poured some water from a water pouch into the bowl.

"Do you see any water?" Elaine held up the bowl.

Jasmine peered into it. "A little below the leaves."

"Could you easily scoop out a handful of water?"

Jasmine shook her head.

"Why not?"

"Because the leaves are in the way."

"You mean the nature Qi, but yes. The leaves are in the way." Elaine poured more water into the bowl, turning it into a leaf soup. "What about now? Could you get some water out?"

Jasmine dipped her hand into the bowl and managed to scoop some water into her palm. A smile bloomed on her face. "I did it."

"Yes, it was much easier when there was an equal amount of water and leaves, right? This is what having a dual-core is like. Not only do you have to comprehend Heaven's whispers from two separate affinities, but you must also keep a constant balance between the two affinities within your own Soul Core. If you have too much nature Qi, your body cannot draw from the water Qi as easily, even if it's there."

Stella found herself listening to the lesson with as much interest as Jasmine.

Diana mentioned many times about an imbalance in her Soul Core. Was she referring to this?

Elaine set the bowl to the side. "Despite the challenges, having two affinities does have benefits. You aren't as easy to counter in a fight. It gives you access to a broader variety of techniques and even different fighting styles."

Jasmine looked down at the bowl filled with damp leaves. "Is nature affinity any good?"

Elaine gave a thumbs-up. "Absolutely. Nature affinity is great, one of the best even. Its Qi is abundant, it's one of the easiest to comprehend as we are surrounded by it, and it's not an abstract concept like spatial or void. In fact, its ease to cultivate is why I would suggest you should pick a second affinity."

"Really?"

That surprised Stella. Until now, having two affinities sounded like a real hassle. There were so many downsides, especially since even with Ashlock's truffles and her bloodline, she still struggled to comprehend even a dozen techniques for a single affinity, let alone two.

"Yeah, though there are some conditions to that statement." Elaine raised her fingers. "One, you have to pick an affinity that is also easy to cultivate. Nothing too rare or complex like my illusion affinity, for example. Because you have to cultivate the two affinities in parallel, you will get held back if one is vastly easier than the other."

Elaine really is amazing, Stella suddenly realized. *She is cultivating void and illusion Qi, both of which are rare, yet managed to ascend many stages in the last Mystic Realm... I really am no expert.*

Stella bit her lip. *I need to improve and faster. Otherwise, I will be a worthless master for Jasmine.*

"Second," Elaine continued, "you need to pick an affinity that works harmoniously with nature. For example, fire or ice would be a no-go. But earth and water would be fine. Lastly, pick an affinity that you think is cool or have an interest in. You will spend many years cultivating and listening to the Heaven's whispers about whatever affinity you choose, so you better find it interesting!"

Jasmine nodded with determination. "I want another affinity."

"Great! Do you have any idea which one?"

"Nope!"

Elaine chuckled and patted her head. "That's fine. It's a big decision. Maybe after trying to cultivate nature Qi for a while, you will change your mind about wanting two affinities. Either way, come back to me when you have decided, and I can advise you if it's a good choice."

Stella smiled wearily at Elaine's words. *I don't think she will change her mind. She seems a bit too stubborn for that.*

Since the conversation seemed to have concluded and Jasmine had no more questions, Stella summoned her flying sword. "Elaine, we will leave now, as I still have some errands to run for Ash. Thank you for this very insightful talk."

"You two are welcome here anytime." Elaine went to sit back down below the tree. Once she closed her eyes and breathed in, the trees around them began to vanish once more.

Stella landed in the White Stone Palace's courtyard and helped Jasmine off the flying sword by holding her hand. During the short trip, Jasmine seemed lost in thought about what affinity to choose, so Stella enjoyed the short silence as she also had much to think about.

A lot has happened today. I wonder how I should teach Jasmine moving forward? If she's always sticking around me, she won't be able to progress her natural affinity, as I will drown the area out with spatial Qi.

Unfortunately, the peace and quiet would never last long anytime Stella stepped foot in this forsaken palace of white stone.

"Welcome, Mistress Stella!" The Redclaw Grand Elder, having likely spotted them flying across the sky from his study, was the first to greet them with a near-horizontal bow.

"Hello, Grand Elder. I hope you don't mind the intrusion. I just have a few things to give you," Stella said.

The Grand Elder straightened up and gave a warm smile. "Certainly. Would you be willing to follow me to the meeting room?"

"I would rather just give it to you here—"

"Please." The Grand Elder's smile faded slightly. "There are two people who are eager to have a chat with you, and I also have some things to discuss."

Stella clicked her tongue. "Who are these two people?"

"Sebastian and Ryker Silverspire," the Grand Elder said as he led the way.

14

MISUNDERSTANDINGS

Ashlock was curious about what the Silverspires could want. They had been quiet since their last meeting under his canopy, where Sebastian had helped pick out the mirror artifact for Stella and contacted a Sage Advisor of the Eternal Pursuit Pavilion to get Diana registered.

It had been one of the first meetings where Stella and the others showed their faces and welcomed the Silverspires more into the inner circle. Of course, they were still in the dark about many things, like the Mystic Realm and the truffles. But Ashlock liked to think their relationship with the Silverspire family scion had strengthened despite the poor results from selling pills thus far.

"Are they mad about a lack of profits?" Ashlock mused. "Or maybe they have concerns about Ashfallen City appearing overnight at the base of the mountain?"

"Why do I have to deal with them?" Stella grumbled as she followed the Redclaw Grand Elder to the meeting room with Jasmine in tow. *"This is supposed to be Diana's job."*

"Sorry, Stella, but Diana is still busy with Julian," Ashlock said. It hadn't been long since Stella and Jasmine left Nox to see Kaida. Diana and Julian still had a lot of things to work out, so they would likely be busy until evening.

"Oh, and I'm not busy?" Stella complained to the ceiling.

"Master, who are you speaking to?" Jasmine tugged on her arm with concern.

Stella clicked her tongue. *"The Immortal. Sorry, I usually speak to him telepathically, but my mind was elsewhere."*

"I wish I could speak to him."

"No, you don't." Stella patted her head. *"Breaking your mind aside, all he does is demand things."*

Ashlock couldn't believe the slander he was hearing. **"I do not only demand things. You are painting a bad image of me—"**

Jasmine pouted. *"Sounds like my mom."*

"Exactly! Would you like it if your mom could nag you from anywhere straight into your mind?" Stella smirked as she looked up at the ceiling. Was this her way of getting back at him for asking her to deliver some truffles and attend a meeting? Just how lazy was she?

"That sounds terrible, Master," Jasmine said, patting Stella on the back.

The Grand Elder, walking up ahead, remained quiet while Stella ranted. Shaking his head, he opened the door to the meeting room and stepped through.

Stella strode close behind with her usual impatience and arrogance as she scanned the room. There were two sofas and two chairs placed around a small table. Sebastian and Ryker Silverspire occupied the far sofa, and a neat pile of spirit stones was on the table.

"Please take a seat." Sebastian gestured to the sofa nearest the door.

Stella reluctantly sat down, and Jasmine sat beside her.

"What did you need to see me for? Is it to do with these spirit stones?"

"Partially." Sebastian pushed the pile closer to Stella. *"I finally managed to sell those artifacts you looted from the bounty hunters last time we met. This is your share of that. Around two thousand high-grade spirit stones."*

Stella didn't show interest as she waved her hand over the pile, making it disappear like a magic trick in a flash of silver light.

"Was that all you needed?" Stella asked impatiently.

Sebastian and Ryker exchanged a glance.

"No, we had another topic we wanted to discuss, but it's quite sensitive." Sebastian glanced at Jasmine, who sat beside Stella. *"May I ask who this is?"*

"This is Jasmine, my disciple," Stella said casually as she crossed

her legs and relaxed. *"Anything you would say to me, you can say to her."*

"You took her on as a disciple?!" The Redclaw Grand Elder stroked his chin. *"What a surprising turn of events! I should inform the other Elders and maids so Mistress Jasmine will receive the appropriate treatment benefiting her new position."*

"Stop being dramatic." Stella rolled her eyes. *"Just get on with the topic you wish to discuss. You are all wearing on my patience."*

"To think the daughter of the Immortal took on a disciple." Sebastian bowed slightly. *"I apologize for questioning your presence, Mistress Jasmine."*

"It's uh fine…" Jasmine seemed flustered by having such powerful cultivators bowing toward her.

"Big sister took on a small sister?" Ryker seemed thrilled. *"Can I also be a disciple of big sister?"*

"No. I didn't come here for this." Stella clicked her tongue. *"If you wanted to have a long, drawn-out conversation, you should have waited for Diana to be free."*

"I was actually hoping to speak directly with you, Mistress Stella, as you are the only one with enough authority under the Immortal to humor my request."

"And what might that be?"

Sebastian leaned closer. *"I am not blind nor deaf. I closely watch the surroundings and the ongoings here in the Redclaws' residence for Ryker's safety and my own."*

Stella narrowed her eyes. *"What are you suggesting?"*

"When I arrived here as the bodyguard for the youngest heir of the Silverspire family, I had low expectations. Ryker is inexperienced as he is only five years old, and he had seemingly drawn a short straw by having to come here to Darklight City. To my knowledge, there was little industry here, and Ryker lacked connections to do large-scale business with other cities or even sects."

Ryker lowered his head as if embarrassed.

"As you know, there is a fierce ongoing competition between Ryker and his siblings for the Silver Core that the Silverspire Grand Elder will shed as he ascends to the Golden Core stage. However, I didn't tell you the real reason behind the competition."

That confused Ashlock. "Since age isn't the defining factor for strength in this world and the Silverspire family is focused on money making, the logic of sending all the heirs out to different cities and having them compete in business seemed like a good idea to test who is worthy of inheriting the Silver Core," Ashlock pondered. It didn't make sense for that not to be the reason.

Stella leaned on her hand, seemingly unimpressed. *"So? What is the real reason?"*

"It's a political maneuver." Sebastian sighed. *"It's well known that whenever someone in the Blood Lotus Sect ascends to the Nascent Soul Realm, they mysteriously die soon after. Sometimes, it's in a sudden war. Other times, they are killed while cultivating. The Silverspire Grand Elder is about to step into this realm, and he's noticed this pattern. So he sent out his heirs to every major city in the sect under the pretense of competition, but really, it's the groundwork for a mutiny."*

Ashlock felt like a bombshell had just dropped. A butler of the second most powerful family in the Blood Lotus Sect openly admitting his family's plan to overthrow Vincent Nightrose, a Nascent Soul Realm cultivator, showed a deep trust.

"Oh, a mutiny?" Stella said, unimpressed.

"Tree, what the hell is a mutiny?" Stella mentally asked. *"I never studied politics stuff."*

"It means the Silverspire family is planning to overthrow Vincent Nightrose," Ashlock replied. **"It's serious to admit that so openly. This is getting interesting."**

The Redclaw Grand Elder studied Stella's bored expression. *"How couldn't I have seen this before? Everything makes sense now…"*

Stella tilted her head to the Grand Elder. *"What now?"*

"Nothing much. I just felt like your lacking reaction to such news solidified a few theories I had regarding yourself and the Immortal," the Grand Elder said.

"What theories?" Stella seemed awoken from her boredom.

"May I speak without reserve?"

"Can he?" Stella asked the ceiling.

Ashlock was curious about what conclusion the Grand Elder had reached, and his oath of loyalty wasn't triggering, so it likely wasn't in bad faith. **"Let him."**

Stella sighed. *"Go on, Grand Elder."*

"When we first met, you claimed that Ashfallen was a secret faction led by your ancestor, right? And the Patriarch was a Grand Elder of the Ashfallen Sect under his control."

"Is that really true?" Sebastian seemed taken aback, and Ashlock could feel the man's Star Core pulse in his chest. He was now on edge.

"Did this old fool really have to bring that up right now?" Ashlock sighed. The Silverspires were about to let them in on a plan to change the Blood Lotus Sect forever, yet he just had to run his mouth. "Why did I let my curiosity get the better of me?"

Stella closed her eyes with a frown.

"Tree, did I say that?" she asked him telepathically.

"I think so? Honestly, I have lost track of what lie we have told who. Best to just play along and nod your head."

Stella opened her eyes and nodded.

"You also said that Larry, the guardian beast, wiped out the Winterwrath and Evergreen families because they discovered the Immortal's existence," the Grand Elder continued.

Stella nodded again.

The Grand Elder turned to Sebastian. *"I believe the Ravenborne Grand Elder, who had just ascended to Nascent Soul Realm, discovered the Immortal and was therefore wiped out by the guardian beast. It wasn't an act by Vincent Nightrose to eliminate competition. Therefore, I suspect that other Nascent Soul Realm cultivators have also been wiped out by Larry because they will discover the Immortal, and his existence is to be kept secret."*

Ashlock had no idea where the Grand Elder had gotten these ideas. Larry hadn't even been the one to kill the Ravenborne Grand Elder. The man had gone supernova.

Yet Sebastian seemed convinced by the story and was ready to draw his sword to fight to the death, and Ryker looked equally terrified. Meanwhile, Stella kept nodding with a bored expression, but internally, she wasn't so calm.

"Tree, what in all the realms is this idiot Grand Elder sprouting? We never did such things!" Stella shouted telepathically. *"Is he trying to ruin our relationship with the Silverspire family by saying such lies?"*

"To be fair, we were the ones who told such a ridiculous lie in the first place and left a lot to be misinterpreted." Ashlock sighed again as he got ready to use Spatial Lock on the Silverspires to prevent them from escaping. This was one big mess. The lie they told got them through the early days when they had been weaker than the Redclaw family. But now, it was a chink in their armor. **"Just keep nodding, but get ready to pull Jasmine out of there. I have no idea where he's going with this, but to shut him up now will forever sour our relationship with the Silverspires."**

"So what you're saying is we have entered into business with the true ruler of the Blood Lotus Sect, the Immortal, who acts from the shadows?" Sebastian asked calmly as he straightened his back.

"Future ruler," the Grand Elder corrected.

"Pardon?" Sebastian rubbed his temples. *"I don't think I am following."*

"You have felt how the Immortal's powers have grown at such a rapid rate while you have been here, correct? His overwhelming presence and power seep through every inch of this mountain range like an ever-present fog."

"That it has." Sebastian nodded.

The Grand Elder rubbed his chin. *"Now imagine this. If you ascended to the next layer of creation and suffered from a severe injury that forced you to return down here to the sect you had once called home with a crippled cultivation, what would you do?"*

Sebastian's expression turned serious. *"Ideally, I would hide where nobody could find me. But if my return was known, I would fake my cultivation level by any means necessary while I ascend back to my peak strength."*

The Grand Elder grinned as he glanced at Stella. *"You have repeatedly mentioned that the Immortal is recovering within the mountain. Anyone that could serve as a threat to discovering his state is quietly wiped out, and the Patriarch is kept at arm's length."*

Sebastian's eyes widened. *"Does the Patriarch not know that the Immortal is weakened?"*

"I always found it strange that as the Immortal's strength recovered, the more antagonistic our actions against the Blood Lotus Sect became." The Grand Elder stood and began pacing the room. *"We caused a war between the Voidmind and Skyrend families. Both sides were carefully weakened. The Voidmind family lost multiple Elders at the alchemy tournament, and we stole their entire city of mortals from*

under their noses. Meanwhile, the Skyrends had their scions killed, and there are rumors from other nobles at the Academy that half of the Skyrend family was mysteriously wiped out on their own mountain by a void beast."

"Say what now? Hey, Grand Elder, you can't say such a rumor so lightly! The Skyrend family was attacked on their own mountain by a void beast? I can only think of one culprit. That was definitely Maple's doing." Ashlock groaned to himself. "And the rest of those were not plans but rather attempts to survive. The Grand Elder is seeing the results but is clueless of the motives behind them, so he's making ridiculous leaps in logic."

The Grand Elder paused beside the window. *"It was almost as if the Immortal is planning for an aggressive change in leadership for the Blood Lotus Sect by slowly wiping out the families most loyal to the Patriarch."* The Grand Elder turned with his hands behind his back. *"If my theory is correct, Sebastian, you have come to the right people. We share a common enemy and goal. To kill Vincent Nightrose and overtake the Blood Lotus Sect. Is that right, Mistress Stella?"*

Ashlock was astounded. **"How can he be so wrong that he went all the way around to be right? That's honestly a talent."**

Sebastian and the Grand Elder turned to look at Stella expectantly.

Stella returned a bored gaze. *"Did it really take you that long to figure out the extent of our plans? You were involved in half of them, and we hardly hid anything from you. I honestly expected better from you, Grand Elder."* Stella smiled. She was clearly having fun with this. *"You were right about most things but have only gleaned the surface."*

The Grand Elder gave a deep bow. *"As expected of the Immortal and his daughter. Even with all the clues he has given me, this was the extent of my insight. If he could enlighten me about the rest of the plans, I could help more—"*

"I don't have the time or patience for that. You can figure out the rest of the plans yourself," Stella waved him off and turned her focus to Sebastian. *"As you heard from the Grand Elder here, we do indeed share a common enemy and goal. The death of Vincent Nightrose is one of our many objectives. So, with that in mind, what was your request?"*

"Good deflection, Stella." Ashlock laughed. **"We've got to keep them guessing."**

Sebastian paused to gather his thoughts. He seemed to treat Stella even more seriously than before, and Jasmine seemed in awe of her master as she kept deathly quiet to the side.

"I have been sending reports back to Ryker's mother. Enough details that she gets the picture of what is happening here, but I, of course, kept a lot of information to myself. She doesn't hold the most authority in the Silverspire family, but with the Grand Elder in closed-door cultivation, she holds some sway." Sebastian glanced at the Redclaw Grand Elder. *"As I said, I am not deaf or blind. The Redclaw family vanishes for a week at a time and returns far stronger. This is also true for Mistress Stella, Diana, and others. Even the Immortal is rapidly regaining his strength."*

"How observant." Stella flexed her Star Core as she stopped slouching and got serious, causing both Silverspires to flinch under the sudden pressure. *"Choose your next words carefully."*

Sebastian gulped. *"From the Qi density, I suspect the Immortal is on the cusp of reaching the Nascent Soul Realm. I reported to Ryker's mother, who mostly keeps to herself in the family, how there was another at such a realm that could help our Grand Elder take on Vincent Nightrose. I also explained how fast everyone here progresses—"*

A black blade wreathed in purple flames materialized next to Sebastian's neck. It pressed against his skin as Stella glared at him. *"You took an oath of secrecy, did you not? How are you able to leak such information?"*

"Only in regards to our business deal and the production of pills," Sebastian replied as he eyed the blade, *"not toward the Redclaws or Ashfallen as a whole."*

Stella clicked her tongue. *"Give me a good reason I shouldn't behead you right now."*

"Please don't, big sister!" Ryker begged. *"We want to be friends!"*

"Friends?" Stella narrowed her eyes. *"I am very selective of my friends, and those that leak information behind my back don't make the cut. The more that word of us gets out, the greater the risk Ashfallen faces!"*

"Please forgive me. I had to get permission from Ryker's mother."
"For what?"

Sebastian placed his hand on the back of Ryker's head, and they both bowed despite the black blade biting into his neck and drawing blood. *"Mistress Stella, would it be possible to welcome Ryker and myself into your inner circle? To share this method of advancement that would far surpass the value of inheriting the Silver Core? We are willing to sign an oath of absolute loyalty, which I hope you understand is a big deal for an heir and servant to undertake. This would turn Ryker's branch of the Silverspire family into a close ally with Ashfallen."*

Silence filled the room.

"Please…" Sebastian begged one last time, and his eyes widened as the sword was withdrawn from his neck.

15
INNER CIRCLE

"**Stella, withdraw your blade,**" Ashlock instructed.

His adopted daughter huffed the hair out of her eyes in annoyance but thankfully listened to him. She wiped the fresh blood off the black metal with a cloth before depositing the sword in her spatial ring in a flash of silver light.

Sebastian hesitantly raised his head now that the instant threat of death had passed and let out a sigh of relief.

"**So you want to join the inner circle,**" Ashlock spoke into Sebastian's mind with {Abyssal Whispers}. Since he had already cast the skill on him the last time they met under his canopy, he could reawaken the connection so long as Sebastian was within the range of his roots. He also projected his words to Stella and the Grand Elder so they didn't have to listen to a one-sided conversation.

Sebastian quickly fished a bottle of Mind Fortress pills from his pocket and popped the cork. He only gulped down a single pill compared to the three he had last time.

"Immortal, as a person in power, I hope you understand how big of a deal this offer is. I am a servant to an heir of the Silverspire family and a prominent member of a branch family in my own right. For the two of us to offer ourselves to you with an oath of absolute loyalty means we place the Ashfallen Sect above our own family. If you were to go to war with my brothers and sisters, I would be at your side with a blade drawn, pointed at my own kin."

Sebastian placed a hand on Ryker's head, and for once, the little rascal didn't raise a fuss. *"Despite Ryker being from the main branch, he is the seventh in line, and his mother holds less power than the Grand Elder's other wives. Even if he received the Silver Core, his position in the family would not be elevated by much."*

"I understand now. You see more potential for Ryker's future under the banner of Ashfallen. Is that correct?"

"That I do." Sebastian nodded. *"It's why I hope you will forgive me for sharing that information with his mother. It took an understandable amount of persuasion for her to agree to let her son swear an oath of loyalty to an unknown sect, knowing that she could one day face Ryker down on a battlefield."*

"I believe in the importance of family," Ashlock replied. "There will always be a spot open for Ryker's mother here at Ashfallen, and I will do everything to ensure the scenario you just presented does not occur."

"That I appreciate more than you know." Sebastian ran a hand through his silver hair.

"Despite your conviction, I cannot welcome you into the inner circle."

Sebastian's hand paused.

"If you swear an oath of loyalty, I will give you and Ryker access to all the resources you seek. Both of your cultivations will skyrocket, and you will be under my protection. Don't misunderstand. I am generous, and I fully understand the sacrifice that you are making for such a leap." Ashlock paused. "But joining the inner circle for now is impossible."

"Why not?" Sebastian stood up and petitioned to the ceiling. *"We share a common enemy. You will have the loyalty of an heir to the main branch of the Silverspire family. One of the most powerful in all of the wilderness!"*

Ashlock knew all that, but it didn't change the fact that he didn't want anyone new joining the "inner circle" because it was nothing like Sebastian was expecting. Everyone was lazy. They didn't have many secret plans like they alluded to, and Ashlock didn't feel like he could be himself with a new person around, especially someone as uptight as Sebastian. Some may call him introverted, but it was the truth. He was happy with his tight-knit group and was adverse to bringing in new people.

Luckily, he had a scapegoat.

"**Anyone Stella disapproves of is not allowed in the inner circle,**" Ashlock said simply, as if it were a fact. "**I may control things from the shadows, but she is in charge while I cultivate. You betrayed her trust, and she drew her sword on you.**"

"But I had to—"

"**There is, unfortunately, nothing I can do. If you earn Stella's approval in the future, perhaps you may be welcomed into the inner circle. But for now, we are happy to take you on as a vassal of the same rank as the Redclaws. You will receive all the same benefits. The only difference is you will live here on White Stone Peak.**"

Sebastian sat back down and eyed Stella across the table.

Stella was seething with rage.

"Tree, did Nox's attack knock out your brain? How are you sprouting even more nonsense than the Grand Elder was earlier?" Stella shouted at him through telepathy as she ground her teeth. *"This is the most ridiculous meeting I have ever been in. I am never agreeing to one of these again!"*

"**Stella, do you want Sebastian snooping around our peak? Sitting on the bench beside you? Telling you off for lazing around? What about having Ryker constantly asking to be your disciple or wanting to train with Jasmine? Does that not sound horrifying?**"

"You're right…that does sound horrifying."

"**The Redclaw Grand Elder and the Silverspires might start asking why Jasmine was let into our inner circle but they weren't. By making you the gatekeeper, your disciple's inclusion is obvious, and if you find anyone else you would like on our peak, you can wave them in.**"

"You know what? I quite like the sound of this." Stella calmed down and resumed her haughty pose as she tapped her chin.

Seeing that his scapegoat was open to the idea, Ashlock went for the finishing blow. "**This also gives you a position of absolute authority in the sect. Nobody will want to get on your bad side as it denies them the possibility of reaching the inner circle.**"

Stella's lips curled up into a smirk. *"You heard the Immortal. Your* actions that put Ashfallen at risk displease me, but your value is notable. Join the sect and work hard, and I may forgive this transgression someday."

Ashlock chuckled as he saw Sebastian's respectful bow. "She plays the part of a haughty princess so well it even tricks seasoned cultivators!"

"Then...we will take you up on this offer." Sebastian sighed. *"An oath of loyalty for power. Turning our backs on family, we pledge ourselves to Ashfallen. I hope, in time, you will recognize our worth and sacrifice, Mistress Stella."*

"I will make a note of it." Stella nodded. *"The oaths will be written up in heavenly ink and delivered to you in the near future. If that is all, I have much to do so—"*

"Just a minute, Mistress. I have another topic to quickly discuss with you and the Immortal," the Grand Elder said. *"Remember how we planned to take on cultivators from Darklight City and have them live here in the White Stone Pavilions?"*

"Yes?" Stella raised a brow. *"What about it?"*

"I was going to propose a tournament is held to decide who should be allowed in as spaces are limited, and it will give us prestige if it becomes known that we have high entry requirements. The tournament could either be held down in the arena by the Academy, or perhaps we could turn the giant market square up here into a makeshift arena?"

Ashlock had actually been thinking recently about how he wanted to rapidly expand the number of cultivators under the banner of Ashfallen while managing secrecy and the sect's resources. He didn't have infinite resources to give out, nor did he want to.

"Once I ascend to the Nascent Soul Realm and don't have Qi to carelessly waste, every fruit I grow will set me back from advancing toward the Monarch Realm. But I also need a lot of cultivators to help me face off against the beast tide in the coming years, so there had to be a balance between investment and reward," Ashlock mused. "What I need is talented cultivators with a hunger to learn and improve while also being able to work in a team environment."

That gave Ashlock an idea.

"Let's have a tournament near the Academy where cultivators are randomly assigned groups. They will then work together to defeat one of my Ents or perhaps an instructor," Ashlock replied to only the Grand Elder and Stella, leaving Sebastian out of the discussion. **"Then smaller-scale duels are held in the White Stone Pavilion market square to decide who gets given the best resources through a leaderboard. This will spur competition among those under our banner and mean the hardest working progress the fastest. I might even allow the top few on the leaderboard to enter the Mystic Realm."**

"I like that idea." The Grand Elder sagely nodded toward the ceiling. *"When would be a good time to hold it? Everything is ready to go. All we have to do is notify the cultivators in attendance at Darklight City's Academy and give them a few days at most to prepare."*

Stella placed a hand on Jasmine's head. *"Could we delay it till next month? I would like Jasmine to participate in the tournament."*

"Master?!" Jasmine's eyes went wide. *"What tournament? I have never fought anything before."*

"Don't worry, you will find out the details later." Stella grinned as she ruffled her disciple's head. *"And there is no way my dear disciple could lose."*

"Master, that's so cruel." Jasmine's shoulders sagged as she sank into the sofa in defeat.

"It might be possible to get her in fighting shape if the tournament is held after a round in the Mystic Realm," Ashlock said. **"Yeah, that works. Have it held in around a month."**

"As the Immortal commands." The Grand Elder stood. *"Then, if that is all, this meeting is adjourned."*

Ashlock withdrew his presence from the room. He had some other things he needed to do today.

"I need to make an ethereal root link between Nox and me so Jasmine has a quick way to get back home. I must also link the citadel to Geb so the Mudcloaks can freely move between those two areas." Ashlock sighed. "Perhaps I should ask Douglas to build a transportation hub."

In the White Stone Palace courtyard, Stella was about to hop on her floating sword when she paused. *I almost forgot the entire reason I came here before getting dragged into that stupid meeting.*

"Grand Elder." Stella turned to face the man, seeing them off with a smile. She pulled off a cheap golden spatial ring and placed it in his palm. "This spatial ring contains a hundred Spirit Root Improvement truffles, alongside a few heart demon–purging ones and a load of other fruits such as Mind Fortress, Lightning Qi Barrier, Enlightenment, and more. Feel free to give the majority of them to your family, and any you don't use give to Kane Azurecrest to be turned into pills."

"I thank the Immortal for his immense generosity." The Grand Elder gratefully took the ring as if it were a treasure. "Have a safe journey home, Princess."

Stella smiled. She liked that title. "We are in Ashlock's territory. What could go wrong? Come on, Jasmine, let's go."

Once her disciple was aboard, Stella pushed Qi into the blade and soared up into the sky. Tilting the sword, she began heading east toward the many human villages.

"Where are we going, Master?" Jasmine asked as they shot down the mountain.

"To find someone I lied to a long time ago." Stella's eyes darted between the tiny dots of brown that were villages, trying to discern which looked the most familiar.

"You lie to people?"

"Did I really lie if I make what I lied about into a reality?"

Jasmine scrunched up her face in confusion. "I…think so?"

Stella laughed as she brought out two white wooden masks. Slipping on one, she turned to hand the other to Jasmine.

"What is this for?"

"Interacting with mortals is bothersome—something you should know since you used to be one." Stella tapped the wooden mask on her face. "This helps hide our identity from them."

"Didn't you wear this same mask when you saved me?" Jasmine asked as she looked down at hers. "Did you find me bothersome?"

Stella hummed. "Possibly." She wasn't paying attention to her disciple as she scanned the land below.

That looks like the village nearest to where I found that kid huddled under a rock from that insect monster. Stella tilted the sword toward it. The location was near the great wall that separated the eastern fields from the rolling meadows of the wilderness. *With Tree's presence and*

Larry's hunting sessions, there have been no incidents with monsters around these parts as of late.

Stella let off the faintest hint of her presence as she arrived above the village and began to descend. All of the doors of the village banged open nearly simultaneously, and middle-aged men and women armed with rusty shovels and rakes ran outside.

"Someone sound the bell to alert the Redclaws!" one of the men shouted as they all glanced around with their knuckles going white from holding the shafts of their tools so tightly. "I sensed a monster."

Is my presence really so frightening? Stella wondered. *And why do none of them think to look up?*

"Calm down, mortals," Stella called out. If they rang the bell, it would cause an unnecessary panic.

All the villagers squinted and covered their eyes from the sun with their arms as they looked up.

"Is this the village with the mortal named..." Stella trailed off and realized she couldn't remember their names or face. *Was it something beginning with an A? No, that doesn't seem right. A W, perhaps?*

A kid with sandy-blond hair dashed between his father's legs, scrambling to get out of his wooden hut. "Miss Cultivator! Is that you?"

Stella squinted at the kid behind her mask. *I have no idea who that is.*

"What is your name, mortal?" Stella crossed her arms as she floated a few meters overhead with the sun to her back.

"Sam!" the body energetically replied. "You told me I could be a cultivator one day if I reached the top of that mountain, and you would tell me the secret to cultivation!"

That name does sound familiar...Sam. I remember him being a half-dead kid who was nothing but skin and bones, but here he is, bustling with energy and life. Is this really the same mortal I lied to? Yet the story checks out. That is what I told the kid, so this must be him.

Stella lowered her sword and hopped off. Leaving it floating there, she strode over to Sam with Jasmine in tow.

"Are you really Sam?" Stella said as she paused before the boy and looked down at him. "You look more full of life than I remember."

Sam scratched the back of his head. "Well, I had been running from that monster for a few days when you found me. But since you left, I have been eating well and training every day because the village has put their faith in me. Even if I still can't cycle any Qi, if I train myself enough, I should be able to climb that mountain to meet you."

Now I feel bad for lying, though I suppose it's motivated him to train. Yes...let's focus on the positives here. At least I get to look generous in front of my disciple.

Stella's spatial ring flashed. A truffle, a bottle of pills, and a parchment that detailed the most basic breathing technique appeared in her hands. "This is for you...because of all your hard work."

"You have been watching?" Sam took the gifts with wide eyes.

"Sure…"

I feel like I messed up this conversation somehow. Stella frowned behind her mask and quickly changed the topic. "Eat the truffle and the pills, and follow that parchment, and you should find it easier to cycle Qi. If you want to try your hands at some combat practice, a tournament will be held in a month at Darklight City. Those with the most potential will be welcomed into the Ashfallen Sect and be allowed to live atop White Stone Mountain."

"A month away…" Sam's excitement faded. "That's too soon."

"There will be more tournaments in the future, so don't worry," Stella reassured the boy. "Oh, and my disciple here will be participating, and as of now, she is not far above you in cultivation level."

"Really?" Sam eyed Jasmine, who was a head shorter than him.

"Yeah, if you beat her in a round, maybe I will even let you replace her as my disciple—"

"Master?!" Jasmine shouted in horror.

"Only joking." Stella ruffled her hair. It was fun seeing her react like this.

Sam clenched his fists, and there was the fire of determination in his eyes. "A month...I can do this."

He does know I was joking, right? I would never trade this random mortal for my adorable disciple, Stella wondered but decided it didn't matter.

"Thank you for blessing my son with such gifts," the man behind Sam, who was likely his father, said with a grin. "The name's Barry, by the way. Feel free to come 'round whenever you need fresh vegetables or a hearty soup."

"It was nothing, really. I was simply passing by." Stella waved the man off and hopped back on her sword. "Thank you for the offer, though. You should check out Ashfallen City, which is near the old mine. It's far closer than Darklight City and would be a good place to sell food."

With that, Stella took to the skies, leaving the villagers behind. There were still a few hours before Jasmine had to go home to her mom, and Stella planned to have her eat every truffle and fruit imaginable.

16
CULTIVATION LESSON

Jasmine felt like her entire worldview had shattered into a million pieces in a single day. She had seen a shadow spirit, met a grumpy ink snake, was taken in as the disciple to the daughter of an immortal, and discovered that the Immortal was a facade and everyone was taking orders from a spirit tree.

If that wasn't enough, she was dragged into a meeting with an heir of the Silverspire family and the Grand Elder of a noble family. They bowed to her with respect. She watched her master effortlessly tame the Silverspires. Then she was told she would participate in a tournament a month from now, having cultivated for only a few days and having no combat experience.

In a daze, she was taken by her master to a mortal village and told if she didn't perform in the upcoming tournament, she would be replaced by this mortal boy, and now she was back in the sky on a flying sword.

Jasmine sighed. *Are cultivators always this busy? I thought they did nothing but sit in caves and meditate all day! Yet it's not even late afternoon, and so much has happened... I am so cold.*

Although she couldn't fall off the flying sword as a barrier was erected around its perimeter by her master, there was no protection from the freezing wind that burned her neck and fingers. Her face was only spared by the wooden mask she still wore.

While she was suffering, her master stood casually at the tip of the sword in a thin cotton attire that looked suitable for training martial arts in the summer. Her ankles and arms were entirely exposed, and Stella didn't even bother to wear shoes. Yet she was unfazed by the winter wind other than occasionally huffing her short blond hair out of her eyes.

"M-Master, I am freezing," Jasmine stuttered as her teeth chattered.

"Stand behind me, then." Stella glanced over her shoulder with a smile. "I'm blocking most of the wind."

"O-okay." Jasmine shuffled closer and hugged up to Stella. Burrowing her head into her master's back, she got some relief from the cold.

Master is so warm.

Her body became less numb, and her chattering teeth stopped.

"We will be at Red Vine Peak soon. Are you okay?" Stella asked.

"Yes, just a bit cold still."

"I could give you a spicy fruit to warm you up, but I think you will struggle." Stella clicked her tongue. "I forgot that you are still quite weak. Give me a second. I will speed up the journey with a portal, and we will do a lot of training when we return."

"Okay, Master."

I hope Master's training isn't as brutal as her negotiations, Jasmine prayed in her mind. The way her master had sneered at the Silverspires as if they were bugs to her was engraved into her mind. *Master is ruthless. I hope that Ryker will be okay.*

Deciding to distract herself, Jasmine tilted her head to the side and looked down at the forest far below. Her eyesight wasn't the best, and the mask wasn't helping, so the many villages surrounded by many fields were nothing but dots of brown.

Everything seems so small and insignificant from the sky, Jasmine thought with a hint of sadness. *To those mortals we just met, that village is their whole lives, yet it's just a smudge of brown on the landscape from up here. Is this how the world looks to all cultivators?*

Jasmine glanced back and saw thousands of stone homes encircling the mountain base in the distance, with the palace of white stone lording over it from above. *Master had to tell those mortals about an entirely new city that had appeared a few hours away. They were so clueless and trapped in their own little bubble.*

"Master, what do you think of mortals?"

"Mm, nothing really. Why?"

"No reason…" Jasmine muttered.

When I went to school back in Slymere, I asked the teachers what they thought of cultivators, and everyone had long-winded answers. Some admired them; others feared them. They would tell me stories about how they met a cultivator once or how their family was killed in the crossfire of a fight. But to a cultivator like Master, mortals aren't worth thinking about.

Jasmine reached up with her fingers, which had gone red and numb from the cold, and touched her wooden mask.

Master told me to wear this as mortals were bothersome to deal with. But if cultivators are so powerful and wise, why would they find mortals difficult to deal with?

Jasmine looked at the fast-approaching mountain, which was Stella's home. Like the white stone palace, it was high in the sky, impossible and out of reach for any mortal.

Why did Master tell that mortal to meet her at the peak when it would be impossible for a mortal to climb so high? She even went out of her way to help him with a truffle. Is it some kind of test?

Lost in thought about her master's profound ways, Jasmine blinked, and they reappeared over the mist wall. The sudden change in pressure, making her ears pop, suggested they had gone through a portal. Landing the sword, Stella hopped off, and Jasmine followed. In a flash of silver, the large sword was sucked into Stella's spatial ring.

"What a frustrating day," Stella grumbled as she removed her mask and gestured for Jasmine to do the same. Luckily, it was warm enough up here due to the fire Qi tree, and the mist blocked the harsh winds, so Jasmine happily gave the mask back.

Stella stowed them away and then placed her hands on her hips. "All right, first up, I should have you eat—"

"Hey, Stella!" someone shouted across the mountain peak.

Jasmine watched her master's face sour in real time as she turned on her heel.

"The hell do you want, Douglas?" Stella squinted into the distance. "Is that a hut?"

Summoning a portal with a snap of her fingers, Stella dragged Jasmine through. Sure enough, on the other side of the rift was a stone hut like the one her family lived in, and beside it was a broad-shouldered man in a beige suit. There was also a strange creature with glowing blue eyes, and the rest of its features were hidden under what looked to be a black cloak.

"You must be Jasmine, Stella's new disciple." The man grinned. "I knew Stella and Ashlock would forget how different the needs of a mortal are compared to cultivators and trees, so I built you this hut. Come have a look inside."

"This is for me?" Jasmine followed Douglas through the door and gave a nod to the Mudcloak, which returned a funny grunt and three-clawed salute.

"Yes, this is for your personal use. The entire hut is engraved with a Qi-gathering formation and is well insulated to keep heat in. There is a padded bed made from wolf fur that you can use to nap or meditate on. Oh, and over here is a storage cabinet for your belongings and food. Finally, in the corner, there is, of course, a toilet. I know you will spend most nights at home, but Stella has a habit of dozing off or going elsewhere, so this gives you a place you can call your own, rain or shine."

Jasmine was speechless. "This is really all for me? Did you make it?"

"With the help of the Mudcloaks, I made it in a few minutes, so don't worry, it wasn't much of a hassle," Douglas said. "The fur I used for the bed is something I bought a long time ago with the intent of turning it into a coat. Oh, speaking of, I have something Elaine wanted me to give you."

"Elaine? The nice teacher lady I met earlier?"

"She's a real sweetheart, ain't she?" Douglas passed her a thick black cloak with a hood. "Apparently, Elaine used this in her youth, so it should fit you. It's standard Voidmind family attire, so maybe don't wear it outside as you might get mistaken, but it's fine to wear around here."

Jasmine slipped into the cloak, and sure enough, it fit her snugly. It was lined with many layers and had big pockets where she could keep her hands. It was perfect for the weather.

"I don't know what to say other than thank you," Jasmine muttered. Today had been all too much.

Douglas laughed. "No need for thanks. I'm just doing what's right. I know your new master rather well. She has a good heart but a poor grasp on other people's limits…" He trailed off, and his gaze turned dark. "Just like the boss who thinks building a city overnight is a reasonable request."

"The boss?" Jasmine wasn't sure who Douglas was referring to, but he sounded mean.

"Oh, don't worry. I am just mumbling to myself. Actually, speaking of the boss, he wanted me to build him a transport hub by the end of today, so I better get going." Douglas walked around her in the small hut and patted her on the shoulder as he left. "Any issues you can come and find me or Elaine. We are always open to lending a good old ear. Good luck, little disciple. May we meet again soon."

"Are you done being dramatic?" Stella was standing outside the hut with her arms crossed.

"I wanted to make a good impression on her before you twist her personality." Douglas laughed as he wandered off. "And now that my job here is done, I'm off!"

Stella rolled her eyes as she walked into the hut. "Twist your personality—what does that even mean?" She glanced around. "Though I must say this is quite a nice little place he made for you. I forgot what having four walls felt like ever since the pavilion was destroyed."

Jasmine watched Stella plop down on her bed and sit cross-legged.

"Come," Stella patted the space before her, "let's cultivate in here."

Jasmine felt through their link that Stella was in a good mood, which was nice. Her master had been the epitome of irritation during the meeting with the Silverspires.

"Okay, Master." Jasmine sat across from her and was surprised at how comfortable the padded bed of fur was. She almost felt too cozy with the cloak wrapped around her and the bed below.

"Now, my dear disciple, tell me," Stella locked gazes with her, "what is cultivation?"

That is such an open-ended question!

"It's a way to get stronger?" Jasmine said hesitantly.

"What else?"

"To become immortal and fly around on swords? Errr, to kill monsters? To protect my family?"

Stella frowned. "You are focusing too much on the results. Cultivation is a long road. I know you are young, but focusing on the process is more important than the outcomes. Understand?"

Jasmine nodded.

"Good. Now tell me what the *process* of cultivation is, not the outcome."

Jasmine remembered Elaine's demonstration. "I have to absorb Qi into my soul."

"That's right." Stella nodded. "Since we are humans, the most efficient way to absorb Qi is to use a breathing technique to bring the Qi into our lungs and then cycle the Qi through our spirit roots until it goes into our soul. Now, what *is* Qi? Do you know?"

Jasmine opened her mouth to answer but felt the words die at her lips. She had gone to a school in Slymere for mortals where she learned to read and write to serve the cultivators like her father in the future, not cultivate Qi or fight.

"I have no idea." Jasmine let out a sigh.

"Don't worry. Despite cultivating all my life, I used to only know the basics until I spoke with Elaine. It's important information as understanding what you're absorbing can help speed up the process," Stella said with a warm smile. "Now let's see…from what I understand, Qi is the manifestation of Heaven's will. You can think of Heaven as a force of change that desires creation over nothingness. So Qi is basically Heaven's energy. When you cultivated earlier today under Nox, what did you experience?"

"There were all these voices shouting at me." Jasmine shuddered. "And the Qi I absorbed felt impossible to tame. It raged around my body and mostly dissipated back into the surroundings. It was almost like trying to contain steam in my hands."

Stella nodded. "That's because you tried to cultivate what we call untamed Qi. Remember Elaine's example of the bowl filled with water and leaves? You were trying to take in all of creation, every strand of Qi around you woven into this reality, and force it through your spirit roots and into your soul."

"Oh…"

"The best way to cultivate is first to work out what type of Qi your body is best suited to handling. In your case, that would be nature Qi. Then other cultivators would have to find a location to immerse themselves in that type of Qi. Such as the Redclaws living on a volcano."

"What do you mean by 'other cultivators,' Master?"

"Here in the Ashfallen Sect, we don't have the constraints others have. Cultivation is hard, so often people use pills and formations to make it easier. We do the same, but to a greater extent. You could almost call it cheating."

Stella summoned multiple fruits and a waterskin from her spatial ring and handed them over. "This is an Enlightenment fruit. It will help awaken your consciousness to the whispers of Heaven. Meanwhile, this is a Mind Fortress fruit, which will help keep you calm and composed, and finally, a Deep Meditation fruit. Now eat up, and then we will continue."

Jasmine bit into the fruits; they honestly tasted amazing with different flavors, and she could feel their effects almost instantly.

"Now, I would have you eat some truffles, but that will have to wait until Diana returns. I'm sure she will want to devour your heart demons, and her water Qi will help with the stench that comes from purging impurities and improving your skin."

Devour my heart demons? Jasmine shuddered at the thought. Diana really was a demoness.

"This should be good, actually," Stella said. "Too much help at the start might hurt you more than help."

Jasmine finished all three fruits and gulped down some water to wash out the nice but overly sweet taste in her mouth. "What now, Master?"

"Shuffle around and show me your back." Stella paused while she turned. "Okay, good. Now, I will help guide Qi through your body since your spirit roots are of rather poor quality and filled with impurities. Just close your eyes and tell me what you see."

Jasmine closed her eyes and felt Stella's palms on her back. The Deep Meditation fruit helped her enter the depths of her consciousness. Breathing in, she felt Qi fill her lungs. Stella helped pull the Qi through her spirit roots and into her consciousness. A myriad of strands flowed all around, but unlike last time, their thousands of whispers didn't overwhelm her. The Mind Fortress fruit was helping keep her calm.

"Master, I see many strands of Qi in my mind. What should I do now?"

"Focus on the strands of nature Qi. It will likely be of a green color, and their whispers will be the most coherent to you."

Jasmine sorted through the many fire, water, earth, and spatial strands as those were the Qi types that dominated Red Vine Peak and honed in on one of the green strands. "Okay, I got it."

"Good, now pull on that strand and try to absorb it into your soul," Stella instructed. "And as you do so, try to listen to its whispers. They contain profound insight regarding your Qi type, and by coming to an understanding with nature Qi, you will reach enlightenment. Only by you and Heaven understanding one another on a deep level will you be capable of enacting your will upon the world and wielding your stored-up nature Qi to perform techniques in the future."

Jasmine didn't quite understand, but she followed her master's teachings. Pulling on the nature Qi strand, she was surprised at how easy it was to absorb compared to the untamed Qi earlier. It flowed through her spirit roots like a calm river and trickled into her soul. While doing so, she also listened to the whispers and slowly learned more about nature.

It wasn't like facts or a conversation with another person. It was a totally indescribable experience. She felt like she understood the world around her on a deeper level that no amount of study as a mortal could ever achieve.

This is why the cultivators see the world in such a different way, no matter their age, Jasmine realized. She was no longer comparable to her clueless self from this morning. Unaware of time passing, Jasmine pulled on more and more strands of nature Qi in her mind and intently listened to the teachings of Heaven.

A light pulse of foreign Qi spread through her body.

"Wake up, Jasmine." Stella's voice tickled her ear. "It's time to go home."

Home? Already?

Jasmine slowly emerged from her consciousness, and all at once, reality hit her. Her stomach felt like it was eating itself from hunger, her mouth was parched, and she was bursting for the toilet. Evening sunlight shone through the doorway, so hours had passed without her noticing.

"How was that? Your first proper cultivation session?"

"Life changing," Jasmine answered honestly. "I see why Elaine told me I should pick a second affinity that interests me. I never knew nature was so fascinating."

Stella frowned. "Don't get too absorbed in the whispers. Otherwise, the Qi will twist your personality," Stella said seriously as she tapped Jasmine's chest. "Your soul is *you*. Not this fleshy body. All that matters is your soul, and allowing Qi into your soul *will* change you for better or worse."

Jasmine gulped. It was only her first cultivation session, and she already felt like a different person with a new way of seeing the world. It was as if a curtain she didn't know was there had been peeled back.

"Come on, your mother will be mad if you spend any longer here." Stella helped her to her feet. Her legs felt numb from sitting, and her eyes were blurry.

"Ugh, having a mortal body sucks," Jasmine grumbled.

Stella chuckled as the doorway to the hut turned into a portal with a wobbly view of her house on the other side. "I had Ash make you a portal home because the transportation hub isn't complete. Diana should be around tomorrow, so I will have you eat some truffles, and we can continue from where we left off. Any questions?"

Jasmine didn't know why, but she stumbled over and embraced her master in a tight hug. Today had been the most crazy day of her life, and it was all thanks to this girl. "Thank you, Master, for choosing me. You are the best master a disciple could hope for."

Stella awkwardly patted her head. "Uhm, thank you…"

Jasmine freed her master from the embarrassment and walked over to the portal. "I will be going now, Master. See you tomorrow."

"Yeah, see you…"

Going through the portal with a smile, Jasmine felt the pressure and temperature change. Once the portal snapped closed behind her with a pop and a gust of wind, she didn't immediately head into her house but rather crouched beside a patch of grass.

Coating her hands in Qi, she frowned at how it was still colorless despite her absorbing only nature Qi. "Is this because I don't have the Soul Core thing Mistress Elaine mentioned?" Jasmine murmured as she ran her hand through the grass. It was pleasant to the touch. She had never cared much for grass, but now it was beautiful. "Will I be able to control grass with my will in the future?"

"Jaz, you're back. Are you talking to the grass?"

"Yes, Mom…I was." Jasmine sighed with exhaustion as she turned to see her mother standing in the doorway with her arms crossed and a spoon in her hand. "I'm back."

17
MONSTER FARM

Evening descended on Red Vine Peak.

While Stella and Jasmine spent most of the afternoon cultivating in the hut, Ashlock had been working with Douglas and the Redclaw Grand Elder on a plan for a transport hub after explaining to them how his new skill worked.

Because of his {Ethereal Roots} skill, his roots could now act like permanent portals so long as he hollowed them out. This was because space within them was compressed, so every step someone took would equate to hundreds of meters in the real world. So traveling through his ethereal roots wasn't quite instant like a portal, but it was close enough. A journey that might have taken hours would now take a few steps.

Since he wanted other people, such as the Redclaws, to use his root network to hunt for corpses out in the wilderness or get around the sect, he didn't want all his ethereal root tunnels to originate from Red Vine Peak.

Of course, since the roots were attached to his body, all would eventually lead to him. But luckily, he could decide where the openings to the hollowed-out roots were. Almost like train stops.

For example, he could have a root with three openings. One near his trunk on Red Vine Peak, one in the White Stone Palace, and a final one in Ashfallen City. Space between these three openings would be compressed, allowing someone to get between the three openings within seconds.

This was how Ashlock came up with the idea of a transportation hub. He wanted a location where all his hollowed-out roots converged, similar to a capital city's train station. Since the place needed to be away from Red Vine Peak and security was a concern, Ashlock settled on the transportation hub being constructed inside the White Stone Palace.

"But where should it be…" Ashlock searched the interior of the palace. The basement was already dedicated to the alchemy lab run by Elder Margret and Kane Azurecrest. The western side of the palace was heavily used as it faced the courtyard, so there were many meeting rooms. Meanwhile, the central section of the palace was dedicated to the Redclaws. "Actually, what about the servant area? There should be room there as this building was designed to house the servants of the Winterwrath and Evergreen families."

Ashlock found a wide corridor lined with unused servant rooms in the palace's eastern wing.

"Okay, this is perfect," Ashlock said to Douglas. **"We will use this area. Have it cleared out."**

"Yes, Boss."

The rooms were all stripped of their furniture to make each room as spacious as possible so many people could wait around for their turn to use the ethereal roots in the future.

"All right, what's next?" Douglas asked as the last of the furniture was carried away by a team of maids to be stored elsewhere.

"Give me a moment," Ashlock replied. **"I need to think of where people would want to go. Any ideas, Grand Elder?"**

"A root to Ashfallen City, Darklight City, and far out into the wilderness would be great." The Grand Elder rubbed his chin in thought. *"Getting to Darklight City for supplies and to see their families is a real pain for the mortal maids we have employed and even for my family. Only us Elders at the Star Core Realm can fly around. Everyone else has to walk up and down the mountain, which takes hours."*

Hearing that made Ashlock glad he had this idea. Keeping a portal open at all times wouldn't have been possible as he slept during the night, and maintaining a portal took constant focus.

"I suppose if I knew about this issue before, I could have had Titus maintain a portal..." Ashlock sighed and decided to keep his realization to himself. It was easy to forget that not everyone could teleport around the sect via portals like Stella did.

Activating his {Ethereal Roots} skill, he brought up a root into each room and hollowed it out to create a tunnel. Qi was drained from his Star Core but refilled as quickly as it left.

"Okay, put a sign on each door for its destination. I made them in the order you suggested," Ashlock said. **"Then, for the final room at the end of the corridor, I will have a root that leads inside Red Vine Peak. I want that room to be guarded, covered in defensive runes, and fitted with a metal door. Only those in the inner circle and sect Elders can use this root. Anyone else risks death on arrival if they use it without permission. Understand? Oh, and it can never be used during the night."**

"As you wish." The Grand Elder bowed. *"Since the roots go both ways, this area must be closely monitored. I will have an Elder alongside some youths guarding this area at all times, and we will take turns."*

"That is a really good point," Ashlock mused. "I had been so focused on how my people would use the roots to leave that I forgot people from outside could use the roots to come inside."

Thankfully, he had subordinates with centuries of experience to realize these security flaws.

"With security in mind, perhaps cover all rooms in defensive runic formations. We have the spirit stones to use after selling those artifacts and robbing the bounty hunters."

"Don't worry, boss. I will get this place secured by the morning." Douglas saluted the ceiling and turned to his small army of Mudcloaks. *"Come on, let's get to work."*

"Work, work, work!" they enthusiastically chanted as they rushed into the rooms. Douglas threw them some spirit stones, and they used their Qi and claws to carve out runic words into the stone walls and floor.

"Sometimes I forget how capable they are," Ashlock thought as he watched them work. "I guess it's to be expected from a race of monsters that built runic cannons capable of killing giant turtles and entire cities underground to resist the superior kobolds. Some simple runic arrays are nothing to them."

After watching for a bit longer, Ashlock decided to return to Red Vine Peak as he still had some ethereal root tunnels he wished to establish.

One out to the grove of demonic mist trees he had made in the eastern demonic forest far out in the wilderness for Diana. He also needed to make an ethereal root between Geb to the south and the citadel so the Mudcloaks could freely move between the two locations.

The one out to the demonic mist grove was simple enough, and he made the opening on the eastern side of his trunk. Basically, there was now a hole in the stone, and if someone jumped into it, they would find themselves emerging a hundred miles away in a forest of demonic mist.

Pleased with himself, Ashlock was about to make the root between the citadel and Geb when he felt something *move* through his root. "What the hell?" A second later, a creature heaved itself out of the hole in the ground. It had the vague appearance of a two-meter-tall monkey with black fur and crazed red eyes. Multiple arms of various lengths sprouted from its back at odd angles, ending in claws, and the skin on its face seemed to be melting with corruption.

The monster turned to stare at him before opening its mouth to let out a shriek, but it never managed as its head was ruthlessly cleaved off. The body stood upright for a second before it toppled forward like a domino, revealing its executioner standing silently behind.

"Thank you, Khaos," Ashlock said to his void Ent. His silent guardian had been so fast that he hadn't even had time to kill the weak monster standing before him. With Larry asleep and expending Qi not an issue for now, Ashlock had tasked his Ents to work around the clock on patrolling the sect for any monsters or bounty hunters. Other than Geb, since he was a bit too big to do such a thing.

Never one to turn down a free meal, black vines emerged from the ground and wrapped around the corpse. It was in the Soul Fire Realm, so there wasn't much point in turning it into an Ent, so Ashlock decided to eat it for credits.

"Khaos, guard this entrance. I am going to take a look at the forest." Ashlock cast {Eye of the Tree God}, and his vision blurred over the endless meadows of the wilderness. Arriving at the vast eastern demonic forest bathed in evening sunlight, he focused on the area shrouded in a demonic mist. Numerous shadows could be seen lurking in the fog, accompanied by the constant howls of monsters.

Ashlock was in disbelief. He occasionally searched the wilderness for any monsters worthy of hunting and only ever found weaklings not even worth the Qi expenditure to eat them.

"Were they all attracted here by the demonic mist?" Ashlock wondered. "Or was it the demonic mist that birthed these monsters?"

Either way, he now had a buffet waiting for him to feast.

[+12 Sc]

A system notification flashed in his mind, alerting him that the monkey had been devoured.

"Let's see, if the monkey gave me twelve credits, how many more do I need to kill?" Ashlock pulled up his status screen and navigated to the requirements for advancing to Nascent Soul Realm.

[Requirements to turn Chaos Nebula into an Inner World:
2577 / 10000 Sacrificial Credits
0 / 1 Absorbed Fire Star Cores
0 / 1 Absorbed Water Star Cores
0 / 1 Absorbed Earth Star Cores
0 / 1 Absorbed Wind Star Cores
0 / 1 Absorbed Metal Star Cores]

[Rewards upon formation of the Inner World:
You will ascend to the Nascent Soul Realm.
The System will be upgraded with new features.
{Transpiration of Heaven and Chaos [B]} will be upgraded.
Your attacks will carry the weight of your Inner World behind them, and your rate of cultivation will increase the more you develop your Inner World.]

"I still need around seven thousand five hundred credits, so I would need to kill something like six hundred of those monkeys to reach the ten thousand credits required." Ashlock glanced back at the demonic mist. There certainly weren't six hundred shadows lurking in the fog, but there were quite a few. "Wait, now that I have unlimited Qi, it's worth hunting anything that will give me credits since I don't have to worry about wasting my Qi! I can even send my Ents or Larry when he wakes up from his evolution to capture the monsters."

Suddenly, the ten thousand–credit requirement to form his Inner World didn't seem so steep. Especially if he went hunting during the next Mystic Realm for some higher cultivation monsters that would net him far more than a measly twelve credits.

"That just leaves the Star Cores I need for my Inner World to worry about. Luckily, I have quite a few options to choose from to gather them. If I have the Redclaws haul back a Star Core–level monster from the next Mystic Realm, that would solve the fire Star Core I need. The same could be done for the Earth one with Douglas. Diana doesn't cultivate Water Qi anymore, and I have nobody for the Wind element other than maybe Kane Azurecrest, so those might be a little trickier. That just leaves Metal… I can ask Sebastian to bring me back a monster as well."

Ashlock was starting to realize that if he focused up, he might reach Nascent Soul within a month.

"Any affinity I can't get my hands on, I can have Diana and Stella hunt a person down through the pavilion. Anyway, worrying about the Star Cores can come in the morning. For now, I want to grab as many credits as possible."

Ashlock was about to open a portal and drag monsters through but realized the demonic mist made targeting the monsters difficult. He could only see their vague shadows as they moved quickly between the trees, and the forest canopy got in the way.

"Should I get Diana to hunt them down? Or perhaps my Ents? Hmm…" Ashlock mulled over his options when he felt another monster decide to travel through his roots. Switching his view back to his trunk, a fresh, headless corpse was ready to be eaten, with Khaos casually standing there.

"Why does this remind me of those conveyor sushi restaurants?" Ashlock chuckled as he devoured the fresh corpse. "I'm not sure why monsters keep trying to go down my ethereal root, but this could work nicely if they keep doing so."

Ashlock created a dozen more ethereal root tunnels leading to various points in the demonic mist forest to see if that would increase the rate at which monsters came through.

"Khaos, kill any monster that appears from these holes and leave their corpses near my trunk," Ashlock instructed and then went to find Titus to tell him to help. With two Ents on guard duty, killing some weak monsters should be a breeze. "Wake me up if any powerful people come through the roots like bounty hunters, okay—"

Two more mutated, monkey-like creatures appeared from the holes. Khaos tore one in half in a split second, and Titus pulverized the other into a paste with a soul flame–coated hand, making the entire mountain tremble.

"Yeah...good job. Keep doing that."

"Tree?!" Stella suddenly appeared out of the hut wreathed in spatial flames and with her sword drawn. *"What in the nine realms is going on? Are we under attack?"*

"Relax. Come take a look. I've found a new way to kill monsters."

Stella vanished and reappeared next to Khaos via Spatial Step.

Four more monsters emerged from the holes, and they were swiftly butchered and added to the devouring heap.

|+18 Sc|
|+9 Sc|
|+15 SC|

Notifications popped up now and then, but Ashlock mostly ignored them.

"What's happening here?" Stella raised a brow. *"Where are they coming from?"*

"The demonic forest to the east," Ashlock explained. **"I made a demonic mist grove for Diana, and when I went to create an ethereal root tunnel to it, monsters started coming through. Any idea why?"**

Stella tapped her chin. "I think it's because monsters are attracted to anything that is a source of Qi, especially demonic Qi. It's why they appear along the routes of ley lines." Stella leaned over and looked down into the hole. "You use your roots to transport Qi around your body, right?"

"Yeah."

Stella nodded in understanding. *"The monsters must think they have stumbled upon a ley line, and when they go down into the hole to feast on the Qi, they end up here."*

That made a lot of sense. It also explained why so many monsters had gathered in the demonic mist. They were attracted there by the demonic Qi floating around, and the fog likely helped weaker monsters hide away and survive, so it was safer than being out in the open.

"Do you want me to go to the forest and slaughter the monsters for you?" Stella asked while two more monsters crawled out from the holes and were killed by Khaos.

"No need. This solution seems to work well at bringing the corpses to me with minimal risk. Though do you think you could watch this area overnight? There's a low chance, but too many monsters may come through at once for Khaos and Titus to deal with."

"Sure, leave it to me," Stella said with a yawn.

"Thank you."

With that sorted, Ashlock had one last thing to do before sleeping.

"I need to make a root between Geb and the citadel. Though I wonder how the citadel is doing? I haven't checked on it for a while."

Ashlock pushed his spiritual senses through his roots into the giant hole running through the mountain. The monolith in the center was covered in a thick layer of moss, and the spiral staircase now led to thousands of rooms built into the mountain. As he had previously instructed, the top section was mostly empty rooms reserved for his sect members once completed, while the Mudcloaks had the rest to themselves.

Going all the way to the monolith's base, Ashlock was surprised to see the Mudcloaks had dug even deeper. They had expanded into the old path the giant worm had taken and had a whole little city down here. There were roads, market squares, two Mudcloaks engaged in a street fight, and rows of restaurants serving moss with spices they had gotten from god knew where. He even saw a Mudcloak wearing a hat and trying to bash another on the head with a stick at an assembly line that made knives.

"Okay, so that's where they got those knives from. I'm starting to wonder if letting these menaces out of the citadel is a good idea. Do they intentionally act dumb so I turn a blind eye as they overtake the world? Surely not..." Ashlock made the ethereal root tunnel at the end of a road that led to a dead end and decided to withdraw from this wacky city thousands of meters below.

The monster farm near his trunk seemed to be going fine, so with the sun setting, he decided to have a well-earned rest under the nine moons. It was a relaxing place that felt like a spa visit, but he did it for another reason despite his lack of need for Qi.

Glancing across the dreamscape, he saw Nox gathering Qi from the moons. If he didn't use his {Nocturnal Genesis} skill at night, it wasn't only his offspring that missed out on the extra Qi, but also Nox.

"What a long day..." Ashlock yawned in his mind as he drifted off to sleep. "Maybe I should dig deeper tomorrow to find one of those ley lines Stella mentioned..."

Sunrise came late as winter approached. The cold made waking up an absolute chore. Weirdly, over the usual sound of rustling leaves in the wind and chirping of distant birds, there was a loud munching noise and snoring.

Idletree Daily Sign-In System
Day: 3598
Daily Credit: 35
Sacrifice Credit: 2787
[Sign in?]

"Those are less credits than I had been expecting..." Ashlock cast out his spiritual senses to see what was happening beyond his bark.

First, he saw Stella sprawled out on the bench like a cat, fast asleep with her leg propped up on the backrest and her head rolling off the side. She was the source of the loud snoring, likely due to her terrible sleeping posture.

Next, he noticed the cocoon of swirling ash that had weighed on his branches was gone...

Following the munching noise, Ashlock glanced at the monster farm and found Larry in all his divine ashen glory with a half-eaten monster hanging out of his mouth.

"Oi, you big spider. What the hell do you think you're doing with my breakfast?" Ashlock asked Larry, and the divine spider dropped the corpse like a dog caught in the act.

18

BEAST TIDE

Ashlock rustled his leaves in anger, causing ripe fruit to rain from his branches like hail. He had gone to sleep and dreamed of waking up to a delicious stack of fresh corpses overflowing with Qi, ready to be consumed. The taste of devouring a Nascent Soul Realm cultivator a few days ago still lingered, making him even hungrier than usual.

So to wake up and find his breakfast not only missing but also catching the culprit in the act made him rather angry for the first time in a while. He had really been looking forward to his breakfast...

"Sorry, Master." Larry crawled away from the corpse he had just been munching on, leaving it near his trunk.

As angry as Ashlock was, he marveled at his first-ever summon to reach S-grade. After all, Maple wasn't his summon. They were simply in a pact to not kill one another.

Larry looked somewhat different after finishing his divine evolution to become a Herald of the Divine Ash. Upon a quick glance, he appeared as a giant spider with silver fur, scarlet eyes, a crown of horns, and a halo of swirling ash. There was also a sense of majesty, as if he were a mythical creature. However, upon looking closer, Ashlock noticed that Larry's body was not made of flesh and bone but a condensed storm of divine ash in the shape of a spider. His horns were also made from dense ash, and his eyes were floating orbs of Qi.

"How kind of you to leave half a corpse for me," Ashlock said sarcastically as a black vine emerged from the ground. "And welcome back, Larry. I missed you."

As his black vine approached the half-eaten corpse, Larry seemed to shrink back as if something terrible was going to happen.

"Mhm?" Ashlock found his summons actions rather strange. The spider only seemed further distressed when he wrapped his vine around the corpse. "Whatever, I am starving—"

The corpse disintegrated into a pile of silver ash the moment it was touched.

"…" Ashlock was speechless as he stared at the remnants of his breakfast. He had already forced himself to accept that his food had been stolen and to make do with the little he had left. But to watch his hopes and dreams crumble into a pile of ash was heartbreaking. "Okay, deep breaths…in and out, in and out. It's fine. Everything is going to be fine."

"Ashlock, what's wrong? Are you hurting somewhere?" Diana asked as his entire canopy lit up and dimmed with lilac flames as if it were his lungs and he was hyperventilating.

"I think he is angry about something," Elaine said while glancing up. *"I wonder what it could be?"*

"Master is angry at Larry." The spider dropped his head. *"I ate his food without asking."*

"Huh?" Diana squinted at Larry. *"You told me he left these corpses for you?"*

"Larry lied."

"I didn't even know you could lie." Diana crossed her arms. *"And you never used to do anything Ashlock hadn't commanded you to do. So I didn't question it."*

Ashlock calmed down as best he could. His breakfast was gone, reduced to a pile of silver ash. There was no point holding a pity party over it, and it was best to move on. Larry had never acted with malice before, and the spider knew how important corpses were to him, so there must have been a good reason.

"Larry, why did you steal my food?" Ashlock spoke to everyone present. Hints of his suppressed rage were carried by his {Abyssal Whispers} skill, so they all flinched as his presence descended on them in a flood.

"When I finished my evolution last night, everyone was asleep."

"**Even Stella?**" Ashlock asked.

Larry nodded. *"She was knocked out on the bench in a deep sleep."*

Ashlock glanced at Stella, and despite everything that had happened with fruit having rained down all around, she was still fast asleep. Either someone had cast a sleeping technique on her, or she was so exhausted from teaching Jasmine yesterday it had put her in a coma.

"Knowing her, it's far more likely that too much socializing put her in a coma than for her to lose to a sleeping technique." Ashlock sighed. He had entrusted her to watch over the monster farm, but unlike his Ents, who mindlessly followed his orders until they ran out of Qi, Stella was still human, even as a cultivator. Sometimes, the mind's need for rest could not be ignored.

"**Okay, Stella aside, what happened next?**"

"It's hard to describe, but I was not myself when I left the cocoon. I had become a small swirling ball of divine ash, almost like a storm. I had the vague shape of my past self, but moving felt entirely different. I floated more than walked and was so small that I threatened to blow away in the wind."

"**You were small?**" Ashlock asked. Larry was definitely a tad smaller than his past self, but he was still massive for a spider at around two meters tall.

Larry nodded. *"About the size of Diana's head."*

"**So how did you get so big?**"

Larry answered by crawling over to the pile of ash formed from the half-eaten monster's corpse. Because he was a storm of ash rather than an actual spider, he crawled as if floating slightly above the ground, which furthered his mythical nature.

Larry stood over the pile of ash. Like metal attracted to a magnet, the ash flew off the floor and into his body, becoming part of the ever-swirling ashen storm in the shape of a spider.

"If I will it, anything within my realm of influence will be decayed into ash," Larry said gruffly. *"Since I was so small and weak coming out of my cocoon and I saw a pile of corpses nearby, I decayed them all to ash and absorbed the ash to reform my body and regain my strength despite knowing these were for Master."*

"So it was for a good reason, then. All is forgiven," Ashlock said, and Larry raised his head.

"Really, Master? Are you sure I should not be punished for a thousand years in Hell for eating your breakfast?"

"A thousand years in Hell? Forget it. There's no need for punishment over something so reasonable. I can always find more corpses for breakfast, but what am I to do if you blow away in the wind, never to be seen again?"

Larry's eyes widened in shock. *"That would be terrible. If not for me keeping you and Stella safe, you would surely perish from laziness!"*

"What…when did you get so silver-tongued?" Ashlock was baffled. Since when did Larry speak back to him like that? Was it something to do with his evolution?

Curious, Ashlock glanced through his system screens and navigated to the section about his summons.

{Herald of the Divine Ash: Larry [S]}

*Having consumed the flesh of a divine being from an upper realm, Larry has unlocked a new path to power. As a **Herald of the Divine Ash**, he will begin his path to become a deity. Alongside unlimited cultivation potential, Larry now has divine authority over ash and decay. He can decay any matter at will within his realm of influence. Also, as a divine being with governance over an affinity, Larry's body has been reformed entirely from divine ash, allowing him to reincarnate from ash and gain immortality.*

"Nothing here says anything about talking back to his summoner," Ashlock grumbled to himself. If it wasn't anything to do with the evolution option he picked, perhaps it was because Larry had reached S grade? He had started being capable of speech at A grade, so maybe it had upgraded?

"Larry, be honest with me," Ashlock said. "How do you view me after your evolution? Are you as loyal as before? What do you feel about being a summon?"

"Since I have outgrown Master in cultivation, I find my mind less restrained than before," Larry said thoughtfully. *"But I am still*

devoted to Master and wouldn't have it any other way even if I was free."

"That's good. I would be sad if you grew to hate me."

"Master, I would never!"

Ashlock gave his past self a big thumbs-up for treating his summons well. To think Larry ascending to the equivalent of S grade would cause the system's leash on him to weaken to the point he could make decisions by himself, such as eating a pile of corpses without being given permission.

A sudden feeling of something moving below ground alerted Ashlock to a monster coming through his roots.

"Something's coming…" Sure enough, a wolf-like creature with two curved horns sprouting from its head and rotting skin appeared a moment later with a confused growl.

Nobody even had time to react as Khaos executed the wolf on the spot. Its death had been so swift and silent that it was almost unbelievable that it had died until its headless body slumped forward in a pool of rancid blood.

"This is even better than food delivery back on Earth." Ashlock chuckled as he wrapped his black vine around the meal and moved it far away from Larry so it didn't disintegrate into ash. "I didn't even have to order anything, and I had food appear. It was even free, too! This is the ultimate way of life."

"If you don't mind me asking, where are these monsters coming from?" Diana asked as the corpse was crushed and dissolved.

"I also wanted to ask about that." Elaine pushed up her glasses. *"I have never seen something like this."*

Diana and Elaine had been there from the start, watching from the sidelines in interest. They had likely been drawn here by the mountain trembling as Titus pulverized monsters like a game of Whac-A-Mole.

"**My ethereal roots allow me to connect two places with a tunnel of compressed space, almost like a portal, but you still have to walk a few steps to travel the distance,**" Ashlock explained. "**The monsters are coming from a demonic mist grove far out in the wilderness that I made for you, Diana.**"

"You already grew it?! And they just crawl down through your roots by their own free will?" Diana seemed baffled.

"Yeah, Stella theorized that it had to do with my roots appearing as ley lines to the monsters."

"That does seem to be the case," Elaine said as she crouched down beside one of the holes and squinted into the darkness. *"However, you must have an insane amount of Qi running through your roots for that to be the case since we are built upon one of the realms' largest ley lines."*

"We are?"

Elaine nodded. *"It's a few hundred miles in width and spans from one end of the realm to the other. It also connects a few of the largest known spiritual springs, so it's a common pathway for beast tides."*

Ashlock had forgotten to investigate or ask more questions about the beast tide since becoming a powerhouse of the region. The level of threat he associated with it had vastly reduced since he grew in power and unlocked his {Skyborne Bastion [SSS]} skill. The fact the sect had also grown, and he had more Ents than ever, further reduced the severity of the beast tide in his mind, so he hadn't put much thought into it.

"Forgive my ignorance, but could you explain more about the beast tides, the ley lines, and these spiritual springs?" Ashlock asked. "Diana has mentioned a bit about it to me in the past, so I know the basics, but…"

"It's widespread knowledge as it's the greatest threat to all demonic sects." Elaine's eyes widened. *"So I am surprised you don't know."*

Diana tapped her shoulder. *"He may look big and sound wise, but Ashlock isn't even a decade old, you know? He was a tiny sapling back when Stella was a child. So he had never seen or experienced a beast tide. Which makes sense—most trees don't survive in the path of those beasts."*

"Not even a decade old?!" Elaine glanced up at his vast canopy and awkwardly coughed. *"Ahem, well, I am always here to answer any questions you have. Let's see…where should I start? I suppose explaining what an actual beast tide consists of would be a good starting place. Simply put, a beast tide is a large gathering of monsters racing along a ley line to the next spiritual spring. It includes monsters of all types and cultivation levels."*

"Even flying monsters?"

"Absolutely, they are the biggest nightmare to deal with." Elaine nodded. *"There are also ones that travel underground, such as giant worms. It's why remaining if the sect isn't strong enough to fight the beasts off is nonsense, as you cannot simply wait for it to pass by hiding underground."*

"How long do beast tides typically last?"

"Depends, some can last a few weeks, while others could take months. They typically come in waves with the weakest at the start and then the strongest at the end."

"Why is that?" Ashlock always wondered.

Elaine grinned as a translucent white flame that shifted between various colors like a rainbow flickered to life around her hand. She tapped the ground beneath her with her hand wreathed in illusion Qi. *"Let me show you…"*

The ground shimmered and changed color as if it were covered in a thin layer of water with dyes poured into it. Elaine clicked her fingers, and the colors gathered into a sparse web of glowing blue lines. Some were very thick, while others were thin. On occasion, they were intersecting each other, causing crossroads.

"What's this?" Diana asked as she stepped back to avoid stepping on the illusion.

"These are all the ley lines I know of. We are based somewhere in the middle on this thick one here for reference. The rest of the Blood Lotus Sect is also built upon this ley line, while the Tainted Cloud Sect is actually built on this smaller one that curves below us from the east to the west."

Only upon seeing the map did Ashlock realize something. Nox had said the Tainted Cloud Sect lay to the west, yet she escaped to the east. He had thought she planned to loop back around, but perhaps she was heading to an eastern portion of the Tainted Cloud Sect on this curved ley line.

"Now, do you see where these ley lines intersect?" Elaine continued, pointing at the map. *"These are called spiritual springs, areas of immense Qi. The largest of these spiritual springs is here to the south, where three giant ley lines intersect and the Celestial Empire is built."*

Ashlock suddenly felt very jealous. He was growing along a single ley line here, but the World Tree got three? "The Qi in that area must be obscene! No wonder the Celestial Empire's people do not need to absorb the demonic Qi from beast cores if they are swimming in the stuff."

Elaine used a stick and pointed at one of the places where two thick ley lines intersected. *"Spiritual springs deplete over time if enough beasts gather to cultivate and fight. Now, what do you think would happen if thousands of monsters gathered in a condensed location like this?"*

"They would fight to the death for supremacy?"

"Some would, but monsters in the Soul Fire Realm and above have enough intelligence to know when to flee." Elaine made the spiritual spring glow red on the illusionary map. *"I will use red to demonstrate the flow of beasts. For a long time, anywhere between fifty and a hundred years, the monsters will wage a brutal war among themselves around the spiritual spring. This is an era of peace for us cultivators."*

The red on the map grew darker and began to pulse.

"However, eventually, the spiritual spring will lose its luster. The stronger beasts begin to fight more fiercely among themselves for the densest spot of Qi, which causes the weaker beasts to leave in fear for their lives and to seek out a better place to cultivate. This is the beginning of a beast tide, the first wave."

The thick ley line that happened to be the one Ashlock's sect was built on slowly turned red as if a river of blood was pouring along it.

"As more monsters flee the spiritual spring, the ones at the front are unable to settle down on the ley line in fear of being devoured by the stronger monsters behind them." Elaine tapped her stick on another intersection up ahead. *"And they are also racing to be the first to the next spiritual spring, which has had a century to recover to its former glory. This is why beast tides are easy to predict. We can see the path the beasts are most likely to take decades in advance."*

Everything was starting to fall into place.

"Let me guess, the original spiritual spring eventually runs out of Qi, so the strongest beasts have no choice but to move to the next one?"

"Exactly. This is the wave of the beast tide that the demonic sects fear. After weeks or months of battling waves, everyone's Qi is exhausted. That is when the strongest monsters attack and entire sects have been wiped out in the past." Elaine pointed the stick at a nearby smaller ley line that wasn't dyed red. *"So the solution demonic sects*

have used for as long as records have existed is to simply move the sect out of the way. It's usually the better option anyway since all the spirit stones will have been mined in this area, and nowhere has all the Qi types a sect needs. Am I talking too much?"

"No, no, this is all very useful information," Ashlock said as he looked at the map. Having built a city in a day, he could see how easy it was to move a sect. Especially considering fighting waves of monsters involved spending years of gathered Qi for little gain. Sometimes, it was best to simply move on…

"But I don't have that choice unless I turned the entire sect into a Bastion and floated away." Ashlock sighed. "I may do that in the future, but for this time around? I don't have the hundreds of thousands of credits I need. I have no choice but to stay and fight. So what I need is practical solutions to help fight off this tide."

An obvious one would be digging down deep to hit this ley line. Considering how it was hundreds of miles wide, hitting it was assured so long as he dug deep enough. "Let's secure a link to it first." Qi and nutrients flowed from his trunk as he sent a hundred roots to sprawl downward at the maximum speed.

While that was going on, he looked back at the map.

"What lies between the ley lines in those dead areas?"

"Qi-deprived lands," Elaine replied. *"There are millions of mortals who live there in vast cities. There are also villages, farmland, animals, and much more."*

Ashlock had not been expecting that answer at all. **"Really? Why does anyone live on the ley lines then if there are beast tides?"**

"Because life—excuse my language—sucks fucking ass in Qi-deprived areas."

Diana laughed. *"It sure does, but to think someone as serious as you would swear. Didn't see that one coming."*

Elaine rolled her eyes but smiled. *"I was being serious. Qi may give birth to monsters by corrupting and mutating animals, but it also gives way to an easier and longer life. For those in the Qi-deprived lands, famine and illness kill most before they are adults, and of those that survive until adulthood, they would be lucky to live till eighty! But on the ley lines, under the protection of cultivator sects, mortals live in comparative abundance without risk of famine or illness for upward of a hundred years due to the ambient Qi."*

Ashlock couldn't believe it. "From the sounds of it, the mortals of the Qi-deprived lands live lives comparable to those in the medieval times on Earth but perhaps even worse."

"Not to mention," Diana said, *"you can never find out if you are a cultivator if you live in the Qi-deprived lands. Without Qi in the air, spirit roots will remain forever dormant."*

Elaine nodded. *"Also, monsters sometimes roam out of the ley lines and slaughter entire villages before their beast cores crack and kill them due to Qi deprivation. The poor mortals can do nothing to the Qi-enhanced beasts."*

"So monsters can't survive for long outside of areas with Qi."

"That's correct. It's the same for humans, but to a lesser extent. They won't die, but once they have spent all the Qi in their core, it's impossible to absorb anymore to replenish it."

Ashlock looked back on the map. If the ley lines were like borders to places of death for ordinary mortals, then in the smaller pockets of land surrounded by ley lines, wars for space between these cities and villages were also likely fierce. As Elaine said…life sucked fucking ass for them.

"To think the mortals under the cultivators had it better," Ashlock mused. "Mhm, but since I can pump Qi through my roots, couldn't I make a Qi-rich city within one of these pockets between the ley lines? That could be a way to move all the mortals of Ashfallen City out of the way, but that doesn't help me. I am stuck here…"

"Elaine, these beast tides are predictable, right?"

"Most certainly! The next one should come down this ley line from the north toward the Celestial Empire in the south in about two to three years. It should be one of the biggest in recorded history, so the last I heard is the Blood Lotus Sect is planning on moving soon."

"The biggest in recorded history…" Ashlock suddenly didn't feel so confident as he looked down at the map that was pulsing red. It wasn't even here, and they were just talking theoretically, but it was starting to feel far more real and a significant threat. **"What would the biggest in recorded history entail exactly, and how would you suggest we could survive it?"**

Elaine laughed. *"Survive it? We would move, of course. Fighting it would be impossible."*

"**Move?**" Ashlock said slowly. "**And how do you suppose I do that?**"

"Eh?" Elaine glanced back at his trunk. *"You would just... Oh. Oh no."*

"We have talked about fighting the beast tides a few times..." Diana shook her head.

"I didn't think you were serious?! I thought you would fight a few waves at the most and then leave!" Elaine shouted. *"That's suicide. Impossible. This tide will contain an entire wave of Nascent Soul monsters. It's accumulated hundreds of years of unchecked monsters since all the last beast tides missed the Celestial Empire."*

"Well, shit..." Ashlock looked to the north. He might need to speed up his own and everyone else's progress if such an apocalypse was on the horizon.

Stella yawned loudly and almost fell off the bench. *"What is everyone shouting about so early in the morning?"*

19

WORLD STAGE

"Morning, sleepyhead," Ashlock said to Stella as she sluggishly got off the bench and wandered over while yawning and rubbing her eyes.

Her hair was disheveled, and it seemed a few fallen fruits had smacked her on the head in her slumber, judging from the variety of colors staining her blond hair.

"Morning Tree…" Stella yawned again before smacking herself awake. *"Wow, I am exhausted. So…why is everyone shouting so early in the morning? Oh, hi, Larry."*

Larry waved one of his legs. *"Hello, Mistress."*

"You look shinier than usual." Stella squinted.

"That's because I am a demi-divine being now."

"Oh…I see." Stella shrugged. *"Good for you."*

"Thank you, Mistress."

"Why is there smashed fruit everywhere?" Stella grumbled as she reached up to comb her hair out of her face with her fingers. *"Ugh, it's even in my hair."*

"Ashlock got a little angry that Larry ate his breakfast. Let me help you." Diana summoned a ball of swirling water to her hand.

"What are you talking about— Agh!" Stella spluttered as Diana hurled the water in her face, drenching her head to toe. *"Diana! What the hell?"*

"Relax…" Diana drew back the water alongside all the fruit juice

and dirt, leaving Stella dry and clean. Discarding the water on the ground, Diana smiled. *"See? Isn't that better?"*

Stella blinked, clearly wide awake now after being splashed with cold water. *"Yes, though I disapprove of your methods."*

Diana shrugged as the water she had just discarded rose from the ground toward her hand. *"I can always give it back."*

Stella vanished and reappeared behind Diana with the blunt side of a dagger's blade pressed against her neck. *"Oh yeah?"*

"I forgot you could do that." Diana clicked her tongue and let the water drop back to the ground.

"Okay, enough nonsense, you two. We were discussing the beast tide and potential countermeasures. Care to join us, Stella?"

Stella stepped back from Diana and spun the dagger in her fingers before it vanished in a flash of silvery light. *"Nah, that sounds like a headache and rather pointless."* She frowned. *"Wouldn't Ash just win against a wave of monsters? Sounds more like a feast than a threat to me."*

"I appreciate your blind trust in me, but this is definitely something we need to plan and discuss. If you don't want to join in, what are you going to do today?"

Stella shrugged. *"Train my disciple, I suppose."*

Ashlock could tell Stella was in a bad mood just by how she spoke and acted. She was likely still exhausted from yesterday and was now annoyed because their shouting interrupted her sleep, and water was thrown in her face.

"Sorry to ask this of you, but could you grab a heavenly contract from Kaida and deliver it to the Silverspires while on the way to pick up your disciple? That's the only task that needed completing today. Oh, and you can return here via a root near Nox."

Stella huffed the freshly dried hair out of her face. *"Fine. But no more meetings. I'm done with those for a lifetime."*

"Sure, I promise," Ashlock said as Stella vanished from where she stood and reappeared at the entrance to the ink Bastion, where Kaida resided.

Now that she was gone, Ashlock glanced back at the illusionary map cast over the stone pulsing red. The beast tide was most certainly a threat, but with two years to go, that gave him dozens of Mystic

Realm visits to power up, and he already had some solutions at his disposal to help him survive.

"You really plan to fight this thing?" Elaine asked seriously.

"What other choice do I have?" Ashlock laughed. **"Worst case, I can teleport all of you to another ley line and face the tide alone."**

Elaine shook her head. *"Stella would kill me if I even suggested leaving you behind. If you are staying, so is she. And therefore, so am I. Whether I like it or not, it seems like fighting this thing is our only option. It may be two years away, but laying down the groundwork for a defense would need to begin today."*

That was true. Some things couldn't be rushed, even with Ashlock's powers and the system. Examples included making Bastions and Ents as he needed to farm the credits and find the necessary corpses. The cultivators of the Ashfallen Sect would also need time to cultivate up to Nascent Soul Realm.

"Be honest with me." Elaine looked up into his canopy. *"What are your strengths? Since you will be the focal point of our defense, Ashlock, we must work to your strengths and cover your weaknesses."*

Ashlock had no intention of sharing anything to do with the system with anyone except Stella and maybe Diana, but he could still give Elaine some clues.

"My strengths? Let's see…I have a massive pool of Qi and can quickly regenerate my reserves by pulling on all my offspring."

Elaine brought out a parchment and made notes. *"Big pool of Qi, and you can…pull on your offspring? What does that mean?"*

"I am linked via my roots to every demonic tree you see, whether on this mountain range or out in the wilderness. I can pull from their Qi reserves to substitute my own. Each may have a small amount of Qi to spare, but it becomes a significant amount when there are thousands of them."

Elaine scratched her head. *"I see. But spirit trees cultivate extremely slowly, right? So this must be a one-time thing you can do. I will note it down as a trump card—"*

"For a typical spirit tree, cultivation may be slow. But these are my offspring. Not only do they cultivate and grow faster than normal, but during the night, I take them to a dreamscape where their cultivation speed can increase upward of ten-fold depending on the moon's position."

"*Huh?*" Elaine glanced at Diana. "*Do you understand what he is talking about?*"

Diana shrugged. "*Not really? It sounds like he takes all his children to an alternate dimension during the night.*"

"*How is that possible? I have never seen him or his offspring go anywhere.*"

"*Trees are mystical beings, Elaine. I have seen him create rifts and drag creatures through them when he was weaker in cultivation than you are now. I stopped trying to understand Ashlock's nonsense a long time ago.*"

Elaine let out an exaggerated sigh. "*Okay, fine. Your main strength is effectively unlimited Qi. That is certainly useful. Anything else?*"

"**Mhm…**" Ashlock ignored his production skills and summons as he didn't consider them his personal strength since they gave him indirect strength through others. But on that topic, he did have something. "**I could technically create an army of Ents and Bastions to fight back against the beast tide.**"

Elaine glanced at Khaos. "*I see. What's the cost of making these, and how many could you control?*"

"**Other than upkeep, they cost me nothing to make. I just need a mostly intact corpse. As for how many I can control, it should be unlimited.**"

"*Unlimited?*" Elaine noted that in disbelief. "*And no cost to create?*"

"**Well, the main cost for me is that I gain power from eating corpses, so those I turn into Ents would become external power rather than personal power.**"

"*I fail to see the downside,*" Elaine grumbled. "*Both options result in more power under your control.*"

Ashlock chuckled. "**I suppose so.**"

"*Right, so you have infinite Qi and the ability to turn the beast tide into your own army.*" Elaine pushed up her glasses. "*Dare I ask, is there anything else?*"

Ashlock thought for a while. Since this would basically be a war, gathering information and holding down locations would be important. "**I can see and project my influence to anywhere within the reach of my roots and unleash my full power through any of my offspring.**"

"Mhm, yes, how reasonable," Elaine muttered as she noted it down. *"So just to be clear, you can fight a faraway battle without even being present? How far do your roots currently go?"*

"That is correct, and if I had to guess, my roots currently go around a thousand miles or so in every direction," Ashlock replied. **"I am also burrowing deeper as we speak to seek out the ley line."**

"Fascinating, anything else?"

Ashlock thought awhile. **"I can kill things with my roots and void tendrils. I can also turn small areas into bubbles of a certain affinity by overlapping a pocket realm. I think that's about it other than the strength of the Ashfallen Sect."**

The scratching sound of Elaine's quill was deafening as she noted everything down. Ashlock felt like he was taking a test and being graded for his worthiness. It didn't help that Elaine kept pulling different faces between disbelief and resignation. She finally laid the quill to rest and pushed up her glasses.

"Despite your ridiculous advantages, survival is still not assured. The weaker waves of beasts can be ignored since you have infinite Qi to deal with them and can create an army of your own," Elaine mused. *"However, there is still the issue of the Nascent Soul Realm and possibly even Monarch Realm monsters. You seem to lack direct attack power compared to your other advantages, so those strong monsters still pose a significant threat."*

Elaine clicked her fingers, and the illusion rose from the ground, becoming a three-dimensional map. She zoomed in by spreading her hands, and Ashlock could see a vague reconstruction of Red Vine Peak with a projection of him at the top of the mountain. Purple glowing lines that he assumed represented his roots began to sprawl through the mountain. Some spread outward in all cardinal directions, while others continued into the depths.

"Unlike you, I don't have my presence spread out for a thousand miles, so most of this is guesswork." Elaine clapped her hands, the map zoomed out to show the ley lines, and Ashlock could see his purple roots sprawl out. *"From the maps I have seen, this is around where I would guess your roots reach as of now."*

It was nowhere near as big of an area as he expected. In fact, his roots barely touched the edges of the thick ley line upon which he was growing.

"No wonder I never saw these mortal cities nestled between the ley lines, as I haven't even left the area of my own. However, I am getting close to the ley line along which the Tainted Cloud Sect is built." Ashlock's gaze drifted to the south. "Meanwhile, the Celestial Empire might as well be on another continent. It's so far away."

When shown his presence on the world stage, Ashlock didn't know how to feel. With Larry's evolution, the Ashfallen Sect was undoubtedly a powerhouse of the region, but there was still so much out there.

"I might have a way we can win for certain," Elaine said as she circled the illusion while biting her thumb.

"Really?"

Elaine gestured to the spiritual spring to the north that was easily ten times further away than his roots currently reached. *"Do you think you could grow your roots to reach the spiritual spring before the beast tide begins?"*

"If I had to guess, I can grow a few miles daily. So yes, I could reach there in a year."

The purple roots on the map spread up the ley line and intersected the spiritual spring to the north.

Elaine tapped the pulsing red area. *"This is where we will fight. As far away from your immobile body on Red Vine Peak as possible. This way, we can fight without risk."*

"How so?" Diana asked while squinting at the map. *"It's pulsing red because it's dangerous. The beasts are concentrated there. It's easier to deal with them when they come in small groups or alone while in the tide."*

"No, I can see what she is thinking. Very clever." Ashlock sighed at how blind and defensive his thinking had been. **"I blame it on being a tree. While you humans instinctively flee danger, I only considered facing it head-on. Launching an assault on the beast tide before it began never occurred to me."**

Elaine nodded. *"Ashlock, your main advantage is turning monsters into allies and being capable of fighting wherever your roots are. This gives you a unique way of fighting. Pardon my analogy, but your fighting style is reminiscent of rot. If you sent Larry or anyone else capable of killing a single Nascent Soul monster through your roots, they could ambush the monster, kill it, and then flee. You could then turn the corpse into an Ent and have it wear down or kill the other*

Nascent Soul–level monsters in the spiritual spring. Every monster that succumbs to your persistent assaults joins your power."

"Slowly, the beast tide would become under my control…"

It was a great plan. One with minimal risk and maximum gain. Ashlock had been ready to hunker down and fight the beast tide on his own terms, but if he could carve out an area of the spiritual spring, grow a forest of demonic trees, and wreak havoc there… It might even be too easy.

"Elaine, this is a great plan. There's just a few slight issues." Diana sighed.

"What are they?"

"Larry's main way to attack is by decaying things to ash. I assume you can't turn a pile of divine ash back into a monster?" Diana asked Ashlock's canopy.

"That's true. I need a mostly intact corpse," Ashlock replied.

"That's what I thought…and although you can fight anywhere your roots are, would you be capable of killing a Nascent Soul Realm monster away from your offspring?"

"No, over my roots, the best I can do is make portals, lock monsters in place with Spatial Lock, and attack them with spatial Qi. Even if I am in the Nascent Soul Realm, I doubt I could defeat such a monster with these methods alone in the spiritual spring, which will be overflowing with other Qi types."

Diana crossed her arms. *"So we need someone that isn't Larry or Ashlock in the Nascent Soul Realm that can go and hunt monsters far away. A few come to mind, such as Maple, the Silverspire Grand Elder, or perhaps one of us if we get that powerful within the next year, but I propose we kill two birds with one stone and make an Ent out of a certain someone."*

"You can't mean…" Elaine muttered.

Diana grinned, showing her fangs. *"Wouldn't turning the Blood Lotus Patriarch, Vincent Nightrose, into an Ent solve all our issues?"*

20
PERFECT FOUNDATION

Stella placed two parchments written in heavenly ink on the table, and the two Silverspires reached to take them.

"The terms of our agreement are written crystal clear on this parchment, so there's no room for you to *interpret* the meaning and continue to share sensitive information with others," Stella said as she made no move to sit down, instead opting to stand there with her arms crossed and looking down at them.

Sebastian's eyes glided over the agreement before he set the parchment down with a resigned sigh. "If the benefits are as great as I believe them to be, agreeing to this would be a no-brainer. But as it stands, this is asking too much and giving too little."

"Is that so?" Stella summoned two root improvement truffles to her hand. "What I have here is a mythical truffle that will permanently improve the quality of your spirit root. It's what turned Jasmine from a mortal to someone capable of becoming my disciple."

Stella placed them on her side of the table. "Sign the oath as we agreed upon, and it is yours. Consider it a signing bonus."

"You really are ruthless." Sebastian shook his head in resignation. "Fine, I had no intentions of backing out anyway, and you just sweetened the deal."

Stella knew she had played into Sebastian's little scheme, but she just wanted them to hurry up. Every moment she spent in this room made her nervous that a meeting would spring out of nowhere and sink its claws of misery and drama into her shoulders, forcing her to sit down and argue over things she had no care for.

Sebastian and Ryker both inserted Qi into the contracts. The words glowed with heavenly light. Lifting off the page, they floated into their bodies.

"Welcome to the Ashfallen Sect." Stella smiled. Knowing they were now under an oath of loyalty gave her more peace of mind. Before, it had felt like walking on eggshells around them as they were only business partners. But now she could be more open about things…if she could be bothered. "If that is all, I will be going now."

"Just one last question," Sebastian said.

Stella slowly turned to him with the fakest smile she could muster. "Mhm?"

"Other than shareholders of the Ashfallen Trading Company, we have nothing else to do here in the sect. Since we have a vested interest in its success, could we help out with selling the pills?"

Stella honestly didn't know the answer. She would ask Tree or Diana, but they were busy having a *meeting*, which she managed to escape.

"I'm sure Julian would appreciate some help. You can find him down in Ashfallen City or around here somewhere." Stella used a tactic she had learned from Ash: pass the problem on to somebody else! It appeared super effective as Sebastian bowed and gave his thanks. Not even giving him the opportunity to say anything else, Stella took her leave.

The hallways of the White Stone Palace swirled with fire Qi, and the defensive runic enchantments installed after the incidents with the merchants made creating a portal inside a hassle, so Stella chose to walk to the courtyard. As the morning sunlight hit her face, she breathed in relief. The courtyard was empty so she could summon her flying sword in peace.

"Mistress!" a voice boomed down the corridor behind her.

Stella's eye twitched. *I am exhausted and annoyed. Now is not a good time.* Glancing over her shoulder, she was surprised by who it was. "Elder Mo?"

"Phew, I heard you were visiting, but to think you would scurry away so soon." Elder Mo grinned. "Don't worry, we are both busy people, so I won't take too much of your time. I wanted to give you this."

His spatial ring flashed, and a short sword appeared in his hand. It looked rather basic, with a simple steel blade and a cloth-wrapped handle. The only noticeable features were that the cloth handle was dyed green and the word "Jasmine" had been etched into the hilt.

As Stella took the short sword, she could feel something tickling at the back of her consciousness, compelling her to swing the sword in a certain way.

"I heard you got a new disciple from the Grand Elder and wanted to gift her this. I used Spirit Fire to imbue my teaching spirit into the sword. As I'm sure you can feel, it compels the user to practice and guides them on proper form. I know it's not much, but I wanted to show appreciation for everything you and the Immortal have done for me and my family."

"This is incredible," Stella said as she weighed the sword in her hand. "What a great gift. I am sure she will be thrilled."

"I assume she will grow out of it quickly, and I didn't have much time to work on it, so the materials are rather plain." Elder Mo grinned. "But once Jasmine grows tall enough to swing a normal-sized sword around, come see me, and I will make her something befitting of the Mistress's disciple."

Stella stowed the sword away. "Thank you. I will ensure she gets this sword when she's ready, and she will know it's from you."

Elder Mo left down the corridor. "As promised, I won't bother you for too long. Take care of yourself, Mistress. Until next time."

"You too, old man." Stella laughed. With her mood lifted, she hopped on her flying sword and flew over to Ashfallen City while enjoying the view of the clear blue skies and sprawling scenery. The once-dull gray mountain range was now a vertical forest of red leaved trees, which made Nox and the field of white jasmine flowers surrounding her stick out.

Sitting crossed-legged under Nox's canopy was a blob of light green hair that Stella recognized as her disciple. Gliding down, she paused overhead, blocking the sun and casting Jasmine in her shadow.

Jasmine stirred from her meditation and glanced up. "Master?"

Stella withdrew her flying sword into her spatial ring and casually dropped down. "Morning, my dear disciple. I see you have already started cultivating."

"Well, it's almost noon," Jasmine said as she got to her feet and patted down the black cloak that Elaine had gifted her. "I was starting to worry that Master wasn't coming today. Did you oversleep?"

Stella snorted. "Absolutely not. I was busy in…meetings."

"I can tell you're lying." Jasmine squinted at her.

Stella blinked. *How?*

"You don't need to put on an act before me, Master." Jasmine beamed. "Just be yourself. Now that I know Master is lazy, I will remember that for the future."

Stella felt the upstanding and dignified persona of a master she had been trying to put on for her disciple crumble away before her very eyes while Jasmine smiled at her with a smug look on her face.

"Tsk, being called lazy by a darn kid." Stella ran her hands through her hair with a sigh. Today was not going how she expected at all. "I was trying to act like a dignified master for you, but if you don't want that, then fine." Stella crouched to Jasmine's eye level. "But you better tell me how you knew. No secrets, remember?"

"Master is no fun." Jasmine pouted. "But if you insist…I can feel your emotions through our master-disciple link. It's vague, but if you are standing before me, I can get a sense of your mood. I know you didn't just come from a meeting because you weren't angry or irritated."

Stella's eyes twitched. "Why can you read my emotions through the link?"

"And now you're irritated." Jasmine giggled. "As for the link, I have no idea. It was like that from the moment I accepted you as my master."

"Strange. I wonder if it's because I was the one to ask, and you accepted me as your master." Stella stood up. "Well, no matter. If you can feel my mood, that's helpful. We should head back to Red Vine Peak. Are you ready to go?"

"Yup." Jasmine nodded and held up a cloth bag. "My mom even made me lunch."

The image of a giant golden tree dropping a fruit on Stella's head appeared in her mind. *Is that how my mother would have given me lunch?* Shaking her head to remove the ridiculous thoughts of the

World Tree being her mother, Stella glanced around. "Now, where is the root Ash was talking about…"

Nox's shadow body emerged from behind the trunk like a ghost and gestured to a hole obscured by the flowers near her roots.

"That leads to Red Vine Peak?" Stella cautiously asked while stepping forward to put herself between Nox and her disciple. Even if Nox was a changed person, she still didn't trust her.

The shadow nodded wordlessly, so Stella walked over to check. "Take my hand, Jasmine. Let's go together."

I wonder how it feels to use one of Ash's roots now. Will we fly through it, or will it feel like a portal?

Stepping down into the hole while holding Jasmine's hand, Stella was surprised. Compared to the tight squeeze filled with sap she had experienced the last time she traveled through the mountain, this was a spacious tunnel. Almost too spacious, as if it was expanded with spatial Qi. The tunnel was lit by light cascading down from the hole above. There was a similar hole letting in light a few steps away.

Walking forward, Stella felt a slight tug on her body, and if she paid close attention, she could see that the tunnel walls were blurring as she moved. Arriving under the next hole in the tunnel within five steps, Stella jumped slightly and felt the tunnel eject her out of the hole.

"Whoa." Stella caught her footing and glanced around. It was unmistakably Red Vine Peak. Jasmine popped out beside her, equally bewildered at how they had covered such distance in a few steps.

Diana waved to Stella and walked over. "Welcome back."

"Is your meeting done?"

"Yeah." Diana glanced back at the illusionary map that Elaine was still walking circles around. "You were right, by the way."

"Oh?" Stella raised a brow. "About what?"

"The beast tide is looking to be more of a feast than a threat." Diana chuckled. "How ridiculous of a statement is that? Of course, there are still some things to work out and do, but Elaine is far more on board about fighting it out than trying to run."

"Good, I wouldn't have let her flee anyway." Stella smirked.

"She knows." Diana glanced at Jasmine. "I see you're here again today. I heard from Elaine that you have the potential to pick a second affinity. Have you chosen one yet?"

Jasmine shook her head. "No, Mistress Diana, I have not. I only just started learning about the truths of nature Qi from Heaven's whispers yesterday. So I am not sure what I should even pick…"

Diana nodded thoughtfully. "It's indeed a hard choice, and there's no shame in learning more and establishing your base in the nature affinity first, as it may give you an idea for a fitting affinity in the future."

Jasmine nodded and fell into thought.

"Talking of establishing her base," Stella patted Jasmine's head, "would you be able to help me give her truffles? There will likely be a heart demon to kill and some impurities to wash away."

Diana shrugged and gestured to the hut. "Sure, I don't have much going on until Julian finalizes the plans for the mortal branch of the Ashfallen Trading Company, so I could help."

Stella decided to stay quiet about how she suggested Sebastian Silverspire get involved.

I'm sure it will work out fine.

Once the three were inside the hut, Jasmine placed her lunch in the storage cabinet before joining Stella and Diana on the fur bed. It was a tight fit with the three of them.

"Let's do the heart demon one first." Stella summoned it from her spatial ring and handed it to Jasmine. Her disciple eyed the black mushroom with caution, which was understandable given its name.

"Negative emotions and experiences condense into what we call heart demons, and they cause bottlenecks to form," Diana explained. "Eating this truffle will force the heart demon out, leaving you with a serene mind perfect for cultivation and accepting Heaven's will for change."

Jasmine frowned with concern. "How does the heart demon get out?"

"It will crawl its way up your throat and emerge out of your mouth," Stella replied bluntly. "But don't worry, we are here to kill it and take care of you. Just trust us and let the process happen. Don't fight it."

"O-okay." Jasmine hesitantly ate the truffle. The three sat there in silence. Stella and Diana stared at her mouth, and Jasmine shifted uncomfortably under their gaze.

"I feel something coming. What do I do?!" Jasmine's eyes shook with fear as she looked between Stella and Diana.

"Relax." Stella patted her hand. "Just let it out."

Jasmine tried her best to relax, and a moment later, she opened her mouth. A tiny black phantom the size of a thumb climbed out, and Diana swiftly grabbed it.

It's so tiny, which I guess makes sense since Jasmine hasn't lived long enough to have many negative experiences.

"That thing was inside me?" Jasmine shuddered.

Diana threw the phantom into her mouth and gulped it down. "They aren't so bad." Diana licked her lips. "Quite tasty, actually."

All the color had left Jasmine's face as she stared at Diana in horror.

Diana seemed to find the reaction amusing as she leaned forward and rested her chin in the palm of her hand. Her nails extended into claws, and her long black hair, tinted with streaks of blue, covered half her face. "If you found something as tiny as that phantom terrifying, you should have seen the one Elder Mo housed, which was the size of you."

"Knock it off." Stella flicked Diana's forehead. "Stop trying to intimidate my disciple. It's perfectly normal to be scared of the horrors that mortal bodies house."

"What could be worse than that?" Jasmine asked as she hugged her legs.

Stella exchanged a knowing look with Diana.

"Well, this next truffle is the spirit root–improving truffle, which you have already had before," Stella said as she placed the mushroom before Jasmine's feet. "It's not as scary as the heart demon–expelling one, but it is far messier."

"I don't think I want to eat truffles anymore." Jasmine pouted as she hugged her legs tighter and side-eyed the truffle on the fur bed beside her.

"Really?" Stella frowned. "After this one, I was going to give you the skin improvement truffle that will give you skin as smooth as ours. But if you don't want to eat any more truffles, then I suppose it can't be helped—"

Jasmine grabbed the truffle off the bed and gulped it down without even taking a bite.

"Or you could do that." Stella smiled at her disciple's sudden change of attitude. "Take off your cloak. Close your eyes and cycle Qi through your body."

Jasmine followed her instructions, and soon, a pungent smell filled the hut as her impurities were pushed out through the pores in her skin. Her clothes darkened as they absorbed the impurities, causing Jasmine to gag.

"Ugh, I smell awful." She scrunched up her nose. "What is this stuff?"

Stella coughed and waved a hand before her face. "Impurities, and there will be a lot. Your spirit roots are of poor quality, so I will have you keep eating these truffles until you have as good or even better spirit roots than me."

"It's almost unfair how good of a foundation you are receiving, Jasmine." Diana hurled water at the girl, causing her to cry in shock. Diana then pulled the water back into a murky ball that floated above her palm. "I am very curious to see how fast you will grow under Stella's guidance and resources."

"So am I." Stella snapped her fingers to create a portal leading outside where Diana could dump the impurity-filled water. "But there's a lot of work to be done."

Splashing Jasmine with water and then pulling it off continued for the next hour.

"I think the process is finished," Diana said. "Jasmine, try to push your Qi to your fist."

"Okay…" Jasmine said absentmindedly. Being drenched and then dried over and over had taken a toll on her. Her hand became wreathed in untamed Qi. It burned brighter than before and held its shape.

"How does it feel?" Stella asked.

"Amazing." Jasmine grinned as she woke from her daze. "It's so much easier than before."

"Great, let's continue truffle eating tomorrow." Stella stood up and stretched. Sitting in such a small hut for so long was tiresome.

"But my skin improvement truffle…" Jasmine grumbled.

"Come on, get up. You can eat that tomorrow."

"What are we doing now, Master?"

Stella glanced outside. "While the sun is still out, it's a perfect time to practice sword fighting. You still have that tournament to fight in a month, remember? Having high-quality roots and good skin won't help if you lack ways to attack, and there's too little time to form your nature Soul Core and learn many techniques."

Jasmine's shoulders sagged. "But, Master, I don't even have a sword."

Stella felt her lips curl up into a smile. "Would you believe I had one made just for you?"

"No way."

"I doubt it."

Jasmine and Diana answered simultaneously.

Stella scowled. "Why not?"

"When would you have had time? You are far too lazy." Diana shrugged. "You were with Jasmine all of yesterday and then slept so deeply last night—"

"Ha!" Jasmine grinned. "I knew Master slept in."

Stella crossed her arms and frowned. "I don't even want to give you the sword anymore."

"You actually have one?" Diana seemed surprised.

"Well, Elder Mo gave it to me as a present for Jasmine." Stella smirked. "But disciples that are rude to their master don't deserve gifts. Take this wooden sword instead."

Jasmine stared down at the tiny wooden sword that was basically a stick in her hands. "Master, I'm sorry."

"Apologize to me by running a lap around the peak and doing five hundred sword swings before evening," Stella instructed. "Maybe then I will reconsider."

"Yes, Master…" Jasmine walked out of the hut and sprinted off.

"Isn't that a little cruel?" Diana asked.

"The sword Elder Mo gifted me will make learning the sword too easy as it was imbued with his will via Spirit Fire," Stella replied as she leaned on the hut's doorframe with her arms crossed and watched Jasmine sprinting into the distance. "I want to spoil Jasmine, but she must understand how big the advantage I am giving her is. It's why I had her practice cultivation before feeding her the truffles and will now swing a practice sword around for a few days before earning Elder Mo's gift."

Diana hummed in agreement. "You actually put some thought into this."

"Of course I did." Stella smiled. "I plan to turn Jasmine into the greatest cultivator that ever lived. That way, I can laze around knowing Tree is safe."

"There it is." Diana walked past her with a sigh. "I wonder how she would react if she knew that was the reason. Anyway, remember she is still just a child."

"Exactly, children are more malleable and are good learners." Stella waved her off. "I will train her personally in sword fighting over the next few days until she meets my standards."

"That's not what I… Never mind." Diana wandered off while shaking her head. "She is your disciple. I can only pray for her."

Why would she be praying for my disciple? Stella tilted her head in confusion.

21
UNWAVERING CONFIDENCE

Ashlock watched as Jasmine stood under his canopy, swinging her wooden sword and dodging the attacks of an enemy he couldn't see.

Elaine had cast illusion magic on Jasmine so she could fight a weakened copy of Stella while the real Stella lay slothfully on the bench under the shade of his canopy, reading one of the many technique manuals she had looted from the Azure Clan's library.

The idea of fighting an illusion had been brought up after Stella found herself unable to hold back during training and broke Jasmine's wooden sword every few minutes. After going through dozens, it was clear another solution was needed. Diana offered Jasmine to fight the phantoms within her mist, but they terrified the poor girl.

Eventually, Elaine offered to let Jasmine fight an illusion created from Jasmine's mental image of Stella. The fight felt real, as Jasmine received some pain if the illusionary version of Stella landed an attack. Which was why Jasmine was fighting the air so desperately. This exercise also allowed Elaine to practice with her illusion Qi, as conjuring up fake enemies that inflicted pain would do wonders in a fight.

Despite massive improvements, Jasmine was still struggling due to her intensive training regimen. While cultivating, she was fed as many fruits and truffles as possible in the mornings. As the sun reached its zenith, Jasmine was expected to run a lap or two of the entire peak and then practice swordsmanship for a few hours. This part was naturally the most fun for Ashlock to watch as he saw her improve in real time.

"Master, it's been a few days." Jasmine panted as she jumped backward. *"Can I use a real sword yet?"*

Stella let the book she was reading lay flat on her chest and glanced to the side at Jasmine. *"Why?"*

Jasmine furrowed her brows. *"So I can defeat the illusion version of you, Master."*

"Wrong answer." Stella picked up her book and flipped the page. *"You fight an illusion rather than something real. The blade you wield makes no difference. Once you understand this, you will be able to defeat the illusion, and only then will I give you Elder Mo's gift."*

Jasmine rolled to the side and scrambled to her feet. *"Master, I said I was sorry for doubting you! Beating you is impossible without a better sword!"*

"Still the wrong answer," Stella replied.

"Master, I don't understand— Agh." Jasmine crumbled to the side in pain. It was short and sharp, so she could recover within a second.

A version of this conversation was repeated during every afternoon sparring session. Ashlock knew Stella had her reasons for training Jasmine the way she did, but he still felt bad for her disciple.

"Jasmine has improved quite a bit over these last few days," Ashlock said to Stella. **"Why not give her the sword imbued with Elder Mo's fighting spirit? It would surely help her improve and defeat the illusion of you."**

Stella slammed the book she was reading closed and set it aside. *"I agree she has improved. However, I hoped Jasmine would see the purpose of this exercise on her own."* Stella swung her legs around and got up. *"But a little guidance may be required. Elaine, could you dismiss the illusion for a moment?"*

Elaine snapped her fingers, and Jasmine collapsed to the floor in relief as the illusion dispersed.

"Let me teach you something, my dear disciple," Stella said, holding out her hand and helping Jasmine to her feet. *"The number-one rule to fighting as a cultivator is not your abilities with the sword, your cultivation level, or even the plethora of techniques at your disposal because these things can be outmatched or overcome by an opponent."*

Jasmine's eyes widened. *"What is the most important thing, Master?"*

"To have unwavering confidence," Stella answered simply.

"Unwavering confidence?" Jasmine tilted her head.

Stella nodded. *"Cultivators have many ways to fight and win. Victory or defeat is never assured for either side, no matter the difference in realms. Certain affinities counter each other. A life-saving artifact could turn the tide of battle or even a lucky hit. There is so much out of your control, so it's important to steel the most important thing you have absolute control over at all times."* Stella tapped Jasmine's forehead. *"Your mind."*

"My mind?" Jasmine frowned as she stared up at Stella's finger.

"Think about it. You have been fighting an illusion crafted from the mental image you have of me. The only thing holding you back from victory isn't this sword, but rather your own mind," Stella explained. *"You believe that if you had a real sword, you would win, and you likely would. However, your triumph would not result from changing sword but because you* believed *in victory."*

Stella withdrew her finger. *"I will give you the sword when you have earned it by conquering your mind and forming unwavering confidence. Until then, defeating my illusion will be impossible, and you are undeserving of Elder Mo's gift."*

"I can really win against you with this flimsy wooden sword?" Jasmine asked.

"You could even win without it." Stella winked as she returned to the bench and her reading. After settling into her slothful pose, she added, *"Elaine, could you restart the illusion and turn up the difficulty?"*

Elaine shot her a confused look. *"Really? You know I can't do that. The illusion is based on Jasmine's mental image. I just feed it Qi."*

Stella hid her face with the technique manual she had been pretending to read all day and used her spatial Qi to carry her voice to Elaine's ear, and Ashlock listened in. *"Just make her believe you did, and the illusion will naturally grow stronger. It's all in her head, after all. Until she learns this truth, she is not worthy of wielding a real sword as she will become too dependent on it. Our mind and bodies are our greatest weapons, not the piece of steel we hold in our hands."*

Elaine smiled and turned to Jasmine. *"On second thought, increasing the difficulty is a great idea."*

Ashlock still felt bad for Jasmine, but he had to agree with Stella's teachings. "I have fought a plethora of cultivators over the years, and the ones that kept a poker face right up until their deaths were the toughest to deal with. For example, even as Nox was turning into a tree and had Stella's sword rammed through her chest, she stayed calm and even grinned. Stella has also bluffed her way through many situations with misplaced confidence."

"Master?!" Jasmine protested in horror. Every inch of her body was in pain, not from the stabs and slashes inflicted by the illusionary version of Stella as those quickly faded but from aching muscles overwhelmed with fatigue.

If Master hadn't made me run two whole laps around this place before swordfighting, I could have won easily. But I am so tired I can hardly react to the illusion's movements! Not to mention, I have this flimsy wooden sword while she has a black blade wreathed in spatial flames that burn my skin! This isn't a fair fight, and she wants Mistress Elaine to turn up the difficulty? I will die!

Elaine smiled as she walked over. "Let's turn up the difficulty, shall we?"

Don't come any closer, you demon posing as a teacher! Jasmine cursed in her mind as she didn't dare say her thoughts aloud. *Nothing good will come of it if I protest. Stella finds anyone who questions her annoying, and my life becomes far worse when she is in a bad mood.*

Jasmine felt like she was going through literal hell. Who knew becoming a cultivator was so intense? But the results did speak for themselves. On the first day, a single lap of the mountain peak had taken the wind out of her, but now she could do two laps without fainting. She could also control the untamed Qi in her body and focus it around her fist for an hour now.

Elaine placed her hand on Jasmine's forehead. It felt ice cold to the touch, as if it weren't even a human hand, and then Jasmine felt the coldness penetrate her skull while something wormed its way into her consciousness. Out of the corner of her eye, she saw a person materialize from the ground.

It was Stella with a haughty expression and her sword casually resting on her shoulder. The illusion did not speak as it stared her down, and Jasmine felt her blood run cold. If she hadn't seen this version of Stella materialize out of illusion Qi, she would have believed it was the real deal.

Elaine patted her shoulder and gave a supportive smile. "Remember, Jasmine, it's all an illusion born from your consciousness. She is crafted from your memories and experiences. The more you fear her, the stronger she becomes. Have some confidence, okay?"

Again, with the confidence? Jasmine wanted to scream, but instead, she nodded and tightened her grip on her wooden sword. Even as an illusion, Stella wasn't one to hold back. She only ever went for the kill.

Maybe her ruthlessness is due to the nightmares I had after our first training session, where she threatened my life constantly while saying I needed to toughen up and keep a calm head in a challenging situation, Jasmine wondered as she watched the illusion's every move. *Ah, here she comes!*

The second Stella lowered her sword, she vanished. Jasmine spun around and tried to meet the blade with her flimsy wooden sword that felt so weak and pathetic in her hand, and as expected, the illusionary blade passed right through and struck her shoulder. Immense pain greater than before sprawled through her entire body, making her yelp and seize up. This had happened before, and it would happen again. Over and over, she would try and fail to fight back.

She really did get stronger, Jasmine thought as the pain faded as quickly as it came. Her sword remained intact, but it was basically useless. *Master really is scary. She is nothing but an illusion and a weakened version, yet she can kill me in an instant.*

The illusion smirked as if it knew her thoughts and vanished again. This time, the pain came before Jasmine even had time to react. The wooden sword in her hands went flying as she crumbled forward in pain from being stabbed in the back.

The pain was already gone by the time she fell to her knees, but the experience of an unavoidable death was still fresh in her mind. Until now, she had fought with a glimmer of hope. She was always a little too slow, or her sword was too weak to block the attack. But just now, she would have died before she even knew what happened.

Why did the illusion get even stronger than before?

"It's impossible," Jasmine murmured as she stared at the wooden sword lying within arm's reach. Frustration began to boil inside her, and she reached out to pick it up and try again but then paused. It had been days at this point, and she only felt further away from beating the illusion. Clearly, what she had been doing until now wasn't working.

Is it really all in my head? Can I really beat something if I just believe I can? That sounds ridiculous.

Although Jasmine *knew* the illusion was fake, it felt authentic. The way it looked at her with contempt, went for the kill without a word, and was ruthless.

Wait, that isn't like Master at all.

Jasmine glanced past the illusion at Stella, the real one. She was lying slothfully on the bench and playfully petting a white squirrel she called Maple. Through the link, Jasmine could tell that Stella wasn't filled with wrathful hatred but was calm and happy.

That's the Master I know. Jasmine retracted her hand from the wooden sword, leaving it there. *Master said I could defeat the illusion without a sword. I just need to figure out how.* Sitting cross-legged, Jasmine cycled her Qi while keeping her eyes glued to the real Stella.

Jasmine could feel the illusionary Stella behind her but made no move to block the attack that she knew was coming.

You can't hurt me. You aren't real. You can't hurt me. You aren't real. Jasmine chanted over and over in her mind while keeping her eyes glued to the peaceful view of Stella. Her heart was pounding, and her ears were ringing as she anticipated the pain. It came a second later —sharp and hot like always, but to her surprise, it hurt less than the last hit.

Stella's resentful look flashed in her mind, but she purged it from her consciousness, and the pain passed. *It's working.* She thought as she imagined patting Stella on her head for a change. Any mental image that made her seem less fearsome was what Jasmine focused on. *If this illusion is as strong as my view of her, I will make her as harmless as that squirrel she's petting.*

However, it was not easy. The illusion didn't take her refusal to participate in their dance of death lightly as it kept slashing and stabbing at her back. Yet, with every strike, the pain lessened.

It isn't even real. Jasmine snorted. *To think I was terrified by a sword that doesn't even exist.*

From a pain that had once winded Jasmine and brought her to her knees, it now felt pathetic. She didn't even need to look at Stella playing around with the squirrel anymore. As a test, Jasmine decided to close her eyes and try cultivating despite the illusion's measly attempts to break her concentration.

Oddly, the pain helped her focus. Perhaps it was because her body felt it was a life-or-death situation, so Heaven's whispers were more vivid than usual, and the Qi flowed through her spiritual roots with ease.

An hour or so passed, and something more threatening than the illusion broke Jasmine's concentration. Her stomach was rumbling. In fact, she was so hungry she feared her stomach would emerge out of her throat and be the one to kill the illusion rather than her.

I guess it's time to finally end this. Jasmine opened her eyes and saw the real Stella watching her from the bench with interest. Giving her master a smile, Jasmine rose to her feet and rolled her shoulders. The slight pinpricks of pain from the illusion's attacks drilling into her back hardly fazed her.

Jasmine's gaze landed on the wooden sword lying on the ground. *I can't believe I was so foolish to think I needed such a thing. Swords really are worthless when I have all I need.*

Untamed Qi gathered in her fist, and with as much force as she could muster from her Qi-enhanced body, she spun around and delivered the most vicious uppercut she could muster to the illusion of her master. Surprisingly, the illusion did not fly through the air like she had envisioned. She had pulverized the illusion out of existence as it faded into nothingness.

Jasmine looked down at her fist with awe. She stood there for a moment, relishing in the victory, and felt a tear streak down her face. Days of pain and fear had been conquered in a single, confidence-filled punch.

"Master, I did it." Jasmine turned to the bench and was almost thrown off her feet as Stella ran over and embraced her in a tight hug. Bewildered, Jasmine didn't know what to say. "Master?!"

"My disciple is so cool!" Stella released her and grinned. "I knew when you opened your eyes that you had conquered your fear of my illusion, but to think you would turn around and deliver such a vicious punch right into what I guess was my face!"

"Um…"

"Honestly, you were a bit hopeless with the sword, and I was growing worried that you lacked what it would take to fight in the tournament so soon. But that punch was excellent," Stella continued rambling. "I know talent when I see it, and to think you were hiding that inside you. Forget the sword. You should just punch people in the face!"

"Wait, what?!" Jasmine was shocked out of her daze as her goals crumbled. She had dreamed of becoming one of those dignified cultivators cruising through the skies on flying swords and engaging in fierce duels. There was nothing dignified about punching people in the face.

"Master, what about Elder Mo's gift? I beat the illusion. So I should get the sword now, right?" Jasmine asked desperately. She heard it would help her train. *Even if I lack the talent with the sword, Elder Mo should be able to save me, right? I don't want to only punch people.*

Stella shrugged. "Sure, you can have it. Swords are a cultivator's best friend, as even if you don't use them in combat, they are useful for flying around. But as your master, I am telling you this is not where your talent lies. As a cultivator that defies the heavens, sometimes it's important to understand and lean into your strengths to get ahead of others. There's no shame in doing so."

Jasmine felt like crying. Why did her master say such reasonable things that made it hard to refute?

Stella's spatial ring flashed with a silvery light, and a sword that looked comically short appeared in her hands. "Here you go. A gift from Elder Mo. You earned it."

"Thank you, Master." Jasmine accepted the sword with her best manners. It felt heavy in her hand, but it didn't fill her with the confidence she had anticipated. Something buzzed at the edge of her consciousness, compelling her to swing it. However, with a sigh, she ignored it and sheathed the blade.

Master is right. My fists are better.

22
RAPID EXPANSION

A few more days passed since Jasmine rejected the sword and embraced the path of the fist. She was here again at sunrise, fighting an illusion Ashlock couldn't see.

Stella intently watched Jasmine's punching form while sitting on the bench and shouting pointers every few tries.

"Lift your hands a bit higher. Yeah, there we go. Keep your head straight. Only twist your upper body here. Yes!"

Idletree Daily Sign-In System
Day: 3605
Daily Credit: 42
Sacrifice Credit: 3288
|Sign in?|

Ashlock shrugged off his sleep with a yawn. The sun rose later, and the winter winds made him sleepier than usual. Days seemed so short now, and as fun as watching Jasmine's progress was, he had work to do. It wasn't easy keeping tabs on the area within his domain when he rapidly expanded in all directions, especially overnight when he had faster growth under the nine moons.

"I should reach the Tainted Cloud Sect later today," Ashlock mused as his consciousness spread throughout his trunk and roots that sprawled out for a thousand miles. Briefly glancing to the east, he confirmed it would still be a few hours, so he checked up on the rest.

Down below, he had yet to encounter a ley line. Still, the Qi density was increasing the further he delved, which boosted his system-given cultivation technique {Transpiration of Heaven and Chaos} as he had to draw Qi up his roots to expel it out of his leaves. There were also sizable spirit stone deposits down here, so he had hollowed out some of his ethereal roots so Mudcloaks could reach these deposits and mine them for the Ashfallen Sect.

"I'm starting to wonder if the ley line is even a physical thing like a powerline or if it's closer to an ocean in how the pressure increases the closer you get to the bottom, but it never solidifies."

Ashlock would keep delving deeper until he broke through to hell to find out. He also intended to verify if the realms were round or flat. Most things pointed to the layers of creation being flat by how they were described to him by Diana, which raised some questions and concerns.

Structure of the realms aside, digging down was overall the least exciting of his expansions. It was just a lot of rocks and dirt. However, he encountered the odd worm-type monster, which he killed and then consumed.

The more exciting direction to expand was into the Blood Lotus Sect.

Previously, he had avoided growing toward the west, where he suspected the other mountain peaks of the Blood Lotus Sect resided, for the simple reason of wishing to remain hidden. Sprawling roots that emitted a large amount of spatial Qi were bound to attract the attention of cultivators, and following his roots to their source would be easy. Exploring was great, and he wanted to see what the other peaks looked like, but he also liked living.

However, with his sect's explosive growth in power and Larry's recent ascension to Nascent Soul Realm, he finally began expanding into the Blood Lotus Sect. His days of hiding away on Red Vine Peak were drawing to a close with the involvement of the Eternal Pursuit Pavilion, whether he liked it or not, so it would be best to grow under his future enemies.

Ashlock cast his vision westward to the newest area he had discovered. Floating above the land with {Eye of the Tree God}, he saw the shadow of the grandest mountain he had ever seen dominate the skyline.

"It seems the peaks are sprawled out in a sort of banana shape curving upward to the northwest. When I went straight west, there wasn't much there except more endless forests."

Ashlock suspected the strange layout was so that all the cities of the Blood Lotus Sect were built within the width of the giant ley line that ran from the spiritual spring to the north all the way to the Celestial Empire in the south.

So far, of the nine cities under the control of the Blood Lotus Sect, Ashlock had encountered three of them. Darklight City, which he now ruled, and Slymere, which was very nearby, were the closest. The mountain in the distance was his latest discovery.

It was around five times the distance as Slymere was to Red Vine Peak, and from some snooping around and listening in to the locals, he suspected this place was Thunderhold Peak—the home of the Skyrend family.

Thunderhold Peak was a place that inspired awe, even in Ashlock. The mountain was relatively flat but kept ascending until it reached the clouds. A vast city built from marble and gold encircled the summit, and every street led to paved squares that were lorded over by towering statues of the Skyrend family members.

"Egotistical bastards," Ashlock muttered at the insanity of how many statues littered the city. It was an obscene personification of pride.

Ashlock had a relatively low opinion of the Skyrend family after his run-in with the now-dead scions Kassandra and Theron during the Alchemy tournament. But he now understood where the arrogance had stemmed from if this was the absurdity of wealth their family could put on display, having settled in this area for less than a century.

"I suppose being able to guarantee the survival of an Elder as they attempt to ascend realms is a lucrative business," Ashlock mused as he floated just below the clouds overhead. He didn't have his roots grow too close to the peak where a palace that might as well be its own city resided as it was decked out in enough defensive runic arrays that he feared they could summon the heavens itself to smite him out of existence if he even looked in their direction.

This made the fact Maple had apparently wiped out enough

Skyrend family members here that they felt justified in a war with the Voidmind family even more impressive. Just how powerful was that darn squirrel?

"If only Maple was my summon and as obedient as Larry." Ashlock sighed. They were in a mutual pact that stopped them from killing each other so they could coexist peacefully, but that was it. Maple was not obligated to help Ashlock or do as he asked, and he was free to attack families if he so wished.

Ashlock's gaze went down the sloping mountain of Thunderhold. Like the much smaller Slymere, the architecture became cruder and denser further down the slope until the industrial sector resided at the bottom.

"I wonder which city I will hit next? I know Darklight City is the easternmost city. I remember there being twelve noble families and only nine cities. Since the Ravenborne, Winterwrath, and Evergreen families are gone from the Blood Lotus Sect, that leaves the remaining nine families. I assume Nightrose City, home of the Patriarch, will be closer to the middle of the sect, so maybe I will hit the cities controlled by the Silverspire, Azurecrest, or even Starweaver families next?"

Either way, expansion into the Blood Lotus Sect was progressing smoothly. After a few more hours of snooping around Thunderhold Peak and carefully directing his ethereal roots around any defensive arrays he spotted to make sure he covered as much of this city as he could, the sun reached its zenith, which meant the Tainted Cloud Sect should be close.

"Before arriving, I should probably ask Nox if she remembers any details about the city," Ashlock muttered as he headed back. "There were multiple Nascent Soul individuals there, right? It would be bad if I immediately alerted them to my presence and invited their wrath. As fun as talking about killing the Blood Lotus Patriarch and turning him into an Ent was, Nascent Soul Realm cultivators are best not to be messed with. Larry has only just ascended, so he is getting accustomed to his new strength, and he is the only one capable of fighting them as of now."

Speaking of Larry, the spider was out hunting. He needed to decay corpses to ash and absorb the ash to increase his size and strength, so he wasn't even around to protect Ashlock if he earned a Nascent Soul Realm cultivator's ire.

Arriving at Ashfallen City, Ashlock passed the area being cleared out for the construction of a grand building that would serve as the headquarters for the mortal branch of the Ashfallen Trading Company. Progress on it had been slow thus far as Sebastian wanted to make a structure a tad more complex than the simple buildings Douglas and the Mudcloaks used to make.

A little further up the mountain, he found Nox growing in her field of white flowers. She had grown in size, now looming over the surroundings, and her canopy of black leaves rustled in the breeze.

Last time, Ashlock had used {Progeny Dominion} to restrain and communicate with Nox because of a misunderstanding. This time, he wanted to go with a gentler approach and try to speak without forcing their souls to merge.

"Nox, can you hear me?" Ashlock had to use {Abyssal Whispers} as Nox had split her soul with her family's Shadow Soul technique to create a dryad out of shadows. This way, he could speak to both halves of her soul at the same time.

"Ah, yes!" Nox replied as the shadow dryad looked toward Red Vine Peak. *"How can I assist the great tree?"*

"Just call me Ashlock, and I have some questions for you. Are you free?"

"Yes, I have all the time in the world... Few mortals visit here besides that one family," Nox said with a hint of loneliness. *"Whenever someone comes close, I try to offer them a fruit, but they run in fear instead. Catherine doesn't seem keen on cultivating, Julian is too busy with work, and Jasmine says hello to me in the morning before using the ethereal root to go to Red Vine Peak. She doesn't even show interest in my fruit or cultivating here..."*

Ashlock saw the shadow dryad's shoulders sag and felt bad. But who could blame mortals for being scared of a shadow spirit appearing from behind a tree and trying to offer them suspicious fruit while being incapable of speaking?

"Huh, I just realized how crazy Stella is to have trusted me so much," Ashlock muttered to himself in disbelief. At least he had Stella to keep him company, but Nox seemed alone in her field of white flowers.

"Sorry, Ashlock, you didn't come here to listen to me ramble on. I will try to answer anything you ask."

"Thank you. How much do you remember about the Tainted Cloud Sect and the Eternal Pursuit Pavilion?" Ashlock hadn't interrogated her regarding this yet, as Nox had seemed somewhat disorientated since becoming a tree, and he hadn't reached the Tainted Cloud Sect yet. But now he needed information.

"I spent most of my life before becoming a merchant living in the Tainted Cloud Sect, so it's a significant part of who I am," Nox replied. *"So I do remember quite a lot, especially from my younger years."*

"Okay, good. What can you tell me about Tainted Cloud Sect east of here? Is that your home?"

"Yes, the Tainted Cloud Sect consists of five very spread-out cities, and the city to the east of here is called Nightshade, my home. All cities have a branch of the Eternal Pursuit Pavilion, but Nightshade's claim to fame is that it's home to the Celestial Warden who governs it. Oh, another fun fact is that the city's name, Nightshade, came from combining the names of the two most powerful families, Duskwalker and Lunarshade."

"Duskwalker is your family name, right? How powerful are you in comparison to the Lunarshade family, and how strong is the Celestial Warden?"

The shadow dryad looked down at the ground. *"The Celestial Warden is at the sixth layer of the Nascent Soul Realm, but he is far more powerful than his cultivation suggests, having lived a long life of battle rather than sitting in a cave for centuries. As for my family, I believe we used to be equal to the Lunarshades, but that seems to have changed recently."*

"How so?" Ashlock asked and vowed in his mind to avoid earning the Celestial Warden's attention. He sounded dangerous beyond his comprehension.

Nox let out a long sigh. *"I fucked it up. I ran away for selfish reasons, and my father was killed in an ambush, leaving my mother, sister, and cousins to run the family. The last time I spoke to my sister Evelyn, she said the family had absorbed a few smaller families to stay afloat. However, if she stops being the Lunarshade scion plaything, the Duskwalker family could be eradicated overnight."*

"That's terrible. Did you like your sister?"

"No—well, yes. It's complicated. There was a time when we were close siblings, but once our father started assigning us roles and as the

more talented one I was told to marry into the Lunarshade family like some sort of sacrifice to keep the peace between the families, it made me resent her. I then ran away and forced that role onto her, so she now resents me."

"What about the rest of your family?"

"I don't remember much about them, to be honest. Once my father died, my mother was hardly seen. Which is about as present as she was throughout my childhood. A few of my cousins were cool, such as the one you likely killed. I heard he was an up-and-coming talent supposed to revive my family."

"Oh…sorry about that."

Nox laughed. *"Don't be. I am the one who sent him to his death to buy time for my escape. As I said, I was the one who brought the downfall to my family. A sin I will bear, I suppose, for eternity now. Though becoming a tree and losing half my memories does lessen it."*

"Doesn't that defeat the point of bearing a sin?"

Nox fell silent for a while. *"Maybe? I do feel bad for Evelyn. I really do. She didn't really deserve the life I forced on her."* Nox's shadow looked to the sky as if reminiscing, and another silence drew between them as they both got lost in thought.

After a while, Ashlock decided to switch topics. **"I had Diana register for the Eternal Pursuit Pavilion—"**

"You did?! No way."

"What's with that reaction?"

"I overheard a Jade Informant registering someone called Diana, which I found strange at the time but passed off as a coincidence. Anyway, sorry, continue."

"Right…I want her and possibly Stella to sell pills and take on bounties through the pavilion. Since the Celestial Warden is present there, would you advise against that?"

"Mhm, he doesn't usually get involved in matters, but he knows Stella's name because of me. Though the Lotus Informants are secretive, they wouldn't hide anything from the Celestial Warden if he asked. So I would advise against Stella doing anything that would earn attention."

"I see. Maybe I should have Stella work in a different city to avoid issues?"

"You could do that, but the Celestial Warden oversees all cities. If

it's an issue in one city, then it will be in another," Nox explained. *"A better solution is using proxies to sell pills. Even if Diana sells your pills, she will earn unwanted attention, you know. It's why I didn't want to sell pills for you guys in the first place and went after Stella's earrings instead."*

"A proxy? I heard about those before. But we don't know anyone we could use as one?"

"Just use my sister. She is ranked as a Crimson Tracker within the pavilion and from a powerful house. Nobody would raise a brow if she started selling pills, including the Celestial Warden."

"Nox, in case you forgot, we have never met your sister, and you are stuck here as a tree. There's no way she would trust or work with us."

"Don't be so sure," Nox replied as her shadow pulled off one of its fingers. It then bent the finger into the shape of a ring. *"Show this ring made from my Qi to Evelyn, and she is bound to at least hear you out. Once you get her attention, offer her a cut of the sales to the pavilion, and she would be more than happy to comply…I think."*

Ashlock took the ring with telekinesis. **"Doesn't your sister hate you? Surely if Stella or Diana showed up to the Duskwalker residence with this ring, they would be killed on sight?"**

"That's a good point…" Nox replied and fell into thought. *"Oh! Take that big spider. Evelyn is terrified of spiders."*

Ashlock sighed. How the hell did that solve anything?

23
TAINTED CLOUD SECT

Stella had a headache as she stared at the strange-looking ring of shadow in her palm.

"So, to summarize these last few hours of discussion," Stella massaged her temples, "you want Diana and me to head to the Eternal Pursuit Pavilion to get registered as bounty hunters. Are you *sure* that is a good idea?"

"Diana has already been registered as an Iron Seeker but needs to appear in person to be promoted to a Crimson Tracker. You, on the other hand, are yet to be registered. Nox is confident you should have no problems as the Lotus Informants are quite professional."

"Mhm, is there no way the Silverspires can register me like they did for Diana?"

"I asked, but apparently, doing it once was already straining their connection. It's a big deal to get a letter of recommendation from such a person. Don't worry, you will be fine. Climbing the ranks should be a breeze for you."

"What about registering in another city?"

"You can, but it will take me a while to reach another city, and apparently, the pavilion in Nightshade is the largest and offers the most missions that you will need to advance up the ranks."

Stella bit her lip. *Diana is already ahead of me with the help of the Silverspires. If I wait around any longer, I will be stuck as an Iron*

Seeker while she is a Jade Sentinel. Not that I am jealous…but I will be left behind.

"Fine." Stella side-eyed Nox's shadow. "So after I register, I then use this shadow ring to have a meeting with your sister, who will likely try to kill us on sight, so we should bring Larry because she is scared of spiders?"

The shadow dryad slowly nodded her head.

"Larry will remain here for now," Ashlock said. **"I will portal him over when he is needed. Remember, we want to avoid too much attention until we can use Nox's family as a proxy. Okay?"**

Stella fastened the jade mask to her face. "Don't worry, I can remain lowkey if I want to."

"Good. My presence over there is limited as my coverage of the city is still quite low, and I have no offspring to magnify my presence through, so you will be on your own for the most part. Do not attract the attention of the Celestial Warden. Now go quickly. I found a quiet place to make the portal."

Stella felt her ears pop as she stepped through the portal Ash had conjured for her to the Tainted Cloud Sect. Not only did the pressure change, the temperature was a few degrees colder.

"Has the sun moved further through the sky as well?" Stella mumbled as she shielded her eyes with her hand and glanced up. It had been afternoon a moment ago, but it was now evening. After a few hours of discussion and preparation with Nox and Tree, it felt weird to finally be here. *This is my first time being so far from Tree.*

"Ashlock did say that Nightshade City was over a thousand miles away," Diana said in a distorted voice as she stepped through the portal, which snapped closed.

"What does that have to do with anything?" Stella asked as she looked over her shoulder at Diana. Like herself, the demoness was wearing one of the jade masks they had looted from the bounty hunters. The masks were inlaid with a runic circuit that distorted one's voice and helped hide one's face.

"The sun appears in different parts of the sky as it travels across the realm. Since we covered such a vast distance, it's as if we went forward in time," Diana said as she walked past and flipped up the large hood of her black cloak. "Anyway, that's not important right now. We should be near the entrance to the Eternal Pursuit Pavilion."

Stella scrunched up her nose as a rat ran past. They were standing near the bins behind a restaurant, and it was filthy.

I'm so glad Ash forced me to change my clothing and even wear shoes, Stella thought as she looked down at the simple black slip-on that matched the dark cloak she was bundled up in. *If only these darn masks blocked smells, that would be helpful right now.*

"This area has a Qi-gathering formation in a nearby building, so it was easier to mask the presence of my portal." Ashlock's voice rang in Stella's mind. **"Walk down that alley to your right and then follow the street to the foot of the mountain that dominates the city's center. It's impossible to miss."**

Stella flipped up her hood and nodded to Diana. "Let's go." The two moved in silence down the alleyway, and sure enough, once they were on a main street with a more open view of the sky, the mountain was indeed hard to miss. Not because of its size, as it was nothing compared to Red Vine Peak, but because it was covered in hundreds of ornate pavilions adorned in shades of jade, and even from here, Stella could feel the power emanating from the place. The air shuddered, especially around the top third.

Those are some impressive defensive formations, Stella thought as they shuffled closer through the busy streets, dodging city folk going about their chaotic and short lives. *I see why Ashlock dropped us off nearby. Wanting to avoid attention aside, it was likely impossible for him. My spiritual sense dissipates when it comes near the mountain, so there's no way I could make a portal from here to the entrance.*

Before she knew it, they were at the gate. It towered over the guards standing before it, processing the many people passing in and out. The bounty hunters of the pavilion were easy to spot due to how they dressed and moved about compared to the more casually dressed merchants and other mortals who wished to enter.

"We don't need to wait in line. I can get us in," Diana said as she flashed the gold-and-black pendant with a phoenix symbol in her palm.

Stella pouted. *Why does Diana get a recommendation letter and a pendant, but I must remain lowkey? Stupid Nox. If only she had removed the 6,000 Yinxi Coin bounty on me before turning into a tree. Though I would still need to watch out for the Celestial Warden. He knows I was the last person Nox went to see, so as time passes, he will grow suspicious of why Nox is missing. Ugh, what a pain.*

Weirdly, she still felt a tinge of excitement. Here she was at the gates of an organization filled to the brim with people who would kill her the moment they learned of her true identity, and as fun as teaching Jasmine was, Stella felt herself getting rusty and impatient. Cultivation progress had slowed to a crawl, and instead of learning techniques, she had been teaching Jasmine the basics.

Stella grinned behind her mask as she passed a line of merchants and stood before a guard.

"Business with the pavilion?" the man wearing shining armor asked in a dull tone. He wasn't even focusing on them as his gaze lingered on the clipboard in his hand.

Diana released the slightest hint of pressure from her Star Core, startling the man enough to almost drop his clipboard.

The guard threw himself into a deep bow, not daring to look up. "Esteemed Elder, I apologize for my manners."

Diana's distorted laughter rang through the mask. "At ease, guard. I am no Elder."

The guard hesitantly straightened up and seemed nervous to say the wrong thing.

Stella glanced between the two and found the situation amusing. *I wonder how the guard would react if he learned that Diana was in her early twenties and not some hidden Elder of a noble family?*

The mask and the cloak made it impossible to tell anything about Diana's identity. The guard's only clue was her general body shape and strands of black hair that snuck out the hood of her cloak.

"May I pass?" Diana was holding out the pendant of a bounty hunter.

The guard glanced at the pendant before nodding. "Such power yet only an Iron Seeker? Ah, my apologies, that's none of my business. Step on through."

The pendant vanished into Diana's spatial ring, and she strode past the guard.

Stella went to follow, but an arm stopped her.

"Business with the pavilion?" the guard asked with a grin. His previous humble demeanor before Diana was gone in an instant, and it felt as if he was trying to pass on his humiliation to her.

Stella felt her eye twitch. *You know I am stronger than that woman you just waved through with your tail tucked between your legs?*

Should I flatten him to the ground with my pressure? Or perhaps chop off his arm as a snack for Tree…

"She's with me," Diana said with irritation, and the man's hand raised faster than it had fallen.

"A guest of the Esteemed Iron Seeker. Enjoy your stay, Miss. Next!"

Stella clicked her tongue as she walked past the guard. A wave of Qi washed over her as she phased through the main defensive array, and the lingering feeling of Ashlock watching her vanished.

It's going to be fine.

Stella felt her heartbeat quicken as she joined Diana on the other side, waiting on a wide, paved road lined with trees that led to a square up ahead that looked like a sea of people.

"I could feel the ripples of Qi near your soul from over here," Diana hissed as they walked. "Remember, we are trying to be lowkey. I don't know what you were thinking, but harming a guard to the lowest level of the pavilion would achieve little. That guy was hardly a step above being mortal. I bet they get replaced all the time."

"Maybe if they had cultivators capable of detecting Qi fluctuations on the gates, they would have fewer casualties," Stella hissed back as they reached the square. "It's not my fault that the bored guard was trying to pick a fight with me."

Diana snorted. "If what Nox told us is true, most Iron Seekers are weaklings. I mean, look around. I can't see a single other cultivator here. It's all mortals moving between the pavilions. That blockhead guard likely took the job to feel superior to people with his meager strength."

Stella glanced around, and Diana exaggerated a bit. The odd cultivator wearing robes and masks was dotted among the hundreds of mortals flowing between giant pavilions

It seems all pavilions in the lower third of the mountain are made of wood and stone, with decorations of white jade. Stella noted as they walked around the square's edge toward one of the smaller pavilions with an iron phoenix hanging over the door.

I wonder why the bounty hunters' pavilion is smaller than the rest. Stella recalled what Nox had told them, but she hadn't gone too in-depth other than explaining how to get past the guards, register, and where the Duskwalker residence was located. Stella scrutinized the other pavilions since there wasn't much else to do as they swiftly walked.

The largest pavilion that dominated the far end of the square had the words "Trade Hall" written over a doorway wide enough for a dozen people to walk through side by side. This was precisely what was happening, as guards in shiny armor controlled the flow of horse-drawn carts loaded with goods into the building.

I could fit that entire horse, cart, and all its goods in my spatial ring. If everyone was using spatial rings, there would be no need to make the place that big. Stella sighed. Sometimes, she pitied mortals.

Other than the Trade Hall, there were a few other buildings, such as the Alchemy Hall and Smithy.

I should check out the Alchemy Hall later. I want to know the standard of our competition and their pricing. There also seems to be a place to sell fruits; I wonder what price Trees' would fetch?

"Are you sure about using your real name to register?" Diana asked, using her Qi to mask her voice. The area near the Iron Seeker's pavilion was quieter, and far more bounty hunters were standing around, so that was a smart move. "Using a persona would help you go unnoticed by the Celestial Warden."

"Yes, I am sure," Stella replied, using her Qi to portal her words straight to Diana's ears so nobody could hear them. "Other than Nox, nobody knows that the Celestial Warden is interested in me. So long as I avoid my name being brought to his attention, I will be fine. I could even lie to the man if our paths crossed and tell him that Nox is recovering from the curse."

"Hmm." Diana seemed skeptical. "Will that really work?"

"I don't see why not," Stella replied. "Any artifacts he uses to verify if she's still alive will show that her soul is still present in this realm, and I doubt he can leave here to verify."

"That's true. Such a powerhouse wouldn't leave this place unattended just to verify your words. At least until the Celestial Warden grows very suspicious."

Stella nodded. "Exactly. I will admit using my real name is risky, but I would argue using a fake name is even riskier. If someone found out, they could use it as blackmail against me because if they reported it, I would be exiled from the pavilion no matter how high ranking I get."

I did suggest using a fake name earlier, but Nox's shadow had shaken her head and told me through Ashlock that so much in the pavilion is tied to the reputation of a name. So joining under a fake identity is one of the most severe crimes. Even if I became a Jade Sentinel, I would be exiled should I be discovered, which would be terrible as this is one of the best places for cultivators to sell their skills and make money.

Diana pushed the door to the Iron Seeker pavilion open, and they strode inside. Dominating the center of the room was a large white jade pillar encircled by a counter manned by numerous Lotus Informants. All of them had long lines except for a woman near the end who was serving a single person. Since it was the shortest line, they joined and waited.

"Look up there." Diana pointed at the jade pillar. Following her finger, Stella saw a long list of active bounties in golden letters. Searching down the list that went from high to low with Vincent Nightrose and the Silverspire Grand Elder at 100,000 Yinxi Coins alongside a few others in that range at the top. Further down, her gaze paused.

[Dead or Alive: Nox Duskwalker]
Target's estimated threat level: Star Core 9
Affiliation with Duskwalker Family: Nascent Soul Realm 6 [Pending Re-evaluation]
Bounty: 30,000 Yinxi Coins.
The bounty is placed by The Lunarshade Family. For more information, consult a Lotus Informant.

Stella noticed that the Duskwalker family was listed as a Nascent Soul Realm powerhouse yet was pending a re-evaluation. *Nox did mention something about her family's downfall since her father died. I wonder what the new evaluation would be?*

There was also a surprising number of high Star Core Elders in the 10,000 Yinxi Coin range, and then there was a slight drop.

[Death of Stella Crestfallen]
Target's estimated threat level: Star Core 1 [Unverified]

Affiliation with Ashfallen Trading Company: Star Core 9
[Unverified]
Bounty: 6,000 Yinxi Coins.
The bounty is placed by Nox Duskwalker, and the target is at the marked location. For more information, consult a Lotus Informant.

Do they think I am still in the first stage of the Star Core Realm? Stella let a small chuckle escape. *How would they react if they found out I just stepped into the sixth stage?*

The rest of the board had low-ranking bounties for mortal merchants and whatnot. Honestly, with only a name to go off, for the pay, they didn't even seem worth the effort. To her surprise, as she was still reading them, every name floated up a spot, and a brand new bounty appeared at the bottom for 20 Yinxi Coins. It was for the kidnapping of a mortal farmer's wife.

Who would even take on such a job? Stella wondered, but then she saw out of the corner of her eye three cloaked people who had been huddled around one of the many tables that littered the room stand up and leave. On the way out, she overheard one of them discussing the name in the bounty.

Trying to get a feel for their cultivation level was impossible as the defensive array heavily suppressed the flow of Qi, but if she had to guess, they were in the Qi or Soul Fire Realm at best.

What lowlifes wasting their pathetic cultivation to bully mortals for such little pay.

"Next, please!" The Lotus Informant rang a little bell to draw their attention.

Diana stepped forward and placed her gold-and-black pendant on the counter. "I wish to be promoted to the rank of a Crimson Tracker."

"Have you completed the requirements?" the brown-haired woman asked with a strained smile.

"What are they?"

The Lotus Informant's face fell, and she let out a long sigh. "Another upstart who thinks they are important. Listen here, cultivator. Very few ever make it to the Crimson Tracker rank, you hear me? Your cultivation stage is irrelevant, as we only want talented people. If you want to advance, you must complete ten missions and pass a combat test."

"Well, I haven't completed any missions."

The Lotus Informant gave a deadpan look. "Then we are done here." She rang her bell and called out, "Next."

Why is this woman so unprofessional? Stella frowned behind her mask. It was clear that the pavilion thought little of the Iron Seekers by how cramped and lackluster this pavilion was, but this was ridiculous.

"The Sage Advisor told me that I would need to come in person to be promoted to the Crimson Trackers," Diana said calmly. "Does this mean an honorable Sage Advisor lied to me?"

Much like the guard, the Lotus Informant's demeanor did a one-eighty as her eyes widened. "May I ask for your honorable name?"

"Diana Ravenborne."

"One moment, please." The woman crouched down and dug through a pile of jade slips before finding the one she was looking for. Getting to her feet and inserting some Qi, she read the words on the slip. "An honorable Sage Advisor did indeed put in a recommendation for you. Diana Ravenborne, you are approved to skip the necessary missions and can advance after completing the combat test, which will be held in the arena behind this pavilion tonight."

"Thank you," Diana replied simply and stepped aside. A few nearby tables began whispering among themselves, and because of their low cultivation, Stella could easily hear that they were displeased by Diana's usage of connections to "cheat."

I see the need for a proxy now. The Lotus Informants for the Iron Seekers are terrible at keeping their voices down in this busy room.

"How can I help you today?" the woman asked as Stella stepped forward.

"I wish to register as an Iron Seeker." Stella tried to use Qi to mask her voice, but an even denser defensive formation protected the Lotus Informants. *I bet it's to prevent mind control techniques.*

"Okay," the woman said, bringing out a jade slip and infusing some Qi into her fingertip. "I will need to know your name. Please note that if you use a fake name and it's discovered, you will be exiled and possibly even hunted down." Her eyes raised, and she stared straight at her mask. "And we wouldn't want that now, would we?"

Stella's spatial ring flashed, and a slip of parchment with the name

"Stella Crestfallen" written on it appeared. She passed it to the Lotus Informant in hopes that it would allow for a quiet registration.

The woman read the note, paused to look at something at the corner of the room, and then gave a sly smile. "Not every day I get a mute cultivator. Just nod if the name Stella Crestfallen works for you."

Mute? What is she on about? I spoke to her a moment ago...

Stella didn't need to be a cultivator to notice how the room suddenly became quieter, and far more heads stared into her back. A few groups even stood from their tables, and someone from the far end strode straight toward her.

What the hell is up with this loud-mouth Lotus Informant? Weren't they supposed to be secretive? Nox told me they would keep the mention of names to a minimum, and I even prepared this parchment slip just in case.

A sigh escaped her lips as she gave the stupid Lotus Informant a nod. Things just got tricky.

24
KILL ZONE

"The registration fee can be paid with high-grade spirit stones, dragon crowns, or Yinxi Coins," the Lotus Informat listed off as she placed the jade slip with her name on it under the table. "What will it be?"

Stella hardly registered the woman's words as she felt blind. The defensive formations in this place were suffocating. Her spiritual senses were suppressed to just a meter, and even cycling Qi through her spirit roots was a chore. So, for the first time in years, she relied on her eyes and ears to feel the shifting and murmuring of people around her.

"Hello? Are you listening?" the Lotus Informant said in a dull tone.

Stella turned to her while trying to keep track of everything going on. To say she was stressed was an understatement. *This was never part of the plan. I was supposed to register and then use proxies for everything else quietly. Where did it go wrong?*

Nox had insisted that Lotus Informants were usually professional and secretive. Had that changed since she was a bounty hunter? The other Lotus Informants nearby seemed composed and respectful to their lines of Iron Seekers, whereas this bitch was incompetent to the point of being malicious. *No wonder nobody was lining up to see her. We should have gone and joined the longest line.*

"If you can't even afford the fee, you shouldn't have come here—"

Stella threw a few high-grade spirit stones onto the counter. "Here."

"Thank you." The woman gave the fakest smile.

Stella was starting to think there was something off about this Lotus Informant. *She didn't mention a price, but I definitely overpaid. Now, to see if you reveal your true colors while I turn away.*

Weirdly, the people gathering behind her stayed at a respectful distance, and other than talking among themselves and hearing a few mentions of her name, they made no move to attack her. *They aren't going to kill me?*

The Lotus Informant took all of the high-grade spirit stones, and Stella caught a flash of golden light out of the corner of her eye as the Lotus Informant bent down to get something from under the counter.

"Here is your pendant," the woman said, placing a black-and-gold, coin-shaped object on the counter.

Stella noticed a golden spatial ring on the woman's hand. *She actually stole my money. I can't believe it.*

"Hey, random question." Stella leaned in closer, resting her elbow on the counter, and kept her distorted voice low. "What is the punishment for an Iron Seeker if they kill a Lotus Informant?"

"Punishment?" The woman tilted her head. "I suppose there isn't one for killing a Lotus Informant specifically."

That was not the answer Stella had been expecting. This woman was being blatant to the point of robbing her, yet there was no punishment if she retaliated by executing her on the spot?

"Hypothetically speaking, I won't be exiled from the pavilion if I cut you down right now?" Stella asked, just to be sure. Killing this woman over this wouldn't be worth the hassle and attention, but this was good information.

"Let me explain something to you, Iron Seeker." The woman rested her chin on her arm and smiled, unfazed by Stella's blatant threat. "You have a juicy bounty on your head yet stand here alive. Now, why is that?"

That was a good point. Everyone kept their distance and didn't show any hostility despite her bounty. "I don't know."

"It's because we have rules that cannot be broken." The woman gestured to the room. "This pavilion is a strict no-kill zone. If not for this rule and the defensive arrays to help prevent fights, there would be a slaughter here every day. After all, you aren't the only one here with a bounty looming over their head, as it's common for bounty hunters to put bounties on their competitors."

Stella glanced up at the bounties listed on the pillar. *I assumed these were all Elders of families, but now that I think about it, wouldn't it make sense for those Elders to be part of this pavilion, too?*

"Your bounty is rather special because of how high the reward is compared to how low your cultivation is," the woman said with amusement. "But in the grand scheme of things, you aren't that special. Bounty or not, someone could kill you out of the blue for free. It's a dog-eat-dog world out there, but it's safe in here."

So she thinks she is safe in here because of the defensive arrays?

"Just out of curiosity, what happens if I break the rule and kill someone in here?" Stella asked. The array did make cycling Qi hard, but she could always cut someone in two with her sword.

The woman's smile reached her ears. "Ooo, that's a fun one. You will be **exiled** from the pavilion, meaning anyone here could cut you down where you stand without repercussions. In fact, they would even be rewarded with every Yinxi Coin left in your balance."

Well, that's concerning. I don't think I could win a fight against all these people with my cultivation suppressed to this extent.

Stella's eyes flicked to the doorway. "What about outside this pavilion? Does the no-kill rule still apply?"

"The whole mountain is a no-kill zone." The Lotus Informant had a sly smile. "And Lotus Informants live on the mountain, so killing one of us will indirectly lead to exile. Though the defensive arrays are weaker outside the pavilions, and accidents can sometimes happen. So do be careful when walking around."

Stella frowned. This woman called out her name and robbed her, but now she was giving good advice. *I can't get a read on her at all.*

"If that's all the questions, let's finish this registration, shall we?" The Lotus Informant pushed the gold-and-black pendant across the counter. "Please draw some blood and drip it onto the pendant."

Stella saw a spike on the pendant, so she used that to prick her finger and smeared some blood on its surface. The pendant glowed with power as it absorbed her blood and Qi.

A strange symbol appeared on the counter around the pendant, and the Lotus Informant studied it. "You have a registered bloodline. How interesting. One moment, please."

"Registered bloodline?" Stella asked as the Lotus Informant searched for something under her counter.

"Yeah, to crack down on people using fake names in recent centuries, we started keeping a record of families' bloodlines." The woman placed a sizeable leatherbound book onto the counter and flipped through the pages. "Since the formation reacted, somebody from your family has registered with us before, and I can now find out if your surnames match."

Stella felt her blood run cold. If she had taken Diana's suggestion and used a fake name, wouldn't she be moments away from exile and being executed by all the cultivators gathered behind her? *Is that why they are all gathered around like vultures? Hoping I lied so they can kill me for the bounty while I am suppressed?*

"Ah, here we go," the Lotus Informant said. "There is indeed another person here, and they also registered under the Crestfallen family name."

What?! Only one other person? Could it be my father...? If the pavilion knows his whereabouts, I can ask him about the claim that my mother is the World Tree.

Groans of disappointment sounded out as a few groups of bounty hunters wandered back to their tables.

Stella leaned forward to see the book, but the Lotus Informant slammed it shut. "With that, your registration is complete. You are now an Iron Seeker of the Eternal Pursuit Pavilion. If you wish to advance to a Crimson Tracker, complete ten bounties or other missions of appropriate levels from the other halls. Any other questions?"

"What was the name in the book?"

"Eight hundred Yinxi Coins."

Stella tilted her head. Had the woman not heard her?

"Everything in this pavilion has a price. Such confidential information about ancestral bloodlines costs 800 Yinxi Coins."

Stella ground her teeth behind her mask. How could information about her own family be confidential? "But I just registered. How am I supposed to have any Yinxi Coins?"

"How is that my problem?" The woman rolled her eyes as she hid the book back under the counter. "Go kill someone or sell something. This ain't a charity for weaklings, you know?"

Stella found this woman insufferable, but she really wanted to know the name in the book. *I could sell some pills...*

"Don't." Diana grabbed her arm. "I know what you are thinking. That information isn't going anywhere. We can get it later."

Stella clicked her tongue. "Fine." Taking the pendant and putting it into her spatial ring, she turned to leave. In hindsight, she didn't want this Lotus Informant shouting out the information about her family, so it was best to leave for today and ask a more competent one tomorrow.

The stares from all the cultivators were unnerving, so she pulled her hood down tightly and made for the exit. *I will leave and vanish into the dense crowd of mortals.*

Registering had been the only goal for today at the Eternal Pursuit Pavilion, and although it had been far more eventful than she had anticipated, it was done. She was now an Iron Seeker, which granted her access to the pavilion's resources, and she could travel to any demonic sects without her identity being questioned.

"A real bitch, isn't she?"

Stella paused and turned to the person who had called out from the shadows. "Who are you?"

A person was leaning against the wall near the doorway with their arms crossed. The thick black robes and full-face jade mask made determining anything about them challenging. *If they hadn't called out and turned their head, I might have missed them by thinking they were part of the wall. I feel so blind without my spiritual sense.*

"By that question, I can tell you are new." The person looked straight at Stella, their features hidden behind a jade mask. "Giving out such information is a quick way to the grave. The Lotus Informant wasn't lying about the dangers. Beyond those doors, assassinations occur more often than she made it sound."

Stella looked at the door and realized those cultivators hanging outside in small groups weren't simply wasting their time. They were keeping track of those going in and out of the pavilion. *The pavilion and mountain may be a no-kill zone, but out in the city? Anything goes. Will they tail me if I leave? Oh, I bet they sell my whereabouts to others, those leeches.*

"For this chance meeting, you can call me Seth." The man stepped forward and offered a gloved hand. "I am happy to answer any questions you have."

Stella made no move to shake it.

"How cold." Seth sighed and lowered his hand.

"Why did you call that Lotus Informant a bitch?" Stella asked bluntly.

Seth laughed. "Is she not? I am sure you noticed, but nobody will line up at her counter except clueless newbies like you."

"How is she still working here if she acts like that?" Diana asked.

Seth shrugged. "She has connections with the Lunarshade family, so nobody dares to touch her, and other than being a bitch and committing some petty crimes, she mostly stays within the rules. Though between you and me," Seth stepped closer and lowered his voice, "she is one of the few Lotus Informants that will take bribes. It's already hard enough to advance to the rank of a Crimson Seeker, so nobody here wants to get rid of someone who could give them an advantage."

So much for staying within the rules. Stella glanced at the brown-haired woman standing alone behind her counter with contempt. *She is rotten to the core. I bet she gets a share of the death of those exiled for using fake names, which is why she shouts them out.*

"Is becoming a Crimson Tracker really so hard?" Diana asked. "Ten missions and a combat test seem simple enough."

With his chin, Seth gestured to a nearby table. "How about we discuss over there?"

"What's the catch?" Stella didn't trust this shifty person one bit. It may be "safe" here, but there were ways around everything. If she was poisoned in here and died outside, would that exile the killer, or would it be written off as another unfortunate "accident"?

"Catch?"

"What do you gain from sharing this information? Do you want something from us?" Diana insisted. Her voice dripped with suspicion.

Seth raised his gloved hands. "Okay, you caught me. I was going to ask you a favor, but you are under no obligation to accept it. I will answer your questions regardless."

"Hmm." Stella looked to Diana, and the woman shrugged.

Nox either forgot or lied, or her information is outdated as she never mentioned the no-kill rule or the bloodline verification, which the Lotus Informant said was introduced in recent centuries. So getting some information and comparing notes would be helpful, but can I trust anything this guy says?

Stella sighed and followed Seth to the nearby table. There was a silver ball in the center, which he placed his hand on and inserted some Qi.

Diana grabbed his arm. "What are you doing?"

"Relax. It's a formation that distorts our voice so others will struggle to listen in," Seth replied calmly. His Qi made the silver ball glow, and sure enough, all the ambient noise around them became distorted. "Now then, can you please let go of my arm?"

Diana withdrew her hand into the many folds of her cloak.

"Quite the strength you have there. I thought my arm was going to break." Seth rubbed the area Diana had gripped.

"My apologies," Diana said. "Now, if you don't mind, could we get to the answers? I have something to do tonight."

"The combat test to advance, right?" Seth said as he relaxed his arm. "With strength like that, you may have a chance at passing."

"What do you mean? Is it really that difficult?" Diana asked.

Seth gestured around. "If it was so easy to advance, do you think there would be this many people stuck down here having to share a space with the disgusting mortals? Everyone here fights tooth and nail to claw their way up the mountain using any means necessary. Don't look down on their struggle just because you got a recommendation letter."

"I see. What does the test involve?"

"It really is a simple combat test—nothing but a duel. However, it's the opponent who makes things tricky. Since the pavilion wants to keep the prestige of the ranks intact, they make us fight and have to win against someone from the Crimson Tracker rank. You have heard the term 'mission' thrown around, right?"

Stella and Diana nodded.

"Defending the honor of the Crimson Trackers is one such mission available to them. There is no pay, but they are eager to participate."

"Why?" Stella didn't understand. Fighting was a risky thing to participate in and also a waste of Qi. If there was no pay, what reason would they have to do such a thing?

Seth chuckled. "Ego aside, there is a practical reason. Iron Seekers need to complete ten missions to have the *opportunity* to advance. However, if we fail the combat test, the number of completed missions is reset, and we must start again from zero. A tough deal, but for the

Crimson Trackers, it's far worse. They need a hundred completed missions to advance to the rank of Jade Sentinel, and they lose all that progress if they fail the combat test. Crazy, right? If they tried to complete the requirements with bounties alone, it would take centuries since there is a short supply of bounties worth the risk and pay to the Crimson Trackers. So they take on the mission of dueling the Iron Seekers to keep us down."

"That is rather harsh," Diana agreed. "Especially since you have to beat someone from a higher rank who may have an affinity that counters you. It's as much luck as it is skill."

Seth nodded. "Do you see now why we are all stuck here?"

"Yeah…" Stella hated to admit it, but her opinion of Nox rose. *No wonder she could run from us and fight for so long. Jade Sentinels are not only strong in cultivation, but they had to have completed at least a hundred missions and beat someone higher rank than them in a duel.*

"This is where my shameless favor comes in." Seth leaned on the table. "I need one more mission to qualify to advance. I have the location of Albis Lunarshade locked down."

Stella glanced at the white jade pillar and quickly found the person in question.

[Death of Albis Lunarshade]
Target's estimated threat level: Star Core 2
Affiliation with the Lunarshade Family: Nascent Soul 6
Bounty: 10,000 Yinxi Coins
The bounty is placed by Corvin Blightbane. For more information, consult a Lotus Informant.

"As you can see, he is listed as being in the Star Core Realm with a bounty of 10,000 Yinxi Coins. That's where you two and especially Stella come in. I may know his location, but I am not strong enough to defeat him. However, with the three of us, I believe we can win."

Diana crossed her arms. "Suppose we agree. How would we split the pay?"

"You both need the Yinxi Coins really badly, right?" Seth stroked his chin under the mask. "How about two thousand for me, and you two can split the remaining eight thousand? Sound fair?"

Stella exchanged a glance with Diana. "The deal sounds good to me. Could you give us a few days to discuss and get back to you?"

"That's fine." Seth shrugged. "It would be best to wait until after Diana has been promoted to the Crimson Trackers anyway, so it counts toward her advancement to becoming a Jade Sentinel. Speaking of which, the duels should begin within the hour. I could lead you there if you wish?"

Seeing no issue with that, the three left the building through the back door toward the arena.

I wonder if Diana can win, Stella thought and then shook her head. If anything, she should be praying the opponent's face didn't cave in from a single punch.

25
OLD ONE

Ashlock felt locked out, and he didn't like it. Sneaking a single root under Nightshade City to that restaurant near the Eternal Pursuit Pavilion's mountain so he could make the portal for Stella and Diana had been risky enough. The mountain was the closest thing to a military base that he had seen so far in this world.

It wasn't the Soul Fire Realm guards at the gates or any walls that made the place impenetrable. It was the endless layers upon layers of formations that simply defied logical sense. To Ashlock's spiritual sense, the mountain may as well be a black hole. If he tried to get close, he felt his vision grow blurry and his Qi getting drawn into the greedy formation that was sucking up all the Qi for miles around. It was why he had felt comfortable with creating a portal so nearby as it was masked by the rivers of Qi being drawn to the mountain.

"No wonder the Duskwalker and Lunarshade families built their homes a few mountains away. There would be no point in cultivating within the center of Nightshade City," Ashlock mused. Since he couldn't watch Stella or Diana, he scoped out the place some more and found the two prominent families' residences. Naturally, he didn't dare get too close for now, especially to the Lunarshade family run by a sixth-stage Nascent Soul Realm cultivator.

Ashlock watched the sun descend behind the Eternal Pursuit Pavilion's mountain from the city's outskirts. The evening was turning to dusk.

"Now that I think about it some more, I bet that drawing in all the Qi for miles around is a feature of the defensive formation. Since it sucks in all the nearby Qi to power itself, trying to launch a siege would be impossible as the attackers would have the Qi forcefully sucked out of their long-range attacks." Ashlock hummed to himself in thought. "Mhm, even with the amount of Qi it's drawing in, it still shouldn't be enough to power so many layers of formations that cover an entire mountain. Are they consuming piles of spirit stones every day? Or perhaps they found a way to tap directly into the ley line? The only other option is having a bunch of Elders sitting in a room and feeding the formation, but there's no way that's the case."

Ashlock stopped mumbling and tried to keep busy by carefully expanding his roots around the city's outskirts and the prominent families' mountains. He would slowly take over the city one root at a time. "Maybe I should plant a few of my offspring in secluded locations? Or will that raise issues? What if I spent some of our earnings and bought up some houses with gardens? That way, people can't raise a fuss if well-behaved demonic trees pop up, right?"

Ashlock sighed as his thoughts drifted. He felt on edge no matter how hard he tried to distract himself. He was especially worried about Stella. Not because of her questionable personality or tendency to cause fights but because of her affinity.

"Red Vine Peak is rife with spatial Qi due to my presence, so she can easily and freely wield spatial Qi. The only other places she has fought were in Mystic Realms drenched with spatial Qi. But out here? She is like a fish out of water."

Ashlock moved his view closer to the mountain peak, and once again, as he got closer, he felt the view of the jade pavilions blur and a distinct tug as if someone was trying to pull out his eye.

"I just want to see inside this stupid defensive formation," Ashlock grumbled. "I wonder what Stella and Diana are up to. I hope they haven't gotten into any trouble."

"That girl is trouble," Seth commented as a person strode into the arena without a mask, showing off their deep violet eyes and silver-tinted black hair. A purple-tinted aura wreathed her body, giving her a ghostly presence that Stella had never seen before.

"Why?" Stella asked. She sat on a bench close to the arena alongside Diana and Seth. The no-kill zone defensive formation still bore down on her, so she couldn't perceive much about the girl as her spiritual sense was heavily suppressed. However, Stella had been told that the inside of the arena was free of suppression so that cultivators could fight at their maximum capacity. The defensive formation acted as a barrier around the arena, protecting the spectators.

"Elysia Mystshroud is a rather notorious Crimson Tracker, you could say," Seth explained. "Her fame gives us the advantage of knowing her capabilities and record."

"Huh? I thought they hid people's names here."

"They do. These people are either participating with fake names or arrogant enough like Elysia to use their real ones."

"Oh, I see." Stella nodded. "So what is Elysia's record and strength?"

"She is somewhere in the mid-stages of the Star Core Realm and cultivates Mystic Qi. Her record is said to be forty-seven wins and a single loss." Seth turned and said seriously, "Stay away from the Mystshroud family. They are a bunch of lunatics and operate more like a cult."

Stella took the warning to heart, but she had never heard of such a Qi type before. "What even is Mystic Qi?"

"It's one of the more obscure Qi types that leans heavily into Dao comprehensions and visualizations. Mystic Qi is only created when a person believes in something so strongly that they can manifest it into reality," Seth explained. "You will see in a moment, but the easiest way to describe it is calling them summoners of their imagination and belief. Mystic cultivators' summons grow stronger as more people believe in their power, hence the whole cult thing and their eagerness to show off in public settings like this."

"Honorable Iron Seekers of the Eternal Pursuit Pavilion," a voice thundered through the arena, carried through the formations. **"Elysia Mystshroud of the Crimson Trackers, sitting at a record of forty-seven wins and a single loss, is now open to challenge. For every victory achieved today, she will ascend closer to the rank of a Jade Sentinel. However, anyone capable of adding a loss to her**

record will be promoted to the Crimson Trackers with immediate effect!"

Elysia looked around with a smirk hanging at the edges of her lips as if inviting the challenge.

"So what if her power is a little strange?" Diana tilted her head to Seth. "I don't see how that makes her troublesome. Is her high cultivation stage the main issue? I can imagine someone of that strength being far above most Iron Seekers."

"That's part of it, but in her specific case, the record of nearly fifty wins in a row is the main driver of her power," Seth said. "The more people she wins against, the stronger the belief in her summons becomes, and the stronger she gets, the more she wins. It's a self-feeding cycle. Her only loss was her first-ever battle. Once she got the ball rolling, nobody has been able to stop her."

Seth sighed. "Looks like nobody will be passing today. You got really bad luck, Diana. I am sorry."

Diana laughed. "Don't count me out just yet."

"Could the first challenger please make their way to the arena?"

Stella glanced to the other side of the arena and saw a person emerge from a hole in the wall that was sealed up behind them. They wore a mask and cloak like everyone else, but their hood was pulled down, showing off their icy blue hair.

"Ivor Frostveil takes the stage. With zero wins and three losses, this will be his fourth attempt at rising the ranks. Please wait while the arena is adjusted to facilitate fair competition..."

The arena trembled as the ground below the two contestants rose a few meters. The bare arena that looked like a sand pit began flooding with water. Once the water reached the two mounds that the cultivators stood on, the water flash froze, turning the arena into a frozen wasteland.

"How is this fair?" Stella squinted at the area as her spiritual senses were blocked. "Where is the mystic Qi for Elysia?"

"It's something that cannot be created on a whim," Seth said. "The Pavilion attempts to make the fights as fair as possible, but they are not gods."

"The battle will now begin! Remember, the intentional killing of the other contestant will count as a loss!"

"Elysia, today will be the day I finally—" Ivor was cut off as he was forced to kneel.

Star Core pressure? Stella's eyes widened. "How is she strong enough to force him to kneel so easily? Is Ivor really weak?"

"No." Seth replied. "Ivor should be a freshly ascended Star Core. The gap between the two shouldn't be this vast, but this is Elysia we are talking about. Her presence carries the weight of her god."

Elysia rose up into the air via a column of purple smoke. Her eyes glowed with power as a giant ritual circle that took up half the arena manifested into existence below her, and she began chanting.

"O' creature that dwells beyond the veil of our reality,

Heed my call and traverse the endless blight.

Through the swirling chaos of time's untold decay,

Emerge from my consciousness, manifest and devour!"

The ritual circle began spinning and pulsing faster and faster as a strange, chilling dread overtook the arena. Ivor Frostveil slowly pushed himself to his feet under the pressure as blood trickled from the corner of his lips. His face was also red as his blood vessels tried to break free from his forehead.

"Crazy bitch," Ivor cursed as he raised his hand, and with a flick, a giant ice spike surged toward the defenseless Elysia, who was busy chanting and pouring power into the ritual.

Elysia sneered and casually slapped the attack away with the back of her hand with such force that the whole spike shattered downward as if it were made of glass, and the ground around Ivor exploded, sending him flying into the wall.

The ritual circle stopped spinning and slowly grew as if trying to consume the entire space.

"By the sigils of the ancients, I continue my bloodline's legacy,

To serve the ones who came before.

In the name of the lost, the forbidden, and the unseen,

I command you break the seal, come forth, and intervene."

Whispers and screams that twisted the mind reverberated like a chorus of misery from the ritual circle. Within the darkness, something began to emerge.

"There is only one way to beat a ritualist." Seth leaned forward and rested his chin on the back of his hands. "Stop them before the ritual completes, or run away. Unfortunately for Ivor, the ritual is complete, and he has nowhere to run. He's already dead."

Stella looked at the arena. Ivor was slumped against the far wall as the eerie purple smoke filled with harrowing screams crept closer. His eyes widened with fear, and he was trying to stand back up, but his leg was likely broken alongside many of his ribs as he howled in pain.

"Even without spiritual sense, I can tell the power stored in that ritual circle should far surpass anything Ivor can conjure up in that condition." Diana sat back and crossed her arms. "It's over."

Ivor, unaware of their thoughts, seemed determined to keep going.

Poor guy. He will have to do ten missions all over again. Stella could see the determination in his refusal to surrender, but this match was heavily one-sided.

"I serve and worship the old one with my entire mind and being. So come forth, show your power, and crush the foolish mortal who rejects your existence," Elysia said coldly as her eyes dimmed.

Something not of this realm slowly hauled itself out from the ritual circle. It seemed to defy the laws imposed by the realm on how things should appear as its body of shifting shadows and tentacles constantly moved and changed as if not entirely present in this dimension.

Ugh, it's an ugly thing. Stella had a slight headache as her mind tried and failed to comprehend what she was looking at. The tentacles that comprised most of its massive body were covered in crazed eyes and mouths filled with rows of serrated teeth dripping with a viscous dark fluid.

"S-Stay back!" Ivor shouted as the ice around him cracked and surged up. He tried to create multiple walls, but the summon monster's tentacles smashed through them effortlessly.

"Don't look if you want to keep your sanity." Seth trembled as he looked straight at his feet.

Stella exchanged a glance with Diana over Seth's lowered head.

"Compared to Neptune, don't you think it's kinda cute?" Diana asked with a laugh.

Stella glanced back at the monster. Now that she got a second look, it was like a cute puppy compared to the cosmic horrors that made up Maple's family. If Neptune and Mars were planet eaters, this thing was nothing but a chained pet to a little girl.

"Yeah, I almost feel bad for it." Stella leaned back in her chair and listened to the sound of smashing ice as Ivor desperately tried to prevent the monster's advance.

"Take his limbs," Elysia commanded from atop her column of smoke behind the looming monster, "so he may do nothing but stay put and revere you."

"No…please!" Ivor shouted. "Stop, stop!"

His cries came a moment too late. Four tentacles smashed through his final layer of ice and pinned him to the wall.

"I give up! I concede!" Ivor cried out.

"The winner has been decided. Elysia Mystshroud has achieved her forty-eighth consecutive victory against Ivor Frostveil."

Stella felt a massive flow of Qi, followed by an ear-ringing howl from the monster as immense pressure descended on the arena.

Did they activate the defensive formation? Stella wondered as she saw the monster helplessly pushed back to where it had come from, and Elysia was forced to the ground from her purple smoke pillar.

"Relax, I wasn't going to kill him." Elysia curled her hair behind her ear, but her sickening smile told a different story.

Ivor fell to the ground face-first in a pool of blood with nothing to hold him up. All of his limbs were gone, so he was helpless to even kneel.

Elysia strode over and planted her foot on the back of his head, driving his bloodied face into the sand. "This is the position you should have assumed when you gazed upon the glory of the old one. Do you understand, weakling?"

Ivor tilted his head to the side and spat out blood. "Fuck you and your stupid old one, you crazy bitch."

"A shame." Elysia reached down and gripped Ivor by the hair. He screamed as she held him up with one hand and wrapped her fingers around his neck with her other. "The old one accepts the worship of all. Even foul-mouthed bastards like you. I took away your limbs so you would know your place, but it seems you have no need for a voice, either."

Ivor gasped out as Elysia tightened her grip.

"As the duel has concluded, the arena is currently a no-kill zone. If you kill Ivor Frostveil, you will be exiled, Elysia Mystshroud."

Elysia clicked her tongue and threw Ivor into the wall as if he were a sack of rotten potatoes. "Fine. Bring on the next Iron Seeker weakling. I must get through at least ten today to satisfy my god." She returned to her starting position, and Ivor was dragged away by an arena representative, leaving a thick trail of scarlet in the frozen sand.

Diana stood up.

"You're up next?" Stella asked.

"I think so." Diana shrugged.

"Don't go," Seth insisted. "Elysia is worse than a demon! Even if leaving here will void the advantage of your recommendation letter, at least you will keep your perfect record, your dignity, and all your limbs!"

"Worse than a demon, huh?" Diana snorted. "I'll be the judge of that."

Diana stood at the opposite end of the arena and stared down Elysia. Without the defensive formation suppressing her, she felt she could finally breathe.

I never realized how much I relied on my spiritual sense until it was robbed from me. Diana cracked her knuckles and rolled her shoulders. This was not going to be an easy fight. *I reached the fourth stage of the Star Core Realm recently, and from the Qi fluctuations reaching me from here, I would guess Elysia is of similar strength. If I used my bloodline, I would win with ease, but showing I am a demon would be less than ideal.*

"Raven takes the stage. With zero wins and zero losses, this will be her first attempt at rising the ranks. Please wait while the arena is adjusted to facilitate fair competition."

The ground rumbled as the mound below Diana's feet lowered, the ice melted, and the arena returned to its neutral self.

I guess they couldn't summon any demonic mist Qi for me

"The battle will now begin! Remember, the intentional killing of the other contestant will count as a loss!"

"Raven? Only cowards use fake names," Elysia sneered as she rose into the air, and that purple smoke spread out to begin the summoning ritual. However, this time, it didn't spin or pulse. The twisted howls and screams that made Diana's mind shudder started straight away.

Does resummoning that monster not take as long the second time? Diana wondered but didn't wish to find out. As Seth had advised, she planned to end this fast. Crouching down, Diana poured Qi into her artifact boots, causing them to become ethereal.

"O' creature that dwells beyond the veil of our reality—"

Blurring forward, Diana arrived before Elysia and enjoyed how her constant smirk was replaced with an expression of surprise and fear. "Don't bite your tongue," Diana said as she reeled back and planted her fist straight into Elysia's face, sending her plummeting to the ground in a shower of sand.

Unwilling to reveal her wings, Diana dropped to the ground nearby and walked toward Elysia. As expected, the girl hadn't suffered much. *If I had used my claws, I could have pierced her brain, but then I would have been disqualified for killing. Tsk, it's such a pain holding back.*

Elysia stood up and brushed the sand off her cloak. "A sneak attack befitting of an Iron Seeker. I thought you were a newbie, so I went easy, but it seems I underestimated you." Elysia's eyes glowed with power, and with a sneer, she pointed at Diana. "Now, kneel."

What the... Diana felt a mountain of pressure press down on her shoulders, almost on Ashlock's level, when he was slightly annoyed. *Was this really enough to make Ivor kneel?* Diana wondered as the ground beneath her cracked.

Elysia raised a brow. "You can still stand?"

"There are few I would kneel before," Diana said casually as her nails elongated into claws within the folds of her cloak, and she felt her fangs grow behind her mask as she tapped into her strength as a demon to walk forward. "And you are certainly not one of them."

"You dare stand before a servant of the old one? The insolence." Elysia clapped her hands, and her hair began floating as power flowed out of her and into the ritual circle. The otherworldly screams from behind grew louder as the creature began to emerge.

I need to finish this up quickly. Diana blurred toward Elysia with the help of her boots, and before the crazy cultist could even react, Diana had her hand gripping her neck and tackled her to the ground.

"Surrender, or I will strangle you until the life leaves your eyes," Diana hissed, and for the first time, Elysia looked genuinely scared as she was strangled against the sand. But even after the roles were reversed, the crazy girl refused.

"The old one will save me even if I die," Elysia gasped as Diana's claws drew blood. The worst part was that her words were half correct; the monster had finished emerging from the ritual and loomed over them.

"Call it off," Diana insisted. "I can snap your neck faster than it can impale me."

Elysia grinned, her eyes crazed. "We both know you won't do that. Life as an exile is one of certain death."

Diana's eyes widened as she realized the fatal flaw with this arena. No matter how fair they tried to make it, the rules and environment would benefit some more than others. As a summoner who relied on a ritual, Elysia benefited greatly from the rules. She was like a god here since she couldn't die while her guard was down during the summoning, and the opponent couldn't run away or group up on her.

"It seems you understand now." Elysia laughed despite her situation. "Once the ritual is complete, there is only one way to win. You have to kill the old one."

Diana reeled back her other hand and delivered the most brutal slap of her life, almost knocking the daylights out of Elysia. With her incapacitated, Diana stood up and turned to the monster from another plane of existence.

It looks like I will have to reveal that I am a demon to win. Diana sighed as she cycled her demonic Qi and felt the power flow through her body.

"Diana?"

"What?" Diana paused. That hadn't been the announcer's voice.

It had echoed straight into her mind, which she only experienced when talking to Ashlock and the Worldwalkers. Glancing up, she noticed the monster wasn't attacking. Its tentacles shifted to the side, revealing a giant green eye.

"Your name is Diana, right?"

The monster was speaking to her, and it somehow knew her name.

26
ILLUSION OF CONTROL

Diana met the gaze of the monster's glowing green eye that was like a contained star hidden within a mass of shifting tentacles.

Yes, Diana is my name, she replied within her mind and was glad the monster seemed to understand her inner thoughts as she didn't want to be seen speaking to the monster while in view of the many pavilion members.

"I thought I smelled the blood of a Ravena, but I wasn't so sure until just now when you leaked your presence."

So it knew about her bloodline. Was this another one of Maple's family?

How do you know my name?

"I watched you training in Hell alongside Neptune... That is the name you realm dwellers gave, right? Neptune? It sounds weird to say." The mass of wiggling tentacles opened up more as the giant green eye drew closer as if trying to get a better look at her. "Anyway, I see you have grown in power since then. I assume that is the work of that spirit tree?"

Diana nodded. *Ashlock's generosity and Neptune's training have helped my cultivation improve by leaps and bounds. I have also grown in understanding of my bloodline, as I am sure you can tell. But to think you watched me suffer through Hell alongside Neptune.*

"Watching is all we Worldwalkers do as there's not much else going on in the void. It's terribly boring, so even overlooking someone's struggles in Hell keeps the mind ticking. Without stimuli, time doesn't pass for us, and we don't progress as beings."

Is that why you listen to Elysia's orders and fight for her? Out of boredom?

"Well, I was also hungry." The eye shifted to glance at the blood-stained sand behind it before returning to stare at her. **"There's nothing to eat out in the void, so a few limbs are a tasty snack and help to progress my cultivation."** The monster let out an otherworldly sigh that made Diana's consciousness quiver. **"I am terribly jealous of Maple, who gets to run around in this realm due to making a pact with that spirit tree. How unfair."**

Diana frowned behind her mask. *If you know Maple, why didn't I see you in the last Mystic Realm alongside Neptune and Mars?*

"Oh, that's because I am what you could consider Maple's little sibling. I am a few decades younger, so he finds me annoying and dislikes including me in things." The monster's tentacles seemed to sag a little as if it were depressed. **"Maple is mean, right?"**

Diana wasn't sure how to comfort a void monster being bullied by its realm-eating siblings. *I cannot comment on sibling relationships, but I do have to ask. Are we going to fight?* Having looked up in the stands, Diana had noticed that some people were tilting their heads in confusion at how they weren't fighting.

The monster laughed in her mind. **"I fear Maple would eat me if I hurt one of Stella's friends, so no, I would rather not fight."**

What about the Mystic Qi that summoned you? Does it not force you to follow Elysia's orders to attack me?

"Oh, you are talking about this stuff?" The monster slammed down a few tentacles into the summoning circle, throwing up a cloud of sand.

Yes. Another cultivator told me that Mystic Qi allows a cultivator to bring a creature from their imagination into reality. Yet you seem to exist outside of Elysia's mind, so how does that work?

"I have no idea. One day, I was floating in the void when I saw a suspicious-looking portal. Neptune and Mars have told me to avoid such cracks in reality as they lead to trouble, but I was *really* bored, so I stuck my head through."

Diana felt like she had heard this before. *Wasn't Maple going through a portal how he ended up in a pact with Ashlock?*

"Something like that... Anyways, as I was saying, I stuck my head through the crack and found myself in what I can only describe as a bubble. It forced me to take on a certain shape and heavily limited my powers, but I was in the lowest realm, facing that Elysia girl surrounded by a ritual circle. I thought about eating her but luckily realized that she was the reason I could appear in this realm."

Elysia summoned you?

"I was not obligated to heed her call, so saying I was summoned is wrong. I prefer the term *invited*."

Okay, so she "invited" you here. Then what?

"Well, the Mystic Qi she used to create the opening severely limited my powers by crushing me into a vessel of Elysia's design." The eye shifted to look at Elysia lying on the ground and groaning. "So I figured if I wanted to exert more power in this realm and feel less suffocated, I needed to open her mind, so I started visiting her dreams. She welcomed my presence, and as I slowly broke and twisted her mind, she created better vessels for me to occupy."

Diana raised a brow at how the monster had said something so horrifying in such a casual way. *Does the Mystic Qi make you follow her orders?*

The monster laughed, shaking her mind. **"Of course not."**

Why do you follow them, then? Diana asked. *Such as when you ate Ivor's limbs when ordered to.*

"I can only manifest in this place if Elysia invites me here. If I give her the illusion of control, she will call upon me more often and feed me more cultivators in the long run."

You're like a well-trained dog. Diana snorted.

"I am not."

Whatever. Diana sighed. *I don't know if you understand, but I am currently in a duel with Elysia. I can't kill her as that will disqualify me, and she won't surrender until I defeat you. But I can't defeat you, and you won't kill me in fear of Maple.*

The monster shifted to loom over her. **"Why don't you surrender, then?"**

I refuse to lose.

"Then I suppose we are at a stalemate."

Not quite. Diana summoned her sword and pointed the tip at

Elysia's neck as the girl slowly stirred awake after being slapped. The red handprint was still visible on her swollen cheek. *I can chop Elysia up and carve fear of me into her mind so deep that she won't be able to summon you again.*

The monster's eye narrowed. **"Are you really capable of such a thing?"**

Diana didn't hesitate as she slashed her sword down and chopped off Elysia's left arm. The girl's eyes shot open as she was shocked out of her confused state, and she screamed out in pain.

Unfazed, Diana flicked the blood off her sword onto the sand and looked back at the monster. *Should I keep going?*

"Haha, good, very good. As expected from one with the Ravena bloodline. How interesting." The monster's voice turned cold. **"But to harm the tool I have spent so long carefully nurturing is deserving of some punishment—"**

Diana dropped to the ground and felt the air rush over her head as a tentacle from her blind spot passed over. If she had remained standing, it would have slammed into her and flung her into the nearby wall—a nonlethal attack but enough to knock her out.

You really are scared of your siblings, aren't you? Diana taunted as she used her artifact boots to barely dodge the barrage of incoming tentacles trying to slap her away. *I can see why Maple finds you annoying. You have such a short temper.*

"I assure you my temper is nothing compared to Maple," the monster replied as the whole arena trembled. A cloud of dust made tracking the tentacles even harder. Diana knew for a fact that the monster was holding back from killing her in fear of Maple, but it was determined to at least smack her around.

"Annoying fly," the monster said, and Diana noticed the tentacles suddenly double in speed.

"Oh—" Diana blinked as a tentacle slammed her in the face, shattering her mask, breaking her nose, and sending her flying. She collapsed into a heap near the wall in a ditch in the sand. Spitting out sand and blood, her ears were ringing, and her head was pounding. *What the hell was that? I couldn't even see it coming.*

Hauling her body up with a groan, she made sure to hide her face with a wooden mask from her spatial ring before glancing over her shoulder at the monster. It kept its distance and didn't seem interested in attacking while she was down as it watched her intently with its giant green eye nestled among a sea of shifting darkness.

Diana straightened her back. *You're just toying with me, aren't you? No, wait...* Diana looked to Elysia, whom it had called a tool and wasn't even trying to protect. *You're not even really angry, are you? You're treating this whole thing as nothing but a game.*

"So what if I am? I can't eat you, so having a little fun is the next best thing, don't you agree?" The monster's eye shifted to Elysia, who clutched her stump and cried. **"She won't die from such an injury, but it would be inconvenient if you damaged my carefully raised tool any further. So how about a deal?"**

A deal? Diana tilted her head. *What do you propose?*

"It's rare that I get to test this form's limitations. Most opponents I face are weaklings like that ice cultivator from earlier. I desire some challenge to see what areas of this vessel need improvement. So the deal is simple. Go all out against me for ten minutes, and once the time is up, I will surrender to you so you may win this pointless duel."

What about Elysia?

"If you try to harm her further, I may accidentally use lethal force. Don't misunderstand, I don't want to kill you, but I will if I have to. Elysia is my only way into the realm, and I have spent years breaking her to this point. To throw that all away for a friend of my sibling's favorite human is not happening."

Diana sighed. *Looks like I have no choice, then. Let's dance.* Demonic mist Qi spread out, and she began to transform. She would not last even a minute if she didn't go all out.

"That's the spirit," the monster said as a wall of tentacles came her way.

"What's going on in there? I can't see anything." Seth squinted at the arena and even cycled Qi to his eyes, but it was useless. The defensive array suppressed any spiritual sense, forcing them to rely on their eyes.

"Who knows?" Stella shrugged. The arena had turned into a sandstorm mixed with demonic mist. Shadows could be seen moving within the mist, and there were the howling phantoms, but the spectators couldn't see much else.

Diana uses the sand and mist to hide her demon form as she fights. But it doesn't make sense. Stella rested her chin on her palm as she mulled over the events. *Why did Diana cut off Elysia's arm? She's never been one for cruelty and dislikes killing unless necessary, so why antagonize the monster that seemed wary of her to the point that she is now forced to risk showing her demon form?*

Seth let out an exaggerated and distorted sigh beside her and leaned back in his chair. "What a bizarre fight. I have seen dozens of duels of Iron Seekers against Elysia, and I have never once seen that monster tremble in fear before an enemy. Just how strong is Diana?"

"Strong," Stella answered simply.

"No wonder she got a recommendation letter from a Sage Advisor. Maybe she is from some hidden clan. Her family name was Ravenborne, right? Do you know anything about it?"

Stella tilted her head to Seth. "You seem awfully concerned with the origins of her strength. Is there a reason?"

"Uh, I was just curious is all. We might be working together soon to hunt down Albis Lunarshade. He was last measured to be in the second stage of the Star Core Realm and is a good fighter, so I am relieved that Diana is so strong."

"Mhm?" Stella squinted behind her mask. "You sound more concerned than relieved."

"Do I?" Seth chuckled. "Well, we may be allies during the hunt, but if Diana wins this fight and ascends to the Crimson Trackers, us Iron Seekers will have a powerhouse stronger and even more ruthless than Elysia to deal with."

"Is that so?" Stella looked back at the arena. *I wonder who would win if we were to fight?*

"The dust is settling!"

Stella looked to the side and saw a group of Iron Seekers commenting on the fight.

"Oh look, the mist is dispersing as well!"

"I can't see any more shadows flying around. Did the monster lose?"

"Don't be ridiculous. Elysia has a single loss and nearly fifty wins. How could she lose to an upstart with no record?"

"I mean, didn't you see the start of the fight?" one of them refuted the other. "She defeated Elysia in the blink of an eye."

"Nobody fears Elysia. It's that monster she summons, which made her the heir to the Mystshroud family, that's the problem. I have seen Elysia beaten up before, but the monster always wins."

"True…"

Stella was also curious about the outcome, so she waited patiently for the sand and mist to disperse. In the middle of the arena, Diana stood tall. There was no evidence of her wings, and her cloak and mask hid any other signs that she was a demon.

Good, she has preserved her dark side from these pesky gazes.

Diana raised her sword and pointed it at the monster. "Surrender."

"Is she crazy?" Seth muttered in disbelief.

Stella was honestly wondering that as well. Things weren't adding up. Diana was panting and seemed injured. Meanwhile, the monster was unharmed and could easily kill her. Instead of attacking, the monster turned and stared straight at Stella in the stands with its green eye that looked so familiar. Where had she seen that look before?

Why is it looking at me? Stella's eyes widened. *Unless it's what I think it is… There's no way that's a Worldwalker, right? I thought Mystic Qi made things from the imagination.*

The monster began sinking back into the darkness of the ritual circle while keeping eye contact, much to the surrounding cultivators' shock. They stood up in disbelief and started discussing theories that were all wrong.

"Interesting," Stella muttered as she crossed her arms. *Diana didn't win. The Worldwalker decided to leave for some reason. But these people don't know that. To them, it looks like she scared the monster away.*

"No, don't go!" Elysia cried out as she scrambled through the sand toward the ritual circle. "Old one! Come back! I order you to come back and fight!"

Diana pressed the blade edge against Elysia's throat, causing the girl to stop in her tracks. "Don't bother. It's over."

The ritual circle collapsed in on itself, and the Mystic Qi returned to Elysia.

"There's no way the old one would lose or surrender." Elysa began muttering to herself as her eyes shook. "It's impossible. I still draw breath."

Diana sighed. "Just surrender—"

Elysia grabbed Diana's sword with her remaining hand, drawing blood. "There's only one explanation!" She looked up at Diana with crazed eyes. "You are also a worshiper of the old ones... No, you are a leader of them! It listened to you over me! That's the only explanation! Come with me to meet my family! You must!"

"Annoying." Diana kneed Elysia in the face, making her head snap back and tumble to the ground, knocking the girl out cold. "Stop sprouting such deluded nonsense," Diana said, turning and walking away through the sand. "You don't even understand the half of it."

"The duel has concluded! Elysia Mystshroud is no longer putting up a fight, which means Raven is the victor! Congratulations, Raven. You are now promoted to the elusive rank of Crimson Seeker with a flawless 1-0 record."

Diana didn't seem to react to the announcement as she swiftly left the arena. Her features were obscured by the white wooden mask she had equipped after getting smacked in the face, so Stella had no way to tell.

Meanwhile, Elysia's unconscious body was carried off alongside her arm.

"Good fight," Stella said once Diana arrived.

Diana snorted. "Quite the opposite," she said with spite. "Come on, let's go."

Stella had expected Diana to sound relieved or excited about her victory, but her voice dripped with anger and annoyance. Had Elysia ticked her off that much, or was it something else?

"Sorry, Seth. I will give you the answer about working together next time." Stella stood up and followed Diana out of the arena.

"Oh, okay...you can find me near the door. I usually wait around there."

"Will do." Stella waved him off, and once they were out of earshot of anyone, she asked, "What happened out there? You're not acting like yourself. Are you not happy about being promoted?"

Diana paused her steps and turned to Stella. "That wasn't a fight. I just wasted a load of Qi and got beaten up for ten minutes for that monster's amusement. Worst of all, when I cut off Elysia's arm to try and convince it to surrender, it did nothing but laugh and say I had embraced the attitude of a person with my bloodline. Everything I did was simply amusing to that monster."

"Was that monster…"

"Yes, it was one of Maple's siblings." Diana sighed. "That was the only reason it didn't tear me limb from limb."

"I see…" Stella bit her lip. Things just got even more complicated. "There is no way the Mystshroud family is going to live this down. You will be targeted by them, especially by Elysia. How could they even summon and control a Worldwalker in the first place?"

"I will explain to you later. First, let's move fast while we are still under the nose of most powerhouses." Diana turned and started walking at a brisk pace. "Let's pick up my Crimson Tracker pendant first, and then we should visit Nox's sister at the Duskwalker residence before nightfall. We don't have time to wait until tomorrow."

"I agree." Stella glanced down at the ring of shadow Qi around her finger that Nox had given her. *I really hope this thing works, as Nox hasn't given the most reliable information so far.*

27
A SHOW OF FORCE

"We are being followed," Stella said to Diana as they briskly walked through the gate at the mountain's base. Since the defensive formation was far less suppressive down here, Stella could use Qi to mask her voice.

"How many do you count?" Diana replied. "I can detect five tailing us."

"You can feel five? I only noticed four."

"My demonic Qi is more resistant to the suppression of the defensive formation. The fifth person is hanging quite far back up the mountain, but they only move forward when we do."

"Oh, I see," Stella said and briefly nodded to the guard that had let them through earlier. After being waved out, they proceeded past the lines and crowds of mortals still trying to get into the Eternal Pursuit Pavilion's grounds despite the late hour. "Let's quicken the pace."

"Where are we going, though?" Diana asked, following Stella a step behind as she weaved through the mortals. "We don't know the way to the Duskwalker residence."

"That's a good point. Should we deal with our stalkers first?" Stella spread out her spiritual sense, and it felt so freeing not to be suffocated by a defensive formation. Sure enough, five masked and cloaked people were following them into the city. They didn't even try to obscure themselves, so Stella could see the purple mist swirling around them. They were all Mystic Qi cultivators.

"Did you notice?"

"That these bastards are Mystic affinity cultivators?" Diana grumbled as they dashed around a corner and jumped over a mortal's cart that had overturned and blocked the street. "What do these crazy people even want? They aren't even trying to hide from our spiritual senses."

They should know Diana is at least in the Star Core Realm, so why chase her so openly? Either they are suicidal or all in the Star Core Realm, which I find hard to believe.

"Should we try talking to them?" Stella asked.

"Absolutely not." Diana shuddered. "We do not want to be associated with them. If they are anything like Elysia, they are all insane, and their power is a farce. Elysia thinks she is controlling the Worldwalker, but it's just bored and learned that listening to Elysia's orders earned it more snacks."

Why does that sound like Maple?

"Mhm, so that's a no to talking, then." Stella summoned a dagger to her hand and hid it in the folds of her cloak with a reverse grip. "Killing in the pavilion isn't allowed, but there's no risk of exile if we kill out here. Let's wait and dispose of them. We can't make our way to the Duskwalker residence with them tailing us—"

"I'm glad to see you two are alive." Ashlock's voice echoed in her mind. **"Did something bad happen? Why are there people chasing you?"**

"We might have attracted too much attention." Stella sighed as she looked up at the darkening sky. "A little help? These people are lunatics."

"Head to the restaurant from before. I will make a portal leading to the Duskwalker residence from there."

Stella nodded to Diana, and they rushed through the streets. She didn't remember the city's layout, but she could sense Ashlock's presence in a certain direction, so she just followed that. A few twists and turns later, they ended up in the filthy area behind the restaurant from before.

"They are gaining on us." Diana clicked her tongue. "Maybe chopping off Elysia's arm was a bad idea."

"You think?" Stella laughed as a rift tore itself into existence. They both dashed through, and a second later, it snapped closed behind them, leaving Nightshade City and the stalkers behind. They were now halfway up a mountain and could see what looked like the Duskwalkers' residence looming overhead.

"This is annoying," Diana said, running her hand through her long black hair and combing it behind her ear with her claw-like nails. "I was worried you would be the one to attract too much attention. To think I would be the one to steal the spotlight."

Stella nodded. "Seth seemed very interested in your background as well."

"Really?" Diana's hand paused and then fell to her side with a sigh. "None of this is my fault. I even made an effort to hide my demon form and abilities from everyone, but that stupid Worldwalker wanted to make a show out of it and wouldn't leave until the dust had settled."

Stella smirked behind her mask. "I must say you did look very imposing telling a Worldwalker to surrender, and it actually obeyed."

"It better have," Diana hissed in anger. "After I endured ten minutes of the torment and pain and wasted far too much Qi, if it had gone against its promise, I would have demanded Maple come here and eat it—"

Another rift suddenly appeared, drawing Stella and Diana's attention.

Larry crawled through in all his silvery ashen glory with Maple riding on his head. The fluffy white squirrel leaped through the air and effortlessly landed on Stella's shoulder.

"Hey, little guy, what's up?" Stella patted his head and stroked behind his ear. "Where have you been all this time?"

After enjoying the head pats for a moment, Maple used his paw to slowly push Stella's hand off and then leaped down to the ground. Suddenly, he exploded upward in a mass of wiggling black tentacles, which morphed into a naked, androgynous humanoid body with no defining features other than long white hair that reached his legs, fluffy ears, and a white tail that curled around his entire form. Maple had taken on his "human" form, loosely based on Stella.

"I was exploring the area and found a good shadowy snack nearby alongside some weaker guards."

Shadowy snack? Did he eat some poor shadow cultivator as a snack? Oh, who cares? He is too adorable, Stella thought as Maple looked up at her with his golden eyes. *He looks like the little brother I never had.*

"Why don't you take this form more often? You are so cute." Stella pulled Maple up into a hug, much to the former squirrel's annoyance.

"Talking in this form uses a lot of Qi. Every word I utter feels like drowning underwater," Maple replied in a completely neutral tone. "But it's easier to speak to you two as a humanoid because telepathy has gotten trickier. You two have built up a considerable resistance to mental manipulation due to Ashlock's questionable way of speaking."

That's true. I no longer feel the need to eat the Mind Fortress fruits when Ash speaks to me.

Stella pouted. "How do you not have enough Qi to spare to stay in this form? Don't you go off for days at a time to feast?"

"Why would I waste precious Qi to take on this unsightly form?" Maple turned his head and looked at Diana with a frown. "Let's get to the point. You met my younger sibling, didn't you?"

"News travels fast in the void, it seems."

Maple shook his head. "I felt the tear in the void from afar."

"You should have come and saved me." Diana crossed her arms. "But yes, I met that monster while fighting a Mystic Qi cultivator. They were pretending to be her summon. What about it?"

"If you can, stay away from them in the future. Every Worldwalker goes through this phase, and it's dangerous to get involved in. Half of all Worldwalkers are said to perish to Heaven's wrath during this thrill-seeking period of their lives. You got lucky this time because they thought I would go out of my way to punish them for harming you."

Diana's shoulders sagged. "I can see why you dislike that sibling of yours. They treated everything like a game to satisfy their selfish boredom. If I had to fight them again, and they were going for the kill, I would lose."

"What's this?" Ashlock's voice entered everyone's mind. **"I feel like I missed something."**

Diana sighed. "I will explain what happened."

What followed was a quick summary of the fight, what the Worldwalker had said about Maple, and Diana's deal to get the Worldwalker to surrender.

"To think we would encounter another Worldwalker capable of

appearing on this realm," Ashlock said. **"Does your sibling have a name?"**

Maple shook his head. "Not one you would understand. Feel free to give them one."

"Diana, did it have a noticeable color?"

"A color?" Diana looked to the ground in thought. "Ah, it did have a green eye. Other than that, it was nothingness."

"Green... Let's see. If I am to keep up the naming scheme, I need a green planet. There's only one with a green tint, and that's Uranus, but that seems too unsightly of a name for a Worldwalker..."

Stella frowned. "Maple, do you know what Ash is mumbling about?"

"Other worlds or dimensions by the sound of it," Maple replied.

"Any you recognize?"

"No. If these places are real, they exist beyond the void, a place the Worldwalkers could never go." Maple's golden eyes narrowed. "Perhaps that dimension is where he draws his impossible powers from—a higher plane of existence that is unreachable to us."

"Somewhere even a Worldwalker couldn't go? Mhm..." Stella closed her eyes as she continued listening in to Ashlock's murmuring. *One day, when I am strong enough to rule over the entire heavens, I will let you share your secret with me, Ash. But until then, until we are safe from anything that could tear us apart from one another, I ask that you keep your secrets for our safety. Just wait for me.*

Stella's eyes opened, and she looked to the darkened sky. "Ash, you're talking aloud, you know? Have you forgotten our promise?"

"Huh? Oh...my apologies. I got carried away and lost in thought."

Diana and Maple looked at Stella with questioning looks, but she ignored them. "Have you decided on a name?"

"Since he is Maple's annoying little brother, I feel the name Pluto fits. What do you think, Maple?"

"I do not know the deeper meaning behind the name. But I am surprised you even thought so deeply about them, considering how lazy you are."

Stella then felt Maple wiggle out of her grasp, and she decided to look away to spare herself the grotesque scene of Maple switching forms. He then hopped up on her shoulder.

"Don't look at me like that. I am not petting you."

"All right, since everyone is here, should we begin?" Diana asked as she replaced her white wooden mask with a black one.

Stella nodded. "Do you remember the plan?"

"Of course I do." Diana chuckled as she walked up the mountain. "If they dare to resist…"

Evelyn Duskwalker stared at the servant in disbelief.

"What do you mean my mother is gone?"

"She went out for a stroll, Mistress, but is yet to return. The guards sent by the residence to tail her have also vanished without a trace." The servant's voice trembled. "Do you think the Lunarshade family is finally making its move? Are we all going to die?"

Evelyn ignored the servants' rambling and began pacing the room. *We have absorbed most of the smaller families in Nightshade City under our banner, so we have multiple Star Core Elders to defend ourselves with, but that won't be enough if **he** decides to make a move. We have nothing capable of stopping a Nascent Soul Realm threat. Only the Celestial Warden can fight him, but convincing that cunning man to move from his mountain is unlikely.*

"Mistress, would it be possible for you to beg your husband to spare us?"

Evelyn paused, glared at the servant, and barely held back her wrath from pulverizing him. "You want me to go beg like a dog and spread my legs for the Lunarshade scion every time we feel threatened?"

The servant didn't dare meet her gaze but uttered under his breath, "Well…"

"Get out."

"As you wish, Mistress." The servant gave a small bow and took his leave, closing the door quietly on his way out. He was a skilled servant, so killing him over voicing legitimate concerns and solutions would be a shame.

Evelyn collapsed on a nearby chair and stared up at the ceiling. "I would go and beg that bastard if I could, but he doesn't have eyes for me anymore, no matter what I do. Since news of Nox reappearing at the Eternal Pursuit Pavilion reached his ears, he has looked at me with even more contempt than usual." Evelyn closed her eyes and listened to the wind rattling the windows as a sense of melancholy overcame her.

What am I even fighting so hard for anymore? Father is dead, Mother is missing, and the cousin I had the most faith in reviving the family disappeared chasing after Nox, who has abandoned me. All I have gained in my long life is command over a dying household on the brink of collapse and forced into a marriage with someone who disdains me.

The door suddenly slammed open. "Mistress Evelyn!"

"What now?" Evelyn snapped as that same darn servant came back in.

"There are two powerful cultivators at the door. They wish to meet with you."

"How powerful are we talking?" Evelyn's eyes widened.

"One of them had a Crimson Tracker pendant, and they both look like bounty hunters," the servant explained.

"Tell them we are busy and to come tomorrow." Evelyn stood up. "With my mother missing, I can't say for certain that I could win against them. We need to buy time—"

"They claim to know Nox," the servant added.

Evelyn clicked her tongue. "More debt collectors? I already paid off that Lightbringer bastard after he threatened to place bounties at the pavilion for only being compensated 200 Yinxi Coins for healing Nox's hand."

The servant shook his head. "The blond-haired one showed a ring made of shadow Qi and claimed it was from Nox. They are more likely to be acquaintances of the Mistress's sister."

Evelyn massaged her temples and let out a long sigh. "I really don't need this right now. Without my mother around, the other families we have taken under our wing may grow greedy. Time is not on my side here. Can you really not tell them to leave—"

Spatial Qi suddenly crackled through the air, and despite the defensive formations built into the residence, reality was torn apart as a rift formed. The air shuddered in protest, and the walls of the room glowed with power as the defensive formation attempted to crush the portal.

What in the nine realms is going on? The amount of Qi needed to forcefully open a portal like that is unfathomable.

A gong began to echo through the residence, alerting everyone to the situation. *I just need to hold on until the other Grand Elders get here.*

Evelyn's Star Core pulsed in her chest as shadow Qi wreathed her body and condensed into armor. She also summoned a sword to her hand and got ready to summon fiends.

From the distorted portal, two silhouettes emerged. Both wore the typical attire of bounty hunters, such as thick black cloaks with many folds and big hoods to hide their features. They also wore masks, but they differed. The blond-haired woman wore a jade mask, while the black-haired woman wore a simpler black wooden mask.

"Pardon the intrusion." The blond-haired one spoke, her voice distorted by the mask as she looked around the room. The portal snapped closed behind her, sending a wave of wind that rustled the intruder's hair and cloaks. The woman then focused on her. "Are you Evelyn?"

Evelyn gulped. "Depends on who's asking."

The two intruders exchanged a quick glance.

"We are acquaintances of Nox Duskwalker." The blond-haired woman showed her finger with a ring of shadow Qi. "We came to make a deal."

"Oh? Would you mind if I verified that ring?" Evelyn stepped closer with a smile and lowered her sword. "It's been so long since I heard from my dear sister. It would sadden me if people pretending to be her acquaintances used her name to take advantage of us."

"Sure." The woman offered her hand.

One more step... She is the dangerous one. I will get rid of her first.

Evelyn didn't show her inner thoughts on her face as she leaned over and pretended to care about the ring. "Well, that's a surprise. You really do have a ring made from our shadow Qi—" Evelyn swung her sword up with all her strength and speed before finishing her statement.

First, I will cut off this outstretched hand of yours and then finish with your head— Huh?

There was a loud clang and shower of sparks as a dagger hidden in the woman's palm flipped out, met Evelyn's surprise attack, and redirected the momentum overhead. Evelyn felt her balance thrown off as her sword tip pointed to the ceiling, leaving her defenseless with both arms raised.

How did she know? Evelyn's eyes widened. *That reaction speed... She saw through my ruse somehow.*

"What a cheap trick. I know you hate your sister." The woman's distorted voice answered her thoughts and was followed by a powerful punch to her gut, sending her flying backward. "I wanted to give you a chance, but it seems a show of force is the only way to make you listen. Just like your sister…"

"Ugh." Evelyn pushed herself up from the pile of destroyed furniture she had crashed through and gritted her teeth. "If you know how much I despise my sister, you shouldn't have come here."

"We have more in common than you would think," the blond-haired woman replied as she twirled the dagger between her fingers. "After all, the Nox you knew is dead."

"Impossible," Evelyn replied before her brain could catch up. Scrunching up her face in disgust, she said, "I hate to admit it, but Nox is far too adept at life as a merchant. Over the years, many bounty hunters have been sent after her, yet she evaded capture every time. Unless someone on the level of the Celestial Warden put his all into hunting her down, she wouldn't fall to the likes of you."

"Oh, but she did." The woman laughed. "She stole from the wrong people and paid the price with her soul."

Evelyn narrowed her eyes.

It was true they had forced their way in here with ease, and she couldn't find any falsehoods in their words. This woman's confidence exuded absolute authority, so maybe she really was telling the truth.

If that's the case, these people have someone on the level of a Nascent Soul Realm cultivator.

"Elder Evelyn! What's happening?" The doors flung open again, and three Grand Elders ran inside.

The one who had shouted her name was the Grand Elder of the Frostveil family. Close behind was the Grand Elder from the Blightbane family with hair as dark as rotting wood and eyes like fading embers. He looked as gloomy as the rest of his family, who cultivated death affinity. The third and final Grand Elder was from the Mystshroud family, which consisted of a bunch of lunatics who occupied the basement of the Duskwalker family residence alongside their cult.

Despite the arrival of the three powerhouses and being outnumbered, the two intruders seemed unfazed.

Evelyn raised her hand to silence the Frostveil Grand Elder. She then glared at the blond woman and said, "Tell me who you people are and what you want with me and my family."

"We are agents of Ashfallen." The woman glanced at everyone in the room. "We come with an offer of collaboration. The Duskwalker family will swear itself to Ashfallen and act as our proxy. In return, we will share our profits from the pavilion and lend you our strength—the strength that allowed us to slaughter Nox for her transgressions against us."

Grand Elder Frostveil stepped forward. "What nonsense are you sprouting? That's absurd! I have never heard of Ashfallen before—" The woman suddenly appeared before him and pressed a dagger against his neck.

"I wasn't asking," the woman said. "Either you join us by your own decision, or we take this place over by force."

"Force? What a lot of hot air." The Frostveil Grand Elder smirked. "Do you really think you can beat four families by yourselves?"

The woman snapped her fingers, and the ground trembled.

Evelyn stepped back as an ethereal black root emerged from the floorboards alongside a sudden pressure. Once again, the air shuddered as it was ripped apart, and a portal formed. However, this time, the silhouette that emerged was that of a monster.

A spider made of shifting, silvery ash crawled through the portal like a mythical creature. The halo of ash orbiting its crown of horns began to rotate, and Evelyn felt her body scream in pain as she was pressed to the floor by a pressure she had never felt before. The other Grand Elders followed a similar fate as they were all forced to kneel before the mythical creature.

Its gaze swept the room, and Evelyn could only look at the floor and tremble.

"No need to be so scared. After all, we are going to be working together soon," the blond-haired woman said with a distorted voice as she crouched before Evelyn and pushed a parchment written in ink along the floor. "Just drop your blood on this. Don't make this harder than it has to be."

Evelyn strained her neck to look up and saw her pathetic reflection in the woman's polished jade mask. "Are you even human? A contract made in blood? This is something a demon would do," Evelyn hissed out.

The woman tilted her head and laughed. "Who knows? Maybe I am less human than I thought. Now sign."

28
COMFORTING SHADOW

Stella tapped the heavenly ink contract Kaida had written for them for a third time as Evelyn made no move to sign it in blood. At a casual glance, the contract written on some yellowing parchment with rough edges and a few simple and agreeable terms looked innocent enough.

- Loyalty to the Ashfallen Sect & Trading Company.
- Secrecy regarding the activities of the Ashfallen Sect and its members.
- Agreement to act as a proxy for the Ashfallen Sect.

I didn't even mention that this is a Heaven-binding contract, and she is already this averse to signing it. Stella's patience was growing thin. *After dealing with her sister in the past, I will not make the same mistake again. Without the curse, Nox would have gotten away with my earrings and the knowledge of what we can do. We now have the power to take the initiative.*

"Why are you doing this to me?" Evelyn trembled, and a single tear rolled down her cheek to the floor. "Was killing my sister not enough for you?"

"Spare me the act." Stella rolled her eyes. "I know all about you and your family's situation. Nox hasn't been present in this family for many years, and you hate her. Yes, we killed Nox, but it had nothing to do with you. Now stop acting and sign the contract."

"I'm not acting! It's just one thing after another!" Evelyn pounded the ground with her fist as the tears kept coming. "What have I done to deserve this? All my childhood, I was treated as a spare. Nox ran away from her responsibilities, and Father died, leaving me to pick up the broken pieces. I became her fucking fiancé's plaything to buy time. After centuries of suffering and torment, I finally started to rebuild my family's strength, and then this accursed night happened. Mother is gone, and now you Ashfallen people show up making cold-hearted demands. Cooperation, my ass. What are you really after? Money? I have none left! You want revenge for something my sister did? Then just slit my neck and let me be done with this miserable existence."

Evelyn's words echoed through the room and were followed by her sobbing.

"Elder Evelyn…" the man with icy blue hair and eyes called out while barely able to raise his body against the pressure. "We stand with you! We won't sign anything until you do—"

Diana slammed the man's face into the stone. "Keep quiet. We only need the Duskwalker family to cooperate."

This is getting out of hand. Stella frowned and looked back to Evelyn, who was still sobbing. *Yet what am I to do? You call us cold-hearted, but I have little trust in those who wield shadow Qi. You are all pathological liars prone to backstabbing… I mean, you tried to take off my head a moment ago despite us showing no aggression. Evelyn, you brought this treatment upon yourself. Do you think I enjoy this? I was open to talking!*

Stella sighed. "Evelyn, we don't want your money—quite the opposite. We want to give you money. Anything you have, we can get ourselves. As for Nox, I am at peace with what happened and do not want revenge against your family. What we need is a proxy to take on the scrutiny for our actions here in Nightshade City and the Eternal Pursuit Pavilion. That is all."

"Who would believe such crap?" Evelyn scoffed and looked ready to collapse as she panicked.

Nox warned us that Evelyn wasn't strong-willed, which is why she was easily bullied her whole life. It seems our arrival, and the sight of Larry has brought her to a breaking point. This is good. I can use this. If I could somehow steer her feelings toward trusting me a bit, I might be able to get her to cooperate down the line of her own volition rather than having to force her at every step.

Evelyn's face scrunched up as she said with disdain, "Who do you work for? The Lunarshades? Did my husband finally tire of tormenting me and send you to humiliate me before finishing me off?"

Stella leaned in closer, held Evelyn's trembling hand, and placed a dagger firmly in her palm.

"Hey," Stella whispered into her ear, "just relax and listen to my voice. I know it sounds unbelievable, but one day, you will remember this moment and feel like laughing. You don't know me yet, but I cherish and care for those I can trust. However, I will kill those who are a threat to me and my family. You are one drop of blood away from joining the former group and receiving salvation."

"You would cherish me and become my family's salvation?" Evelyn hissed through gritted teeth. "The silver-tongued words of a demon. There is no such kindness in this cutthroat life."

"I disagree," Stella said calmly. "Kindness really does exist. You were just dealt a bad hand in life and stuck with it till the bitter end, for better or worse. You can resent Nox all you want, but she made the wise choice to run away from this fate. With the powerhouse of your family dead, this was always the inevitable outcome—at my hands or that of another. The Duskwalker family would fall into obscurity as other powerhouses took its place."

Evelyn violently shook her head. "We were so close to restoring our power! If we can find my mother, who was about to break through to the Nascent Soul Realm and bought a few more decades, it would be possible…"

I fear your mother is already dead, Stella thought as she recalled what Maple had said about finding a powerful shadow cultivator to snack on. *God darn it, Maple. Just because we are in a new area and can be more brazen doesn't mean you can eat anyone that looks tasty.*

"What if she doesn't come back?" Stella asked. "And even if she does, do you think the Lunarshade family will sit around and let her get strong enough to contest them?"

"No. I refuse to believe this is happening." Evelyn glared at the dagger in her hand. "I worked so hard…gave up so much. Was it all for nothing?"

"How can you refuse to believe something that is happening before your eyes? Now, calm down and think logically. We really are here to cooperate despite my heavy-handed approach. You can blame the distrust sown into my heart by Nox for that."

Evelyn took the words to heart and tried to calm down. Her breathing slowed as she took in deep breaths, and she stopped trembling as much. "Of course, it's the bitch's fault. Everything in my life is," she muttered before raising her head. Her eyes were red and puffy, and her hair was disheveled—she looked awful.

"You know it was Nox who asked us to help you?" Stella said.

Evelyn's eyes widened. "Liar."

Stella tilted her head. "It was her dying wish for us to save you."

"The selfish words of a dying bitch. I don't need saving. I *was* fine. Everything was under control. I just needed a little more time to push through."

"And you still can. We aren't here to take over your family, you know? We just want to offer you resources and support in return for selling things for us."

"That's really all you want?" Evelyn muttered.

A man kneeling before Diana with deep violet eyes and silver-tinted hair like Elysia coughed to draw attention. "I think we should agree to their terms. The Mystshroud family deeply appreciates the support the Duskwalker family has given us and our cult, but we are not blind. Our necks lay on the chopping block and are at the mercy of the Lunarshade family's mood toward Elder Evelyn. If there is a day the Celestial Warden leaves for another city, nobody in Nightshade City will be left to hold him back from destroying us. I have not heard of this Ashfallen group before, but if they have a mystic cultivator capable of summoning and controlling such a divine monster, I can only kneel in awe."

Stella raised a brow behind her mask. *Does this old man think Larry is made from Mystic Qi?*

"It's as you say, Grand Elder Mystshroud," Evelyn looked to the floor in despair, "I did everything I could and still fell short like always. I am not as good a leader as my father, as talented as my sister, or capable of bringing all of you together under one banner like my mother. I can do nothing right…"

"Elder Evelyn, sign the contract," the gloomy man with long black hair like rotting wood, which hid half his face, said in a deep voice, drawing everyone's attention. "A person's dying wish is a legacy to be carried out by the living. To embrace their departing words is to give peace to the deceased soul, but to reject that legacy is to condemn that soul to endless suffering."

"Good," Evelyn hissed. "That's what Nox deserves—"

The man slowly opened his eyes. "Elder Evelyn, as someone who cultivates death and has spent my life listening to the regrets of the departed, I cannot follow someone who rejects a dying wish. Just because someone is a criminal does not make them a bad person. It's all about perspective and context, something the dead can no longer provide."

"But..."

"I know what you are thinking, Evelyn," the man said slowly as his eyes flickered between Stella and Diana. "The killing intent around these two is nonexistent, so their aggression is manufactured out of distrust. They have come to honor a dying wish with good intentions." The man narrowed his eyes at Evelyn. "Meanwhile, I can sense the aura of death hanging over you. If your imminent death isn't the result of anyone here, then there is only one possibility." The man's gaze turned serious. "You are planning on killing yourself to escape this seemingly hopeless situation."

Evelyn's head shot up, and her eyes widened. She tried to say something, but the words wouldn't come out.

"Am I wrong? Your eyes are hollow as if you have already made peace with your decision." Grand Elder Blightbane shook his head. "Are you that desperate to meet your sister in the afterlife so soon?"

"Meet my sister? Why does it always come back to her?" Evelyn began to manically laugh as her eyes widened further. "You compel me to live, but what do I have to live for, Grand Elder Blightbane? Tell me. I can only take so many centuries of being treated like shit and ordered around before I give up. The only thing keeping me going all this time was the faintest hope that my efforts would be rewarded someday, but these Ashfallen bastards have shattered my delusions. I am weak and always will be. Forever at the mercy of someone else." Evelyn raised the dagger to her own throat and glared at Stella. "You said you needed me, and that bitch of a sister's dying wish was for me to live on, right? Well, fuck you, and screw her, too. I won't live on in misery to please others—"

Stella moved entirely on instinct, faster than even her mind could process. As the blade bit into Evelyn's neck, Stella gripped the tip with two fingers, stopping it from digging further. A trickle of warm blood ran down the blade and hilt before wetting Stella's hand and dripping onto the contract below.

"Get away from me," Evelyn hissed.

The words written on the parchment glowed with heavenly light and rose off the page to enter Evelyn's body. A pressure belonging to the heavens washed over the room as if verifying the contract had been made.

Stella pulled the dagger away from Evelyn's neck, throwing it to the floor, and embraced the woman in a tight hug. The woman froze in her embrace, clearly confused about what was happening.

I don't really know why I felt the need to hug you, either, Stella thought as she stared at the far wall. *It just felt like the right thing to do.*

Evelyn eventually slumped into her embrace as her body seemed to give up.

"I'm sorry I put you through that," Stella said. "But it was hard to tell if it was all an act or genuine. Without an oath of loyalty verified by the heavens as some assurance, I wouldn't feel comfortable even telling you my name."

Evelyn hummed in agreement.

Good, she seems to be accepting me more. Now for the final push…

"I know how it feels to be alone and have nobody to talk to. It drives one crazy and makes the world appear bleaker than it really is. I said we are similar, remember? Trust me when I say this: life can get better, and I will make sure it does for you. Okay? This is not the end for your family, but rather a new beginning."

"Do whatever you want," Evelyn mumbled. "I give up."

Stella tilted her head and looked at the other Grand Elders. "What about you lot? Will you join the Duskwalker family on this path?"

"Do we have a choice? If Elder Evelyn has signed the contract, then we should, too," Grand Elder Blightbane said as he slit his hand and let the blood drip onto the contract.

"So this chain around our soul is a heavenly oath," the Blightbane

Grand Elder muttered as he patted his chest. "I have heard about them before but thought they were usually spoken aloud."

The other Grand Elders in the room followed suit after exchanging nervous glances.

Once the heavens verified them as loyal to the Ashfallen Sect, Larry released his pressure on the room.

The hard part is over. Now that these Grand Elders cannot outright betray us, we can try to win them over to our side with rewards.

"Good. Let's start this again from the beginning with less violence and threats." Stella pulled back from the hug and stood up. Taking off her mask, she smiled at Evelyn while outstretching her hand. "My name is Stella. It's a pleasure to be working with you."

"You're younger than I expected." Evelyn sighed as she rubbed her eyes. "Now I feel even more embarrassed for showing such a display to a junior."

"We all have our moments of weakness. There's no shame in it. I am just glad I managed to stop you in time." Stella clasped Evelyn's hand and hauled the woman to her feet. "To continue introductions, this mythical beast is Larry. He is the pet of my father and is not a creature made from mystic Qi. Sorry to disappoint you, Grand Elder Mystshroud."

The spider waved one of its legs to Evelyn, making the woman smile slightly in amusement.

"Unbelievable," Grand Elder Mystshroud muttered as he circled Larry, stroking his chin. "Your father was able to tame such a creature? He must be on the level of an immortal."

Stella simply smiled and didn't give a straight answer. It was unlikely these people would interact much with the main sect back on Red Vine Peak, so the stronger they believed them to be, the better.

Diana also removed her mask and gave everyone a fang-filled grin. "My name is Diana, and as you can see, I am a part demon. I apologize for smashing your face into the stone, Grand Elder Frostveil. No hard feelings, I hope?"

The Grand Elder laughed with fear in his eyes. "N-None at all! But if you don't mind me asking, what did you go through all this effort to achieve? You mentioned something about us being proxies, right?"

Stella nodded as her spatial ring flashed, and a few pill bottles appeared. Handing them out to each Grand Elder, they eyed them with a mixture of suspicion and curiosity.

"These are the pills we plan to sell to the Eternal Pursuit Pavilion for Yinxi Coins. Due to their potency and rarity, if people were to figure out their source, it would bring trouble. That is why we want to lean on the reputation of the Duskwalker family and have them sell the pills for us," Stella explained and patted Evelyn on the shoulder. "This is where my promise to bring you salvation comes in. Each bottle contains eleven pills. You can take one from every bottle for yourself to use or sell. You can also keep ten percent of the Yinxi Coins you get for each sale. However, the rest must be transferred to me or Diana each week."

"A fair deal if these pills are as rare as you claim," Grand Elder Blightbane said as he inspected the bottles in his hand. "The Lunarshade family is bound to catch wind of this as they have deep ties within the pavilion."

Like that Lotus Informant I had the displeasure of interacting with earlier.

"How many of these bottles can you give to us to sell each week?" the Frostveil Grand Elder asked, his fear clearly turning to greed.

"As many as you feel comfortable selling," Stella replied simply.

"So many rare pills… Just who are you people?" Grand Elder Frostveil ran a hand through his icy blue hair in disbelief. "Even the Lunarshade family hoards their pills and buys up whatever stock comes on sale."

"I never thought about the implications that whatever pills we sell could also be bought by our enemies." Ashlock's voice echoed through Stella's mind. ***"We should keep the selling of the pills to a minimum while we look to weaken the Lunarshade family as soon as possible."***

Stella nodded and turned to Evelyn. "We should focus on building up Duskwalkers' strength, and for that, I need you to feel free and clear-minded. Tell me who your husband is. We can get rid of him first."

"What?" Evelyn was shocked out of her depressed mood. "That's…"

"Do you not want him dead?"

Evelyn shook her head. "I do, I really fucking do. His name is

Albis Lunarshade. There's a bounty on his head, I believe, for 10,000 Yinxi Coins, but nobody would dare take it."

Stella realized she had heard that name earlier today. It was the person Seth was trying to track down and kill.

"Leave it to me." Stella smiled at Evelyn. "He will be dead by the end of the week."

29
DEMONIC MEAL

Evelyn had no idea what to say.

How can Stella say something so ludicrous with such certainty when so many have failed? My tyrant of a husband dead by the end of the week? Can such a reality even exist?

"Stella, I don't think such a thing is possible..." Evelyn felt her skin crawl, and a chill spread through her body as the image of her husband came into mind. Albis Lunarshade was a towering figure with broad shoulders and round features. He was also bald—hairless from head to toe—and had pupilless eyes so white they mirrored the emptiness of his soul. He was evil to the core, someone who relished another person's suffering and seemed to find no pleasure in anyone's company.

That was the person she was forced to pleasure to survive all these years, and his father, the Grand Elder of the Lunarshade family, was even worse. He was a grotesque man who shared similar features to his son but was more round than tall and spent most of his time bathing in a moonlit pond while being tended to by a team of maids like a stranded animal. He would hurl insults at her whenever she walked near—calling her a whore that only came when she needed something and laughing in her face about the downfall of her family and pelting her with spirit stones.

Albis is that man's son. There's no way he could die... It's not possible... Those two sit upon a mountain of corpses and dictate the lives of everyone else. Only the Celestial Warden can hold a candle to their power...

"Eat this," Stella said, dangling something before her eyes like a hypnotic coin.

Evelyn blinked away the visions. "What's this?"

"This truffle is the raw ingredient used in our higher-grade pills." Stella smiled, but with how crazed her eyes were, it was hard not to feel uncomfortable. "It's rare and expensive for us to grow, and it has a miraculous effect."

"What's the effect?"

"This is the Heart Demon Expelling truffle. I am sure you can guess its effect from the name." Stella lightly grabbed Evelyn's hand and placed the truffle into her palm. "Usually, I wouldn't hand them out like this, but I can tell from your actions and gaze that you are plagued by inner demons that stagnate your cultivation and cloud your judgment. This won't be an immediate fix, as you have a lot of mental hurdles to overcome, but it will help."

Evelyn looked down at the truffle in her palm. *This thing is far too precious... How can I possibly afford it? Our family looks prosperous, but I am barely scraping by and owe rogue cultivator gangs in the city thousands of spirit stones and a few bounty hunters Yinxi coins.*

With a heavy heart, Evelyn went to give it back.

"What are you doing?" Stella asked.

"I don't have any money to buy it from you." Evelyn sighed. "And I don't want to be in anyone's debt. Just give me some time... I will sell lots of pills for you and scrape together the mon—"

"Oh, *that's* what you were worried about? I said I take care of those who are loyal to me, remember? So there's no need to repay me for this. It's a gift from me." Stella firmly handed the truffle back. "Now eat it. Diana and I will return to the Ashfallen Sect soon, and I guarantee you will want to eat it while we are still here."

"You're really giving me this for free?" Evelyn couldn't make sense of Stella at all. *What is her motive? Actually, does she even have one? Her actions are all over the place and are nothing like the other scions from noble houses I have interacted with over the years.*

"Just eat it," Stella insisted with a frown.

Evelyn hesitated. "Could you tell me why I should want you two to be here while I eat it?"

"Admitting that ruins the fun," Stella said as she slowly raised her hand.

Unable to muster any more strength or care to resist, Evelyn reluctantly threw the truffle into her mouth and gulped it down. "Bleh." Its distinct earthy taste made her wince.

Stella stepped back to join the ranks of the Grand Elders, who were watching on from afar as if she were about to explode any second.

Meanwhile, Diana strode forward, licking her lips. "This is going to be a big one."

"What do you mean—" Evelyn choked as she felt something surging up her throat. A sense of terrible *wrongness* flooded her body, making every muscle spasm and tighten. *Something* was trying to get out, and it made her scream in agony and fear.

"The truffle forces the heart demons to gather and leave your body out your mouth," Diana explained, but her words felt distant to Evelyn as her ears rang. "And since you have led such a miserable life, there are bound to be many negative emotions that have condensed into the heart demons plaguing your soul."

"Help…" Evelyn gasped out. "Please help me…"

"Just let it happen," Diana replied. "It will be over soon."

Evelyn let out a howl as she threw her head back. She tried to claw at her throat as an extremely itchy burning sensation swelled upward, but nothing she did helped ease the horrific discomfort. Once the burning reached her mouth, it forced her jaw open.

"What in the nine realms is that?!" Evelyn heard Grand Elder Frostveil cry out. The other Grand Elders also seemed to shout and step back.

"That is a heart demon. A phantom made entirely from demonic Qi created from Evelyn's negative emotions twisting the world's Qi," Diana said. "It lived within her soul and is the main cause of her bottlenecks. All of you will also have one festering inside you, though it's unlikely to be this big."

"Demonic Qi?" the Mystshroud Grand Elder said with concern. "How will we kill this thing before it kills Evelyn? Demonic Qi reacts violently to other Qi types, and since it's a phantom, physical attacks won't work."

Diana snorted. "Did you forget I am a demon? I will handle it."

Evelyn felt the thing being pulled out of her throat. The terrible wrongness that had been making her want to escape her own skin vanished alongside the burning sensation. She blinked away the tears and glanced around.

Diana stood in the middle of the room, holding a phantom of shifting darkness in her claws. It was huge, about the size of a human child, and almost reached the floor. Gazing upon it made Evelyn want to throw up at the thought of that thing having been inside her.

"Thank you for the meal." Diana grinned as she raised the phantom over her head. A mist curled up her arm and engulfed the phantom, making it screech as it melted. Diana opened her mouth wider than should be possible, stuck out her pointed tongue, and savored the liquified phantom that dripped down into her throat.

Evelyn shuffled backward and diverted her gaze from the display. *Diana really is a demon! Who in the nine realms have I sworn my loyalty to? I thought only Stella was insane, but they both are!*

Diana side-eyed Evelyn while licking her lips. "That was delicious."

"I-I'm glad you enjoyed it...?" Evelyn had no idea what to even say to that.

Stella strode over and crouched down before Evelyn. They locked eyes, and Stella grinned. "Looks like it worked!" She patted her shoulder enthusiastically. "That dead look in your eyes is gone. Try to cultivate and let me know if you feel any different."

What is she on about? How did my eyes look dead... Evelyn let out a sigh and began reluctantly cycling Qi through her body. To her shock, she immediately started going through a breakthrough to the next stage in the Star Core Realm. Her Star Core greedily pulled in all the Qi within her body and the room as shadows pooled toward her. It then rapidly expanded in size, letting off a pulse of Qi that made the Grand Elders take a step back.

Evelyn exhaled as she stabilized her new cultivation at the third stage of the Star Core Realm. The bottleneck that had halted her cultivation had been removed, and now, it seemed like an unobstructed path to power lay ahead.

"Did Elder Evelyn just break through after all these years?" Grand Elder Blightbane asked as he stroked his chin. "How unbelievable... Forgive me, but is there any way this old man can get his hands on that truffle you gave Elder Evelyn? I have likely formed quite a few heart demons myself after years of listening to the dead and would love to have them purged and this bottleneck that had troubled me for years gone."

Stella smirked as she stood up and faced the Grand Elder of the death affinity. "I don't hand them out so freely. As the leader of the Duskwalker family and you lot, I felt it important that Evelyn had a clear head and less depressive thoughts. Hence, there was a need for such an extreme solution as consuming a heart demon–expelling truffle."

"Ahem, as much as I respect Elder Evelyn, she is not our leader," Grand Elder Mystshroud said. "We were brought together under Grand Elder Duskwalker, Evelyn's mother."

"She's dead," Stella casually replied. "And so is Nox. Which makes Evelyn the next in line, right? So she should now be promoted to the Grand Elder of the Duskwalker family."

Evelyn's eyes widened, and she felt her heart pound in her ears as she jumped to her feet. "Dead? How can my mother be dead?"

Stella sighed as if explaining things annoyed her. "Was she out on a stroll with guards when she went missing earlier today?"

"Yes…" Evelyn hesitantly nodded. "How do you know that?"

Stella tapped her nose. "The same way I know she's dead. Though don't be mistaken, I wasn't the one who killed her or had anything to do with her death. Nor is the Ashfallen Sect. The killer won't cause us any trouble, though. We are in a mutual pact of sorts. It was an unfortunate…accident. But don't worry, with our protection and resources, the Duskwalker family will soar to heights unreachable by relying on your mother to ascend."

"I…guess that's true?" Evelyn massaged her temples. This was all far too much to take in. How was she even supposed to feel about this?

Mother has been distant my whole life and even more so since Father's death. She locked herself away for years at a time in an endless pursuit of cultivation for a vain dream of revenge against the Lunarshade family. Whenever she did emerge from closed-door cultivation, she would demand more cultivation resources, even going so far as to empty my spatial rings and sell anything we had to the pavilion. I put up with it because she was the strongest in the family and our only hope at rising up again, but now that the Ashfallen Sect is here…

Evelyn briefly closed her eyes to offer a silent prayer for her mother.

You may have been a terrible person and an even worse mother, but I hope your death wasn't too painful, and don't worry. I will continue your revenge in your place. Rest in peace, and don't bother Grand Elder Blightbane with your nonsense—the poor guy has enough lunatics to listen to.

Opening her eyes with a sigh, Evelyn glanced at the gathered Grand Elders. "Assuming my mother and sister are dead, that makes me next in line. I may be inadequate compared to those who have led this family in the past, but I hope you can give me a chance." Evelyn gave a brief bow. "Of course, if either return alive, I will relinquish this temporary position. Is that acceptable?"

The Grand Elders exchanged a glance.

"Fine with me," Grand Elder Frostveil said.

"Me too," Grand Elder Mystshroud added. "Without your talentless mother around, we might have a chance to escape our terrible debts. The fear of your mother wouldn't keep those savage debt collectors at bay for much longer. They have already started putting bounties on our juniors' heads and torched the fields. It was only a matter of time until they came for us."

Evelyn nodded. "And what about you, Grand Elder Blightbane? Do you approve of me as a leader?"

The man briefly opened one of his eyes and studied her. "Hmm, for now."

Evelyn let out a sigh of relief. "Thank you."

Stella clapped her hands to draw everyone's attention. "Okay, with that sorted, let me tell you about the pills since Grand Elder Blightbane has already expressed interest. The pill bottles that I handed out earlier contain pills made from fruits we grow." She then held up one of the bottles with a flower emblem engraved into the porcelain. "This one is called Florist's Touch. It helps with the harvesting and handling of plants and would be heavily sought after by alchemists."

That does sound useful, but it's not very impressive, Evelyn thought as Stella showed a bottle with a sun emblem. *I wonder what that one does…*

"This pill dramatically increases the chance of enlightenment and comprehension of Daos." Stella then held up the other two bottles. One had the emblem of a root with spikes, and another had the emblem of a person sitting in a cultivating pose. "Neural Root pills help the cultivator feel and control every part of their body and boost their reaction time and control. Meanwhile, the Deep Meditation pill helps drown out the unnecessary whispers of Heaven while cultivating."

Evelyn was far more impressed with these pills. *Such powerful effects, and I get one pill for free with every bottle I sell? No way...*

"These are our low-range pills." Stella laughed at the Grand Elder's shocked reactions as she brought out a wooden box from her spatial ring and opened the lid before the Blightbane Grand Elder. "You asked if you could get your hands on that truffle, Grand Elder Blightbane? Well, here is your answer. It's a pill made from a quarter of a Heart Demon Expelling truffle, so the effect is less severe, but with multiple, you could achieve the same result Elder Evelyn experienced. Just make sure someone is nearby to help you dispose of your heart demons once they break free."

The Grand Elders shot glances at Diana, who licked her lips in return.

Stella snapped the lid shut. "These pills are far too dangerous to sell as of now, as even the Duskwalker family will struggle to shrug off the scrutiny if we sell them."

"Really?" Grand Elder Mystshroud said. "They just remove heart demons. That can't be enough to start a war..."

"What about a pill that permanently improves your spirit roots? Or an ointment that makes anyone beautiful?" Stella laughed. "You don't even understand the miracles our high-range pills can achieve."

Grand Elder Mystshroud gulped. "Even the 'low-range pills,' as you call them, have effects that sound far too good. I am sure they will sell for a high price, even at auction."

"Auction?" Stella tilted her head.

The man nodded. "Once verified, the pills are evaluated and sold in one of two ways. They can be sold through the Trading Hall or at an auction."

"Oh, really? What's the difference?"

"The Trading Hall is better for wholesale stuff, so if you plan to sell hundreds of cheap things, you will get the most eyes as it's where the merchants go to buy and sell. Meanwhile, an auction is better for selling one-off items or things with rarity."

"Interesting…"

"Um," Evelyn said, drawing Stella's attention. "I could take you to get the pills verified at the pavilion tomorrow? I know a Lotus Informant that is trustworthy."

Stella smiled. "Sure, that sounds good."

The portal in the middle of the room began to flicker as if inviting attention.

Stella chuckled. "Well, I better get going. My father is getting a little impatient the longer I hang around here, as he hates staying up at night, and he's the one keeping this portal open, so enjoy the pills, I guess? See you tomorrow!"

With that, Stella strode through the portal with Diana and Larry, the mythical spider in tow. The portal snapped closed, sending a cloud of dust and rustling the robes of the Grand Elders.

They exchanged a silent nod and dispersed toward their cultivation rooms to test the new pills.

Meanwhile, Evelyn collapsed into a nearby chair, too tired to even think. Her body and mind were in shock, and her life had changed.

"Well, that was something," she muttered as she stared up at the ceiling.

30
PILL EVALUATION

Stella pulled the hood of her cloak tighter over her masked face as she followed the group through the sea of mortals, shifting between the various halls of the pavilion open to them.

They had flown over here from the Duskwalker residence first thing in the morning. Once they had reached the city's outskirts, the group walked the rest of the way down winding backstreets to avoid their origins being known once they reached the Eternal Pursuit Pavilion.

I was going to offer to use Ash's portal, but I was curious how the others handled arriving at the pavilion in secret, so this was a good but tedious learning experience.

Elder Evelyn, the shortest of them, led the group. The other Grand Elders were also present, and they seemed to be in good spirits with a spring in their step.

"Diana, are you the one who was a Crimson Tracker?" Evelyn's voice tickled Stella's ear without her looking back. The defensive arrays weren't as powerful outside the halls, so they could use Qi to conceal their voices from others as they walked past thousands of mortals shouting at one another.

"Yes, I achieved the rank yesterday. Why do you ask?" Diana's voice was carried by a faint mist that made the inside of Stella's hood a little damp.

"My trustworthy informant operates out of the Crimson Tracker area. All of us are of the Crimson Tracker rank, so it's no problem for us to get in, but Stella will need to follow in as someone else's guest if she wants to use this informant as an Iron Seeker."

Stella clicked her tongue. "I won't be an Iron Seeker for long."

"Oh? Is that what you were scheming about last night with Ashlock?" Diana asked as she slowed her pace to walk alongside Stella. "I could hardly get any cultivation done with you chatting away on the bench."

None of the Grand Elders reacted to Diana's words, so they were likely directed solely at her.

"Well, I apologize, but Ash had a lot of questions and wanted to be caught up on everything that had happened." Stella smiled as she recalled how he had reacted to her stories from the day.

"So what's the plan? You didn't have time to fill me in yet as you were busy giving a quick morning lesson to Jasmine before we headed over here to join the Grand Elders on this trip to get the pills evaluated."

"A few things," Stella replied. "Ash wants me to scope out and accept as many bounties or missions as possible. He will then complete them on my behalf so I can meet the requirement to become a Crimson Tracker as soon as possible."

"Ashlock is going to do the missions for you?" Diana said with surprise and turned to face her, though her expression was hidden behind a black wooden mask.

Stella shrugged. "He said he was bored, so it would give him something to do."

"Bored? Can trees even get bored?" Diana chuckled. "Though I do wonder how he plans to complete the tasks on your behalf."

"What do you mean?" Stella tilted her head. "Ash can send Khaos to hunt down bounties, and he can grow any herbs an alchemist wants. Funnily enough, he would make a very good bounty hunter despite being a spirit tree so far away. If not for needing to win a duel within all these defensive arrays that keep him out to advance, I'm sure he would reach the Jade Sentinel rank before any of us."

Diana snorted. "That feels like cheating."

"Says the person who got a recommendation letter," Stella snapped back. "Some of us have to earn our ranks, you know?"

"Sure, sure. Whatever you say, Iron Seeker." Diana patted her shoulder. "Though for how long you two were talking, that's not all he asked of you, right?"

Stella flicked Diana's hand off her shoulder and huffed, "Of course not. He also wants to learn the value of the various currencies and how Yinxi Coins relate to them."

"That shouldn't be too hard with Evelyn here to ask." Diana sped up and tapped Evelyn on the shoulder.

"Yes?" Evelyn asked. "The Crimson Tracker area is just ahead. We will be there soon."

Stella glanced ahead and realized that while talking to Diana, they had gone down a path between the Iron Seeker pavilion and the massive Trading Hall that was the focus point of the mortal commerce on this mountain. This street was far emptier, with a few people loitering around, and at the far end, she could see a gate guarded by two cultivators with their swords openly drawn.

"I just wanted to ask you about the current value of a Yinxi Coin," Diana said, and her voice reached everyone. "We are new to the pavilion and are more used to trading in spirit stones or crowns, so we don't know what would be a good price for our pills."

"Oh," Evelyn said, turning her head over her shoulder to also look at Stella. "It's quite simple. A Yinxi Coin is worth around the same as a High-Grade Spirit Stone or three Dragon Crowns. But it's impossible to trade another currency for Yinxi Coins directly. You can only acquire them by selling goods and services to the pavilion or completing bounties and missions, so they are sort of more valuable."

So one Yinxi Coin equals a High-Grade Spirit Stone? If I remember correctly, you can buy a full meal for a High-Grade Spirit Stone, Stella mused. Having gone on a few shopping trips with Diana to Darklight City, she had slowly worked out the value of the different currencies.

Despite their fancy name, a High Grade Spirit Stone was still just a thumb-sized piece of rock with some untamed Qi inside. The high-grade part of the name was decided based on their color. If they were pure silver, they were filled with Qi and therefore considered high grade. Whereas if the color was dulled, they were worth far less and called low grade.

But apparently, because mortals struggled to sense Qi to determine the quality of a spirit stone and carrying around a bunch of rocks was inconvenient for mortals without spatial rings, they used Crowns, which were metal coins. They were far less valuable overall, with a Dragon Crown being worth a third of a High-Grade Spirit Stone.

Diana told me that cultivators trade almost exclusively in spirit stones since they can also be used as portable Qi sources or to create arrays. Cultivators also hate being tied to a currency regulated by mortals based on arbitrary values of metals, which differ depending on the region and local supply. Spirit stones, on the other hand, can be found beneath the earth along any ley line and will hold value so long as cultivators roam these lands.

It was all a bit of a mess, and Stella still struggled to understand the value of things, especially since the vendors often made up prices on the spot depending on the customer and their mood. *Most of the time, it's easier to just shrug and pay the asking price. Diana is much better at haggling than me, so I usually leave it to her.*

"Identify yourselves," the guard at the gate said sternly, which took Stella out of her thoughts. "This gate leads to the Crimson Trackers area and is off-limits to those who do not possess the necessary rank."

Evelyn was the first to step up, and Stella could only tell her apart from the others due to her height. Everyone wore identical black cloaks and jade masks, making differentiating them from behind a challenge. Only Diana stood out with her wooden mask.

We need to buy her a new jade mask once we have sold some pills. Stella held back a laugh at that thought. How had they *still* not sold any pills?

A silent exchange occurred between Evelyn and the guard as they both used Qi to conceal their voices. Evelyn showed the guard her pendant, and he checked something on a jade tablet before waving her through the gate. The Grand Elders lined up and underwent the same procedure before being waved through.

"Next!" the guard said, and Stella stepped up alongside Diana. "Two of you?"

Diana nodded. "Yes, she is my guest."

"All right, that is fine. They can stay for a day at most." The guard noted something on his jade tablet and glanced up. "What is your name and rank?"

Diana presented her pendant. "Diana Ravenborne of the Crimson Trackers."

The guard took her pendant for a moment to compare it against something on his tablet and nodded. "Everything checks out. You are free to pass." He returned the pendant to Diana and eyed Stella. "I have marked your guest with the defensive formation. It will force her out of the area by this time tomorrow."

Stella reluctantly nodded and followed Diana through the gate. A wave of Qi washed over her body as she felt the defensive formations relax in their suppression.

I guess they don't want to spend as many resources powering the defensive formations up here when there are so few people compared to near the Trading Hall, Stella thought as she looked around the Crimson Tracker area. The buildings were made from black wood and covered in lavish red and orange jade decor. It gave the place a sinister vibe as they walked down the wide, paved street as a group and passed by a few black-cloaked figures going about their business.

Entering the central square, Stella's eyes widened at what she saw planted. It was a large black bark tree with a canopy of lush scarlet leaves—a demonic tree. Red berries grew in clusters from its branches, and there was a potent acidic smell from the soil as they passed.

"That's not Ashlock's offspring, is it?" Diana asked in a hushed whisper.

Stella shook her head as she felt nothing from the tree. It didn't have a developed Soul Core, so it was just a typical demonic tree that could be found out in the wilderness, not a spirit tree. But she was still surprised to see one planted here. *I guess they grew one here for the aesthetic they are going for? Either way, I will let Ash know about this. Maybe he could turn it into his offspring without earning the attention of the pavilion.*

Demonic tree aside, the square was just as spacious as the one in the Iron Seeker area but was far less busy. There were the same pavilions and halls as before, but they were smaller as there was no need for mortals and their horse-drawn carts. There were only cultivators here, and if the pressure Stella felt when she passed one was to be believed, they were all in the Star Core Realm.

Taking a left, they headed toward a pavilion with a giant red phoenix made from jade hanging above the door. As with the Iron Seeker pavilion, shifty groups of cultivators were hanging out near the entrance and watching them as they passed.

Entering the Crimson Tracker pavilion, Stella felt a suffocating pressure that forced the Qi cycling in her body toward her Star Core. *I didn't know an array could get this powerful. This feels awfully like I am drowning. No wonder there are so few people hanging out in here.*

The room was practically deserted except for a red jade pillar in the center of the room with the bounties listed. Many Lotus Informants stood behind a counter encircling the pillar, but none had lines.

Evelyn gestured for everyone to wait while she spoke with a black-haired man. After conversing for a while, the Lotus Informant emerged from behind his counter and led them down a corridor to a private room in the back. Due to a large table in the center, it was hardly big enough for them to fit inside, but as the door closed behind them with a click, everyone began taking off their hoods and masks.

"Don't worry." Evelyn smiled at Stella and Diana as she noticed their apprehension about following their lead. "This person here is a distant cousin of mine and is trustworthy. There are also formations that protect the room, so we can't be spied on."

Trustworthy? Is it even possible for someone from your family to be trustworthy? I don't believe it, Stella scoffed in her mind but remained respectful when speaking aloud.

"We will be keeping our masks on," Stella replied. "Don't mind us."

"That's fine," Evelyn replied, turning back to the black-haired Lotus Informant. "Mark, we have four sets of pills we wish to evaluate today."

"Very well," Mark said, placing his hand on the round table. The runic formation inlaid into the wood came to life. "The cost of a pill evaluation is 10 Yinxi Coins unless the pill is of a new type unrecorded by the pavilion, in which case the fee is waived, but we will need to take a pill for testing."

"Always greedy for knowledge." Evelyn sighed as she brought out the four porcelain bottles. "These are the four we want to be evaluated."

Mark took the bottles, popped open the cork, and tipped them so a green-tinted pill rolled out into his palm. He inspected it closely between two fingers while humming. "Good coloring, and the scent is strong. This pill is of high grade and made by a talented alchemist with good ingredients." He placed the pill on a highlighted area in the center of the table, and a golden diagram appeared floating in the air alongside a list of ingredients.

"Qi Flowering Grass, Starlight Lotus…" Mark rotated the diagram, showing the inside layers of the pill and how it was made while muttering off the list of ingredients. "Hold on, what is this at the center?" He frowned as he brought out a jade tablet. "This fruit isn't listed in our records. What is it?"

"Does the pavilion buy such information?" Stella asked.

Mark shook his head. "Not here. All I can do is not charge you for this evaluation and pay you for the pill we have to take for testing. If you don't tell me about this fruit, I can't approve it for sale within the pavilion."

So this is how the pavilion acquired such a wealth of knowledge over the years. They make it sound like they are doing you a favor by not charging you their internal currency, which you can only acquire by playing by their rules.

"Fine," Stella said. "That is an enlightenment fruit. When diluted into a pill, it gives a small boost that helps a cultivator reach enlightenment and a deeper comprehension of Daos."

Mark noted what she said and nodded. "I see. Can you tell me where and how this enlightenment fruit is grown?"

"Does that affect the evaluation?"

Mark shook his head.

"Then I will not."

"Fair enough." Mark noted that down and put away the tablet. "I will need to take this pill away and feed it to a test subject to determine the extent of its effect. Many wealthy cultivators will pay high prices for anything that gives them an edge over others when it comes to cultivating, no matter how small, so I can guess this will be a popular one."

"You said you would buy the pill before feeding it to a test subject, right?" Stella asked. "What value would you guess this pill has?"

Mark stroked his chin, thinking. "If we are to go off the market value of a high-grade pill with this effect, I would say 10 Yinxi Coins per pill would be reasonable. Of course, it could be higher or lower after I verify the effect. Do you want to wait or get paid now?"

So 100 Yinxi Coins per bottle. Not bad at all, considering we can make an unlimited number of them.

Stella shrugged. "It's Evelyn's pill, so she can decide. I am fine with waiting till after the evaluation."

"Me too," Evelyn quickly replied. "I believe it will be worth more than only 10 Yinxi Coins."

"Very well, then." Mark stored the pill away in his spatial ring and handed back the porcelain bottle before moving on to the next bottle. "Let's continue the evaluation for these three."

Stella licked her lips. She could almost smell the money they were about to be rolling in.

31
A DARK GOD

"**Welcome back,**" Ashlock said to Stella and Diana as they stepped through a portal with {Abyssal Whispers}. Neither girl so much as winced as his presence bloomed in their minds. "**Stella, did you complete the tasks I gave you?**"

"You bet." Stella yawned as she stretched her back. *"Though that was more exhausting than I expected... All the pills were evaluated, I scouted out a list of bounties and missions, and I figured out the value of the currencies."*

"**All in a single morning? Good work,**" Ashlock replied. "**Catch me up and then go check on your disciple before she has to go home for dinner. She's cultivating in her hut and said she had something to show you.**"

"Oh? I wonder what my dear disciple has to show me." Stella side-eyed the stone hut as she strode to sit and relax on the bench under his vast canopy. As her spatial ring flashed with power and she lined up four pill bottles, the later afternoon sunlight made her short blond hair glow slightly as the wind played with it. She hummed to herself a tune as she prepared her little presentation for him.

"**I've missed having you around over the last few days,**" Ashlock said. Was this how parents felt when their children went to university for the first time? Home suddenly felt so quiet and empty without the usual people around.

Stella glanced up at his canopy of rustling leaves with a smile.

"That sounds funny coming from you. Aren't I loud and annoying to the point you drop fruit on my head to shut me up?"

"That's true." Ashlock chuckled. **"But without you around, the silence is deafening."**

"Well, I will bother you more than usual to make up for it." Stella smiled. *"Though you don't have to worry so much. Once the Duskwalker residence is all set up as our proxy and I have reached the Crimson Tracker rank, I will have little reason to spend much time at the Eternal Pursuit Pavilion. I have a disciple back here to look after and other things to focus on."*

"That's true. But what about reaching the rank of Jade Sentinel?"

Stella shrugged. *"What benefits are there to reaching a higher rank anyway? I want to escape the Iron Seeker area because it's full of corrupt Lotus Informants, too many mortals, and too limited in the missions and bounties I can take. As for becoming a Jade Sentinel? Since I must complete a hundred missions, it will be a grind that will take some time. It's better for someone like Diana to focus on reaching that rank for now than me."*

"I agree," Ashlock replied as he looked at the demoness standing nearby, watching the sun hover over the distant mountain range with her arms crossed.

Glancing over her shoulder at Stella's words, Diana grinned. *"Yeah, just leave it to me. I'm sure there are some unforeseen benefits to reaching the top rank of the Eternal Pursuit Pavilion that are yet to be discovered. If that is all, I will head off now."* Her giant raven wings of feathered darkness sprouted from her shoulders, and she took to the skies. *"I am going to check on how the mortal branch of the Ashfallen Trading Company is coming along now that we have rough values of the pills. See you two later."*

With that, she was gone, soaring through the sky toward Ashfallen City.

"That reminds me," Ashlock said, returning his attention to Stella, **"where is Larry? Why didn't he follow you two through the portal I made?"**

Stella snorted. *"Funny story, actually. Remember how I told you about Elysia? The crazy Mystshroud girl that fought Diana with one of Maple's siblings?"*

"Yeah?"

"Well, she forced her way into the meeting room alongside those people who had been chasing us to inform the Grand Elders about Diana, and then she saw Larry. Despite Grand Elder Mystshroud's efforts, Elysia couldn't be convinced that Diana didn't make Larry out of mystic Qi."

"Elysia thought Larry was Diana's summon?" Ashlock felt a headache coming. **"I hope the misunderstanding was cleared up."**

"Nope!" Stella held back a laugh. *"Elysia promptly prostrated herself before Diana and begged to be her disciple."*

"What the…? How did Diana respond?" Ashlock asked. From what Stella had told him, Elysia had displayed a cultivation level comparable to Diana during the duel, and Diana knew nothing about mystic Qi, so it would be a rather fruitless master-disciple relationship.

Stella failed to hold back anymore and burst out laughing. *"Oh heavens, I wish you were there, Tree. I have never seen Diana so disgusted. She looked down at Elysia as if she were a dead bug on her shoe and outright refused her, saying she wasn't even worth looking at. I think Diana was harboring some pent-up frustration from their duel and took it out on her."*

"That does make sense…" Ashlock chuckled. **"Elysia refused to surrender by abusing the duel's rules, forcing Diana to waste a lot of Qi and become Pluto's plaything for ten minutes. So it's no wonder she would have such a reaction, though I fail to see what this has to do with Larry."**

"Oh, I was getting to that." Stella leaned back on the bench with a big grin. *"It seems that pet of yours has gotten smarter since his evolution. Larry stayed behind after Diana rejected Elysia to convert the Mystshroud family's cult into worshiping him and you."*

"What…Larry has become a cult leader?" Ashlock imagined Larry in a dark cave surrounded by a cult, all praying to him. **"I suppose that's fine? It's probably for the best that Larry stays protecting the Duskwalker residence for now anyway while we get everything set up."**

Stella nodded. *"That's what I thought."*

"Anyway, we are getting off track. What did the pavilion evaluate the pills at?" Ashlock asked with a hint of excitement. He felt like a student waiting to hear back about a test he thought he did very well on.

Stella glanced down at the lined-up bottles of pills. *"Err, the Enlightenment and Deep Meditation pills were both evaluated at 10 Yinxi Coins per pill, if I remember correctly. However, this number should be far higher once the effect of the pills is fully tested. But the Lotus Informant said that was the competitive price for pills that directly help with cultivation."*

"Interesting. Though I doubt the price will change much after the evaluation."

"Really?" Stella tilted her head. *"I thought it might go a little higher, considering how high quality the ingredients you grow are."*

"My fruits are impressive for a cultivation resource, but we use one fruit to make ten pills, greatly reducing the effect. It's for the best. We don't want to attract as much attention with these mass-produced, low-grade pills," Ashlock replied. **"That aside, how much are Yinxi Coins worth?"**

Stella looked down at her hands and started counting on her fingers. *"According to Elder Evelyn, one Yinxi Coin is equivalent to around one High-Grade Spirit Stone or three Dragon Crowns, which is enough to buy a full-course meal. But trying to convert between them is rather pointless as Yinxi Coins can only be used within the Eternal Pursuit Pavilion."*

"I see," Ashlock replied as he fell into thought.

"Due to how bountiful food is in this world of Qi, meals should be rather cheap. From what I have seen by scouting out the menus outside restaurants in Darklight City, you can get an entire meal for the equivalent of around ten dollars back on Earth," Ashlock mused. "So that means one Yinxi Coin is worth around $10? With that in mind, a single one of these pills sells for $100 or $1,000 for an entire bottle of ten… and I can produce hundreds of bottles a day of these watered-down pills. Who the hell said money doesn't grow on trees? I am about to be a very rich tree!"

"Tree? What are you so happy about?" Stella raised a brow. *"I can see your branches wiggling slightly."*

"Ahem, nothing much." Ashlock dismissed Stella's words with a cough. **"What about the other two pills?"**

"Not quite as high. Neural Root was valued at five, while the

Florist's Touch was valued at two Yinxi Coins per pill." Stella shrugged. *"Apparently, alchemists hate buying pills from others, hence the lower value. Whereas Neural Root needed more testing to determine a good price."*

Ashlock was honestly surprised anybody would be willing to pay the equivalent of $20 for a pill that let them handle plants slightly better. The fruit's full effect was quite useful, but it was quite weak when split between ten pills.

"Honestly, it's surprising how expensive being a cultivator is," Ashlock mused. "No wonder only noble families that exploit mortals for labor can afford to cultivate to the higher realms. Just a small Qi-gathering formation needed a thousand High-Grade Spirit stones, so around $10,000 in Earth money, and that's not even factoring in labor! It took Douglas and Stella a few hours, and I bet cultivators aren't usually cheap to hire as they have to use up their Qi. Hell, that technique manual Stella bought from the merchants that contained the knowledge of short-range portals was a thousand Dragon Crowns, or around $3,000." Ashlock snorted in his mind. "For a book that was more poetry and nonsense than an actual guide and once learned only let the cultivator make portals between their hands, that was a steep ask."

"Regarding bounties and missions, I noted down quite a few," Stella said, drawing his attention as she pulled out a parchment. *"I told Seth today that I would be going along with him tomorrow to kill Evelyn Duskwalker's husband, Albis Lunarshade."*

"I don't trust him at all. Be extra careful, and remember I can't help you directly."

Stella rolled her eyes. *"I know. I don't trust him, either, but he seems to be the only one with a lead on Albis, and it's hard to say no to that 10,000 Yinxi Coin bounty."* Her eyes then widened. *"Oh, I forgot to mention I saw a demonic tree planted in the Crimson Tracker area. You should totally make it one of your offspring!"*

"Is that even possible? What about the defensive formations?"

Stella shrugged. *"I noticed the defensive formations were weaker in the Crimson Tracker area than in the Iron Seeker area. Although Qi is quite suppressed on the mountain, I don't think people would find it too strange if the demonic tree there turned into a weak spirit tree."*

"Okay, I will look into it."

Ashlock knew nothing could stop his ethereal roots, not even the extensive defensive formations of the Eternal Pursuit Pavilion. It was just that he didn't want to earn the ire of a Nascent Soul Realm cultivator like the Celestial Warden, but if a demonic tree was already there that he could sneak a root to, that made it easier.

"As for bounties and missions, you wanted me to focus on people or monsters with fire, water, earth, wind, and metal affinities, right?" Stella asked as she looked down at the parchment in her hand.

"Yes, I need to devour cultivators or monsters with those affinities to form an Inner World and advance to the Nascent Soul Realm," Ashlock replied. He wanted to form his Inner World as soon as possible, ideally before the Mystic Realm later this month.

"Huh, I thought cultivators formed an Inner World at the Monarch Realm?"

"Really?"

Stella shrugged. *"It must be a tree thing. You are already ageless, so I suppose there's not much interest in forming a second soul to escape the deathly grasp of time. Wait, if my mother is the World Tree, does that mean I won't age, too?"*

"You are growing up so fast that I sometimes wonder where the little girl who was so clueless about the world went." Ashlock sighed. **"I wouldn't put too much truth on that cosmic being's words until we find your father."**

Stella nodded. *"Eight hundred Yinxi Coins, and I might get a lead by learning his name from the bloodline records. Killing Albis tomorrow will give me enough money, but if that doesn't work out, the first payment collection from the Grand Elders selling our pills should be enough."* She looked to the horizon momentarily before returning her attention to the parchment. *"Anyway, I found quite a few suitable bounties and missions for you…"*

"Quite a spectacular sight…" Ashlock mused. He was using {Eye of the Tree God} to gaze down at a fissure running through a mountain range as if some godly being had tried to crack the mountain apart like an egg.

At the mountain's base and near the opening to the fissure, he could see a fortified town protected by formations populated mostly by mortals with a few cultivators here and there. It was a mining city, evident by the constant stream of mortals hauling bags of rocks on their backs out of the fissure and into the town.

Stella had given him a long list of bounties and missions, and he had chosen a mission that had led him here.

Bounties were more problematic for him to pursue for now as he wouldn't be able to recognize his target even if he saw them standing out in the street. Tracking down a bounty required a lot of talking to those close to the target or stalking places they were known to frequent. It was not his area of expertise, but hunting down monsters and gathering plants? That he could do.

"This looks like the right place. Ironclad town south of the Tainted Cloud Sect." Ashlock shifted his view away from the town and followed the line of mortals into the fissure. Evening sunlight barely reached here, so the mortals relied on lamps hammered into the silvery spirit stone veins for light.

The pay for this mission was terrible, considering it was to kill a Star Core–level wyvern, but Ashlock didn't care. The monster apparently possessed the wind affinity, one of the affinities he needed to form his Inner World. The fissure was also home to a metal affinity flower he planned to harvest when nobody was looking so he could make a grove for Ryker and Sebastian.

"Night draws near! Keep your eyes and ears open!" an earth cultivator supervisor shouted over the constant beat of mining. *"The wyvern may show up again tonight. If it does, remember to run for your lives and leave the spirit stones behind. The wyvern only seeks your flesh and blood. We can collect the dropped spirit stones tomorrow. Do I make myself clear?"*

There was a chorus of agreement that came across as fatigued and depressed. Ashlock went closer to one particular miner who was discussing something with the person beside him.

"We have already lost so many to that beast," the man hissed through gritted teeth as he raised his pick overhead and swung down, dislodging a piece of dulled spirit stone. *"It's too dangerous. Why do they keep us mining instead of dealing with that fucking wyvern?"*

The other man grunted. *"The leader claimed he sent a request to the Eternal Pursuit Pavilion for help, you know?"*

"Don't make me laugh." The man snorted and shook his head as he picked up the spirit stone he had mined and chucked it into a sack at his feet. *"Whatever reward that frugal bastard offered would be far too low for a competent bounty hunter to travel all the way out here. It's not until we are all dead that he might consider it a problem worth hiring a Crimson Tracker to deal with."*

The other man shrugged. *"And what will you do about it? Run away, only to get caught and used as a test subject for pill experiments or target practice? Don't make me laugh. Just keep mining if you want to keep your head and your family fed—"*

A roar from a great beast echoed through the fissure, and Ashlock could sense something fast approaching through the darkness like an arrow. A howling wind threw up a wave of dust, announcing the arrival of the monster he had come to kill.

"It's coming!" the earth cultivator shouted before he began to sink into the stone, leaving the mortals behind to their deaths.

"Oh shit." Both miners he had been listening to exchanged looks, dropped their pickaxes, and turned to run alongside the hundreds of others slaving away below. *"We are going to fucking die!"* one of them shouted as he scrambled toward the light.

The wave of dust was pushed aside as a looming shadow revealed itself to be a dark green–scaled wyvern. It was around the size of a bus, with a maw of shark-like teeth. A ball of condensed wind was gathering like a dragon's breath within its mouth, and if fired, it would annihilate everyone trying to escape.

Ashlock needed the monster's corpse in good condition so Stella could prove completion of the mission and he could guarantee enough Star Core wind Qi to satisfy his Inner World requirement, which limited his attack options.

"First, I need to stop this dumb lizard from moving," Ashlock muttered as he surged spatial Qi through his roots and opened up a massive rift above all of the fleeing miners. Through it, he glared at the wyvern with his {Demonic Eye} and slammed his entire presence down upon it.

The wyvern let out a strange cry as its eyes widened in horror. It lost control and veered to the left, smashing into the side of the fissure and diving down to the ground in a shower of rubble.

Ashlock used telekinesis to pause all the flying rocks from pulverizing the fleeing mortals before hurling them back at the downed wyvern.

"This almost feels unfair," Ashlock thought as hundreds of black vines shot through the giant portal and wrapped tightly around the injured wyvern limbs. The wyvern struggled and thrashed around, which was annoying, so Ashlock crushed its neck with his vines. It let out a final shriek as the life left its eyes. With the corpse secured, he used a mixture of his vines and telekinesis to haul the monster through his rift and back to Red Vine Peak.

"I should grab some flowers while I am here." Ashlock hummed to himself as he used his vines to smash at the rock and free a few flowers, which he also floated through his rift. With the goods secured and the mortals safe, he thought, "I wonder how the mortals are reacting to my benevolence…"

He looked through the portal with his {Demonic Eye} and saw hundreds of miners had frozen in fear. They were all looking up at the rift looming overhead with blood tricking from their noses and wide eyes.

"A dark god has come to save us," one of them muttered, starting a chain reaction. In a wave, the miners all started speaking about a dark god, and some even began prostrating before the rift and calling him the all-seeing gaze.

"I think this is my hint to leave," Ashlock said, closing the rift and withdrawing his presence from the area. Back on Red Vine Peak, Jasmine was poking her head out of the doorway of the hut with a look of awe at the dead wyvern.

32
CIVIL UNREST

Jasmine shouted back into the hut, *"Master! Your dad brought back a big lizard."*

"Already?" Stella called from inside. Trudging out of the hut, she yawned and looked at the dead beast with some surprise. *"That was faster than I expected. How did the hunt go?"*

"Pretty good. Once I arrived at Ironclad town, I was lucky I didn't have to wait long for the monster to appear. Though in my haste to down the beast and reduce casualties, I might have caused trouble for you."

Stella narrowed her eyes at his trunk. "What did you do?"

"I might have accidentally started a cult of demon-worshiping mortals who believed I am a dark god who came to save them."

Stella slowly nodded. *"Right...I thought something like that might happen."*

"What is that supposed to mean?"

Stella shrugged. *"I didn't even need to see your fight to guess how they came to such a conclusion... Despite your best intentions, all of your techniques and ways of using them come across in a certain way that could lead to such a misunderstanding. If anything, I am surprised this didn't happen sooner."*

"I feel oddly insulted," Ashlock grumbled. **"Sure, some of my techniques are a little sinister, but to call me a dark god feels a little…"**

"Master, what are you talking about?" Jasmine asked with big eyes as she looked up at Stella and tugged a little on her sleeve.

"Mhm?" Stella glanced down at her disciple with a smile. *"I am talking telepathically with Tree. It seems he started a cult by accident. Don't you agree he fits the theme of a dark god quite well?"*

Jasmine looked at Ashlock's towering trunk, the wyvern still bound in black vines covered in thorns, and then finally back at Stella. "Yes."

"Don't agree with her!" Ashlock sighed. **"She didn't even hesitate…"**

Stella walked over to the wyvern corpse, laughing and with a dagger in hand. *"Good answer, Jasmine. Now come help your master."*

Jasmine scampered after her master and eyed the shifting, thorn-covered vines and dead wyvern with concern.

"What do you need my help with?"

Stella stood before the corpse and read a parchment in her hand. After triple-checking it, she nodded and pocketed it in her spatial ring. *"To complete the mission, I need a wyvern scale, tooth, and eye to prove its death. The pavilion will independently verify with Ironclad town if the wyvern threatening them is also gone."* Stella glanced over her shoulder. *"Could you pick a wyvern scale for your master? Make sure it's in good condition."*

"O-Okay." Jasmine approached the wyvern and touched its dark green scales. *"It's beautiful,"* she muttered as she ran her fingertips along the scales, tracing the bumps and drips in each one. *"I thought all monsters were scary, but this one is cool."*

Stella watched her disciple with a light smile tugging at her lips.

Jasmine's hand fell to her side, and she turned around. *"Master, I feel bad for the monster."* She watched Stella's reaction intently. *"Is that wrong?"*

Stella shook her head and patted Jasmine on the head. *"It's a naïve view, perhaps, but not a wrong one. Why do you feel bad for it?"*

"You asked me to pick which scale is best, but every one of its scales is so intertwined that taking one out would ruin it."

Stella looked at the wyvern from head to tail and nodded. *"You're right. It would ruin its majesty. But my dear disciple, I can't complete my mission and advance in rank if I don't tear one off and show it to the pavilion. You understand that, right?"*

Jasmine looked at her feet. *"So you killed this majestic wyvern for* a mission? It feels like such a waste. It could have grown into an even cooler dragon one day if given the time."

Stella crouched before Jasmine and put a hand on her shoulder. *"You're right. One day, it could have become a majestic dragon lording over the skies, but we robbed it of that future to progress our own. That's just how things are sometimes. The strongest are the ones that decide the fates of others."*

"It still feels unfair."

"Life's not fair," Stella said seriously. *"The sooner you learn and accept this truth, the easier your life will become. Sometimes, you will have to kill others to live or leave those you love behind to survive. Life is full of difficult choices that you will have to face and decide for yourself how to deal with them. Think back to Slymere. Your family was caught up in a fight that had nothing to do with you, right? What happened?"*

"Dad almost died," Jasmine mumbled.

"He should have died, but Tree saved him. If not for our intervention, there's a good chance all three of you would be dead, and you would have never become a cultivator. But what about the other families of Slymere that didn't get saved because we just so happened to be focused on you three at the time? Is it fair you survived and they died?"

Jasmine slowly looked up and locked eyes with Stella. *"No…"*

"See? Life isn't fair, but there are ways we can prevent being bullied by the world and our fate." Stella gestured to the wyvern with her chin. *"This fella got greedy. He would still be alive if he had devoured a few mortals and then moved on to another feeding ground. Instead, he earned the ire of the mine owner and had a bounty placed on his head. It would have been fine if he was a Nascent Soul Realm dragon, but he is a weak wyvern, so his fate was sealed. Do you understand the lesson I am giving, disciple?"*

Jasmine nodded. *"Don't attract unnecessary attention or be so strong it doesn't matter."*

"You're so smart!" Stella ruffled her hair. *"Now, do you think you could pick a scale for me?"*

Jasmine nodded and meticulously inspected every scale within her reach as the wyvern's corpse towered over her, casting a looming shadow.

While she did that, Ashlock had analyzed the metal flower he had taken from the fissure. It was called an Ironclad Rose, likely the reason behind the town's name. Expending some Qi, he created a grove on the mountain ridge and would inform Sebastian and Ryker about it later.

"This one," Jasmine said eventually, pointing at the dark green wyvern scale before her.

Stella smiled. *"Good choice, Jasmine. Why don't you try and pull it free?"*

"Okay." Jasmine wrapped her fingers around the scale's edges and tried to pull. She grunted as her muscles strained and her face reddened. Green-tinted Qi wreathed her arms and legs as she put her whole back into it, but the scale refused to loosen. With one final pull, she lost her grip and fell on her back, panting. *"I give up."* Spreading out her arms like a starfish, she glanced over to Stella. *"Sorry, Master, it's impossible."*

Stella shook her head with a laugh. *"Nothing's impossible, Jasmine."* With that, she walked over and effortlessly pulled free the scale with one finger as if it were some loose wallpaper and waved it over her disciple. *"See?"*

Jasmine pouted. *"I loosened it for you."*

"Uh huh." Stella smirked. *"If you say so."*

"Stella, could you stop showing off and hurry up with the harvesting? I can't hold back my hunger forever, you know," Ashlock said, half joking. He was itching to see what absorbing the wind affinity soul would do, and this wyvern corpse was making his vines drool.

"Oh, my bad, Tree." Stella deposited the scale into her spatial ring and jumped up onto the wyvern's back. She walked along its spine to its head and crouched next to its eye. *"Wakey wakey, wyvern."* Stella forced its eyelids apart and plunged her hands in with a crazed grin. Using telekinesis to keep it together, she removed the wyvern's eye, which looked like a blood-filled jelly ball, and stowed it away. Burning away the eye juices on her hands with soul flames, she hopped down to its mouth.

Jasmine watched all of this from the floor in horror. In seconds, her face had shifted from bright red to ghostly white.

Unaware of her disciple's expressions, Stella picked out a random tooth the size of Jasmine and easily ripped it free. It was stored away in a flash of silver, and the harvest was complete. *"Okay, Tree, all done. Enjoy your meal."*

"Thanks." Ashlock didn't hold back and began to devour the corpse. Digestive fluids were secreted from his vines, dissolving the thick scales and tough flesh with a hiss. There were also the sounds of bones cracking as the vines tightened their grip.

"Isn't it time you returned home for dinner, Jasmine?" Stella asked the girl.

She slowly nodded. *"Yes...though I have lost my appetite."*

"Why?" Stella tilted her head. *"It's not good for a growing girl like you to skip out on meals. Go home and make sure to eat a lot."*

"Okay..." Jasmine got up, and on wobbly legs, she walked past the dissolving wyvern and jumped down into the ethereal root tunnel that led to Nox near her home.

"Poor girl." Stella shook her head as she went to sit on the bench. *"Reduced to such a state after trying to free a wyvern scale."*

"I'm not sure if that was the root of the problem…" Ashlock replied.

"What is, then?" Stella asked sweetly.

"You looked rather insane while taking the wyvern apart. Maybe you scared her," Ashlock suggested.

Stella snorted and waved him off. *"I have no idea what you are talking about. If anything, your way of eating is likely the reason."*

"What, no way!"

"Then we can agree to disagree," Stella said, lying horizontally on the bench and closing her eyes. *"I'm going to grab some rest. Today was too much for me."*

"Wait before you sleep. What did Jasmine want to speak to you about?" Ashlock asked.

"Oh, she said she still didn't know what affinity to pick and wanted to experience some more things to give her ideas." Stella looked up at his canopy with a smile. *"I am glad she is putting so much thought into it. I will have her speak more with Elaine and maybe show her some things like alchemy to see if that interests her."*

"Good idea."

"Mhm," Stella hummed in agreement as she closed her eyes again and started breathing softly after a few minutes.

"Have a good sleep," Ashlock muttered to himself as he had

already withdrawn his presence from her mind. The sun was setting, so he would also sleep soon under the nine moons. But first, he needed to deal with the system message that had appeared in his mind.

[Absorb Wind Star Core for Inner World? If so, you will gain no Sacrificial Credits.]

"No sacrificial credits? Hmm, I suppose that makes sense since all the Qi I absorb will be going toward my Inner World."

Ashlock accepted the prompt and looked within his own soul at the cloud of untamed Qi, which the system called a Chaos Nebula. Once he fed it the required Star Cores and Sacrificial Credits, it should form into an Inner World.

He watched as wind Qi flowed through his roots and into his soul, but instead of being transformed into spatial Qi and joining his Qi reserves, the wind Qi phased through his soul unchanged and mingled with the Chaos Nebula. With the introduction of wind Qi, the previously static cloud of untamed Qi began rotating inside his soul and gaining speed until it turned into a full-on storm.

His system was then updated.

[Requirements to turn Chaos Nebula into an Inner World:
3429 / 10000 Sacrificial Credits
0 / 1 Absorbed Fire Star Cores
0 / 1 Absorbed Water Star Cores
0 / 1 Absorbed Earth Star Cores
1 / 1 Absorbed Wind Star Cores
0 / 1 Absorbed Metal Star Cores]

[Rewards upon formation of the Inner World:
You will ascend to the Nascent Soul Realm.
The System will be upgraded with new features.
{Transpiration of Heaven and Chaos [B]} will be upgraded.
Your attacks will carry the weight of your Inner World behind them, and your rate of cultivation will increase the more you develop your Inner World.]

"One down, four to go. Not bad. The others shouldn't be too hard to come by. The bigger concern is the sacrificial credits," Ashlock mused. "The monster farm has been netting me a few hundred credits a day, so it's only a matter of time, but it's still far too slow."

Luckily, he had a solution. Using telekinesis, he floated up a parchment lying near his root and read the list. It was the bounties and missions that Stella had written out for him. A lot offered really crappy pay, which was likely why they had been left unclaimed by other bounty hunters. But he didn't care about that. Some of them had details regarding locations with lots of monsters, and they also gave him a good reason to break into and assassinate the Elders of other families in Nightshade City.

"I will complete some of these tomorrow, but now it's time for sleep." Ashlock activated {Nocturnal Genesis}, and he entered the dreamscape. Looking up at the moons, as usual, one was lit with a purple glow while the others were dull. "So it has nothing to do with my Inner World, then. How can I get the other moons to change their affinity?"

A mystery for another time.

Glancing over to the north, he saw Nox in her field of white flowers. Under her canopy was her shadow dryad looking up at the sky in the dreamscape while a shadowy hand rested on her bark.

"Enjoying the view?"

Nox seemed startled as she looked around. *"Ashlock?"*

"Yes, it's me."

"Oh, hello." Nox's shadow waved in his direction. *"Did you need something from me?"*

"Nothing in particular, I just came to check on you. Have you got anything to tell me?" Ashlock yawned. It was so relaxing and pleasant in the dreamscape that the weight of sleep was heavy and warm. He felt ready to drift off.

Nox's shadow looked down the mountainside where Ashfallen City was in the real world. *"I do have some concerns. I know I was only tasked with protecting this place from our enemies, but there is a lot of civil unrest in the city. I fear if things go on, a war is more likely to start from within."*

"Really?" Ashlock paused. **"I thought the Redclaws were handling it."**

"They are trying their best but are outnumbered thousands to one. The mortals fear to raise concerns with the cultivators, and the cultivators don't know how to deal with mortal disputes except with violence or money." Nox's shadow lowered her head. "Gangs have already started to form, bullying others for their share of the free food and selling it in bulk to Darklight City."

Ashlock didn't understand. He had saved these people and given them free food and shelter, and he even sent the Redclaws to police the city, so where had it gone wrong?

"I have even protected a few mortals from being kidnapped on this mountainside as they are nearby enough for me to send my shadow fiends after them," Nox continued. "But from what I can tell, the situation is far worse down in the old mines. I can even sense some Qi types other than fire Qi that might be escaping the senses of the Redclaws."

"So rogue cultivators have finally started moving in under my nose…"

Ashlock realized his fears had come to fruition. A freshly formed city of a hundred thousand people was bound to breed a darker side. The question was how should he fix this issue? He had the power to turn the city into a paradise or hell. He could come in with a heavy hand or turn a blind eye. With so many options, was there a correct solution?

"Thank you for telling me this, Nox. I haven't given the city the attention it deserves recently, and you have given me a lot to think about."

Nox's shadow bowed. *"I am just happy to have been a help, and if you don't mind me asking, how is my sister?"*

"Being well taken care of," Ashlock assured her. **"Duskwalker will soon rise once more under the banner of the Ashfallen Sect. In fact, Stella will be killing Albis Lunarshade tomorrow."**

"That's a relief. Evelyn will finally be free from that monster." Nox's shadow leaned against her bark, gazing at the nine moons. *"I would love to meet Evelyn again one day and say I'm sorry for forcing that fate onto her."*

Ashlock hummed in agreement. **"That day may come sooner than you think."**

33

SOLVING POLITICS THE STELLA WAY

Stella was in a terrible mood.

It was the crack of dawn, evident by warm sunlight streaking through crude glass, illuminating the bare stone room. She sat at a table with other central figures of the Ashfallen Sect on a wooden chair with no padding that dug into her back, successfully aggravating her mood further.

*How did I get dragged into **another** meeting? I thought I told Ash to leave all meetings to Diana, yet here I am in another stupid meeting. Maybe I should just stand up and leave. It's not like anyone would stop me…*

"Master," Jasmine whispered as she tugged at her sleeve, "if you frown all the time, you will get wrinkles."

Stella side-eyed her disciple, who was sitting beside her. "Who taught you to make jokes like that?"

Jasmine tilted her head. "Joke? I'm being serious. My mother told me it was true."

Stella snorted. "Well, unlike your mother, I have access to unlimited skin improvement truffles, so I don't fear wrinkles. I can frown as much as I want."

"If you say so." Jasmine shrugged and looked away.

Stella felt her eye twitch. Was she really being made fun of by a kid whose feet couldn't even reach the floor right now? *Why did I think bringing Jasmine to this meeting would make it more tolerable?* Stella scowled as she crossed her arms and leaned back on her chair. As she swayed back and forth, causing the chair to creak, her scowl slowly dissipated, and she relaxed her facial muscles. *Will I really get wrinkles?*

"I'm sorry for the delay, everyone." Elder Brent quickly walked into the room and sat on the opposite side of the round table. "There was a dispute with the farmers today who were unhappy with how we were taking their crops to feed the citizens, but it has been resolved for now."

There was a moment of silence before a sudden pressure descended on the room.

"Now that everyone is here, we can start." Ash's voice thundered through Stella's mind. She was unfazed alongside Diana, Douglas, and Elaine.

The Redclaw Grand Elder, Elder Brent, and Sebastian took out Mind Fortress pills and downed them. Meanwhile, Julian, Ryker, and Jasmine glanced around in confusion as Ash had spared them from his technique.

Elder Margret finished gulping down the pills and spoke to those left out. "The Immortal just contacted us telepathically. I will relay what he says to you three via my Qi so as not to bother the others," she said with a smile.

Julian gave her a nod. "That is appreciated. Though I have to ask out of curiosity, if this is a meeting regarding the city's development and future, what is my daughter doing here?"

"Dad!" Jasmine shouted at her father.

"Don't get me wrong, Jaz. I don't disapprove of your presence here, but I thought you were busy practicing cultivation from dawn till dusk. So I wondered what the purpose of you attending this meeting is."

Jasmine glanced back at Stella. "Actually, I had the same question, Master. Why am I here?"

Stella smirked. "How else will I have you attend these meetings in my place in the future? As my disciple, it's only right that you have to suffer, ahem, I mean attend these meetings with me."

"Master," Jasmine loudly whispered, "you are letting your true thoughts out."

"I'm about to let a lot more of my true thoughts out if this meeting drags on any longer than it has to because of pointless questions." Stella glared at Julian.

Julian backed off with a smile. "Looks like you have your work cut out for you, Jaz."

"What is that supposed to mean?" Jasmine grumbled at her dad.

Elder Brent coughed awkwardly. "I agree with Mistress Stella. We are all busy people, so let's not focus on unimportant details. Immortal, if you may, what have you summoned us here for today?

"Stella, stop causing trouble."

"I am not—"

"Ahem, getting on topic, last night, I was notified by Nox that there is widespread civil unrest among the populace of Ashfallen City, with gangs starting to form that have attempted kidnappings and even stolen food. There are also unknown cultivators gathering in the mines with unknown origins and goals," Ash said. The mood around the table turned more serious. *"I have brought you all here today to work out a solution to this civil unrest, how to deal with the cultivators, and to improve the lives of those in Ashfallen City."*

Stella glared at Elder Brent and the Grand Elder. "Isn't the security of the city your job? What has your failings got to do with me?"

The Redclaws exchanged a glance.

Elder Brent bowed toward the table. "I apologize deeply for my failings."

"Apologies are useless. I want solutions," Ash said. *"Elder Brent, in your opinion, what led to this lack of control? Feel free to speak your mind, and don't hold back."*

Elder Brent straightened up and coughed into his hand. "If I may really speak freely, then I have a few thoughts."

"Go ahead."

Elder Brent took a breath to steel himself before addressing the room. "The biggest issue we have faced so far is that we are heavily outnumbered. At any one time, around thirty cultivators from our family are patrolling and watching over the city. Even with spirit sight, they can't catch everything happening to a hundred thousand people."

"A lack of manpower rather than outright incompetence, then?"

"Well…" Elder Brent scratched the back of his head awkwardly. "I will admit I have had some trouble getting the youngsters to take their roles seriously. Most of them see it as a waste of time, and even when the mortals ask for help, they often cause more trouble. It's been getting slowly better over time, but there's a reason the noble families usually leave the mortals to police themselves."

"You're speaking too much," the Grand Elder hissed under his breath.

"No, this is a good discussion. It's better to admit to problems than keep quiet about them to save face," Ashlock rebutted, silencing the Grand Elder. *"In conclusion, Elder Brent, and tell me if I am mistaken, the Redclaws are both outnumbered and ill-suited for the job I have tasked them with. Is that correct?"*

Elder Brent slowly nodded. "A fact I hate to admit, but it's true. I should have told the Immortal about this issue sooner. Please punish me as you see fit."

"There is no need for punishment. My oversight led to me assigning cultivators to a job better suited for mortals. Could someone tell me how a city like Darklight City keeps crime under control?"

Julian stood up and bowed respectfully. "If I may, having lived as a mortal in a city overseen by cultivators and also walking the streets of Ashfallen, I have some insight."

"Just spit it out," Stella snapped. "The Immortal isn't going to eat you for speaking out of line, and this is a meeting. It's what we are here to do."

"Right… Wait, eat me?" Julian gulped. "Um, Darklight City is run by a council of mortals. Usually, cultivator families only care about what they can get out of a city, such as spirit stones or labor, rather than how it's run, so they let a group of mortals govern the city so long as the production quotas are met."

"I see, that makes sense. What about crime?"

"Crime?" Julian seemed confused by the question. "Every city has rampant crime because of rogue cultivators."

"Why?"

"I can answer that." Douglas stood up. "For those here that don't know, I used to be a rogue cultivator drowning in debt until I was taken in by the Ashfallen Sect. I did many things I am not proud of to survive and grow in power. It's a cutthroat world of crime out there, so strength is all that matters to staying fucking alive. However, the noble families are greedy bastards, no offense. They buy up and hoard all the cultivation resources, leaving little to go around for the rest, and as you can imagine, the resources left aren't going into the hands of upstanding members of society…"

The Grand Elder chuckled. "'Greedy bastards' is one way to put it, but he is right. We set quite high quotas for the city to meet each month, so they have little to spare for anyone else."

"See? Greedy bastards." Douglas grinned. "Though I have to say I can't blame you now that I live in your shiny shoes. Life is much nicer up here atop a hoard of wealth."

"So the rogue cultivators that Nox detected are likely the source of the crime?"

Douglas crossed his arms and drummed his fingers. "If I had to guess, they are either a bunch of upstarts or a smaller gang that got driven out of Darklight City by the powerhouses and then found Ashfallen City. Although there's little here, there's much to be gained from being the first to take over an area."

Stella had been leaning back on her chair and picking at her nails while listening in. With a sigh, she looked up from her nails at Douglas. "Then we have a solution. I will go slaughter them all, and then no more problem."

Douglas shrugged. "Yeah, that would work."

"No." Elaine shook her head from her seat beside Douglas. "I understand you want the meeting to end quickly, Stella, but that's a short-sighted solution. Unless you want to purge the city every week, they will keep appearing like cockroaches."

Stella narrowed her eyes. "What would you suggest, then?"

Elaine pushed up her glasses as she hummed in thought. "Douglas, you mentioned stronger gangs driving out other rogue cultivators. What if we hired someone to act as a gang leader to prevent other rogue cultivators from acting in the city and then have the mortals police themselves?"

"That could work," Douglas agreed.

"Any idea for who we could hire?"

Douglas looked up at the ceiling. "I do, actually. I think Mister Choi would be the perfect man for the job."

That bald guy we hired Douglas from who runs the Golden Springs noodle shop? Stella wondered as the image of the man appeared in her mind. If a mountain could be a human, that was Mister Choi. His bulging muscles had been barely hidden by the purple silk robe embroidered with golden koi, and his shark-tooth grin was enough to make her nervous. *I think he was stuck at the ninth stage of the Soul Fire Realm. With a few truffles, he would be quite a formidable cultivator under our control.*

"Mister Choi could work," Ashlock agreed. **"Could you contact him for me, Douglas? I'd like to offer him a heavenly loyalty contract and many benefits for joining. Your growth in cultivation should be proof enough that our methods work."**

"I will try my best." Douglas sat back down.

"That just leaves the council of mortals and hiring of guards to maintain order within the city. Julian, could you handle that for me?"

"Yes, my lord." Julian bowed. "But if I may add, Ashfallen City will collapse soon and descend into a civil war even without the rogue cultivators."

"Why's that?"

Julian cleared his throat. "People have been living off the free food and traveling to Darklight City to purchase things they need to live, but eventually, people will run out of Crowns they earned back in Slymere, and with there being no jobs in Ashfallen City, it's only a matter of time before crime becomes more rampant."

"Right, that's a good point. We should focus on having people employed in industries related to farming, manufacturing pill bottles and boxes, guards, and education. Giving people jobs also benefits us as the money will flow back to us when they purchase our pills."

"Are you going to let mortals become cultivators?" Jasmine asked with a sparkle in her eyes.

"Not quite. I don't have the truffles to turn a hundred thousand people into cultivators at your level. But I can make diluted pills from the truffles such that if they ate enough, they would eventually be able to cultivate."

"Good," the Grand Elder said. "Mortals becoming cultivators is unheard of, so anything stronger than that will attract a lot of attention. Your disciple and her family should remain as a unique case unless you want every noble family seeking us out."

Stella ruffled Jasmine's hair. "Hear that? You're special because of your benevolent master here."

Jasmine just pouted as her head was rocked back and forth.

"If you don't acknowledge your master's greatness, you might regret it."

"Master...please...stop...rocking...my...head."

"Okay, it looks like we are mostly done here," Ashlock said. **"Those who want to stay behind and help create the mortal council and the jobs, you are free to stay. The rest of you are dismissed."**

Stella was the first to stand up. "I have never heard something better in my life."

"Hold on, Stella. I still need you to purge the rogues in the mine. No reason to turn down a meal that's causing me trouble."

Stella's smile widened. "Killing some weaklings will be a good warm-up for tonight. Come on, Jasmine, let's go."

"Eh?" Jasmine's eyes widened. "Why me?"

"This is the perfect opportunity to get some fighting experience before the tournament later this month. There's nothing like some life-and-death fights to get the blood pumping!"

"What?! You can't be serious."

As it turned out, her master had been serious.

Jasmine stood before the entrance to the mine wearing the black cloak Elaine had gifted her, and a white wooden mask covered her face. Stella, standing beside her, had a similar setup, and they were attracting a lot of attention. Many mortals passed by, stealing glances at the two.

"Master, am I really ready for this?" Jasmine asked.

"Sure, why not? I will be here to help you, so don't hold back." Stella's ring flashed, and a blood-red fruit appeared in her hand. "Actually, I have a gift for you. Since you have chosen the path of the fist, this will help you."

"What is this?" Jasmine took the small fruit from Stella.

"I think it was called a Vampiric Touch fruit. After eating it, as you punch the shit out of someone, you will steal their Qi for yourself. That should help you believe this is possible, right? Punch someone enough times, and they will be weakened to your level."

"Um...that wasn't what I was worried about."

"Then what's worrying you?"

"We are going to kill a person."

Stella tilted her head. "Not quite."

Jasmine felt a ray of hope. "We aren't?"

"We are going to be *slaughtering* people." Stella giggled and patted her shoulder. "Now come, my disciple, the fun awaits."

This is fun for her? Jasmine stood there, dumbfounded. She watched Stella as she strode toward the cave entrance and drew her sword.

But I have never killed anyone before... Jasmine looked at the blood-red fruit in her hand. *Could I even kill a person?*

A man emerged from the dimly lit passage and stood in Stella's way. He was wearing a brown robe stained with dust and blood. A long sword was strapped to his back with leather straps, and his fierce gaze was barely hidden by a fringe of black hair.

"Miss, you are drawing quite the crowd." The man grinned as he surveyed the mortals, and they all avoided his gaze in fear. "May I ask your business here?"

"It's simple, really." Stella shrugged. "You and your friends have become a stain on Ashfallen City that needs to be purged."

The man's grin faded and twisted into a sneer. "Oh, yeah? And who are you to decide that? This area is under the control of Brax, a Star Core cultivator! You and your short friend over there should run along if you don't want to get killed for entering the boss's territo—"

"Blah, blah." Stella swung her sword upward so fast it was nothing but a blur as it cleaved the man in two. "Noisy people like you are the worst." The two halves of the man fell to either side, and Stella casually walked through the gap, trailing blood with every step.

Silence filled the area as nobody dared to make a sound.

Jasmine felt her heart pound in her chest at how effortlessly Stella executed a cultivator far above her strength. Her gut was also doing somersaults from the gruesome sight, and she was struggling to hold back from puking into her mask.

Hold it together, Jasmine... If you faint here, it will look bad for your master. Just...don't look... Ugh, it's so disgusting.

A sudden ripple of power across the sky distracted her from the terrible scene as a rift formed overhead. Black vines she knew belonged to Stella's father drooped down and curled around the pieces of the dead man, much to the horror of the surrounding mortals. They all screamed and began running for their lives, curiosity be darned.

Jasmine let out a shaky sigh. *How does the Immortal not understand why people see him as a dark god when he does stuff like this?*

"Hurry up, Disciple!" Stella waved to her with a bloodstained sword in her hand. "If you dawdle for too long, I will have killed them all without you!"

I didn't want to kill them anyway! Jasmine shouted in her mind and clenched her fists. She forced herself to walk forward while muttering under her breath, "She's insane. My master is absolutely insane."

34

MONSTERS IN HUMAN SKIN

Stella was in a fantastic mood, humming a pleasant tune as she descended into the mine.

Her eyes were closed as she saw the world in a series of interconnected grids in the spatial plane. A black metal sword embroidered with a golden star pattern that Ash had gifted her floated at her side with telekinesis. With a flick of her finger, it shot through a portal like an angel of death, followed by a pained cry that echoed through the mine and two thumps as a headless body fell from a hole hidden in the ceiling.

Jasmine at her side jumped at the sudden sound of falling bodies.

"Relax. These are all Soul Fire weaklings, barely above the realm of mortals." Stella ruffled her hair and laughed. "I don't even need to fight them directly, see? I can slaughter them from afar with my sword."

It was honestly a bad matchup for the rogue cultivators. Against most enemies, the cramped tunnels in the rock would give the rogue cultivators a way to attack from blind spots, set up ambushes, or even run away. However, the rock became trivial to Stella due to Ash's roots spreading throughout the mine and drenching the place in spatial Qi. It might as well be air to her and now only served as a trap for the rats trying to flee her sword.

Stella went back to humming as she waved her finger around. It may look like she was drawing runes or something in the air, but in reality, she was just pointing at the next target in the spatial plane and guiding her bloodstained sword through portals to get the job done.

The distant cries and thumps were music to her ears.

A sudden ripple of power spread through the spatial plane, and Stella could only marvel at the display of control as rifts were torn open above the corpses, and Ash began feasting.

"You don't need to waste so much Qi for each corpse, you know," Stella yelled at the ceiling. "I can gather the corpses for you after I am done killing that Brax guy."

A laugh echoed in her consciousness. ***"Using this much Qi is trivial to me. In fact, I should be the one killing the rogues, as this is wasting your Qi."***

Stella waved him off. "Nah, this is a good warm-up for tonight, and I barely have to expend any effort to purge these weaklings."

I am a bit worried about Jasmine, though, Stella thought as she glanced over her shoulder at the green-haired girl meekly following her. The girl kept her eyes on the ground and seemed to tremble at the distant cries of slaughter.

Perhaps feeling Stella's gaze, Jasmine raised her head. "Master..."

"That's me!" Stella cheerfully replied in an attempt to brighten the girl's mood. The tunnel down to the mine was a bit dreary, with the low lighting, lack of scenery, and terrified mortals running past them. It was no wonder Jasmine was in a bad mood. *There's no way she would prefer the meeting over a stroll with her master, right?*

"I have some questions," Jasmine said.

Sensing a hint of resolve in her voice, Stella toned down the cheerful act. "I am your master. We don't keep any secrets from each other, remember? If you want to know something, just ask."

"Okay..." Jasmine paused before responding, "How can you kill people so easily?"

"What a strange question." Stella tapped her chin as she continued her casual stroll. No enemies were left alive for the next hundred meters, giving her time to mull over her disciple's question. After some thought, she settled on an answer.

"I can kill people so easily because I am stronger than them." Stella shrugged. *There's not much more to it than that. What else could be holding me back than a lack of strength?*

Jasmine seemed displeased with her answer. "Do you not value human life?"

"An even stranger question." Stella frowned. "I suppose it depends on who they are. You are precious to me, for example. I would go to war with the heavens to save or avenge you. The same goes for Diana, Elaine, and maybe Douglas. He can be a bit of an arse sometimes, but he works hard for the sect, so it's difficult for me to hold a grudge against the guy for how badmouthed he was when he first arrived…"

Stella realized she was going off on a tangent and fell quiet. Jasmine joined her in the silence. Only their footsteps, the panicked breaths of mortals as they ran past, and distant screams as Stella returned to killing accompanied their stroll into the underworld of Ashfallen City.

Jasmine's questions made Stella wonder if what she was doing was somehow wrong. It was clear that many people disapproved of her methods, which was why she disliked meetings the more she attended. They treated her respectfully due to her relationship with Ash and her strength but rejected her methods and ideas as too rash.

Anything that causes harm to Tree's plans should be dealt with swiftly like this. The others like to spend too much time trying to come up with answers that could easily be solved with violence. The maids that wanted to kill me wouldn't have listened to reason, nor would the Dao Storm that almost killed Tree. Sure, talking can work sometimes, but the one with the bigger stick wins in the end, and we have the biggest stick around.

"Do you see humans as different from monsters?" Jasmine asked, breaking the silence.

Stella snorted. "Humans are *far* worse than monsters."

Jasmine tilted her head. "How, Master? I don't understand. Monsters are scary, you know? At least, that's what Mom taught me. Monsters are the reason we hid behind walls and obeyed the cultivators. I know some humans turn to crime, but how can that be worse than something like a wyvern?"

"Stop thinking like a mortal." Stella flicked Jasmine's forehead, and she yelped. "A monster comes at you with open intentions. It wants to devour you to progress its cultivation. Nice and easy to understand, right? But humans? They are cunning monsters in familiar skin." Stella ran her nail along Jasmine's neck, leaving a faint red line to show a point. "Cultivators will betray you at the first opportunity and approach you as a friend with a kind smile before ramming a dagger through your heart. They can plot, plan, and deceive. They can even control others to do their bidding and work together. Do you understand, my disciple? It is not the monsters you should fear the most but fellow cultivators."

"Are humans really that bad?" Jasmine muttered through her mask.

Stella stopped walking and put a hand on Jasmine's head. "Remember that man at the entrance, the one I cut in two?"

Jasmine shuddered under her hand. "Y-Yes…"

"If I was a monster, do you think he would have stood there so casually talking with his weapon strapped to his back?"

Jasmine thought for a moment and then shook her head. "No, Master, he would have fought or ran away."

"Exactly, but he believed he could talk things out because my intentions were unclear, and I wasn't openly flexing my cultivation. Little did he know I planned to kill him the moment I saw him. That's the difference between cultivators and monsters. Do you see now?"

"Mhm." Jasmine nodded.

Stella stood back up. "The world is dark and cruel. You can try to be nice and work with others, but just because you have good intentions doesn't mean that others do, and they will exploit that weakness. One bad apple in a sect can bring it down if people aren't cautious."

"I never realized it was so bad…" Jasmine looked back to the floor.

"That's because you are spoiled," Stella said bluntly. "You've lived a life as the daughter of noble mortals in Slymere, and now you are a cultivator being raised in a safe environment with access to the greatest cultivation resources in this realm. It's not your fault, but you have been sheltered and protected from the darker side of this world."

A sheltered flower like you won't survive out there. Stella delicately combed her hair and readjusted the white flower behind her ear. *I don't want my first-ever disciple to wither and die. You should grow tall and strong like a tree. So forgive me for being harsh and showing you such horrible things, Jasmine. One day, you will understand.*

Jasmine balled up her fists, but Stella could tell her heart still wasn't fully into it.

Let's see what she thinks after witnessing what this Brax fella is up to.

Stella snapped her fingers, and a portal formed. "Let's hurry this up. I have a shitty husband to murder and secrets about my past to uncover this evening. Dealing with these dregs is a waste of my time."

Jasmine felt her ears pop as she followed Stella through the portal. The air here was far staler and reeked of sweat and dried blood. It took a moment to adjust to the darkness of this cavern as it was even less well-lit, but once she did, her stomach began to churn again.

A man with a thin body, wispy white hair, and cunning eyes sat casually with one foot propped up on a cage, picking at his teeth with a toothpick. A family of mortals was restrained inside the large metal cage under the cultivator. A man, woman, and son were cramped into the space with sunken eyes and disheveled hair. Their clothes were also torn in places, and the mortal man had a swollen face that was shades of black and blue. They didn't even look up at Jasmine and Stella as their dull gazes stayed on the floor.

Jasmine took a step back, horrified at what she saw. *How can humans treat other humans like animals? The Voidmind family leaving us to die is one thing, but this is something else.*

Other than the white-haired man sitting atop the cage, dozens of other cultivators were in the room. Some were meditating on top of a Qi-gathering formation while a group of men and women surrounded a man strapped to a chair, force-feeding him bundles of what looked to be pill ingredients. The mortal's screams had obscured their arrival, but the man sitting atop the cage soon noticed their presence and eyed them cautiously.

"Who are you two?" He flicked the toothpick to the ground. His voice drew the attention of the other cultivators in the room, and noticing the two newcomers, they began to slowly encircle them with blade tips poking out of their cloak folds.

"Are you Drax?" Stella strode forward with confidence that befitted her overwhelming strength.

"The name is Brax, not Drax." The man clicked his tongue, stood up, and wreathed himself in earth Qi.

"Does it matter what I call a fraud?"

Brax narrowed his eyes. "What do you mean?"

"The loudmouth at the door said you were a Star Core cultivator, but you're only a half step." A sword appeared in Stella's hand. "Your Star Core hasn't finished forming yet. How disappointing."

Jasmine's eyes widened. *They really do deceive, just like Master said they do. How dishonorable do you have to be to lie about your cultivation?*

Brax mirrored Stella's aggression by drawing his sword in a flash of gold from his spatial ring. Compared to Stella's beautiful blood-stained blade of dark metal, Brax's sword was crude and chipped.

"So you got past Frank guarding the door. That's impressive, but how do you plan to defeat all of us when there are only two—" Brax coughed up a mouthful of blood and looked down at the blade tip poking out of his chest.

Jasmine blinked as she realized Stella had suddenly disappeared in a pop of air and reappeared behind Brax, stabbing him through the heart with a dagger.

Stella pulled back the dagger and elbowed Brax to the floor. He fell flat on his face with a groan, and Jasmine watched the flicker of life leave his eyes.

Despite how terrible this person seemed, his sudden death still made Jasmine sick to her stomach. This was all so wrong.

"You killed the boss?! I will fucking kill you, bitch!" a woman screamed as she ran toward Stella with a sword wreathed in blue soul flames. Her cloak hood flew back, revealing a middle-aged-looking woman with brown hair and a twisted scowl.

Stella effortlessly sidestepped the overhead sword swing as if it had been in slow motion, grabbed the woman's face, and rammed it into a nearby rock.

Jasmine screwed her eyes shut to avoid witnessing another gruesome death, though the crunching sound of bone painted a clear picture in her mind. *This is a nightmare. I just want to go home.*

A whistling noise shot past Jasmine's ear, followed by a gasp and thump. Slowly opening her eyes and turning around, she saw a cloaked figure pinned to the wall behind her with a dagger through the throat.

"Pay attention to your surroundings, Jasmine," Stella said as she casually fought off three people at once. Her arms blurred, and sparks flew as she parried every attack.

She protected me while fighting all those people. Jasmine narrowed her eyes at Stella and realized these people she was fighting were weaker than the man at the gate she had so effortlessly cleaved in two. *Is she using them as practice before killing them off? Or maybe she finds this fun...*

"You won't do," Stella muttered. Her speed suddenly doubled, to the surprise of her attackers, and she twisted her sword to kill one of three by shattering their sword and cutting them in half horizontally. The remaining two cultivators, one a woman and another a man, stepped back in fear, their swords trembling in their grasps. "Your technique was too good, so you have to go as well." Stella teleported behind the woman and punched her so hard in the back that she went flying into the wall, dead on impact.

Jasmine gulped down rising vomit and wished she could crawl back through the portal. The smell of fresh blood tickled her nose, and there was nowhere she could look without seeing a corpse. Her knees grew wobbly, so she struggled to even stand.

"S-Stay back, you monster," the final person standing stammered as he slowly stepped backward over his fallen comrades with his sword tip pointing at Stella.

"Calling me a monster? That's rich coming from you, considering you kidnapped people and were even using them as living pill furnaces, though I suppose it's a matter of perspective," Stella said dryly as she flicked the blood off her blade before stowing it away. She then glanced around the room and locked eyes with the mortals. She brought up her hand wreathed in spatial flames, and with a simple hand gesture, the cages containing the mortals were ripped apart, and the braces keeping the man affixed to the chair snapped.

"Go through the portal." Stella gestured to the rift with her chin. "You are free now."

"Thank you..." the man strapped to the chair wheezed as he dragged himself alongside the terrified family to the portal and left.

The remaining cultivator also stepped toward the portal, but Stella flattened him with her presence. "They were free to go, but not you. At least not yet."

"Y-You might l-let me go?" the man gasped out.

Stella didn't answer him straight away. Instead, she strode through the blood and corpses to sit atop an empty cage. Having taken her throne, she let her legs swing as she declared his fate.

"Throw your sword aside."

"Yes, Mistress." The cultivator, far stronger than Jasmine, was reduced to a servant before Stella. He threw the sword aside without hesitation.

"Good, I knew I picked the right one."

"I am honored—"

"Don't be." Stella snorted. "I picked you because you had the most pathetic fighting techniques, and I felt you would suit the role of a punching bag for my disciple here."

Jasmine and the poor cultivator her master had picked out exchanged a glance.

"Here's how this is going to work," Stella continued. "I will grant you freedom if you can stay standing after twenty attacks from my disciple. You cannot fight back and must keep your arms behind your back. If I see any hint of you attempting to harm my disciple, your head will fly before you even realize what happened. Nod if you understand."

The cultivator hesitantly nodded, and the pressure on him vanished, allowing him to stand. Per the instructions, he put his hands behind his back and towered over Jasmine.

"Master, this feels wrong," Jasmine called out as she saw the man's terrified face.

Stella shrugged. "Jasmine, if you don't want to fight him, then this man has as much purpose as the corpses on the ground, and I have no reason to keep him alive. This is a chance to get real-life combat experience and see if your plan to use your fists against a real opponent will work."

The man grew even more terrified and bowed. "Little disciple, please give me a chance to live."

"O-okay…" Jasmine hesitantly raised her fists. *What kind of twisted situation is this?*

"Don't forget to eat the Vampiric Touch fruit!" Stella said. "Now is a great time to test it. Oh, and don't hold back, Jasmine, for every punch you do that doesn't knock him down, that's five laps of the mountain peak you must do today."

"Master?!" Jasmine said in horror. *Does that mean Stella will make me run a hundred laps today if I don't knock this man out?*

Jasmine gulped down the blood-red fruit and gave the man a bow. "I'm so sorry, but I will be more dead than you if I fail."

The man returned a weary, tooth-filled grin. "Let's both do our best to please the monster, then."

35
HELLISH PUNISHMENT

After eating the Vampiric Touch fruit, Jasmine felt a strange hunger clawing through her body toward the tips of her fingers. Despite the low lighting, she couldn't help but look down at her hand, fully expecting to see small mouths growing through her skin.

"Phew," Jasmine sighed in relief. Her hand hadn't turned into some monstrous appendage, but the hunger was getting to her. Her hand trembled, and it was tempting to scratch at her face and feast on her own Qi...

What the hell did Master make me eat?! Jasmine had never felt so out of control of her own body before. *Do monsters feel this urge to devour as well? If so, I can hardly blame them for mindlessly going after cultivators. It's maddening.*

While Jasmine was trying to regain control, the last cultivator Stella had left alive for her to practice punching on wreathed himself in murky brown soul flames that matched his stained and ripped robe.

Jasmine unconsciously licked her lips. That Qi was far above her own level and smelled so enticing. *What in the nine realms is wrong with me?*

Unaware of her intentions, the man took his stance.

"I-I'm so sorry." Jasmine reeled back her fist and directed all the Qi she could muster into this attack. *I will knock him out in one punch to the chin so he doesn't suffer, and I won't have to run so many laps.*

As promised, the man had his hands behind his back, leaving his face wide open. He even leaned down to give her a better shot. "Do your worst, little disciple."

Jasmine narrowed her eyes on the spot she planned to punch and took a deep breath. *You can do this, Jasmine. You fought with Stella's clone hundreds of times, and this is no different. It's just real flesh this time instead of an illusion.*

"Take this!" Jasmine shouted to hype herself up and twisted her body to deliver the hardest-hitting uppercut of her life straight to the man's chin.

There was a howl of pain followed by a thump.

"Wow, he defeated you with his chin alone." Stella burst out laughing. "Elaine told me about the appeal of a chiseled jawline, and I failed to see it before, but now I know what she was talking about!"

Jasmine pouted as she cradled her throbbing hand while lying on her butt in a pool of someone else's blood. *Forget the chin. That felt like punching solid stone.*

"That's five laps, Jasmine," Stella added after she calmed down from laughing.

"You're a demon!" Jasmine shouted back.

"Six laps."

"Wha—"

"Seven laps."

Jasmine clamped her mouth shut and silently seethed. Clearly, her master had become possessed by a heartless demon and wanted to watch two people suffer for entertainment! With a grunt, she pushed herself up and ignored the dampness of her clothes due to the blood. Her master really would make her run a hundred laps of the mountain peak, which would take until tomorrow morning to finish if she didn't find a way to win.

I found fighting Stella's illusion with my fists easier than a sword because I had to run around, dodge, block, and punch back. Whereas this is a test of raw power against a living brick wall. A sword wouldn't have helped as I haven't yet learned how to externalize my Qi, so I can't empower weapons. It would just bounce off this man's skin. I also don't know any techniques, leaving me with one thing...

Jasmine looked down at her fists. They still hungered like before, but that intense feeling had dulled due to the pain and failure to even make the man blink with an attack she poured everything into.

Is the gap between a Qi Realm and Soul Fire cultivator really this vast, or is it because he is an earth Qi cultivator that focuses on defense? Jasmine wondered as she flexed her fingers, and as the pain faded a bit, she noticed something. *Why is there some earth Qi in my fingers?*

Jasmine recalled Stella's description of the Vampiric Touch fruit's capabilities. *If I punch the shit out of someone enough, they will be weakened to my level.* A small smile tugged at her lips as some hope of winning became clear. *I thought the fruit only let me steal Qi from my opponent, but if I can force this earth Qi to protect my fingers, punching him shouldn't hurt as much.*

It took far more effort than moving around her own untamed Qi or nature Qi, which she had become rather attuned to. But after some effort, the earth Qi had strengthened her fingers.

The earth cultivator seemed to sense what she had done as his eyes widened a little. "Interesting," he said gruffly. "I thought that punch took more Qi to defend than it should have. The idea you stole my Qi never occurred to me—"

Jasmine swung her fist into another uppercut as he talked to hit the same spot on his chin, a tactic she had learned from her master. Yet, unlike her master, who effortlessly cleaved people in half, her feeble attack only silenced the man and caused her another round of pain.

"Ow, ow, ow." Jasmine wasn't thrown to her butt this time, and the pain wasn't crippling, but it was still bad enough to make her regret striking. *This isn't working. Although it didn't hurt as much, the man didn't even flinch. What the hell am I supposed to do? I will have to run over a hundred laps at this rate before he reacts to my punch. Mom, save me...*

"That's twelve laps now, Jasmine," her master happily reminded her. "If you don't want to run until you pass out today, try to use your head more than your fists."

Is she calling me stupid? Jasmine was about to retort but remembered to keep her mouth shut. *Wait, maybe I am stupid. Am I missing something here? As mean as Master seems, she wouldn't give me an impossible challenge, nor does she want me to hurt myself like this.*

Jasmine calmed down and looked her opponent up and down. Since the start of the "fight," he hadn't moved a muscle, and his arms were behind his back. There was no time limit on the fight, only a limit on the number of attacks Jasmine could do before the cultivator won.

Think, Jasmine, think! What is Master trying to teach me here? That using my fists is a bad idea? No, she wouldn't have given me a fruit that makes fighting with my hands better if that was the case. Jasmine glanced at her master, sitting casually on the cage and playing with a dagger. Her expression and everything was hidden by a mask, but even if it looked like her master wasn't paying attention, she knew that her master had the whole cavern under her control.

If I had a dagger and could empower it with my Qi, I could poke a hole in the cultivator and have him bleed out until he fainted. Jasmine looked at her nails. *If I think of my hand as a dagger, couldn't I drain him of his Qi instead of his blood and then knock him out with one punch? But punching him hurts and steals so little Qi each time... Hold on, who said I have to punch him?*

Stella had talked about punching, which was a very Stella thing to suggest. That was certainly the most violent option and would work if she was the stronger one here, but when faced with an immovable mountain, what else was there to do other than chip away at it slowly?

Jasmine stepped toward the cultivator but didn't curl her hand into a fist. Instead, she placed her palm on the man's chest near his heart and pressed down.

"What are you doing?" the man asked with a hint of concern.

"Just stand there and watch," Jasmine said. She closed her eyes and began pulling on the man's Qi through the power of the Vampiric Touch fruit. Earth Qi flowed into her body like a raging river, and she tried her best to hold onto and control some of it, but she leaked the rest into her surroundings.

"This is impossible," the man muttered as his soul fire flickered like a dying flame. "How are you taking in so much of my Qi?!"

Jasmine barely heard the man as she was too busy directing the flow of the earth Qi through her body and expelling it into the surroundings; otherwise, she felt like she would explode. *If my spirit roots were any less pure, this would indeed be impossible. Did Master foresee this, which is why she fed me a Spirit Root Improvement truffle daily?*

"No! Stop!" The man stumbled back a step. "Get away from me! I spent years accumulating this Qi..."

"Don't take another step if you want to keep your head." Stella's cold voice echoed through the room, and Jasmine saw the dagger her master had been playing with floating beside the cultivator's neck.

"This is cheating," the man protested. "How does this not count as an attack?"

Stella shrugged. "I wouldn't consider a palm on your chest as an attack. If you are so concerned, then make an effort to stop her. Flood her with Qi or have better control over your own."

"I can't," the man hissed through gritted teeth. "My spirit roots are too impure to flood her with Qi, and she somehow has greater control over mine!"

Stella laughed at his misfortune. "Your earth Qi is so murky it might as well be swamp water infested with heart demons. How many beast cores did you consume while forcing yourself to cultivate a Qi unsuited to you?"

"What?"

"Don't play dumb with me." Stella tilted her head, and her blond hair fell across her mask. "There's a reason I picked you out of all the cultivators here to teach my disciple a valuable lesson. You are the perfect example of someone who rushed their foundation for a quick boost in power and paid the price for it. Look, you are losing a battle over your own Qi to a little girl who is an entire realm below you right now."

"The fuck do you know?" The man spat to the side and glared at Stella.

"When was the last time you had a breakthrough despite gobbling down beast cores every week?" Stella snapped back. "A few years ago, I bet. Oh, and how is that injury to your left arm?"

"How did you kno—"

Stella snorted. "When we fought, I noticed all the power behind your two-handed swings came from your right side."

"So?" The man grunted. Sweat dripped from his forehead onto Jasmine's arm as she kept draining his Qi. He didn't dare move as Stella's dagger floated a hairs-width away from his neck.

"Here's my theory." Stella crossed her legs and rested her chin on her palm. "You forcefully cultivated earth Qi because it's one of the stronger and easier affinities to cultivate, right? You then rocketed in cultivation with the help of beast cores, never bothering to train or hone your foundations. Always winning through brute strength alone. But then, after many decades, the heart demons consumed your soul. Your cultivation stagnated, and you reached a bottleneck." Stella traced a line through the air as if showing his life story. "Eventually, your rivals surpassed you and came back for revenge. You lost horribly and ran with your tail between your legs to Ashfallen City. Am I right?"

The room fell into silence, and Jasmine was speechless. To her, it had seemed like her master was messing around and having fun while slaughtering these cultivators, but she had been paying such close attention to every detail?

"You're right," the man admitted as his head fell.

"Jasmine, did you hear all of that?" Stella asked. "This is a pathetic excuse of a cultivator and a fate all too many demonic cultivators reach. It's why they turn to horrible acts like using mortals as pill furnaces to try and create miracle pills that are pathetic versions of the Heart Demon Expelling truffle. They always looked for shortcuts in life and paid the price for them."

"I understand, Master." Jasmine nodded. "I won't slack off on training my foundation."

"Good." Stella clapped her hands once. "You can kill him now."

"Huh?" Jasmine glanced at her master, wondering if she had heard wrong. The man also looked back in confusion.

"He has served his purpose and taught you many lessons. Now strangle him or rip out his eyes. Anything works." Stella hopped off the cage. "Don't forget a hundred laps are awaiting you if you slack off."

Jasmine ran through the rules of the duel that Stella had stated and realized something. The only way for the man to survive was if he survived twenty hits from her, but if she failed to down him in those hits, she had a day of hell ahead of her.

This man is evil, but I don't want to be the reason he died. Is that so wrong? Jasmine bit her lip as she debated what to do. *Running a hundred laps may be hell, but I don't want to live with the fact I actually sent someone to Hell.* With some resignation, she withdrew her hand from draining the man of Qi as his soul flames had died out, and he could barely stand.

Pulling back her fist, Jasmine reduced the amount of Qi gathered and punched him in the chest. This time, it was the man who stumbled back and grunted in pain while Jasmine's fist felt rock solid, empowered by all the earth Qi she had absorbed.

Jasmine glanced at Stella, but her master made no comment about her lack of lethal violence, so she went for another punch and then another. Always making sure to use just enough Qi to make it look like she was trying while not causing the man to pass out or fall, which would guarantee his death at Stella's blade.

Just bear with it. I am going to give you a chance at freedom, Jasmine thought as she let off two more punches. The man almost tripped over a corpse as he wiped blood from his broken nose. *Only a few more to go...*

"That's twenty hits," Stella said coldly.

Jasmine lowered her hand and eyed her master cautiously. Stella hadn't said a word as she beat the man, so she wasn't sure if Stella had noticed she wasn't giving it her all. *Who am I kidding? There's no way she didn't notice.*

"Master, I..." Jasmine lowered her head.

"It seems you have made your choice," Stella said dismissively as she approached the man. "The question now is will you come to regret it? Either way, a promise is a promise. Mister cultivator, you survived twenty hits from my disciple, so I grant you freedom."

A portal rippled to life before the man.

"There you go, a rift to the surface. Good luck to you."

"R-Really?" the man asked, and Stella gave him a silent nod.

The man hauled his broken and bloodied body through the portal, and Jasmine's eyes widened as she finally recognized the other side. *That's Red Vine Peak. Why would Stella send him there? No...wait...*

Through the rift, Jasmine saw a black vine ending in a spike impale the man and lift him into the air. He coughed blood and hung there limply as his body began to dissolve.

"Master?!" Jasmine turned to Stella. "You said he would be free if he survived twenty hits. Why are you killing him?"

"Me?" Stella tilted her head. "What a strange thing to say. I am standing next to you without moving a finger. I only ever promised him freedom. I never said anything about protecting him from others who may want him dead."

"But…" Jasmine watched in horror as the man she had steeled herself to save was devoured before her eyes.

"If a meteor crushed him, or a monster suddenly appeared and was eating him, you wouldn't expect me to go save him, would you?"

Jasmine glared at Stella with tears rolling down her cheeks. "You never planned to let him live, did you?"

Stella took off her mask and ran a hand through her blond hair. "No, I didn't, and you should have suspected that." She sighed. "I told him our names, mentioned the truffles, and worst of all, he used people as pill furnaces. Do you even know what those are, my sheltered disciple? They create pills inside a person's stomach and use their Qi, body, and sometimes soul as ingredients."

Jasmine felt genuine rage through her master-disciple link.

Stella's face twisted into a scowl aimed at the chair the mortal man had been strapped to. "Why would I let scum like that live after he has served his purpose? I am more concerned with your naivety, my disciple."

Jasmine lowered her head and balled her fists. *I disappointed Master.*

Stella clicked her tongue. "It looks like I need to double your training. But first, you need to absorb that Qi you stole and then think about your actions while running a hundred and two laps."

"Yes, Master," Jasmine answered dejectedly. Despite her effort, it looked like they had both gone to Hell anyway.

Jasmine wiped the sweat from her brow with her sleeve as she huffed out clouds of cold air. It was already midday, and she had only run ten of her hundred laps. Yet she didn't feel that tired.

Thanks to the Qi I absorbed from the man, I ascended two stages in the Qi Realm and am now at the fourth stage overall. Jasmine remembered how excited she had been to tell Stella about her progress to the second stage yesterday. *To think I would double my progress in a single fight.*

Jasmine ran near Ashlock and glanced at the bloodstained stone where the man she attempted to save had dissolved into a puddle. In hindsight, she realized how foolish it had been to try and deceive

Stella, but a small part of her was still glad she wasn't the one who ended his life.

That aside, the fight had given her a lot to think about concerning her fighting style.

If I can somehow harness the power of the Vampiric Touch fruit as an affinity, wouldn't that work wonders once I reach the Soul Fire Realm and start manipulating plants with my Nature affinity? Rather than getting so close to the enemy to drain their Qi, what if I could achieve the same thing through a vine wrapped around their foot? Wouldn't that let me fight people far above my strength and be helpful to everyone?

Once her master was less disappointed in her, Jasmine planned to ask if she could see how the pill was made. Thus far, she had laid awake at night debating on what other affinity to pick, but none had sounded good enough to her to halve her cultivation speed, as sitting still and absorbing the heaven's Qi was already a chore.

Jasmine had debated the basic elements like earth, water, wind, and even fire, but none fascinated her as much as this fighting style she now had in her mind. *Maybe I should also ask Elaine what she thinks...after I have passed out and slept for a week from these laps around the mountain peak.*

"Ugh!" Jasmine shouted in annoyance across the empty, silent mountain peak. All she had for company was her heavy breathing, clouds of breath, the rustling of the leaves, and the occasional bird chirping. Everyone was off doing work for the sect, leaving her all alone to endure her punishment. "This sucks."

Guilt aside, maybe she was starting to regret being so foolish after all.

36
ALL SEEING EYE

Ashlock enjoyed the afternoon sun as he idly watched Jasmine complete her laps. Judging by her cursing at the skies, she seemed to think she was alone up here, but that was not the case.

"Don't you think over a hundred laps is a bit too far, Stella?" Ashlock asked his adopted daughter, who was hiding away from her disciple in his canopy.

Her eyes were closed as she rested her head against his trunk and listened to his rustling leaves. It had gotten colder as winter approached, but the cold didn't bother cultivators. Stella wore her usual white clothes, which looked more like pajamas, and no shoes—a getup that would cause a mortal to shiver in this cold, but Stella was unfazed.

"It was her choice. She should live with the consequences," Stella murmured without fully waking up. *"Do you not agree with my methods, Tree?"*

"I wouldn't have gone along with your plan of devouring the man as you granted him 'freedom' if I disagreed with the lesson you were trying to teach Jasmine, but she is still an eight-year-old mortal girl. Running a hundred laps in this cold is too much."

Stella stirred awake with a frown. *"She isn't a mortal anymore."*

"I suppose that's true," Ashlock hesitantly replied. **"But she is only in the fourth stage of the Qi Realm, right? Isn't that a level of**

cultivation mortals could naturally reach by the end of their lifetime if they live in a Qi-rich area?"

Stella stretched her back with a yawn. *"The fourth stage sounds a little high for a mortal to naturally reach, but that's not important. She's not a normal cultivator, either."*

"How so?"

"There are diminishing returns, but I have fed Jasmine a Spirit Root Improvement and Heart Demon Expelling truffle every single day to give her a flawless foundation." Stella pushed Ashlock's leaves aside and peered through his canopy at Jasmine in the distance. *"Foundation aside, she is also keen to learn and listens to me most of the time, which is rare for someone so young."*

"She does seem like the perfect student for you," Ashlock agreed. "Do you think she is on track to be able to compete in the Darklight City tournament in a few weeks' time?"

"I don't see why not," Stella said, returning to sitting against his trunk and hiding from her disciple. *"Her cultivation speed is coming along nicely, and she shows promise in combat after fighting my illusions. I would even go so far as to call her rather talented at cultivation, but she has a fatal flaw. No matter her cultivation level and capabilities in a fight, it's all useless if she's unable to go for a killing blow when it matters."*

"Jasmine is too naive." Ashlock sighed. "Kindness to a foe could lead to the death of a friend."

Stella nodded. *"A lesson I would prefer she learned without having to cradle the corpse of a loved one in her arms. She may call me a heartless demon of a master or be cursing me right now as she runs those laps, but one day, she will thank me."*

"You know, I will admit I had low expectations, but I am starting to think you are not so bad as a master."

Stella smiled. *"Thanks, Tree."*

"I still won't admit you are the best master until you win the bet, though!" Ashlock laughed. "Remember, Jasmine has to beat Amber Redclaw in a duel for me to admit that."

"Yeah, yeah." Stella waved him off. *"I will train her well, and in the end, even she will have to admit I am a great master—"*

"Master…is a…demon!" Jasmine shouted to the sky from across the peak between deep breaths. *"I'm going…to…die…"*

"**Are you sure about that?**" Ashlock asked, and Stella's eye twitched.

Eventually, Jasmine passed out after sixty laps, and Stella took her to sleep back at home before heading over to the Duskwalker residence with Diana to prepare for the killing of Albis Lunarshade later tonight.

Meanwhile, Ashlock looked down at the Eternal Pursuit Pavilion from above with {Eye of the Tree God}. Stella had told him a demonic tree was growing in the Crimson Tracker area, and he fully intended to see if he could link his root up with it.

For the last few hours, he had been pouring Qi into an ethereal root, and so far, it had easily penetrated every layer of defensive formations as it rose through the center of the mountain. Sometimes, he had to narrowly direct it around a room built inside the mountain to avoid drawing attention to himself. If a tree could sweat sap, he would be drenched right now.

"This sure is risky," Ashlock mumbled. "But there is no sign of them noticing my root yet, and I should be drawing close."

The defensive formations couldn't stop his ethereal root. However, they suppressed his spiritual sense, so he had to eyeball where the Crimson Tracker area was from outside by the vague colors he could see through the formations. It was far from ideal, and if anyone caught on and alerted the Celestial Warden, he would have to abort the mission as fast as a tree could, which was a speed comparable to a slightly alarmed turtle.

"Just a few more meters…" Ashlock took his time as the afternoon turned to evening. Just when he thought Stella might have been mistaken, his ethereal root made contact with another tree's roots, and judging by the acid it secreted into the soil, it was definitely a demonic tree.

Intertwining his roots, Ashlock knew it would take at least a day before their roots fully fused and this demonic tree joined his offspring. But he still wanted to look around, so using the demonic tree as cover, he poked his ethereal root out of the soil within a gap under one of the tree's exposed roots.

Expanding out his spiritual senses, he was surprised that the suppression was less up here than when traveling through the Iron Seeker area. "Everything is so blurry, though," Ashlock grumbled as he glanced around. He could only see a few dozen meters in every direction, and what he assumed was the Crimson Tracker pavilion was completely impenetrable.

A few figures wearing black robes and red jade masks strode past, neither paying the silent demonic tree in the middle of the square a second glance. "This reminds me of when I first came to this world. Blurry vision, distorted voices, and unable to do much."

Luckily, he didn't have to rely on only spiritual sight. Casting {Eye of the Tree God}, his view shifted to the sky above the demonic tree. With a clear view of the Crimson Tracker area, he could now appreciate how big the demonic tree he was hiding under was.

"Strange, a tree this big should have developed into a spirit tree of at least the Qi Realm by now," Ashlock wondered and then remembered how the defensive formations on this mountain were like a black hole in how they sucked in all the surrounding Qi. "This poor tree has been starved of Qi its whole life. No wonder it's so far behind on its path to becoming a spirit tree."

That aside, Ashlock was happy. He now had peace of mind as he could watch over his sect members as they caused havoc here in the Eternal Pursuit Pavilion. "I will also be able to help them once I fuse my roots with this demonic tree and can use my full power through it via {Progeny Dominion}. Oh, actually, I have an idea…"

Ashlock began to hollow out the ethereal root. "This will give Stella and Diana a way to quickly escape here if needed. I will keep the top of it closed for now as I don't want some random bounty hunter falling through, but I can open it when needed."

Now that he had secured his adopted daughter an escape route, it was time to scout out her workplace to ensure everything was safe. Humming to himself, he checked out each building in the square. If he had to guess based on the signs, these were trading halls, such as the alchemy hall, with a pill bottle carved into its sign.

Unfortunately, he couldn't venture into any of the buildings and was stuck looking down at them from above. Although {Eye of the Tree God} may allow him to ignore the defensive formation suppression, he could not look through walls with it.

Ashlock sighed. "If only my spiritual sight wasn't so suppressed, I would be able to freely look inside the buildings. Whatever, let's check out the rest of this place."

Besides the trading halls, he found an arena behind the Crimson Tracker pavilion. "This looks far more impressive than the Iron Seeker arena that Diana described, which sounded more like a sand pit." Ashlock was grateful they had gone for an open roof so he could look inside. The easiest way to describe what he saw was an arena befitting of Hell with black and red everywhere.

There was still a sand pit, but it was blood-red sand this time. Meanwhile, the stands seemed to be made of a rock similar to obsidian and covered in veins of silvery spirit stones that interconnected to create a vast formation. "I bet that protects the spectators from the battle."

From his understanding, Crimson Trackers were often in the Star Core Realm, so such precautions made sense. Qi Realm cultivators could only empower their bodies with Qi, and Soul Fire Realm cultivators could imbue their Qi into weapons like swords or long-range attacks. Child's play in comparison to Star Core Realm fights where combat was taken to the skies on flying swords, and their exerted presence alone was enough to make weaker cultivators kneel.

"It makes me wonder what a fight between Nascent Soul or even Monarch Realm cultivators would look like," Ashlock mused as he moved on to another area. "It's a level of power that is hard to fathom despite being on the cusp of ascending to that realm myself."

Beyond the square, all Ashlock found were other smaller shops and houses.

"People live up here?" Ashlock wondered. "Oh yeah, they did mention that the Lotus Informant that shouted out their names lived on the mountain peak, so they couldn't easily get revenge on her. I suppose it makes sense. Those Lotus Informants know too much information to be allowed to walk around freely."

In the residential area, everyone walked around wearing the same black cloak and mask, so it was hard to differentiate who was a Lotus Informant and who was a cultivator. There were also guards patrolling the area, who stood out as their black cloaks had giant red phoenixes embroidered on their backs and were openly carrying weapons.

Ashlock looked around some more. Besides restaurants and more shops, he didn't find anything of interest. Since the evening drew near, he decided to check on Stella at the Duskwalker residence.

Having searched the entire residence and coming up empty, Ashlock eventually found Stella in a rather peculiar situation in the basement. She was standing beside Larry, and the two were putting on a show for dozens of cultivators from the Mystshroud family. Stella was using her spatial Qi to make the air ripple and bend to her will, while Larry's body, made from silver ash, was shimmering and shifting, making him look like a divine deity as they stood on a podium.

"**Stella, what the hell are you doing?**" Ashlock asked in confusion. "**I leave you two alone for a few hours and come back to this nonsense...**"

"Oh, Tree. Great timing," Stella replied mentally. *"I got bored talking to the other Elders, so I came to see what Larry was up to, and it seemed fun."*

"**Right...what is he doing exactly?**"

Stella shrugged. *"Dunno. These idiots seem to think he is some divine being, but none of them can understand the ancient runic language, so he has done nothing but wave his legs at them, which seems enough to earn their awe."*

"**I see,**" Ashlock muttered as he looked over the crowd. They all had distinctive silver hair and deep violet eyes. However, one girl stood out from the rest as she was right at the front and seemed far more into it than anyone else as she slammed her head repeatedly into the floor. "**Who's that crazy girl at the front?**"

Stella glanced down. *"Ah, that's Elysia, the one corrupted by Maple's sibling."*

"Mhm, having such devotion from someone capable of summoning a Worldwalker would be useful," Ashlock mused. He hadn't put a lot of thought into this whole cult thing as it felt disingenuous as he wasn't really an evil god, but if the people were happy to trick themselves into believing he was, how could he turn down such a beneficial relationship?

"Heavenly loyalty contracts are great to prevent betrayal, but they don't force the person to devote their whole being to me like a cult member would. Maybe I should lean more into this. What did those mortals in the mine call me? The All-Seeing Eye?"

Ashlock continued watching the zealous devotion and realized he could reward devotion with pills. "Actually, no evil cult is complete without a secret language. Since Larry can only speak the ancient runic language, I should have them all become fluent with Language Comprehension fruits. Oh! I also want to be able to speak to them directly, so I should have them eat Mind Fortress fruits. Their minds are already broken from mystic Qi, so without the help of the fruit, they might even die."

Since mystic Qi let them create things from their imagination, he would give them an experience they would never forget.

"Hey, Stella."

"Yeah?"

"Let's start a cult."

Elysia Mystshroud wiped the blood off her forehead. The cold stone beneath her knees was cracked and pounded into the shape of her face as she had continuously bowed as deeply as she could since last night.

Her plan was simple. If she pounded the glory of this divine monster into her consciousness, perhaps it would recognize her, and its teaching would become clearer. The spider, made from a cloud of shimmering divine ash, had uttered incomprehensible words of wisdom thus far and shown them how to pray to it by waving its legs.

If only I could comprehend a speck of its divinity, I'm sure I would be able to peer further into the beyond! Elysia got giddy just thinking about it, so with all her strength, she bowed once again, smashing her face into the rock.

"Rejoice!" A woman's voice carried by Qi filled the room, silencing everyone.

Who dares? Elysia straightened her back and was surprised to see the words had come from the cloaked woman beside the divine spider.

"Your devotion has been acknowledged by the Herald of the Divine Ash, his highness King Larry of the nine realms!" the woman continued as she raised a black dagger and pointed it to the ceiling.

"As such, you have earned the right to be gazed upon by the Immortal who summoned him, the All-Seeing Eye!"

Elysia's entire body trembled in anticipation as she slowly rose to her feet. *Yes, yes, yes, yes, this is it! The divine spider finally accepted my faith! My self-torture was not in vain!*

A sudden pressure descended on the room, making everyone buckle slightly. Elysia grunted as she strained the muscles in her neck. She refused to miss the arrival of this All-Seeing Eye.

"Suffer under the gaze of the All-Seeing Eye! Those worthy should step forward under its scrutiny to receive his profound words."

The air above the woman holding the dagger cracked and rippled before a rift like no other, reaching all the way to the ceiling, slowly opened. Peering through it was an eye that would dwarf a human and contained an indescribable gaze.

This is... Elysia's mouth opened and closed as she tried to find the words to describe what she saw. *The eye of man contains desire, lust, and pain, while the eye of a beast is shrouded in rage, insanity, and hunger.* Elysia felt all the hairs on her neck stand at attention, and an ice-cold shiver ran down her spine like no other. *This gaze is different. It belongs to a being beyond such trivial emotions and seems capable of peering straight into my soul and judging it. Something alien and incomprehensible to my puny mind!*

Elysia cycled mystic Qi and opened her mind to a full mental assault. The edges of her consciousness shuddered and cracked as if something was trying to claw its way in from the other side. Even as she coughed up blood, she let it continue.

The more broken my mind, the greater my power! Elysia grinned with bloodstained teeth. It was the truth her summon had whispered to her at night as it showed her horrifying visions. The less she resisted the terror, the easier it became, and the stronger her summon also grew.

Laughing manically, she strode forward toward the eye and the portal, along with a few others trailing behind.

The dagger-holding woman and the divine spider stood aside and revealed a second, smaller portal that seemed to lead to a forest enshrouded in fog. Without fear, Elysia stepped through and felt her ears pop, and a cold wind blew past.

Is this demonic Qi mist? Elysia wondered as she glanced around.

She could still feel the eyes gaze on her, so looking up, she saw the moon in the sky, which had been eclipsed by the eye peering at her through another portal. *It really is the All-Seeing Eye. Not only can it glimpse into my soul, but it's always watching wherever I go.*

A while passed, and a small group of cultivators from her family had been deemed worthy and managed to step though the portal. Some were coughing blood while others were tearing out their hair, but overall, they seemed as sane as usual.

Elysia had since calmed down and almost felt comforted by the gaze that replaced the moon.

"Okay, now that you are all here," the woman announced and pulled off her hood and mask, revealing her short blond hair and crazed pink eyes, "my name is Stella, and I will be guiding this service today for the cult of the All-Seeing Eye. If you want to reach the next level of acceptance and to receive his divine word, you must first eat these fruits to shield your mind from breaking beyond repair and another to understand the teachings."

What fruit? Elysia wondered but was soon answered when two fruits fell through the portal in the sky and floated before her. Reaching out, she devoured both without another thought. One tasted sweet, the other sour. She felt a calming wave pass through her consciousness and also heightened attention to those speaking around her.

"Everyone done? I hope so. Otherwise, you may never be sane again." Stella laughed as the tree behind her suddenly extruded a presence similar to the one from before and burst into purple flames that reached the skies. "Now gather close. You don't want to be left out."

Elysia obeyed the words of the cult leader and huddled with the others below the burning tree. A bubble suddenly spread out, engulfing them in another dimension filled with mystic Qi.

Stella was gone, leaving them alone with the tree.

"*I have deemed you worthy of joining the cult of the All-Seeing Eye.*" A thousand voices echoed in Elysia's mind, and the surrounding mystic Qi seemed to mirror the being's thoughts as it transitioned from an aimless purple mist to a dense forest of towering demonic trees casting a looming shadow.

Everyone else was gone; it was just her kneeling before the All-Seeing Eye.

Despite her surroundings, Elysia could feel the encroaching darkness barely held off by the fruit she had eaten and a million eyes on her.

The floating eye shifted and looked at her more closely. ***"I can feel great potential in you, Elysia Mystshroud. More than the others as you have seen things others have not."***

Elysia planted her head on the ground. "I am honored by your praise." The eyes and thousand voices sent visions through her mind as if existence bent to its desires. *Am I going through enlightenment?*

"I appoint you as the new cult vice leader under Stella," the voice declared. ***"Serve me well."***

Elysia looked up and met the eye's gaze. "It would be an honor."

37
PRINCESS OF ASHFALLEN

Uninterested in being drowned in mystic Qi and having her mind wholly torn apart, Stella left Ashlock to his evil god antics and headed back through the portal to the basement of the Duskwalker residence and upstairs to the meeting room. Her hand paused on the doorknob as she overheard the voices from inside; it didn't sound like politics- or finance-related speech, so with some hesitation, she turned the knob and walked inside.

Everyone was here except the Grand Elder of the Mystshroud family. Despite his claimed superiority over the other mystic Qi cultivators, he also fell for Ash's scheme and was deemed worthy of joining the cult of the All-Seeing Eye.

"Oh, Stella, just in time." Diana stood up from her chair. "We should leave to meet Seth soon."

Stella smiled at her best friend. "Yeah, it's almost dusk, and he should be waiting for us at the meeting point in Nightshade City. It wouldn't be good to leave him waiting."

Evelyn looked between them with concern. "Are you two really sure about this? I know you are both stronger than anyone knows, but there's a good reason the bounty reached as high as 10,000 Yinxi Coins despite Albis Lunarshade's cultivation level."

"I was actually going to ask you about that," Stella said. She pulled out her pendant and inserted some Qi into it, revealing the bounty she had saved was on its back in golden letters.

> **[Death of Albis Lunarshade]**
> **Target's estimated threat level:** Star Core 2
> **Affiliation with the Lunarshade Family:** Nascent Soul 6
> **Bounty:** 10,000 Yinxi Coins
> **The bounty is placed by Corvin Blightbane. For more information, consult a Lotus Informant.**

"It says here that the bounty was placed by Corvin Blightbane." Stella glanced at the Grand Elder of the Blightbane family, who sat hunched in a chair beside Evelyn. Like fading embers, his eyes peered through a curtain of hair as dark as rotting wood, and he let out a small sigh.

"Corvin Blightbane was my father. He placed that bounty on Albis before his death."

Stella raised a brow. "How did he die?"

"The same way you two are about to—he hunted down Albis Lunarshade after that crazed bastard kidnapped his wife and ended up perishing at the hands of the Lunarshades' Grand Elder." The man let out a sad chuckle. "My old man was so blinded by rage he pulled the rest of us down with him. Most of us died seeking vengeance. Only a handful of the Blightbane family are left now to live on as a sad husk of our former glory."

"So this 10,000 Yinxi Coin bounty was placed before your father's death and still remains?" Stella asked.

The Blightbane Grand Elder nodded. "We could request the Eternal Pursuit Pavilion to give us a portion of the money back, but we have not bothered. As angry as I am with him, that bounty is his legacy. He wanted nothing more than the death of Albis Lunarshade, so I have left it alone."

Stella's eyes widened a little. *I forgot how much this family of death Qi cultivators cared about the legacies. Now, it all makes more sense.*

"Why hasn't the bounty been completed thus far?" Diana asked Evelyn, who still looked concerned. "Is it because it's similar to Nox, where people feared the person standing behind them too much to dare complete the bounty?"

"That's part of it," Evelyn agreed, "though plenty have tried to kill Albis despite the risk of angering the Lunarshade family. Those fools were convinced they could skip town before news of the bounty being completed reached the ears of the Lunarshade Grand Elder."

"What happened to those who tried?" Diana said.

"All died," Evelyn said bluntly. "No matter their cultivation level, they never came back. I appreciate what you two are trying to do for me and this partnership, but I still think this is too risky. There are other bounties or missions you can take Stella to reach the Crimson Trackers, and in time, you will make those 10,000 Yinxi Coins from selling pills. It's not worth it in my eyes."

Stella and Diana exchanged a glance.

"It should be fine, right?" Diana asked, a hint of skepticism in her voice.

Stella tapped her chin and hummed as she thought this mission over.

"It should be fine. Since it's happening outside the Eternal Pursuit Pavilion, the immortal can lend us his assistance," Stella reasoned. "I can tell this is a trap from a mile away, believe me. The question is how and who."

"Seth is certainly suspicious." Diana stroked her chin. "But he is our only way to supposedly find this man, as even Evelyn doesn't know where he is most of the time."

"It's true," Evelyn said as her face twisted into a scowl. "And I prefer it that way. I only visit the Lunarshade residence to ask where he is when times get tough or I must mellow them out of acting against us. What that bastard does in his free time is of no interest to me."

Stella nodded. "Makes sense. Also, Diana, Seth may be suspicious of your true strength, but he still believes me to be an early-stage Star Core cultivator at most with subpar skills, as I didn't get a recommendation letter like you did. We can use that to our advantage."

"Fine." Diana sighed. "I don't see how they beat us with the Immortal's support unless the Lunarshade Grand Elder is there. In which case, we can only hope Larry or Maple can save us."

Stella held her cloak's hood in place from billowing in the cold winds with telekinesis as she soared over Nightshade City, standing on her sword. To her side was Diana, who was also on a sword rather than using her wings, as they didn't want to attract that much attention. Two Star Core cultivators with uncommon affinities flying around here already raised eyebrows, but a gliding demoness would earn the ire of the pavilion.

"Tree, are you there?" Stella asked the air.

"Always," he replied, his presence blooming in her mind. Ash's voice used to break her mind, but now it was the most comforting voice in the world to her.

Stella pouted. "That's a lie, and you know it."

"Hey, I am cutting into my sleeping time to watch over you. Is that not proof enough that I am always here?"

Stella rolled her eyes. "You are so unbelievably lazy. The sun hasn't even fully set yet, and you are talking about going to sleep."

"For a tree, I would argue that I am quite productive! I mean, I just established a cult in a single evening. Is that not impressive?"

Stella snorted. "Impressive? Are you trying to take credit for other people's work again? Larry was the one who gathered them all, and you didn't even come up with the cult name yourself! You stole it from some mortals that got scared by you."

"Fair...but Larry is technically my summon, so his achievements are mine, too."

"Uh-huh, sure they are." Stella couldn't believe what she was hearing. *This is why I want to train Jasmine as soon as possible. Life is so easy when you can have others do the hard work and then appear at the last moment when you are needed.*

"Can you two get serious for a minute? We are almost there," Diana said as she gave Stella a side-eye before tilting her sword and beginning her descent into the city.

"I am always serious." Stella clicked her tongue and followed Diana.

"Anyway, why are you two going alone anyway? I may watch over you and have the Ents and Larry on standby, but why not take the other Elders with you?"

Stella shrugged. "Seth said if we had too big of a group, it would cause Albis to flee while his goons fought us off. Apparently, he only takes on fights that he believes he can win."

"What about the fact you guys are hunting down a lunar affinity cultivator during dusk? Wouldn't he be weaker during the daytime?"

Stella tapped her chin. "Err, I think Seth said that Albis only appears in public under the moonlight."

Ash sighed. *"How convenient... This is beyond sketchy."*

"I agree." Stella nodded. "But it should be fine. We are far stronger than Albis believes. My bounty claims I am at the first stage of the Star Core Realm when I am actually at the sixth."

"That's true. I worry about you, but I must admit you have grown in strength at an impressive rate," Ash said, warming Stella's heart. *"On that note, how do you feel about the chances of your bloodline activating during this mission? Have you had any further insights into how it works?"*

"I think I have it mostly figured out." Stella nodded. "After some self-reflection, I believe for my bloodline to activate, I need to feel like my *pride* as a ruler is threatened rather than a location like your trunk or my life."

"Mhm, that's the conclusion I reached, too. Do you have any idea why it's your pride specifically? It hasn't activated in times your life was threatened, which I would think is more important than your pride. What use is pride if you're dead?"

"The cosmos told me those of my bloodline have ruled the realms since time immemorial," Stella explained. "Which wouldn't make sense as cultivators at the top have lived too long for an ordinary person to catch up and make them bend the knee. But my bloodline helps me bridge the gap by letting me tap into the knowledge and skills of my ancestors, so long as I maintain the pride of the Crestfallen bloodline."

"Interesting, so you believe your ancestors will lend you their aid to overcome adversity if they believe it will bring shame to their legacy."

Stella nodded. "Yeah, something like that. It makes me even more glad I didn't use a fake name when registering with the Eternal Pursuit Pavilion because I bet my ancestors would be less happy to assist me if I had. Also, I noticed they provide me with more help the greater the challenge I face."

"I see you have been putting a lot of thought into this since the duel with Diana," Ashlock replied. *"So do you believe you have a way to activate your bloodline on command now?"*

"Yeah, and I plan to test it during this bounty hunt." Stella frowned. "However, I still don't know how to activate my ancient bloodline's ultimate state, where I summon the celestial library and gain unlimited access to all my ancestors' knowledge."

"Considering how its presence basically crippled you, I don't think you are ready to use that on command anyway," Ashlock reassured her, and that seemed like a plausible explanation.

Although it made Diana back up in fear, I was so overwhelmed by the presence of the library and the cosmos that guarded it that I wouldn't be able to deflect an attack. For now, it's probably best that I focus on mastering the active part of my bloodline.

Stella disliked her bloodline as it felt like borrowing another person's power, unlike Diana's, which directly empowered her. However, she did retain some of the skills she exhibited while under its influence.

The more my ancestor's knowledge lives through me, the stronger I grow. It's only a matter of time before I can harness everything stored in that celestial library as my own strength. Just you wait, Cosmos. I will prove I am not an ant unworthy of your knowledge.

Armed with determination, Stella landed beside Diana, and they made the rest of their way to the meeting point on foot.

Stella stood in an alleyway near a main street alongside Diana and Seth. They used the secret keyword "Bitch Lotus Informant" to verify each other's identity as all of them wore their masks and thick black cloaks to obscure their body shapes.

"Okay, now what? Where is Albis?" Stella asked impatiently. They had been standing here in silence for a few minutes as the sky darkened and the coldness of night approached.

Seth poked his head around the corner while answering Stella's question in a whisper. "At the end of this street is the Holy Moon Gambling house. It's owned and run by the Lunarshade family, where Albis likes to spend his nights indulging in sin. An event is scheduled for tonight, which starts once the moon rises." He pulled back and turned to face them. "This street is locked down by guards of the Lunarshade family. We will need to get past them first."

"So, a slaughter?" Stella drew her sword. "That's easy enough."

Seth raised his hands. "Whoa, hold your horses. All of the guards wear artifacts that will activate an alarm in the gambling house if they are killed. It's best to try and have them all attack you at once so you can kill them all in one go and then storm the gambling house."

Diana sighed. "What a load of nonsense. First, you tell us to bring a small fighting force of only two of us to avoid attention, then make us wait until the moon is out, and now you are telling us to draw attention?"

"Not to mention, you seem to know far too much about all this…" Stella added, narrowing her eyes behind her mask.

Seth shrugged. "I am a bounty hunter and have spent months tracking Albis's activities. Meeting the requirements for the Crimson Trackers aside, I have personal reasons I want him dead, too. You are free to back out of the plan now, and I can find someone else, but this is 10,000 Yinxi Coins from which you are walking away. It's just a dozen family guards. I am sure you can handle them."

He deflected all of the questions. What a sly bastard.

"Well, thank you for the questionable information," Diana said as she stepped past Seth. "You can leave now. We will take it from here."

Seth tilted his head. "I'm coming with you, too. Who else will identify Albis once you are inside? Don't worry, I won't get in your way. I will hang back and cover your escape path."

"This guy is up to something. It's best to keep your friends close but your enemies closer," Ashlock said in Stella's mind. **"I will keep an eye on him for you, so don't worry."**

Stella nodded and patted Seth on the shoulder. "Whatever, let's go."

"But…" Diana groaned.

"Diana, hang back for now as well. I need to test something." Stella stepped out into the street, her sword resting on her shoulder, and began strolling toward the majestic building in the distance.

Diana walked a step behind and hissed under her breath. "Stella, what are you up to?" She used Qi to hide her voice from Seth, who followed close behind.

"Seth said we need to draw the guard's attention, right?" Stella said via her Qi without having to turn her head. "I also want to test my bloodline by drawing attention to myself, so this will kill two birds with one stone."

"What nonsense are you on about?" Diana huffed. "This is a bounty from which nobody comes back alive. We should take this seriously."

"I am?" Stella said with confusion. "I am at my strongest when my bloodline is active. Without it, we would be at a significant disadvantage. The only problem is what I must do for it to activate."

"Oh? You found out how to activate it on command?"

"In theory, yes. Have you ever heard of noble cultivators defending their family's honor by entering duels?"

"Yeah, a bunch of prideful idiots." Diana shook her head. "You say one off-handed comment about their family, and before you know it, they are throwing a glove at your face and demanding a duel to the death. Those Skyrend bastards were the greatest offenders of this, according to my father."

Stella smiled wearily behind her mask as she noticed several cultivators surrounding them in the spatial plane. "Well, um…"

Diana paused her steps. "Don't tell me… There's no way in hell that the way to activate your bloodline is what I think it is."

"Sometimes the worst answer is the right answer." Stella sighed.

"Identify yourselves!" A white robe man hopped down from a nearby roof, blocking their path. Many others followed, and soon, a dozen gathered between them and the Holy Moon Gambling house. They all drew swords that glinted in the moonlight.

Stella estimated that a few were in the early stages of the Star Core Realm. Slaughtering them would be a breeze, making this the perfect time to test her theory. She stepped forward and slowly removed her mask, revealing her face to the enemy. As the cultivators studied her face, she felt a slight tingle. *It seems showing my face is enough to awaken it a little,* Stella thought with relief.

"I do not recognize you as a friend of Lord Lunarshade," the man at the front insisted as he raised his sword higher. "Identify yourself. I will not repeat myself again."

"My name is Stella Crestfallen, first princess of the Ashfallen Sect." She raised her chin at them and stared at them condescendingly. "Your 'Lord' is a stain on my domain that I wish to eliminate. Do you dare prevent my passage now that you have heard my name?"

Diana groaned behind her, but Stella could feel it working as the tingle turned to whispers.

The man glanced confusedly at those beside him, who shook their heads. Looking back at her with a reddened face, he bellowed, "Woman, are you sane? I have no knowledge of the Crestfallen family or this Ashfallen Sect. If you are so eager to die, I welcome you to impale yourself on my sword for speaking so rudely about my Lord."

Despite being faced with many antagonistic opponents, Stella felt that familiar calmness spread through her body as the whispers in the back of her mind grew irritated as if they had taken that insult personally.

Her bloodline had activated, but there was a problem. Other than the calm state, she felt nothing else. *Either my ancestors aren't insulted enough, or they don't deem this enough of a challenge to bother lending their aid.*

Stella stored away her sword and had an idea. *I want to teach Jasmine some better fist-fighting techniques, but I never really learned any. I have always relied too much on my sword.*

Raising a single finger, Stella smirked at her enemies. "If I, Stella Crestfallen, cannot defeat you all with a single finger, then may my bloodline be forever mocked."

Her mind suddenly opened up to a flood of information about a technique that forced its way into her mind like a raging river. It was overwhelming, and her head began to throb with a pounding headache. Her vision blurred, and standing up became difficult. She started swaying and trying not to throw up.

"Arrogant bitch." The man's face twisted into a scowl, and he charged forward. "You think you can defeat the head of the Lunar-shade guard with a mere finger while drunk? You can hardly even stand! How laughable—"

Stella swayed to the side, narrowly avoiding his overhead sword swing. Her hand blurred as she burrowed her Qi-wreathed finger like a dagger into his temple, piercing his brain. There was a second of realization on the man's face before the life left his eyes, and he collapsed to the floor in a heap.

There was a brief moment of silence as all the guards looked on in shock at how their commander had died in such a way before it was broken by a loud gong noise originating from the Holy Moon Gambling house. The alarm Seth had warned her about had activated.

Diana sprang into action, leaping over her head with her giant feathered wings of darkness growing from her back and claws. She landed among a group of cultivators and began ripping them apart. That group tried to fight her off, while another group decided to rush Stella.

Stella closed her eyes and entered the spatial plane, muttering, "It looks like I have no reason to hold back anymore. To please my ancestors and learn this new technique, they will all perish at my fingertip."

38
WRATH OF THE KING

Stella charged toward the Lunarshade guards, but it was hard to focus. Headache aside, it was rather distracting to have the philosophy and teachings of the **Supreme Nirvana Finger** technique forcefully passed down to her via the chorus of her ancestors.

Humans fear scorpion tails and ant stings, so why wouldn't the gods fear the wrath of humankind's finger?

It's not about the size of one's weapon but its capability to kill.

Swords breed fear in the enemy, raising their guard. Nobody fears a finger.

Through all the conflicting lessons shouted at her and the tingling feeling of the technique returning to her like an old trained muscle, Stella inferred that the Supreme Nirvana Finger technique had multiple stages.

Stage one was all about understanding Nirvana. From the visions and memories playing in her mind, it seemed that cultivators of this technique usually began by meditating on the concept of Nirvana, learning to detach from desires and emotions, which helped stabilize and purify their inner energy.

As lofty as that sounds, this really means purging the body of heart demons and maintaining a clear mind while fighting, as the technique demands an immense amount of Qi to be concentrated into a single point before striking, Stella mused. *I have Ash's truffles to purge my heart demons, the passive effect of my bloodline keeps me calm in battle, and my spirit roots are so pure that I can freely control the Qi in my body with ease. Why do I feel like I am cheating sometimes?*

Having already completed stage one, Stella focused on stage two, the art of Qi Gathering. This was the main part of the technique and was quite simple. All she had to do was condense her Qi into an extremely dense state in her finger, allowing explosive power to be channeled through minimal physical movement.

When I killed the first guard, I rammed my finger all the way into his brain, but against weaklings like these, a simple tap should be enough.

Deciding to test the technique on the fly, Stella calmly stepped within strike range of a Lunarshade cultivator at the forefront of the group rushing toward her. His face was red, twisted in rage, and he bared his teeth as he went for a wide swing. "Die, you crazy bitch!" he shouted as a white glow reminiscent of condensed moonlight covered his entire body and sword.

He is being empowered by the moonlight but is only in the late stages of the Soul Fire Realm, as I don't feel the pressure of a Star Core. This will be a good test of this technique's piercing power. Stella took a half step backward and leaned back so the sword harmlessly passed her over her chest. Straightening up with a grin, she reached forward and gently placed her index finger on the man's forehead as he tried to recover his stance from overswinging.

"Goodbye," Stella said.

"Wha—" The man's eyes widened before Stella unleashed all the dense sixth-stage Star Core Qi she had condensed into a single point at her fingertip. The spot on his forehead rippled as the spatial Qi pulsed out. Unable to resist the attack, the moonlight energy shrouding him dispersed in a wave, and his head exploded backward, showering the other cultivators in blood and cutting them with shards of flying bone.

The headless corpse collapsed like a sack of potatoes at Stella's feet to the beat of the gong from the Holy Moon Gambling house. The alarm was still ongoing, so it was up to the people hiding inside to either come out and fight or flee.

Despite the easy victory, Stella frowned as she looked at her finger. *I guess it works, but I could have achieved the same thing with a punch or sword swing for a tenth of the Qi. Also, I have to direct all my Qi to my fingertip, leaving the rest of the body less defended. I suppose this technique would be ideal for assassinating people or piercing someone's defenses, but against these weaklings, this is a real waste.*

Stella leaped backward to put some space between herself and the Lunarshade guards as her Qi recovered. Now that she was further away, she realized another issue.

Unlike a sword, a finger has no range. I had to get up close to use the technique, which was fine against these guards. But what if I was against a void cultivator? That would be far too risky.

Stella sighed as she calmly gazed at the other Lunarshade guards, who were wide-eyed from the shock of seeing one of their own killed in such a brutal way. Their faces and white robes were stained red from the blast, and there was a carpet of blood between them and Stella.

Unfortunately, she had run her mouth and promised to defeat everyone here with a single finger, so she would have to shed her tears over the wasted Qi later and suck it up for now.

"Come at me," Stella said as if bored, beckoning them to come closer with her finger. The five cultivators all stared at her gesturing finger, which she had used to kill the last two, and didn't dare step forward.

"Got cold feet? Fine, let's make this quick and easy, then." Stella used the Supreme Nirvana Finger, drawing most of the Qi in her body toward her index finger.

Now, who should I target this time? Stella narrowed her eyes at the Lunarshade guards. In the middle of the group was an older-looking woman who was bald and had no eyebrows, which Stella found rather odd. *She also seems to be the strongest left in the group as a first-stage Star Core, so I should eliminate her next. Once all of these people are dead, I will have fulfilled my promise to my ancestors and can go back to using my sword instead of this wasteful finger technique.*

Stella used Spatial Step to close the gap, but to her surprise, she was flung out of the technique early, stumbling before the bald woman instead of appearing behind like she had intended. Barely managing to catch her footing, she found herself surrounded and confused.

What the hell happened? Stella wondered and searched for the answer by looking within. All of her Qi was greedily consumed by the Supreme Nirvana Finger technique, meaning there wasn't enough left over for a Qi-intensive technique like Spatial Step.

Having found the problem, Stella faced a more imminent threat.

She was surrounded, and the bald woman staring her down was in the Star Core Realm. Although a few stages below her, Stella's life was in danger as she had recklessly consumed all of her Qi.

Luckily, her bloodline kept her calm in such a situation, so she worked without hesitation to eliminate the strongest target. Armed with nothing but a death's touch, Stella moved her body to ram her finger into the woman's chest with the intent of blowing her heart to pieces.

The bald woman answered her attack in kind by reaching up with her free hand and grabbing Stella's wrist, holding it an inch away from her robes. To Stella's surprise, she didn't have the strength to wrestle out of the woman's grip.

"You caught the other two by surprise," the woman mocked as she pushed Stella's hand away to a safe distance. "But now that I know your trick, what will you do?"

Stella twisted her wrist and curled her finger so it touched the woman's wrist. "I will do this." There was a moment of realization on the bald woman's face before Stella unleashed the stored-up Qi straight into her hand. A pulse of spatial Qi erupted out, making the air ripple —washing away the bald woman's moonlight protection and obliterating her hand and part of her arm in a shower of blood.

That should buy me some time— Stella shelved that thought as the bald woman was unfazed by her missing hand and used her other to swing her moonlight-wreathed sword downward— *Oh shit.*

Stella managed to tilt her body to the side to avoid the blade from splitting her head open like an egg, but the sword came too fast to entirely avoid and bit into her shoulder. She hissed through gritted teeth as a sharp pain like no other informed her of the deep wound and broken shoulder bones.

At this moment, Stella finally realized she had been blinded by arrogance. These opponents were indeed beneath her in terms of cultivation. But she had handicapped herself to bait her ancestors into giving her a technique she was undeserving of, that she had no experience using, and learning its limitations in actual combat.

She dropped to one knee, as she didn't have enough Qi within her body to resist the downward force of the bald woman's sword. She noticed the surrounding cultivators raising their hands, and after a flash of moonlight energy, her body was encased in ice. It burned her skin and made her want to scream.

"Stella!" Ashlock's voice thundered in her mind.

"Tree...help..." Stella gasped out.

"Muttering nonsense before your execution?" The bald woman sneered as she raised the sword above her head. Her eyes were ice cold, and Stella noticed the woman's hand rapidly regrowing from the moonlight. "I will bring your head to the Lord so he may claim your bounty."

No! I don't want to die. Stella's eyes widened as she pushed as much Qi as she could muster into her earrings. The woman glaring down at her briefly faltered under Stella's gaze, which was what she had hoped for. However, due to the earrings' activation, the calmness of her bloodline faded alongside the whispers, as she had gone against her promise of only using her finger. Perhaps as punishment, she now had a pounding headache reminiscent of the backlash she suffered from overusing her ability at the alchemy tournament.

Movement techniques are fine, but outside help from an artifact seems to have angered my ancestors. I guess they dislike borrowing power from someone else. Stella frowned. She had not only shamed herself but also her bloodline, which she didn't think would bother her, but weirdly, it did.

A sudden wrathful pressure blanketed the area, carried by a howling wind that made all the Lunarshade guards stumble back and cover their faces. Meanwhile, Stella could only look up as a crack appeared in the sky and the wind rustled her hair. For a moment, she thought it was her ancestors deciding to smite her down, but to her relief, her opponents had angered an evil god.

Looks like my carelessness has made Tree angry. Stella smiled wearily through the pain and felt rather pathetic having to be saved by her dad while fighting such weak opponents, but it would be a lie to say she wasn't relieved.

"What is happening?" the bald woman shouted to her subordinates as she blinked away the madness and ignored Stella in favor of watching the sky being torn apart into a colossal rift.

"We don't know," one of the other cultivators replied.

"Contact the Grand Elder!" another shouted. "Tell him his son is about to be attacked by an unknown powerhouse."

"By who, though?!" a third one shouted.

"You hurt a princess," Stella muttered over the chaotic wind. "So now you face the king."

The bald woman glared at her, unable to get close due to the wind. "Still uttering such delusions, you crazed drunk?" She pointed to the sky and screamed over the howling wind, "That's the power of a Nascent Soul Realm or even a Monarch Realm cultivator, not some fake king of your unknown Ashfallen Sect. I know the name and powers of every reported Nascent Soul Realm cultivator, and none of them can open such a rift! How can you look so smug? You are going to die alongside the rest of us."

Stella looked up at the rift with a warm smile as her hair was tossed about in the wind. "I wouldn't be so sure."

"Oh yeah? I will cut you down myself, then."

"Threatening me in this situation is a bad idea," Stella said simply, angering the woman further.

"What nonsense—" A shadow loomed overhead, followed by the entire ground trembling as the bald woman was pulverized under a fist of black wood.

Stella grinned at the towering Ent of black wood, which looked down at her with two burning eyes of lilac flames. "Thank you, Titus!"

"M-Monster..." One of the Lunarshade guards dropped his sword and turned to run. A smaller portal appeared behind him, and a black vine ending in a giant spike shot out and impaled him. He let out a loud gasp as the air escaped his lungs and was then dragged away back to Red Vine Peak.

The other guards met a similar fate, including the ones Diana was battling with. In a mere moment, Ash had come in and wiped the battlefield clean.

Stella sighed in relief. "Phew, that was almost bad..."

"Are you all right, Stella?" Ash asked in a panic. *"Just hold on. I am sending more help."*

"What?" Stella shouted in surprise. The battle was over. "There's no need—"

Alas, her overprotective dad wouldn't listen to her.

The ground trembled again as Ents began raining from the sky and surrounded her. Sol kneeled before her, fished out multiple wisps of light, and pressed them into her body to heal her wounds.

"Tree, this is embarrassing," Stella grumbled as Titus channeled spatial Qi into her body, and Zeus carefully used his lightning to melt away the ice encasing her.

"This is the least I can do. They dared to hurt you, so now I will kill them all," Ash replied nonchalantly.

"But it was my fault." Stella sighed. *I was also the one brutally killing them in the first place...*

"Stella, there is only one thing I care about in this world: those under the Ashfallen Sect. Let me show these moon-loving bastards what this false king can do when they hurt one of my own."

He is serious. Stella gulped. This was the most angry she had ever heard him.

The doors to the Holy Moon Gambling house swung open, and a giant, bald-headed man with pupilless eyes adorned in an extravagant bathrobe, assisted in walking by a group of beautiful cultivators, stepped outside and glared up at the rift overhead.

"Who dares slaughter my guards?" the man bellowed to the sky, his voice carried by Qi.

"Is that Albis Lunarshade?" Ash asked.

Stella shook her head. "No."

"No?" Ash questioned while barely holding back his rage.

Stella summoned her sword to her hand and rolled her shoulders. Thanks to Titus, she was now filled with enough Qi to fight. She turned on her heel and used Spatial Step to catch up to a fleeing Seth.

Seth turned in time to meet her sword with his own in a shower of sparks. After the brief exchange, they parted.

"How did you know?" Seth asked as the wind from Ashlock's pressure made his hood fly back, revealing a bald head.

"Where do I even begin? You knew far too much about Albis Lunarshade for an Iron Seeker bounty hunter. The robes barely managed to hide your broad figure, and weirdly, the bald woman guard knew about me and my bounty as if she had been warned beforehand, which only you should have known about. However, most importantly," Stella pointed her sword to the moon, "even though you haven't revealed your soul flames once, I noticed you grew in strength and speed once the moon appeared. From all of this, I deduced you are Albis Lunarshade, which means the fat bastard that just came out of the pavilion must be your father, the Grand Elder of house Lunarshade."

Albis Lunarshade removed his mask to reveal his hairless face and pupilless eyes, which made Stella shiver a little at how soulless and creepy he looked. *Evelyn had to endure this person for so many years? No wonder she hates Nox with a burning passion.*

"Smart girl," Albis said with a shark-like grin. "After hearing the Lotus Informant we pay off shout out your name, I had hoped to claim your high bounty for myself without getting my father involved. But now that you have killed his guards and insulted him, I fear this has escalated beyond my original intentions. It was nice knowing you, but there is no hope for you to leave this place alive."

He speaks as if he will survive after angering Tree. Stella shook her head. *What a foolish man.*

"Bold words for a family about to face extinction."

Albis raised a hairless brow at her bold words, but his smile soon faded as a second pressure descended upon the battlefield, and the sky darkened even further. The stars and moonlight vanished under a sprawling cloud of silver ash originating from the rift.

Stella smiled as the guardian beast of the Ashfallen Sect graced the battlefield with his presence, and the cloud began to condense into the shape of a spider that loomed overhead.

"What in the nine realms is that?" Albis muttered in disbelief.

Stella kept quiet, enjoying his confusion as His Highness King Larry, the Herald of the Divine Ash, descended to eliminate those who stood in his master's way.

Tonight, there would be a slaughter.

39
AVATAR OF MOONLIGHT

As a tree spread across a thousand miles, the little things no longer bothered Ashlock. It took a lot for him to feel anything and stir his fading humanity into action, let alone explode with rage.

But it had happened. A group of pathetic weaklings had taken advantage of his adopted daughter's recklessness and pushed her to the brink of death. If not for his interference, Stella would have died such an easily preventable death. Just the thought of these moon-loving bastards taking the thing he cared about the most in this world from him made him seethe with rage.

Uncaring of controlling himself, his peak Star Core flared up like a god's furnace, turning Red Vine Peak into a beacon of lilac soul flames reaching for the heavens. The mountain range glowed with power as spatial Qi surged down his ethereal roots like a dam spillway toward the Tainted Cloud Sect in the east.

Sensing their father's rage, every demonic tree for a thousand miles copied their progenitor by igniting their leaves with soul flames and pouring their Qi into the network. Millions of birds fled to the skies in terror, and a chorus of monstrous roars to the moon spread across the continent. In Ashfallen and Darklight cities, the mortals were gathered in their thousands out in the streets, confused at what was happening, while some pointed toward Red Vine Peak.

Darklight City and the mountain range were lit up with orange soul fire, but much of Ashfallen City was shrouded in darkness due to Nox, who was also aflame with shadow soul flames. Under her canopy of darkness, Jasmine was huddling with her mom.

"Nox, what's happening?" Jasmine asked, tears in her eyes. *"Did something bad happen?"*

The shadow dryad, which had taken on a more human appearance than before, looked into the distance and spoke using Qi. *"Someone has managed to anger the one being in this realm they should not."* Nox turned her head and locked eyes with Jasmine. *"Whoever it is, I pity them. They have not only earned his ire but will now face the full wrath of Ashfallen. I can feel it through the roots. The realm trembles from his anger."*

Ashlock was uncaring of his unrestrained fury's effect on the continent, as his focus was above Nightshade City. Since the bounty mission had turned into a full-out war with the strongest family in the Tainted Cloud Sect, he had no plans to hold back. Having blanketed the area in his pressure through his roots, he was surprised that it seemed to carry wind affinity, likely due to his unformed Inner World.

The cat was out of the bag, and the Grand Elder of the Lunarshade family had already taken center stage. If Ashlock wanted to win, holding back even a little would guarantee a loss.

"Who are you people?" Grand Elder Lunarshade bellowed again, his Qi-infused voice shattering every window down the street and making Stella wince. *"Tell me, Albis, my son. Who have you foolishly led to our doorstep this time?"*

Despite being stared down by a storm made of divine ash emerging from a colossal rift in the sky and Ashlock's tallest Ents Titus and Zeus, the Lunarshade Grand Elder seemed mostly unfazed. An arrogance that was expected from a man who believed he was the strongest in the region at the sixth stage of the Nascent Soul Realm.

"Father," Albis took a respectful knee, *"before you is the supposed Princess of the Ashfallen Sect. An unknown powerhouse that recently became known through a bounty placed on Stella here by Nox Duskwalker."* Albis raised his head and grinned. *"Seeing that the bounty was placed by my ex-fiancée who dared to run away from me, I naturally took an interest in her."*

"I see." The towering man who stood only a head shorter than the Skyrends rubbed his hairless chin. He seemed totally hairless, and having fully white eyes without pupils was the defining feature of this

family of freaks. *"Well, come over here. It's dangerous for you."* His eyes narrowed at the Ents and Larry in the sky. *"These people aren't to be trifled with."*

Albis stood to his full height and brushed the dust off his cloak. *"As you wish, Father."* He gave Stella, surrounded by the Ents, a light smile and strode confidently toward his father. There was no hint of fear in either of their eyes, something Ashlock planned to change.

Sending a quick message to Ashfallen's executioner, Ashlock allowed Albis to enjoy his last walk in the realm of the living undisturbed. Titus and Zeus slowly swiveled their heads as they watched him confidently walk toward his father.

"Father, I have returned." Albis gave the Grand Elder a light bow as he stood before the man at the bottom of a dozen well-maintained stone steps.

The giant man gave his son a grin. *"Very good—"*

"Now," Ashlock said simply. Upon his orders, Khaos, the reaper of Ashfallen, silently emerged from the void behind Albis. It was a two-meter-tall creature similar to a wendigo, with long, spindly limbs ending in claws that might as well be swords and deer antler–style horns growing from its head.

The Grand Elder's eyes widened, and his entourage of beauties made hesitant steps back toward the building behind them.

"What's wrong, Father?" Albis asked. Confused after not receiving an answer, he turned around as he likely sensed nothing with his spiritual sense and came face to face with his death.

Khaos burrowed a void-coated claw straight into his chest and pulled free his still-beating heart. **Fear**, the emotion Ashlock had anticipated, finally appeared in the man's eyes.

"That's my," Albis gasped as he tried to reach for his still-beating heart, but his hand fell limp, *"heart."* He collapsed at Khaos's feet.

The unfazed Ent, honoring its master's orders, crushed the heart over Albis's dead body, making blood stain his robes and bald head

"Good," Ashlock said, his rage only slightly sated by the gruesome death of the one who had orchestrated this trap for Stella. **"Now, test the Grand Elder's defenses."**

Khaos silently returned to the void, reappearing behind the Lunarshade Grand Elder a second later with void-wreathed claws as instructed. Since there was more than an entire realm difference between the two, Ashlock didn't expect this to be enough to kill the man, even with the usual strengths of void affinity.

"Let's see if that arrogance of yours is deserved," Ashlock muttered as Khaos rammed its claws into the Grand Elder's back.

The Grand Elder was unfazed. Gentle wisps of moonlight that coated his skin warded off the void as if it were an impenetrable wall. Switching tactics, the Ent tried slashing and clawing at him, but the Grand Elder ignored the attacks. His pupilless gaze was locked onto his dead son at the foot of the stairs, who lay on the ground with his hand outstretched as if reaching for salvation.

"Do you have any idea," the Grand Elder slowly looked up at the moon, which dominated much of the sky despite the rifts and Larry's divine ash, *"what you have just done?"*

Sensing this wasn't working, Ashlock said quickly, **"Khaos, get out of there."**

The Ent vanished into the void, but to Ashlock's surprise, the Grand Elder raised his moonlight-wreathed hand and used some form of telekinesis to drag Khaos back to reality. He held Khaos by the neck with an iron-like grip as no matter how much the Ent struggled, it couldn't break free.

"Only one person has the right to kill my son." The Grand Elder pointed his finger to the moon, and Ashlock noticed the celestial object glow a brighter. *"And that would be me."*

The Ents were disposable in the grand scheme of things, but Khaos was one of the most useful Ents in his collection, so Ashlock quickly shouted to the guardian of Ashfallen, **"Larry, go! Stop him—"**

"Perish before the moon and let it free you of sin," the Grand Elder said before Ashlock could finish.

A beam of concentrated moonlight pierced the sky and bathed Khaos in its wrath. The Ent uttered a silent scream as it evaporated into black smoke. The beam vanished as quickly as it came, and the Grand Elder dropped his now-empty hand to his side. Khaos was nowhere to be seen, and the stone below the man's feet had become ice. Just like that, in a mere second, the reaper of Ashfallen was gone.

Ashlock didn't hesitate. He quickly created portals and pulled a bewildered Stella and Diana to the safety of Red Vine Peak with his vines.

"Holy shit. If that moonbeam attack had been aimed at Stella or

Diana, they would have died before I could even react, as it came instantly without warning." Ashlock wasn't that familiar with the strengths and weaknesses of lunar affinity and the capabilities of a Nascent Soul Realm cultivator. Hence, he used Khaos to test those limits, which turned out to be greater than anticipated. The Grand Elder easily resisted void attacks and straight-up pulled Khaos out of the void, which was beyond expectations.

Having annihilated his son's murderer, Ashlock noticed the Grand Elder's milky eyes shift to the sky at the giant ash spider descending toward him. Stepping forward, moonlight began to gather around his body, and the ground around him froze over and cracked from the pressure.

"Hang back for now, Larry. I know you are immortal so long as some of your ash remains, but this person is powerful," Ashlock said, then instructed Titus, Zeus, and Sol to attack. "No matter a cultivator's strength, they are beatable once they run out of Qi. I should use my Ents to weaken him before Larry goes in for the kill."

Clouds crackling with golden lightning began to gather in the skies, and the night briefly turned to day as Sol shot multiple light beams at the Lunarshade Grand Elder. Flashes of lightning and roaring thunder soon followed as Zeus pointed his finger at the Grand Elder. All the attacks landed, with the light beams having a noticeable impact as they ate away through a few layers of moonlight but never so much as singed the man's bathrobe.

Titus strode forward, and with spatial flame-wreathed fists, he swung down both hands to pulverize the Grand Elder.

"Do not mock me." The Grand Elder answered Titus with a flick of his finger, sending a wave of force up through Titus's arms, shattering them in a shower of black wood that rained down and causing the titan of wood to stumble back and collapse onto a group of nearby houses. The Grand Elder then vanished and reappeared before Zeus, planting his hand on its leg; the Ent was instantly flash-frozen into a statue of ice. Then, with a flick, the towering Ent reminiscent of a marble statue exploded backward as chunks of ice, obliterating an entire line of houses and anyone within them.

Ashlock took the brief moment that the Grand Elder was distracted to pull Sol and what was left of Titus away from the fight and reassess the situation. He felt like he was playing a game of chess where the repercussion for failure was death. If he could, retreat would be the best option. But there was no way this Nascent Soul Realm cultivator would let the murder of his son rest, and he now knew the name of the people behind it. Fighting here and now while the Grand Elder knew little about Ashfallen's capabilities and was far from Ashlock's trunk was for the best.

"So far, the Lunarshade Grand Elder has displayed teleportation and telekinesis, both spatial-type techniques, and he can even drag things from the void. His moonlight beam is similar to a powerful light attack, but it froze the ground, so lunar affinity likely also carries the dao of ice," Ashlock quickly summarized. "Sol's light attacks so far have shown the most damage, so light is likely his weakness, but Sol is too weak and unfocused on combat to make much of an impact on his own."

Ashlock had paid for this lesson by sacrificing Khaos and Zeus so far, but he had gotten the Grand Elder to show some of his moves and secured the 10,000 Yinxi Coin bounty by dragging Albis's corpse away when the Grand Elder wasn't looking.

"Right now, my trump card is Larry, who should be in the upper stages of the Nascent Soul Realm." Ashlock glanced at the living storm of divine ash in the shape of a spider looming in the sky. "But that might not be enough. If only the Grand Elder was near one of my trees, I could unleash my full potential as a near Nascent Soul Realm cultivator and help... Wait."

It was risky, but he had just devised a plan—an insane one with a low chance of success, but it was better than no plan at all.

Grand Elder Lunarshade felt his blood boiling with rage beneath his cold, calm facade. His spiritual sense was spread across the entire city, but he couldn't locate the spatial cultivator coordinating this attack from the shadows.

Where the fuck is that bastard hiding? Such a display of Qi should have a focal point somewhere nearby, but according to my spiritual senses, the entire city is bathed in spatial Qi right now, which doesn't make any sense. The Grand Elder looked up at the living storm. *That* monster is also concerning. Is it made from mystic Qi, or does this Ashfallen Sect have a divine beast on its side?

Either way, it didn't matter. It needed to be defeated while he had the advantage of fighting under a full moon, and then he could track down and destroy this Ashfallen Sect. Taking a deep breath to calm himself and feel the flow of lunar Qi surging through his body, he knew he would have to use a technique that would wipe out months, if not an entire year, of his cultivation progress. But to avenge his favorite heir and squash this upstart sect that seemed to think he was trivial to bully, he would go all-out.

"Soul manifestation," he said as he activated the technique that let Nascent Soul Cultivators use their infant souls to fight. His infant soul expanded outward, and soon, an avatar of moonlight surrounded him like a giant suit of armor. The air around him turned to snow that drifted in the howling winds from that spatial cultivator's pressure.

Let's get this over with quickly, the Grand Elder thought. Fights between high-level cultivators were very Qi intensive, so extended fights were ill-advised as gathering Qi became harder as one advanced, slowing down progression through the stages.

As a Nascent Soul cultivator, he could fly without assistance, so he floated up to meet the spider as a titan of moonlight with the plan to pulverize it in one punch. The spider glared at him with blood-red eyes under a crown of horns with a halo of ash swirling around it. The halo began to spin faster, and the Grand Elder felt a tremendous pressure weigh down on him equal to his own.

A sixth stage as well? The Grand Elder frowned. *This is going to be harder than I hoped.*

"You hurt the princess and angered my master," the spider roared in an almost indecipherable accent, but the Grand Elder recognized it as the ancient runic language. "For that, I will slaughter you and then your entire bloodline."

It can speak?! The Grand Elder gritted his teeth. *How dare an arrogant creature from some start-up sect ignorant of the world threaten my bloodline, which I have spent millennia building into a powerhouse of the region?*

Not only had they so ruthlessly killed the most prized heir of the Lunarshade family, whom he had spent far too many resources and time into raising, but now they uttered such threats after he had unleashed a year's worth of cultivation to manifest his soul?

The Grand Elder reeled back his avatar's fist and planted it in the spider's face, but it felt like punching a gathering of flies. *Is this similar to a Dao Storm rather than a living monster?* he wondered.

The monster opened its maw and devoured his fist.

What is that going to do? The Grand Elder sneered, but then his face fell as he saw his avatar's fist, which could destroy cities or swat powerhouses out of the sky, crumble to silver dust that blew away in the winds and joined the snowfall. The decay then rapidly spread down the rest of his arm, crumbling it to dust. That arm alone wasn't just a year or two of gathered Qi but rather a century at least.

I thought this monster had an affinity for ash, but is it actually a bringer of decay? All the blood left his face as he panicked and withdrew his avatar's arm. Thankfully, once out of the monster's mouth, it stopped decaying, leaving him with a single arm.

The spider dove down at him, obviously intent on devouring his real body rather than his avatar. It came faster than expected, and its maw dwarfed him. Gritting his teeth, the Grand Elder poured out lunar Qi into the surroundings, creating a bubble of moonlight, but it wouldn't hold for long. Innumerable ash spiders poured out of the divine spider's maw from other dimensions and surrounded his bubble.

He needed to think of a solution quickly. Luckily, he had dealt with Dao Storms in the past and knew the best way to deal with them. Their scattered bodies were both a strength and a fatal weakness. He channeled the moon's power and unleashed his control over gravity and tides to tear the spider-shaped storm apart.

The divine spider howled as the millions of ash spiders were expelled, and its body was forced apart, but he wasn't done. Harnessing the cold of the moon, a wave of ice Qi shot from his avatar's hands. The flecks of silver ash that made up the spider decayed the frost but were consumed in the process, forcing the spider to retreat to a safer distance, giving him some breathing room.

Most importantly, forcing the spider apart gave the Grand Elder a clear view of the moon, empowering him more.

"You like that?" The Grand Elder hissed through his teeth as the spider retreated but couldn't flee due to his gravity. "It's always fun to crush incompetent bugs like you. Though I wonder how the supposed master of this weakling will compare?" He grinned from ear to ear. "Once I have killed you both, I wonder how that princess tastes—"

The Grand Elder stopped laughing as his spiritual sense detected a focal point of spatial Qi coming from above. *Has the spatial cultivator finally made their appearance?* He glanced up to see the silver ash storm part and a black rock in the shape of a large ship surrounded by a shield of spatial Qi emerge.

"Huh?" The Grand Elder narrowed his eyes and noticed the demonic tree growing on the rock wreathed in lilac flames, which was the source of the immense pressure and spatial Qi. *A flying tree?*

Moving his avatar's arms, he tried to stop it, but some weird plants growing from its side shot out spatial explosions that blew his arm out of the way. "Oh…" He didn't even have time to react as the ship slammed him to the ground.

While pinned to the ground with the ship on top of him, the Grand Elder felt something invade his consciousness. A white fog appeared alongside visions that he easily ignored. However, he couldn't stop a tree of twisted black wood that bloomed in his mind, and its trunk split to reveal an eye.

A mental attack? No…is this telepathy?

"Who are you?" the Grand Elder asked the spirit tree in his consciousness. It seemed his family had earned the wrath of a rather unique being.

"The one who will bring ruin to the Lunarshade family," a chorus of a hundred voices echoed in his mind. ***"Your death will appease me and fuel my ascension, so be glad."***

"So you are the master behind the Ashfallen Sect." The Grand Elder grinned. "The pleasure is all mine."

40

DRUMS OF WAR

The plan had worked. Ashlock realized that to have a chance of contending with the Lunarshade Grand Elder, he would need to fight the man with his full power through his S-rank skill {Progeny Dominion}. So, using it on Willow's Bastion back at Red Vine Peak, the next issue was getting the Bastion close enough to the Grand Elder without it being destroyed.

Since Bastions weren't that fast, even over his roots, Ashlock needed to give the Grand Elder as little time as possible to react to its arrival. The solution he devised was to have Larry obscure its arrival through the rift by dominating the sky with his body and drawing the man's focus.

Willow was ablaze with spatial flames as Ashlock channeled every last drop of Qi he could muster into the Bastion's Core. The shield surrounding the ship was so thick it looked like a bubble of lilac liquid, and three times more artillery flowers were blooming from the cracks than usual. They were also notably larger as they all swiveled to aim at the pinned Grand Elder.

Having activated {Consuming Abyss} ahead of time, the surface of the Bastion was already covered in a void lake and a squirming mass of tendrils and thorn-covered vines dripping with digestive fluid.

Ashlock had no delusions that a lump of rock with some Star Core–level capabilities would be enough to hold the Grand Elder down for a long time, so to buy a few more seconds, he cast {Abyssal Whispers} first.

"His mental defenses couldn't resist my entry?" Ashlock had expected to bounce off the Grand Elder's consciousness due to the vast gap in cultivation, but for whatever reason, he could weasel his way inside. Trying to fight for control in a Nascent Soul Realm cultivator's own consciousness proved a somewhat fruitless endeavor, as expected, but he did manage to say a few sentences before being forced out.

Happy that the seed had been planted in the Grand Elder's mind and could be called upon later in the fight, Ashlock proceeded to the next part of his plan: devour the Grand Elder alive. With Larry overhead reforming his body and once again blocking out most of the moonlight, the Grand Elder pinned under the Bastion was weakened slightly.

Ashlock's Star Core fragment within Willow then began to pulse out with intentional frequency as he used the Spatial Lock technique they had stolen from the Azurecrest family to block the Grand Elder from using teleportation to escape his carefully laid trap.

"Trying to keep me here?" The Grand Elder sneered as he caught onto Ashlock's plan. He maneuvered his infant soul avatar's remaining hand and hammered away at the spatial shield surrounding the Bastion. Ripples spread across the dense shield as Ashlock felt an immense pull on his Qi reserves to keep the shield intact under such an assault.

Thankfully, if there was one thing Ashlock had to spare, it was Qi.

"This is going to be a battle of attrition," Ashlock mused as he sent forth hundreds of void tendrils and vines through the Bastion's shield to coil down the avatar's arm like snakes. "The one who runs out of Qi first loses, and if we were to compare the size of our Qi pools, yours is a vast lake of moonlight while mine is an ocean of spatial chaos. I'm sorry, Grand Elder, but your loss is only a matter of time."

Unaware of his musing, the Grand Elder screamed in pain as the void devoured his avatar. Khaos hadn't made much of a dent into the Grand Elder's defenses earlier, but that was an illusion of sorts.

"Every attack Khaos inflicted stripped away a layer of the Grand Elder's defenses, but the Qi surrounding his body was so dense it gave the illusion that he was untouchable," Ashlock muttered as he enjoyed the Grand Elder's screams. "He acted unfazed but actually had his guard up the entire time and was hiding his strength. What a sly bastard."

Ashlock's void tendrils were also of the ninth stage rather than the fourth, and instead of a few void-coated claws, he had hundreds of tendrils that he was expending sacrificial credits to empower. But the hefty cost was fine because the Grand Elder's sixth-stage Nascent Soul tasted *divine*.

|+100 Sc|
|+130 Sc|
|+ 122 SC|

System notifications flashed through his mind as he devoured the Grand Elder's avatar.

"His avatar also seems weaker than his main body, likely due to its inflated size, making it weaker to defense piercing attacks like void tendrils..." Ashlock's thoughts paused when he noticed his sacrificial credits in the corner of his eye start rapidly depleting faster than before despite the inflow from devouring the Grand Elder's infant soul. "Shit, what is he doing?"

There was so much Qi flying around, and the Grand Elder was constantly moving his avatar about, trying to tear away from the vines and tendrils wrapped around his arm, so it was hard to find why his sacrificial credits were suddenly depleting.

Looking closer, Ashlock noticed the digestive fluids coating his vines, which were tightly coiling around the avatar's arms, beginning to freeze. His vines were also moving slower as they became stuck together by the ice. While his vines only needed nutrients and Qi to operate, the void tendrils eating away at the ice to try to continue devouring the lunar Qi that made up the avatar required him to expend sacrificial credits every minute.

Void Qi worked on the law of mutual destruction, similar to antimatter. One "atom" of void Qi would destroy one atom of any other Qi type, consuming itself in the process. When fighting stronger enemies or trying to pierce the defenses of an earth cultivator, for example, it was worth the high cost. Yet void Qi would be quickly overwhelmed when faced with an easy-to-cultivate affinity with a high volume like water.

Unwilling to be drained of all his hard-earned sacrificial credits, Ashlock needed someone else to help him quickly break through the avatar of lunar Qi to reach the Grand Elder's main body.

"**Larry!**" Ashlock called on his most powerful summon's help.

The floating spider-shaped storm of silver ash that was blocking out the moon and staring down at the fight with eight orbs of red light serving as eyes and suppressing the Grand Elder with his rapidly spinning halo of ash turned his head toward Willow.

"What do you command, my master?" Larry asked, his voice thundering through the city. *"Should I turn him to dust?"*

"**Yes.**"

Larry condensed into a smaller form and dove down at the Grand Elder. His maw opened, and a sea of ash spiders poured out. Larry then used his silver ash to decay the thick ice encasing the vines and tendrils while the spiders poured in through the gaps into the lunar Qi. Most perished instantly, but their corpses floated around in the lunar Qi avatar, corrupting it with ash.

Ashlock was surprised by how furious Larry had sounded and acted. Only then did he realize it wasn't just Larry who was angry. The root network was overwhelmed with the rage of every demonic tree across the land.

He usually tuned out the emotions of his offspring, as the feelings of entire forests flowing into his mind were a quick path to madness. But since his mental blocks had loosened due to his hyper-focus on the situation in Nightshade City, he hadn't realized how much the emotions of his offspring had been feeding back into him.

"I need to calm down." Ashlock knew such strong emotions would cloud his judgment, and having every demonic tree ablaze with rage was bound to cause issues and attract unwanted attention. On that thought, something dawned on him

"Wait, didn't I link up with a demonic tree inside the Eternal Pursuit Pavilion?"

Quickly switching his view through his roots, he emerged near the demonic tree in the central square of the Crimson Tracker area. Sure enough, the veins of its leaves were glowing with colorless untamed Qi and had attracted quite a crowd of confused Crimson Trackers. The doors to the pavilion off to the side opened, and a Lotus Informant strode out with a jade tablet in her hand and a concerned look.

"Everyone, stand back," the Lotus Informant demanded, and the black-robed bounty hunters stepped aside to let her pass. *"This tree is now under investigation, so please leave this to us."*

"Does this have anything to do with the fight occurring outside?" a cloaked bounty hunter asked.

"I cannot disclose such information without a payment in Yinxi Coins."

"I'll pay. Just put it on my tab." A tall black-robed bounty hunter stepped forward and handed the Lotus Informant their pendant from the folds of their cloak.

The clearly annoyed Lotus Informant took the pendant, but seeing something on it made her eyes widen. Handing it back to the person with a newfound respect, she gave a small bow. *"Yes, we suspect the tree has a role in the battle occurring beyond the pavilion's defensive formations."*

"Do you know who is fighting?" another asked. The Lotus Informant glanced at the tall person as if asking if they really wanted to throw thousands of Yinxi Coins away for a Q&A session.

After receiving a casual nod from the person, she answered, *"Yes, we believe it's an outside powerhouse known as the Ashfallen Sect. They are fighting the Lunarshade family in an all-out war."*

That information caused the crowd to grow restless as they began discussing among themselves. A few smaller groups of the crowd broke off and rushed elsewhere.

Meanwhile, Ashlock was starting to realize just how big of a deal fighting the Lunarshade family was. "I knew fighting a war on the doorstep of a realm-spanning information guild was a bad idea, but the fact they have gathered so much intel so fast is concerning. It's not like I am listening to an emergency meeting between the top brass. This is a random Lotus Informant in the Crimson Tracker area selling live information to a crowd of bounty hunters…"

"Has the Celestial Warden said anything yet?" the tall person inquired.

The Lotus Informant's eyes narrowed. *"Even you don't have the funds to pry into the Celestial Warden's affairs."*

"Bullshit." The person laughed. *"That's as good as admitting he has placed a hush order on this whole affair, as I have bought trivial*

information regarding the Celestial Warden before. But his intentions are easy to read now that I have confirmed this fact." The person turned to face the crowd. *"I found it strange that no bounties were placed on the attackers when they started causing destruction to Nightshade City. Damage to the roads and death of mortals is bad for business, you know?"*

The Lotus Informant frowned but remained tight-lipped.

"The Celestial Warden wants to sit back and watch the Lunarshade family be wiped out, doesn't he?"

That caused an explosion of discussion between the bounty hunters. They didn't even use Qi to hide their voices as they asked one another about the Ashfallen Sect and what would happen if the Lunarshades, who had remained dominant in the region for a long time, fell.

"Now I dislike the Lunarshades just as much as all of you." The tall person began to walk toward the pavilion. *"But having the Tainted Cloud Sect's strength reduced by an outsider with a Beast Tide on the way leaves a sour taste in my mouth."*

During the conversation, Ashlock split his focus between the fight and learning more about the situation within the pavilion. Neither looked too good. The ice was proving an issue to get through as much like the void, Larry's silver ash that caused decay was a bad match against such an easy-to-repair defense. Meanwhile, this discussion in the pavilion was deeply concerning.

"What are they planning to do?" Ashlock wondered as he saw the rich person vanish into the pavilion but was soon answered when everyone brought out their pendants. Looking over someone's shoulder, Ashlock read what appeared in golden letters on its back.

|Mission: Protect the Lunarshade Grand Elder from the Ashfallen Sect until sunrise|
Mission's estimated threat level: Nascent Soul [Unverified]
Bounty: 5,000 Yinxi Coins per participant with a meaningful contribution upon completing the mission.
The mission is commissioned by the Golden Dragon Alchemy Guild and will take place in Nightshade City. For more information, consult a Lotus Informant.

Ashlock read the mission's description intently as an equal amount of fear and dread overcame him.

"Clearly, this very wealthy alchemy guild throwing around Yinxi Coins like they are free is displeased at the idea of their largest client being wiped out," Ashlock concluded. "But isn't this good news? The Celestial Warden, who is the only person I feel threatened by, seems uninterested in making a move against me until the Lunarshade Grand Elder is killed. To the point that an outside entity felt the need to use their own funds to get the bounty hunters to spring into action."

As he finished his thoughts, the bounty hunters had also finished reading the new mission, and from their mad dash toward the exit, the 5,000 Yinxi Coins were too good to give up.

Which was a bit of a problem.

Ashlock's spatial shield around the Bastion was already maxed out defending against the Grand Elder's attacks, and Larry couldn't get distracted having to hold off a horde of greedy bounty hunters, so Ashlock quickly created a portal beside Willow that led to Red Vine Peak and another to the Duskwalker residence.

"You aren't the only fuckers that can call on an army, you know." Ashlock had the Grand Elder pinned down, and the two were in a stalemate, so he was less worried about the Grand Elder striking down his allies with a stray moonbeam compared to earlier.

Switching to Red Vine Peak, he found Stella panicking under his aflame trunk. He had to admit he was a rather scary sight as a pillar of unrestrained power that burned into the night sky. His canopy was particularly imposing as it burned with his rage.

"Stella, I need—"

"Tree! I already know!" Stella waved the pavilion's pendant in her hand. *"Some bastard dared to put a bounty on us! I mean, we were planning to do it ourselves, but that's beside the point. This calls for a slaughter, don't you agree?"*

"**Right…**" Ashlock had forgotten she was a bounty hunter and received the same mission notification as every other bounty hunter across the entire realm. "**Gather everyone. We are going to war.**"

Stella nodded and then vanished as she rapidly used Spatial Step across the mountain toward White Stone Peak to gather the Redclaws. On the way, she told Diana, Elaine, and Douglas about the situation.

She even quickly stopped under Nox to reassure Jasmine that everything would be fine.

Meanwhile, Ashlock's vision blurred toward Geb. His people would need a suitable base of operations, and what better choice than a walking fortress?

41
WALKING FORTRESS

Douglas rushed through the dark stone corridor with Mudcloaks clinging to both of his legs for dear life while another hung from his back like a cape. However, unlike a cape, its claws dug deeply into his suit, and it made terrified whimpers in his ear.

"Guys, can you get off me?" Douglas pleaded. "I know the mountain is trembling, but your 'protection' is unnecessary."

"We will die for the king!"

"Protect the king!"

"Scary mountain!"

Douglas let out a sigh at the little menaces' chants. It didn't even make sense. The Mudcloaks would only get in the way if something could kill him. They *were* getting in the way right now as he headed down an emergency corridor he had built a while ago that led straight to the illusion grove where Elaine should be cultivating.

I have no idea what is happening, but please be safe, Elaine. Douglas had never felt Ashlock unleash this amount of Qi, so clearly, something terrible had happened. The Qi is actually flowing downward toward the east through the mountain. Perhaps a battle is happening?

Whatever happened must be above him as he was yet to be informed. Douglas knew Ashlock could speak to anyone he wished at any time with telepathy, so he must not be deemed worthwhile enough to know.

The corridor suddenly shook even more as the roots growing along the walls flashed with power, and pieces of rock rained down on him, pummeling his back. The Mudcloaks cried out as the two clinging to his legs were smacked off by stray debris, but Douglas kept going despite their protests.

Up ahead, at the end of the corridor, he could see a wooden door inlaid with a runic formation. As he reached it and inserted some earth Qi, the door unlocked, and he pushed it open. Emerging into the moonlight, Douglas clambered out of the leaf-covered hole and glanced around. He was on the side of the mountain path that connected Red Vine Peak and the White Stone Peak. Many small paths winding through the trees led off either side of the mountain path to the groves, and in the distance, he could see some Redclaws fleeing back to the White Stone Palace.

"Douglas?!"

He spun around at the familiar voice and saw Elaine running toward him.

"Hey— Oof." He stumbled back a step as she threw herself into his open arms and nestled her head into his shoulder. Douglas was bewildered for a moment. His arms slowly closed around her, embracing her in a hug, and he patted her head.

"Elaine?"

The blob of light pink hair replied with a hum before she tilted her head up to look at him, and they locked eyes for a moment. She looked a little shaken, and her glasses had been pushed off center. "S-Sorry about that." She lightly stepped back, and Douglas released her from his embrace. "I'm so glad to see you, Douglas. I was worried something terrible might have happened to you when I was thrown out of my cultivation and the mountain was ablaze with Ashlock's wrath."

"Nothing happened to me. I am fine." Douglas was relieved to see she was also fine, but he could see the deep concern on her face. "Are you all right?"

"I'm good, but..." Elaine looked over his shoulder, and he followed her gaze. The night sky was illuminated by a column of lilac soul fire that seemed to reach for the heavens. A vortex seemed to surge up Ashlock's trunk before merging with his vast canopy, where every leaf burned bright with power. It was a breathtaking display that made Douglas's soul tremble from inadequacy.

So that is what the peak of power looks like. It feels like if Ashlock directed even a fraction of that wrath toward me, I would spit blood as I died a pathetic death. His own inadequacy aside, something serious must have happened to cause the usually lowkey Ashlock to go all-out.

"Do you know what happened?" he asked Elaine.

Elaine lightly shook her head. "No, I was hoping you would."

Let's think, what could have happened? All I can think of is that Stella and Diana left for the Tainted Cloud Sect to hunt down that Albis Lunarshade person.

Douglas suddenly had a dangerous thought, and the blood drained from his face. Turning to Elaine, he almost choked on his words. "Y-You don't think something happened to Stella, do you?"

Elaine's eyes widened. "Oh no, that's the worst-case scenario. If Stella got hurt or even died, I fear Ashlock would destroy everything in rage."

Douglas wholeheartedly agreed with that assessment. Ashlock was relaxing to be around and likely the most reasonable spirit tree in the realm when he was in a good mood. But at the end of the day, he was still an incredibly powerful demonic tree with a hunger for flesh and blood and an inescapable reach.

If Stella really did die, I wouldn't be surprised if he slaughtered everyone.

Douglas glanced down one of the side paths, and through the gap in the trees, he got a clear view down the side of the mountain of Darklight City in the distance. Not only was the entire forest between him and the city ablaze with soul flames but so were the trees within the city.

A terrible feeling brewed in his gut, and he clenched his fist. Ashlock was usually so careful, constantly restricting the flow of information and keeping his existence a secret from the wider world. Few things could shake that foundation, and Stella's death was undoubtedly one of them. Would this be the end of the sect as he knew it—

"Yo!" A blond girl wreathed in spatial flames materialized before him, causing his heart to almost leap out of his chest. Stella patted his shoulder with a shit-eating grin on her face. "Just the man I was looking for. Are you ready for war?!"

"War? With who? Huh?" Douglas's mind blanked. "You're fine?"

Stella tilted her head. "Why wouldn't I be? Are you okay? I hope puffing away on all those spirit stones hasn't turned your brain to mush."

"I only have to do that because of unfair workloads." Douglas scoffed as his shock and relief at Stella's appearance quickly turned to annoyance.

"Stella, we thought something bad happened to you," Elaine said as she appeared beside Douglas and glanced between them. "Glad to see you are fine."

"Why would something have happened to me?"

"Oh, I don't know. Maybe it's because the mountain range is trembling, the cities are bathed in soul flames, and Ashlock is pumping enough Qi into the land to turn this place into a spiritual spring?" Douglas listed off with a slightly irritated tone. To think he had been so worried for this ditz of a person. How could she be so clueless about the world around her?

Stella lowered her arm from his shoulder and looked around. Her mouth made an *O* as she realized what was happening. Eventually, she looked back at Douglas and shrugged. "Ash is just overreacting. Don't worry your rock-filled head about it."

"Something did happen, then?" Douglas narrowed his eyes, ignoring the insult.

Stella avoided his gaze and pouted. "I *might* have almost died because of my recklessness, so I suppose this is *partially* my fault. But that"—she pointed at Ashlock illuminating the sky—"is an overreaction."

So she did almost die. Douglas grimaced at the thought. *Wait, did she just admit to being reckless?*

"Right..." Douglas rubbed his temples, feeling a headache from the shock of such a revelation. "What was this about a war, then?"

Stella brightened up. "Oh, yeah! Ash went to war against the Lunarshade family, who hurt me."

"As one would." Douglas nodded as if that made any sense at all. Who started a war with a powerful, well-known family like that over someone getting hurt? If Stella had died, it would have been more understandable, but for someone who supposedly almost died, she seemed fine and dandy to him. There wasn't even a scratch on her body.

Stella dug for something in her pocket and pulled free a pendant.

"We also seem to have made an enemy of the Golden Dragon Alchemy Guild, as we are now also at war with the bounty hunters of the Eternal Pursuit Pavilion."

"What?" Douglas raised a brow. The Lunarshade family was one thing, but how were an alchemy guild and the pavilion also involved? What the hell had happened in the span of one evening?

Perhaps sensing his confusion, Stella handed him the pendant, and he read the mission's details on the back. Elaine leaned on him and read the pendant over his shoulder. She hummed with disapproval the whole time, and he could feel her warm breath on his neck. Now that they were so close, he could also smell the floral scent of the Dreamweaver Orchids.

We only shared a bed once, and progress has been slow since then because we have both been so busy. They were definitely closer than just friends, but neither had tried to take their relationship to the next level yet. *Maybe I should ask her out on a date soon... Wait, now isn't the time for this.*

His peaceful thoughts of dating and going about his usual routine were now secondary to a war he wanted nothing to do with. The Tainted Cloud Sect was so far away that it might as well be another continent or realm for him.

"So let me get this straight. We are now at war with the Lunarshade family, an alchemy guild, and bounty hunters are after us now?" Douglas clicked his tongue, handing back the pendant while trying his best not to shout in her face and call them both idiots. What in the fucking lowest realm of Hell happened to remaining low-key? "How did you even anger them? How many pills did you sell to force their hand like this?"

Stella blinked in confusion. "Sell pills? We haven't sold any yet. They are still awaiting approval."

Douglas felt the anger leave his body as he let out a controlled breath. How could he stay mad at such an absurd situation? That would just be a wasted effort and give him gray hairs.

"I see, so what are we doing about all this?"

"A slaughter, of course!" Stella said with a childlike happiness that was hard to describe. It was as if she had been restrained or told no by a parent for so long and was finally given the go-ahead to run loose.

Douglas looked to the ground and scratched the back of his neck.

This wasn't how he had expected his night to go, and this was all a lot to take in.

Stella stepped closer and looked up at him with intelligent eyes clouded by a haze of insanity. "You don't seem thrilled." She narrowed her eyes as if studying him. "We don't have to hide in the shadows anymore, so don't you think it's about time we went to war. Why are you not overjoyed?"

"Should I be?" Douglas shot back. "What is war good for, anyway? We have plenty of land, access to the Mystic Realm, and pills to sell for money. Ashlock has also made efforts to create groves for various affinities so everyone can live and cultivate here in peace. What could the Ashfallen Sect possibly gain from a war that it doesn't already have?"

Stella stepped closer—no longer smiling. "You may not see it, but the Ashfallen Sect is built on a mountain of corpses. You speak of the exploits of Tree and the lovely life you have here in the sect but ignore how it came to fruition." Stella's eyes flickered between Douglas and Elaine, and her voice dropped to a harsh whisper. "With every corpse, Tree grows stronger, and fewer people in this world will dare to stand against him. So we fight today for a better tomorrow. I've done that my entire life alongside Tree and will continue to do so."

Douglas could see the absolute resolve in her eyes. Just what kind of life could foster such fierce loyalty to another in a person?

I had feared what Ashlock would do if Stella were to die, but maybe I should be as concerned about what Stella would do if Ashlock perished. Douglas felt a shiver run down his spine. *It's as if their fates are tied, as they will live and die for one another.*

Douglas realized his fleeting thoughts about a date with Elaine paled in comparison. This wasn't a pointless war. He had merely joined the sect during a period of relative peace and enjoyed the fruits of Ashlock and Stella's past efforts. Now, it was his turn to wield his sword for the hand that fed him.

If not for them, I would be toiling away in the shadows of Darklight City, forever slaving away to pay my crushing debt. Yet they took me in, paid my debts, and made me stronger than I ever thought possible.

"Don't fight, guys—" Elaine began, but Douglas gently cut her off by raising his hand.

"No, I was wrong." Douglas gave Stella a bow. "I would be

honored to slaughter all who stand against the Ashfallen Sect. It's the least I can do to repay yours and Ashlock's kindness and make the sect stronger and safer for all of us."

Stella searched his eyes as if looking for a hint of lies. Finding none, her scary expression faded, and a light smile took its place. "I knew you were a good guy." She put her hand out for a handshake. "Anyone willing to put their life on the line to empower Tree is someone worthy of my respect."

Douglas felt a warm acceptance as he grasped Stella's far smaller hand and lightly shook it. "Thank you."

"I have other people to inform." Stella looked between them. "I wish the both of you good luck." She then shot Douglas one last smile and nod before she vanished in a pop of air and a small burst of spatial Qi.

Douglas let his hand fall to his side and stared at where Stella had been. With a sigh, he looked up at the endless sea of stars. It had been a stressful few minutes. *Had Stella always been that intense?* He paused on that thought as the memory of her dangling him head first through a portal for fun flashed through his mind. *Never mind.*

"If you're going, then I'm going, too," Elaine said as she slid her hand into his and leaned against him.

"Are you sure?" Douglas didn't deny her. He was just concerned. "You haven't formed your Star Core yet, have you?"

Elaine shook her head a little. "No, and neither have you." She clenched his hand. "But I can't let you and the others fight while I sit around here worried. I have Void Step to escape if anything goes wrong. I will be fine. You will need my help for anything involving strategy."

"Okay, let's go together…" Douglas began walking toward the burning tree dominating the sky but then realized, "How do we get there exactly?"

A familiar presence suddenly bloomed in his mind, followed by a thundering chorus of overlapped voices that threatened to tear his mind apart. **"Douglas, what the hell have the Mudcloaks done to Geb?"**

"What?" Douglas was surprised by the sudden question as a portal tore into existence before him.

"Come take a look."

Douglas exchanged a confused glance with Elaine before he stepped through with Elaine in hand.

"King!" A Mudcloak wearing a strange uniform of black-and-red cloth gave him an enthusiastic salute.

Douglas absentmindedly returned the salute as he looked around. They were in a command room with a large table in the middle with a constantly changing realistic model of the surroundings. The mountain range was complete with a forest of stone trees and a replica of the White Stone Peak. Even little stone people were walking around, but the most impressive was the giant stone tree glowing with power atop Red Vine Peak: Ashlock, the demonic tree that lorded over it all.

"This looks similar to the Bastion," Elaine muttered at his side and pointed at a smaller table to the side. "Look, they even have a Mudcloak managing a shield and another controlling a cannon."

"Cannons…" Douglas furrowed his brows. "Did Geb always have cannons?"

"No," Ashlock replied in his mind, making him wince. *"Nor did he have a fortress city built on his back."*

"Huh?" Douglas walked toward the giant, runic-enforced window that dominated the command room, and the many Mudcloaks, all dressed in the same uniform, wobbled aside to let him pass unimpeded.

Gazing out of the window, he realized he was high above a city of mud and stone nestled among the forest of red bark trees ending in golden brown leaves growing from the mountain-looking shell on Geb's back.

"What is all this—" Douglas turned, and the words died in his throat as he saw all the Mudcloaks on one knee and looking toward him with their glowing blue eyes. One wasn't on a knee, and it spoke to him clearer than the others.

"Kingdom for the king!"

The stone crown on his head suddenly felt heavier than usual as every other Mudcloak echoed the chant.

"Kingdom for the king!"

"Kingdom for the king!"

"Kingdom for the king!"

The Mudcloak strode toward him as majestically as a Mudcloak could, holding up a ring with its stubby little arms. Douglas took the offering and slid it on with some confusion. The stone ring that could have been a bracelet for the Mudcloak barely fit his finger.

The Mudcloaks cheered and did happy dances once he put the ring on.

"What is this ring for?" Douglas asked with concern. Had they scammed him or something.

"Key for the kingdom!" the smarter one of the lot informed him. "Control everything!"

Douglas went back to looking out the window. Holding the ring up, the moonlight illuminated it. Much like his crude stone crown, it wasn't awe-inspiring. *This is going to be so embarrassing if it doesn't work.* Douglas raised his finger and pointed.

"Move," he said intently, almost falling forward as Geb lurched forward with a massive step. *It worked?!*

Elaine came to stand beside him while balancing herself on a nearby table. "It looks like your subjects have built something impressive for you. I never knew they were so capable."

"Bah! The queen insults us!" one of the Mudcloaks shouted, and the rest went into an uproar. "We Mudcloaks very smart!"

"No, no, I didn't mean it like that." Elaine desperately left his side to try and calm them down.

"You can control it?" Ashlock asked in his mind.

Douglas nodded. "I can."

"Good, then proceed through the portal. The cult of the All-Seeing Eye will join you. Your mission is simple: kill them all, and don't you dare die on me."

Douglas cracked a grin. "Understood."

Reality was torn apart as an immense rift formed right before Geb. Through it, Douglas could see what he assumed was the mountain of the Eternal Pursuit Pavilion, judging by how a swarm of cultivators emerged from it on swords wreathed in a myriad of soul flame colors and heading toward the portal's location.

"Shields up," Douglas commanded, and he felt the Qi surge through the colossal fifth-stage Star Core beast as a murky-brown shield manifested over the city. "Walk forward."

Geb trudged toward the portal, and Douglas grinned as he saw streaks of crimson flames soar overhead through the portal. If he counted the number correctly, all the Redclaw Elders were also heading to battle.

"This is going to be a shitshow." Douglas grinned as he stood at the center of it all. "Might as well arrive in style."

42
MAGNUS

Magnus Redclaw, Grand Elder of a family that used to dominate wars across the realm and was feared by all, had fallen to ruin during a peaceful era. Without war, his family slowly faded into the background of the Blood Lotus Sect. As the decades passed, respect toward his family sharply declined, causing others to eye his family's lands. In the following internal conflicts, many of his Star Core Elders were slain, leaving his family weak like mangled dogs.

They had needed to seek a new path to revival, but looking back now, Magnus realized he had been far too stubborn and short-sighted. He had seen professions like alchemy or blacksmithing beneath his family and solely believed that his purpose in life was upholding his title as Magnus the Inferno Sovereign.

Magnus still vividly recalled the day Elder Margret groveled at his feet, sobbing and begging him to stop seeking war in a realm that was at peace. Finally coming to his senses after locking himself away in meditation for a decade, once he emerged, he discarded his old name, Magnus Redclaw, and beseeched everyone to refer to him simply as Grand Elder Redclaw. His sole purpose, moving forward, was to lead his family in this era of peace and rise once more from the ashes.

A decision that had led to this moment.

He stood on his sword of crimson flame with a stoic expression. His hands were clasped behind his back as his dark red robes and hair flapped in the cool nightly winds. His seventh-stage Star Core hummed softly in his chest as he soared under the endless sea of stars alongside his Elders.

Standing with a similar stance on a sword to his right was Elder Margret, a person he deeply respected for her intellect and alchemy skills. She had never been one for war, but having recently ascended to the second stage of the Star Core Realm, she would be a valuable fighting force. Hanging from her robes was a sword imbued with the fighting spirit of Elder Mo, who was to his left.

The old man, who had been crippled by his heart demons due to the lack of war and purpose, had been cured due to the Immortal's kindness and had taken up blacksmithing after receiving an inheritance. It was almost poetic how all of his Elders had turned their backs to fighting and picked up the skills he had looked down his nose at in the past.

But when war calls, I see hints of their past selves shine through.

Elder Mo looked enraged. His loyalty to Ashfallen was a step above the others, and he had almost jumped into the sky without a second thought after Stella informed them of the situation.

"Old friend, can you feel it?" the Grand Elder said with a hint of nostalgia as his voice was carried along the winds by his Qi. "The coming of a new age."

Elder Mo nodded thoughtfully. "As always, the cycle of war is inevitable. Peace breeds the opportunity for a new powerhouse to emerge that will challenge the old families' status quo. It just so happens that we are the aggressors this time."

The Grand Elder hummed in agreement as he looked to the distance. Dominating the night sky like a beacon of power was the Immortal of Ashfallen. His wrath bathed the heavens in a lilac hue, and the mountain trembled as its ruler went to war in a distant land. The endless forests that blanketed the land mirrored the great tree's rage as they also burned fiercely, causing streams of Qi to spiral and rise into the air.

Such a breathtaking display of power assured the Grand Elder once again that he had sworn loyalty to the right Patriarch.

If only all of us were here like the old times.

Aside from those who had died over the years, Elder Brent remained behind in Ashfallen City as he wasn't at the Star Core

Realm. However, a fourth person was with them, trailing a little behind and clearly a bundle of nerves.

"Amber, calm yourself," the Grand Elder said. "Remember, unwavering confidence is a cultivator's greatest strength. When you show a hint of weakness, the enemy will realize they are your superior and will go all-out. Conceal your power, keep your cards close to your chest, and the enemy will remain cautious."

"Y-Yes, Grand Elder." Amber, their family's prodigy who had only recently reached the Star Core Realm, replied as respectfully as possible. Having grown up in peaceful times when their family was at its weakest, she clearly lacked the confidence that the war veteran Elders had. Something that would need to change fast: the coming of a new age of war was upon them, and it was time for the Redclaws to reclaim their former glory.

Soaring past the moving fortress below them that trudged forward, the Grand Elder led his Elders and Amber through the most enormous rift he had ever witnessed. It was so large it seemed to bend the world toward it and drew him in the closer he got. Passing through, he noticed the air grow colder as his ears popped. Strangely, the Immortal's presence was almost as strong here despite being so far from home.

Glancing down, he saw a Bastion, a spiritual ship created by the Immortal to exert his will on the world from afar. Atop it was a demonic tree ablaze with flames shrouded by a thick lilac shield that constantly rippled as it was pounded by the fist of a lunar titan pinned below.

"That must be the Lunarshade Grand Elder," he muttered to himself. "So that is what a Nascent Soul Realm cultivator is capable of. What a fearsome man."

Even from way up here, he felt a wave of pressure threaten to knock him from his sword every time the Lunarshade Grand Elder slammed his avatar's fist onto the Bastion's shield. He was also fighting off the Immortal's constant bombardment of spatial attacks, void tendrils, and the guardian beast.

It was hard to tell who was winning as this was a battle between beings in a higher realm of power to him, but it seemed the Lunarshade Grand Elder was slowly losing. However, that would soon change. Above the fight, a *dozen* Star Core Elders from the Lunarshade family had arrived and were busy setting up a grand formation in the sky above their pinned Grand Elder.

Their bald heads and white robes gleamed in the moonlight overhead, and ethereal energy flowed between them as words of power flashed into existence and began rotating in rings between them and the moon. Six floated on swords in a circle, controlling the formation while the rest defended from external attacks.

Portals, likely from the Immortal, kept opening and closing all around them.

Black vines coated in thorns surged through the rifts alongside a swarm of swords, but they could not stop them. The Lunarshade Elders froze the vines with frost, effortlessly deflected the swords with their own in showers of sparks, and the portals were snuffed from existence by descending moonbeams that also struck the Bastion's shield.

The edges of Magnus Redclaw's lips curled up in a crooked smile as he took in the chaotic sight—the careless use of Qi and the clangs of swords over the shouts of the cultivators. This was the familiar sound of war, something he had missed dearly. His spatial ring flashed, and the cold metal of his sword that had slain thousands weighed in his hand. A wave of crimson flames left his soul core and danced along the length of the blade.

Breathing in a deep breath, the Grand Elder turned the tip of his sword toward the foes of Ashfallen. *My sword may be wielded for a new Patriarch, but it burns all the same. Those that stand in my way shall taste hellfire.*

"Grand Elder Redclaw—" the Immortal's voice thundered in his mind.

"Immortal, please refer to me as Magnus Redclaw from now on," the Grand Elder said, smiling at his old friend's shocked reaction. Elder Mo and Elder Margret stared at him as if they saw someone rising from the dead.

"Very well," the Immortal said, honoring his request. **"Magnus Redclaw, I need you and the others to deal with the incoming bounty hunters from the pavilion."**

"Not the Lunarshade Elders?" Magnus asked, raising a brow. If the Lunarshade family managed to free their Grand Elder, the tide of the fight would turn against them.

"You are not strong enough to deal with this group, and any fire

attacks risk damaging my shield or harming Larry. I have others coming to deal with them. Rather, I need you to work alongside Stella and Diana to slaughter the incoming bounty hunters."

Speaking of the devil, Stella, riding on a sword, flew through the portal alongside Diana, gliding at her side with her feathered raven wings that had an impressive wingspan.

Magnus wasn't sure who this other group of people that could take out a dozen Lunarshade Elders could possibly be, but he wasn't one to question the Immortal's will.

"As you command." Magnus nodded to the new arrivals and his family before facing the horizon. Dominating Nightshade City was the Eternal Pursuit Pavilion, and many people wearing jade masks and black cloaks soared toward them on swords. Soul flames of various affinities wreathed their forms, allowing Magnus to pick out a suitable opponent.

"As the strongest and most experienced one of us," Stella said as she floated her sword beside his, "would you do the honors of leading the charge?"

"How could I say no to such a request from the princess?" Magnus grinned as his stoic and calm facade crumbled to ash. He was a man of war—a slaughterer—and a bringer of destruction. *I may have mellowed out and managed to suppress the raging desires of my flames due to Immortal's truffles, but the embers remain. All it will take is a single spark, and the old Magnus will be back. I will be back.*

He raised his sword and pointed to the sky. His seventh-stage Star Core, which had been quietly humming in his chest until now, understood his intent. It began to roar as the floodgates opened. Fire Qi rushed up his arms in a blazing inferno, igniting his sword as a beacon of power, much like Ashlock back home.

More, I need more. Magnus's eyes widened as more Qi than he had ever been capable of unleashing continued to gather and gush unrestrained through his clear spirit roots. Unable to contain it all on the sword alone, the fire rose up further and began condensing into a miniature crimson sun. *More, more,* **more!**

As the night turned to day by the blazing ball of fire Qi, Magnus slowly lowered the tip of his sword and pointed his creation toward the incoming swarm of cultivators.

"In an era of peace, my name faded from the tongues of those who once stood against me. But hear me now, enemies of Ashfallen, for you face the might of Magnus Redclaw, the Inferno Sovereign." Magnus's lip curled up into a sneer as words he had wished to say for decades left his tongue in a whisper. "Incinerate."

Heaven honored his word and carried out his will. The ball of flame he had put so much of himself into exploded toward the cultivators, setting the air aflame as a sea of fire blanketed across the sky.

Many weaker cultivators tried to retreat toward the heavily defended pavilion but found the flames catching up. Screams filled the air as many were incinerated against the pavilion's defensive formations. Others tried to escape the hellfire by flying to the sides, but nowhere was safe as the tide of fire spread in all directions before Magnus. It caught up to the fleeing rats, consuming them in crimson flames, and they dropped to the city below like dead flies.

Magnus watched the carnage of his hellfire from a respectful distance alongside the others from Ashfallen. The heat was so intense it felt like the very air was melting to the ground as it shuddered and distorted their pain-filled deaths.

Portals rippled into existence below the falling corpses, and black vines dragged the bodies through.

Magnus lowered his sword and relaxed. He didn't wish to show it on his face, but that had taken a lot out of him. Around two-thirds of his Qi had been given as tribute to the attack, but in his eyes, it had been worth it. Not only had he tested the limits of his newfound strength, but he had also wiped out the weaklings of the bounty hunters and created an area saturated in fire Qi for his fellow Elders and Amber to have an advantage.

Stella whistled at his side, clearly impressed.

"This brings back old memories," Elder Mo added with a grin matching Mangus's own. "You never were one to show restraint, always arriving on a battlefield and unleashing a single attack, leaving the rest to me as you were drained of Qi."

"Some things never change, old friend." Magnus chuckled as he sheathed his sword and clasped his hands behind his back. "I will handle things back here and watch your flanks. Those who remain in the hellfire will have spent a considerable amount of Qi or perhaps a defensive artifact to survive. With their numbers reduced, the risk of getting grouped on has lessened, so you should all be able to seek out opponents of comparable strength."

Elder Mo clicked his tongue. "Show off."

"How do you think I became known by a title across the land while you remained nameless?" Mangus smirked, knowing this was a sore spot for his old friend.

"Bold words coming from a man who threw away his name in shame." Elder Mo scoffed, became wreathed with blue spirit flames, and flew into the fire. Elder Margret and Amber closely followed behind Elder Mo.

Magnus felt his eye twitch at his old friend's departing words, but to his own surprise, he could contain his usually short fuse. Fire cultivators weren't known for being the most cool-headed people, as the fire Qi corrupted them. *Is this because of the truffles, or perhaps my decades away from war and focusing on controlling myself?*

"We should go, too," Stella said with her eyes closed. "I can sense a group that managed to avoid your attack heading straight for us." Her eyes slowly opened. "They are strong."

"Jade Sentinels." Diana clicked her tongue as her nails elongated into claws. "How many?"

"At least five, maybe more." Stella's expression turned serious. "All of them are near the peak of the Star Core Realm and have varying affinities, including a metal and fire cultivator."

"Metal?" Magnus stroked his chin. "There shouldn't be any metal affinity cultivators out here unless they are from the Silverspire family."

"I don't care who or what family they are from." Stella tilted her sword and flew off in a direction. "Everyone here is an enemy. I will need your help to fight them."

"As you wish, but are you sure the Immortal won't need help with the Lunarshades?" Magnus asked as he looked back at the chaos occurring below.

"Don't worry, he has it under control!" Stella shouted over her shoulder as she continued flying toward the north of the city along the edge of the still-burning sky. "Douglas and the cult of the All-Seeing Eye will decimate them."

"Douglas and a cult will?" Magnus wondered but then felt a rush of air followed by a pop as reality knit itself back together. The portal to Red Vine Peak had closed, meaning the giant tortoise that was a moving fortress had finished waking through the portal.

Geb turned its titanic head toward the Lunarshade Elders, and its maw slowly opened. A cannon of shining metal emerged from its throat as if sticking out its tongue, and earth Qi flowed through the colossal Ent toward the mouth cannon. An immense amount of power began to gather as the Ent's throat glowed silver due to the runic formations.

What in the nine realms? Since when did Ashfallen have such a weapon?

Squinting his eyes, Magnus saw Douglas standing near the window of a tower rising from the fortress city. One hand rested upon his walking stick, while the other was raised as if ready to point at something. Elaine stood at his side and was directing him.

"Douglas is controlling this massive thing?" Magnus was impressed. He had always found the man to be a hard worker and deserving of respect, but this was on another level. "Is he going to shoot the cannon?"

The Lunarshade Elders seemed to notice the sudden threat. To Magnus's surprise, they stopped focusing on the formation to free their Grand Elder and appeared to deem the Ent a more significant threat as they all flew toward it at immense speed while wreathed in lunar flames.

Douglas frantically lowered his arm, and the cannon fired at the incoming Elders. A metal rod shot out faster than Magnus could even track with his Qi-enhanced sight and took out two Elders, impaling them. However, the weight of two fat, bald cultivators and the impact threw off its trajectory, and the rod continued until it slammed into the Bastion on the ground, taking out its shield.

The other Lunarshade Elders made contact with Geb, and its shield barely resisted a single combined punch as it was thrown backward and almost toppled over.

"Well, that can't be good—" Magnus shut his mouth as he watched the now-defenseless Bastion being thrown off as if a sleeping titan had found it a nuisance. Slowly turning his head with a terrible feeling, he saw the Lunarshade Grand Elder's avatar stand at its full height and turn to look directly at him.

43
BROKEN MIND

Ashlock was utterly astounded by what he had just witnessed.

"Did I mess up?" Ashlock wondered as he saw the world on its side due to the Bastion being thrown off by the Lunarshade Grand Elder.

The group of Lunarshade Elders had been far too strong for the Redclaws and the girls to defeat as they outnumbered them two to one while empowered by the moon. There had also been the pressing matter of the swarm of bounty hunters on the horizon that he didn't want to get too close.

"I thought the Lunarshade Elders were less of a threat as they were more focused on freeing their Grand Elder than outright attacking. I hadn't expected them to drop their progress and go after Geb."

Some remnants of the lunar formation remained as whisps of moonlight hanging in the air, but the whole thing collapsed the moment the Elders went after Geb—not that it mattered. The Lunarshade Grand Elder had taken advantage of the friendly fire, briefly knocking out Willow's spatial shield, and successfully escaped.

"Magnus? Is that you?" the Lunarshade Grand Elder shouted to the sky as he rose to his full height. "Has the Blood Lotus Sect finally decided to make a move and send your old face after me?"

The many frozen vines that had once been coiled around the avatar crumbled and rained to the ground in large chunks of ice. Silver ash sprinkled the fallen ice as the many spider corpses corrupting his form were expelled. Larry kept up his assault by reforming into a dense spider form of equal size and mounting the Lunarshade Grand Elder's back.

Ashlock readjusted his spiritual sight and glanced up at Magnus. The man floated overhead on his sword, wreathed in crimson flame with a stoic expression—seemingly unfazed by the taunts of a Nascent Soul Realm cultivator. His hands were clasped behind his back, and he stared down his nose at the bald and round avatar made of lunar Qi.

"I wield my sword for a new master," Magnus replied simply. "Though it seems an era of peace has treated you well. Not only has your cultivation soared to unimaginable heights, but so has your waistline."

The colossal man grinned with a twisted smile as he tried to wrestle off Larry. "Cultivation is surprisingly easy when all you have to do is sit around eating good food and enjoying the company of jade beauties. Not that you would know if your lack of cultivation is anything to go by."

"Even in an era of peace, some of us still had to fight for our place." Magnus sneered. "Not all of us title holders from the war era gave into the sins of sloth and greed, Dorian Lunarshade, the Phantom Moon's Heir."

"Now that's a name I haven't heard in a while." The man laughed as he fell onto his back, attempting to crush Larry. A bad move, as the spider dispersed to either side and then quickly reformed on top of the man and continued trying to decay the avatar.

Ashlock hadn't remained idle while listening to the conversation between two Grand Elders who seemed to know each other from a previous era. Having restored the shield around Willow, he looked at the projectile shot from Geb that had managed to ruin his plans. It was sticking in the ground beside the Bastion like a flag pole after losing its momentum from destroying the Bastion's shield.

"It's got a heavily Qi-filled stone core wrapped in a metal casing that is heavily runically enchanted. Ah, I see what happened. Spatial Qi is especially unstable when interacting with other Qi types, which is why I can't redirect attacks with portals as the moment another Qi type hits it, the portal becomes unstable," Ashlock mused. "Though Willow's shield isn't a portal, it's still made of spatial Qi, which has this weakness. This metal rod had too much concentrated piercing power for the spatial shield to remain stable no matter how much Qi I forced into the Bastion's Core."

With his faith somewhat resorted to the shield's ability to defend, he got to work on getting those from the Duskwalker Residence to come as reinforcements. Splitting his attention between multiple things, he spoke directly into Elysia's mind while using telekinesis to pick up the metal rod to pull the two dead Lunarshade Grand Elders from it.

The still-alive Lunarshade Elders were almost finished breaching Geb's shields, so it was time to make some Ents and fight back with everything he had.

Elysia lay on the ground, staring up at the stars. She felt drunk as the world spun in and out of focus. Her soul and mind felt disconnected as she wondered who she was. She tried to follow a trail of thought, but it would get lost in the cracks of her utterly destroyed and fractured consciousness.

"I could drift here forever." Elysia giggled as she turned to meet the gaze of the giant green eye that belonged to her summon, the Old One. Never before had they been so close, her mind's defenses gone during the initiation to the All-Seeing Eye. Compared to its power, the Old One seemed like a cute pet.

"The spirit tree did well," the Old One mused as it floated closer, consuming her vision. **"Your consciousness is well and truly broken. It's like taking a pleasant walk in the park. I feel so unrestrained and free in here."**

Her summon expanded in size within her consciousness, and unlike before, when her mind would fight back to contain the madness, the shattered remains of her defenses were knocked aside by hundreds of incomprehensible tendrils.

Inhuman laughter echoed as the Old One poked a tendril past the boundaries of her mind. It appeared in the real world, emerging from her forehead and blocking out her spinning view of the stars.

"Yes, this is perfect," the monster continued, slowly emerging and forcing its way out of her mouth. Elysia felt a tug on her Star Core as mystic Qi was drawn to form a bubble around the tendrils.

She was being used to allow the Old One to take form in the realm world.

Rather than stop her summon, she felt ecstatic.

I have become one with the beyond! Now, there is truly nothing to limit my power! Her eyes widened manically as blood trickled from the corners of her mouth and eyes. Her head pounded with a terrible headache that furthered the spinning, and her ears rang terribly, but she laughed all the same.

"Come forth, Old One!" Elysia yelled to the stars as she felt her broken soul lose its grip on reality, sending her falling through the floor—but then she felt something fluffy land on her forehead.

It was a bit fatter than a squirrel should be, but it definitely had the form of one. It was breathtakingly beautiful, with white fur as fresh as snow and golden eyes glimmering like liquid honey. The mystical creature raised a paw and slapped at the tendril emerging from her head, forcing it back into her consciousness with immense force.

The Old One howled in rage. **"Who dares deny my escape from the void?!"**

"Pluto, what are you doing?" the squirrel hissed, and the Old One fell silent.

"Brother Maple..." the Old One eventually wheezed out. **"It's not what it looks like."**

Maple, the mythical squirrel, raised a brow. *"You know Stella and Ashlock have taken an interest in this human. No matter how broken she is, I won't allow you to kill her. Understand?"*

A flash of pure rage overwhelmed Elysia's unguarded mind, involuntarily making her gnash her teeth. Her nails dug lines into the dirt, and she snarled like a rabid dog. None of these emotions were her own. They came from the Old One, and without the ego to resist, she was at his mercy.

Maple shook his head. *"What a sorry state you have found yourself in, human. Power comes at a cost, and heart demons are one thing, but to destroy your own sense of self to such a point to welcome in the power of another will only lead to your death."* The squirrel placed a claw on her forehead and carved a symbol into her flesh. Warm blood streaked down her face alongside terrible pain that made her howl out and arch her back in agony.

"Stop! Please stop. Agh!" Elysia begged as every muscle in her body spasmed. "What are you doing to me?" The process seemed to last forever, and she was about to pass out when the squirrel finally answered her.

"Creating a third eye." Maple withdrew his bloodstained claw. ***"A doorway to the outside that you can open and close at will to let my dear brother here emerge into the real world. I rerouted your spirit roots to this passageway, so if Pluto tries to force his way out through your broken mind, he will perish to reality without the protection of your mystic Qi."***

Elysia's body relaxed as the strange power swirling around her body was withdrawn. She sat up and coughed a mixture of blood and bile a few times onto the dirt beside her before collapsing onto her back. Her lungs burned from a lack of breath, and her throat was in agony, but she couldn't help but grin at the squirrel that had taken perch on her stomach.

"Are you another one of the All-Seeing Eye's heralds?"

Maple tilted his head at her words as if contemplating them. ***"I suppose?"***

Elysia wiped away the drool at the mythical squirrel's answer. "Then this eye is a gift from the All-Seeing Eye himself!" She reached up and tried to pry it open with her nails. "If I can get a better look at you, maybe I can summon a monster of your grace."

Maple's fluffy tail swished in apparent amusement. ***"You are quite insane, even for a human."***

"Agh," Elysia hissed in pain. "Why isn't it working?"

"Close your eyes and focus on your third eye," Maple replied as he curled his tail around his plump body and rested his chin on it.

Following his instructions, Elysia closed her eyes and meditated. It took a while, but eventually, she managed to locate the passage and found it had been burned into her very soul. No mystic Qi could flow out except through this eye. To open it, she shifted her cracked soul apart and felt mystic Qi flow out unrestrained through the hole.

The Old One, who Elysia now knew was called Pluto, surged toward the opening and stuck his green eye through. The force of the action caused Elysia's neck to almost snap as she was jolted upward.

"Brother! How can you mess with the vessel that I spent so long nurturing? She had finally reached the state of perfection! So broken in every way that I was unrestrained!"

Maple strode up Elysia's stomach and chest before perching on her chin.

Elysia's breath quickened as she felt both of Maple's claws plunge into her third eye and hold Pluto in a terrifying grip.

"I mess with it because your fun and games with this broken toy will cause problems for Ashlock if I do not intervene. Elysia is an important pawn in his upcoming plans, and her demise would spell his ruin."

Pluto seethed with rage, but Elysia didn't feel it as strongly this time. *"Why do you care about that spirit tree, Brother? You are bound by a pact of co-existence. You are not his slave! Let it die and roam this world freely with me!"*

"Oh, foolish brother of mine, you are shortsighted." Maple effortlessly hurled Pluto deeper into Elysia's consciousness, which bordered on the void itself. *"I assist Ashlock not because I am bound by the heavens but of my own free will. I see his vast potential to tear down this god-forsaken reality that has resisted our existence since its inception."*

"Then why are you here?" Pluto howled from the depths. *"Shouldn't you guard Ashlock until he realizes this potential you are hallucinating?"*

Elysia felt blood leaking from her ears as the two mythical monsters used her mind to conduct their argument.

"Your ignorance shows your youth," Maple sneered as he stepped back and sealed her third eye. *"If I intervene in his affairs, it will only weaken him. One can only grow stronger through trials of the mind and body. To deprive him of such experiences would curse his fate."*

Elysia shivered as a sudden pressure overcame them, which she was growing familiar with. Looking up, she saw a rift tear open and shivered as the All-Seeing Eye gazed down upon her.

A twisted tree of black bark and crimson leaves bloomed in her mind alongside a haunted white fog that seemed to unnerve Pluto as he floated further away.

"Cultists of the All-Seeing Eye! Wake up and gather for a grand crusade in my name! We are at war with the Lunarshade family."

The chorus of voices from the All-Seeing Eye rang in her mind as Elysia staggered to her feet. Her family members scattered around the forest also slowly woke up and groaned as they nursed their heads. The experience in that bubble of dense mystic Qi had been intense for them all. Only Elysia had managed to maintain her consciousness.

A portal rippled into existence near the tree that was still ablaze with lilac flames, but the intense presence had moved elsewhere.

Elysia gathered her family like a good vice cult leader and led them through the portal after a quick prayer to the All-Seeing Eye, after which they downed pills and fruits to try to get into fighting condition.

"What in the nine realms happened to you?"

Elysia turned to see Grand Elder Blightbane standing next to Evelyn Duskwalker. The other Grand Elders were filtering in through another portal and looked at her strangely.

"What are you talking about?" Elysia gave the Blightbane Grand Elder a blank stare.

"You're beyond fucked up," the Grand Elder said gruffly as his piercing gaze peered through the curtains of his hair. "Blood and bile stains your clothes and skin, your eyes are unsettling, and that mark on your forehead is no mere tattoo. It's as if an evil god carved its existence into you—"

"You can tell?!" Elysia wanted to squeal with glee. "Yes, I pledged my very soul and being to the All-Seeing Eye. His herald even carved this mark into me as proof of my belief."

Grand Elder Blightbane turned away as if disturbed while the other Grand Elders looked on at her with a mixture of concern and pity.

"You just don't understand his greatness." Elysia clenched her hand so hard her knuckles went white as she restrained herself from kotowing and singing the Eye's praises. "Just you all wait. Soon, you will bear witness to powers beyond our grasp."

Elysia turned away from the judgmental stares and looked around. They were standing on a tilted slab or rock with a blazing spirit tree growing from it. A lilac shield surrounded them, and in the distance, she could see a group of bald men and women wearing white robes attacking some city.

"Everyone gathered here. You have one task." The chorus of voices spoke once more, making Elysia shudder with excitement. ***"Eliminate the ten remaining Lunarshade Elders."***

"Impossible," Evelyn muttered. "There are ten of them, and they are empowered by the moon."

"Don't worry, you won't be fighting alone."

Two corpses floated to the shield's edge with telekinesis and were made to kneel before the spirit tree. Two thin black roots then emerged from the stone and snaked across the floor before going through the shield and down the corpse's throat.

"Those of the Blightbane family should step through the shield and surround the two corpses."

The Blightbane Grand Elder exchanged glances with those from his family before the group of withered people with hair as dark as rotting wood and eyes like fading embers trudged through the shield.

What is about to happen? What miracle is the eye about to honor us with?

A sudden wave of death Qi smashed into the lilac shield, and the Blightbane family dropped to their knees in reverence as the two Lunarshade corpses began to twist into new monstrous forms of wood.

44
DIVINE LAND

Ashlock gathered his forces from the Duskwalker's residence under the safety of the Bastion's supercharged spatial shield, which practically glowed with power as he routed an entire forest's worth of Qi into it.

While the Grand Elders from the Duskwalker, Mystshroud, Frostveil, and Blightbane families discussed among themselves, Ashlock noticed that one person stood out from the rest. Elysia Mystshroud was attracting attention for all the wrong reasons.

"Maple, what did you do to her, and where have you been all this time? I could have used your help," Ashlock asked the squirrel perched on one of Willow's many branches, curiously observing the humans below with his golden eyes.

"My strength is not something you have the right to wield," Maple replied. *"So where I am and what I do is of no matter to you."*

Those were two of the longest sentences Ashlock had heard the squirrel say to him outside the void.

"What does that mean? I know you aren't my summon, but you were able to devour the arm of an Elder from the Azure Clan who should be a league above the Lunarshade Grand Elder in strength. With just a hand wave from you, I could win this battle without difficulty!"

"If I interfere, it will only cripple you in the long term. There is only one person that is in need of my protection." Maple vanished into the void without another word.

Guessing where he went, Ashlock glanced over at Stella, and sure enough, Maple was perched on her head as she faced down multiple Star Core bounty hunters.

"Why does he speak so cryptically like some old master?" Ashlock grumbled. "The longer this fight goes on, the more Qi I waste, and the higher the chance of someone I care about dying. I am also attracting far more attention than I had hoped, and there's no guarantee the Celestial Warden won't make a surprise appearance if he deems me a threat."

Ashlock watched Maple slap away a sword swing aiming for Stella's head from what appeared to be a metal cultivator. "Whatever, at least he will keep Stella safe so I can focus on things here. Though I do hope I will be able to find the useful corpses among the rubble later on."

Leaving Stella, Diana, and the Redclaws to hold off the wave of incoming bounty hunters and Larry to keep the Lunarshade Grand Elder occupied, Ashlock focused back on the Bastion and began thinking up ways to turn the tide of this chaotic battle in his favor as Maple was refusing to contribute.

"Now let's see... These two Lunarshade Elder corpses will definitely be useful." He brought them closer to Willow using telekinesis but left them just beyond the shield. The death Qi released during an Ent's creation was no joke. Targeting them and activating {Necroflora Sovereign}, he watched two thin roots slowly emerge from the black rock like snakes and slither toward the corpses.

"Wait, this is a rare opportunity for the Blightbane family to experience such a concentrated burst of death Qi." Ashlock quickly told the family to stand beyond the shield. They complied with his request and gathered around the two corpses in confusion. As that skill got to work, he wondered if there was anything else he could do, as he had fought long enough in this world of immortals wielding Qi to understand the basics of how a war *should* work.

One of the first lessons he learned was how important the types of Qi available in the environment were. If the giant celestial object looming in the sky, illuminating the world in moonlight, was anything to go by, the Lunarshade family were definitely at an advantage here.

If they had fought with them during the day, Ashlock was convinced that Larry alone would be enough to defeat the entire Lunarshade family. Yet under the moonlight, the Nascent Soul cultivator could defend against Larry and Ashlock long enough for his Elders to arrive and attempt to turn the tide of the battle.

Luckily, Ashlock had a few skills in his arsenal to manipulate the environment to his advantage, but he hadn't had a chance to use them yet.

{Dimensional Overlap}, despite all its potential, had the issue of friendly fire. For example, if Ashlock had tried to summon a light pocket realm while the Bastion pinned the Lunarshade Grand Elder, the bubble of foreign light Qi would have eaten away at his void tendrils, costing a considerable amount of sacrificial credits. Then, when Larry joined the fight if he had summoned the pocket realm, it would've harmed both Larry and the Grand Elder.

There was also no point in using it now, as he had been thrown a fair distance away from the Lunarshade Grand Elder, and he would end up harming those from the Duskwalker residence who were taking shelter under the spatial shield.

So, with {Dimensional Overlap} off the table to turn the environment in his favor, the next best thing was to turn the enemy's strength into his own through {Necroflora Sovereign}, which he desperately needed to do as his people were spread too thin.

Despite his efforts to level everyone up with the Mystic Realm visits and truffles, the combined fighting power of the Ashfallen Sect and all its vassals was outmatched by the Lunarshade family, let alone the addition of the bounty hunters from the Eternal Pursuit Pavilion.

Ashlock observed as the roots went down the throats of the Lunarshade Elder's corpses and deposited the seed somewhere in their upper bodies as their lower bodies and legs had been obliterated by Geb's attack.

"This is using a similar tactic to the one we devised to deal with the beast tide: divide and conquer. Turn the enemies against themselves like a spreading rot as the more that fall, the more join my ranks," Ashlock mused as the expected wave of death Qi exploded out from the two legless corpses. The black miasma of death washed over the spatial shield, making it crackle and ripple, and he noticed the color drain from many of the weaker cultivators' faces as they huddled under the shield.

Meanwhile, the Blightbane family dropped to their knees, eyes wide open in awe. The Blightbane Grand Elder greedily breathed in the sickening miasma of death, and Ashlock saw his pupils slowly turn black like an eclipse. His nails yellowed, and he seemed to rapidly age and wither away.

"Is he dying?" Ashlock grew concerned as he saw the same happen to the others from the Blightbane family. It was as if they were perishing under some life-draining curse.

"Are you all right, Grand Elder Blightbane?" Ashlock asked the man directly.

"All right?" Despite his withered state, the man jumped to his feet like a spring chicken. *"I am more than all right. I feel elated. Never better!"* The miasma of death leaked out his mouth with every word as he frantically dashed over to the corpses and analyzed them with his eyes that appeared dyed with oil. As he jumped around the corpses, he muttered to himself, *"Usually, death Qi is slowly absorbed by the land as the corpse lets go of its lingering regrets and moves on from this realm to its next life. But you pulled it out in such a brutal way that only a god should be capable of."*

Ashlock did remember even Senior Lee being impressed with his Necroflora Sovereign skill. It was undoubtedly one of his more outlandish skills obtained from the system's gatcha draws.

"I wonder how he will react to— Ah, there we go." Ashlock laughed as the Blightbane Grand Elder jumped back in fright and collapsed to his knees in reverence as the corpses rapidly grew upward in a spiral of twisted, pale white wood. Within seconds, the corpses had turned into twenty-meter-tall Ents rivaling Titus in size.

They had dome heads with eyes of white flame that stared wrathfully into the distance. A thick line of black flowers glistening with frost grew down their backs as if representing the dark side of the moon. They had long, spindly arms ending in three fingers, but unlike his other Ents, these two didn't have legs. Instead, they had many thick roots sprawling out that they could use to move slowly around.

"I suppose that's due to the corpse missing their legs," Ashlock concluded. The two Ents were both in the mid-stages of the Star Core Realm and, on his command, became wreathed in the moonlight.

"To summon such monsters from the corpses of the nonbelievers.

This is the unparalleled capabilities of the All-Seeing Eye!" Elysia cried out as she kotowed and smashed her head into the floor, causing even more blood to fly from her wounds. *"He can create life from death, peer into our souls, and wield power from the beyond! A true divine being!"*

Ashlock felt rather embarrassed and was about to correct her but didn't get the chance as every Grand Elder from the four houses exchanged a nod and took a respectful knee. Seeing their leaders take such a stance, the rest of the Elders from each family followed suit, and soon, he had dozens of cultivators bowing toward his creations.

"Well, this is rather awkward…" Ashlock muttered but then felt a shiver run through his bark as an immense pressure passed over him back on Red Vine Peak. Switching view and looking up to the skies, he saw the golden eyes of Heaven glaring down at him.

[You have been recognized as a deity by cultivators under the heavens.]

Ashlock was stunned by the system message floating in his consciousness. He had created the cult and posed as a fake evil god to gather more loyal followers and perhaps spread his name under another pseudonym.

"To think it had more meaning…" Ashlock whispered as golden light danced in the night sky like a divine version of the northern lights and drifted down to his canopy. His leaves that had been burning with lilac flames as his Soul Core unleashed his power in an unrestrained manner greedily absorbed Heaven's offering.

The divine energy flowed through him like a cooling wave, washing out any impurities. With no way to store it, Ashlock directed it toward his Chaos Nebula and watched as the divine energy merged with the swirling winds already there.

[Red Vine Peak is now a land blessed with divine energy. Those on the land who revere the local deity will be favored by the heavens.]

Heaven's eyes receded into the beyond, and the divine light show faded, but echoes of its presence remained on this now-blessed land.

Ashlock could feel it with every breath through his leaves all the way down to his deepest roots. This land was now Heaven-touched. However, the divine presence was subtle and did little more than make his offspring more lively and slightly empower his Chaos Nebula.

"I need more worshipers if I want to receive more divine energy." Ashlock now realized a new path to power. But first, he needed to keep his worshipers alive as a god was nothing without those to bow at its feet and sing praises.

Douglas felt Elaine's hands grasping his arm tightly as she stared out the window with a pale face. He understood her fear as he was also questioning if this would be his last day alive.

The command room and the entire city on Geb's back trembled as the thick brown shield overhead rippled and cracked under the assault of the ten Lunarshade Elders. Moonbeams blasted the shield from above alongside crescent moon slashes and moonlight-wreathed fists.

Under Douglas's command, Geb had hunkered down into the ground and greedily drained the earth dry of its Qi in a desperate attempt to power the shields long enough for Ashlock or someone to come and save them.

Earth cultivators were known for their high defense, but there were limits. Geb's Star Core had dimmed to a fading ember of its former blazing glory. The Lunarshade Elders were too close for Geb's cannon to hit them, as the Ent's head couldn't twist that far back.

"King!"

Douglas glanced at the Mudcloak standing at his feet, staring up at him with glowing blue eyes through his black-and-red cloak.

"What is it?"

"King should take Queen! Run!" the Mudcloak said desperately. "Leave Mudcloak behind! We defend the king."

Douglas shook his head as he steeled his heart. Even if he *could* run, he would not. The Mudcloaks had entrusted him with this fortress city as their king, and he had failed them.

There's no way I would leave them behind as sacrifices. If we are to die, then we will die together.

Turning on his heel, he called out to a Mudcloak frantically hitting glowing stones on a table. "How much longer will the shield hold?"

The Mudcloak let out a shriek. "No time!"

"No time?" Douglas almost lost his footing as the whole tower swayed to the side. "Whoa."

"Careful." Elaine caught him and helped him find his footing. They looked out the window, and sure enough, the earth Qi shield shattered into a million pieces and faded into the air.

"Are we going to die?" Elaine whispered loudly into his ear as the ten bald Lunarshade Elders, wreathed in moonlight and flowing white robes, floated down toward them on swords.

Douglas clenched his teeth in grim determination. "Maybe—" The words died in his throat as his whole body went cold. The feeling of looming death washed over him down to his very soul.

What the hell was that? Douglas wondered. *Am I really that afraid of death that my body would react in such a way when I face it?*

The ten Lunarshade Elders paused and turned in unison to look behind them. In the distance was the Bastion, the last stronghold of the Ashfallen Sect in this foreign land. Before it, two monstrosities of white wood rose up and began gathering moonlight on their dome heads.

Elaine collapsed to her knees beside him and seemed short of breath.

We weren't prepared for the wave of death Qi that comes when the immortal births one of his twisted creations. Our guard was down, and Geb's shield was destroyed.

Douglas helped Elaine to her feet. "Looks like the Immortal has saved us in the nick of time."

Elaine shook her head and replied between breaths, "All he's done is draw their ire upon himself. Those two Ents won't be able to win by themselves." Her eyes flickered to the other fights happening on the horizon. "Larry is suppressing the Grand Elder, and the other key figures of Ashfallen are engaged in battle with the pavilion."

Douglas clenched his hand. She was right. This was a losing battle, but there had to be *something* he could do to help. "Mudcloak, get the cannon ready to fire!" he shouted to the one most capable of speech,. "This time, I won't miss so badly."

The Mudcloak waddled off to fulfill his orders.

"Who will you aim at?" Elaine asked as Geb slowly rose from his turtled position.

Douglas pointed his finger toward the Lunarshade Grand Elder in the distance, wrestling with Larry. Geb turned his titanic head in the direction and slowly opened his mouth.

"I will take out their king." Douglas decided.

45
LIFE-DEATH EQUILIBRIUM

"That seemed to have drawn their attention." Ashlock sighed with relief as the Lunarshade Elders turned their backs on the now-defenseless Geb and were enthralled by the monstrosities birthed from their fallen comrade's corpses.

No matter how much his {Necroflora Sovereign [SS]} skill had altered them into new forms, some resemblance to their past selves remained. The dome head and flickering lunar flames told the Lunarshade Elders all they needed to know.

They were fighting *themselves.*

As the only one who wasn't fazed by his words, as she was already too far gone, Ashlock spoke to Elysia Mystshroud.

"You should lead the charge against them— Shit."

All of the Lunarshade Elders vanished in flashes of moonlight and reappeared before his freshly spawned Ents.

"Defend yourselves," Ashlock quickly commanded of his Ents, and they surged lunar Qi into their defenses and raised their lunar-wreathed arms.

The Lunarshade Elders decided to group up on the left one.

Crescents of moonlight from their silver blades cut deep into the Ent's layers of lunar Qi, leaving deep indents in the wood and outright obliterating chunks from its arm. Once the Ent's arm fell loosely to its side, they went for a round of punches to topple it despite its titanic size and wide-spread roots for legs that should have kept it stable.

"No way…" Ashlock muttered in disbelief as the twenty-meter-tall Ent fell backward and collapsed onto the Bastion's shield, making the Bastion tremble and throwing up a cloud of dust. He tried to slow its descent with telekinesis, but the flickering lunar Qi coating its form interfered. The spatial shield barely held up as the Ent lay against it, looking up at the encircling Lunarshade Elders with fading eyes.

"Accursed creation," one of the oldest-looking Elders snarled as he raised his hand to the moon. *"The moonlight will cleanse you."*

The other Elders raised their hands to the moon in unison and called down a tactical strike of moonbeams. The world went blindingly white and then deathly silent. Much like Khaos, the lunar Ent was obliterated, and all that remained was a layer of ice coating the spatial shield resembling its outline and a flash-frozen crater.

The ten Lunarshade Elders floated overhead on their swords of moonlight with their hands clasped behind their backs under their flowing white robes that fluttered in the nightly breeze. Despite their calm appearance, Ashlock could tell from the flickering of lunar Qi between them that words were most certainly exchanged as they eyed the second Ent.

"Shit. This isn't good. I need to stop their ability to teleport. Otherwise, they might go and assist their Grand Elder before I can stop them." Ashlock cast Spatial Lock on the Elders and started trying to match their frequencies simultaneously but quickly learned this was a single target technique rather than one that could be used on a large group with differing cultivation levels.

Ashlock knew he needed to go on the offensive quickly, so he was about to go and inform the gathered Grand Elders to make a move, but to his surprise, someone decided to take matters into their own hands.

"You bastards dare defile my god's children!" Elysia screamed as she burst through the spatial shield of the Bastion on a pillar of purple smoke. A soul-crushing pressure filled with wrath and a hint of divinity exploded out of the girl, and her eyes glowed with power.

The Lunarshade Elders eyed the newcomer with contempt. Yet their arrogance faded as Elysia's wave of pressure smashed into them, slapping them out of the sky with immense force. They plummeted to the ground like asteroids striking the moon, and the ground exploded upon their impacts, leaving craters. Even the Bastion's shield rippled and groaned under Elysia's soul pressure.

"I remember Stella telling me that Elysia's presence carries the weight of her god. Before, she believed Pluto was a godly being, but now she believes in me," Ashlock muttered in amazement as he watched dozens of spinning ritual circles manifest above Elysia, dominating the night sky. "Is this the type of pressure I will be able to wield once my Inner World is formed?"

Elysia looked to the stars, spread out her arms, and began chanting.

"O All-Seeing Eye, whose godly gaze pierces the veil of my soul,
In your ever-loving sight, I accept the splintering of my whole.
Let the fragments of my psyche be the mosaic of your grace,
Each piece a testament to the depth of your embrace."

The bloodied carving of an eye on her forehead slowly opened, and tendrils of an eldritch being not of this world slithered out of her third eye alongside mystic Qi that leaked out and coiled around its form.

Unfazed by the monstrosity emerging from her forehead, Elysia continued the chant with her passion, reaching new heights. Blood leaked from her nose and eyes as the ritual circle forming overhead began spinning faster, and the pressure further increased.

"In the abyss of your scrutiny, I concede,
The fractured pieces of my broken mind.
Non-believers have arrived at the gates,
Allow me to show them your welcoming embrace!"

Pluto *emerged* in his entirety, wreathed in a shroud of mystic Qi, and descended on the pinned nonbelievers. Ashlock wasn't entirely sure what Pluto was supposed to look like, but he seemed far more ominous than the descriptions he had been given.

"He looks like the embodiment of the All-Seeing Eye. It's as if he has become a manifestation of me."

Pluto was nothing but a giant floating green eye surrounded by a ring of wriggling tendrils. He had no mouth, limbs, or body to speak of. He was a truly alien creature born from a twisted mind devoted to Ashlock. Under Elysia's reverent shouting about killing the nonbelievers, Pluto loomed overhead, unleashing a barrage of tendrils upon the Lunarshade Elders.

Unfortunately, despite Elysia's immense presence by wielding the name of her god, she could not pin the Lunarshade Elders down for long as they blinked in and out of existence along the streaks of moonlight. Ashlock glared at the celestial object that dominated the sky with annoyance, which was letting them teleport around.

"If Larry could be freed from dealing with the Lunarshade Grand Elder, he could blanket the sky with his body and stop their teleportation." Ashlock sadly couldn't depend on Larry, so he decided to use Spatial Lock one at a time to cull the Lunarshade Elder's numbers.

Locking onto a bald woman first, he matched his soul pulses to hers, causing the moonlight to fail to recognize her and refuse her passage through its light. She stumbled in confusion before a stray tendril from Pluto smacked her right in the stomach, dispelling the moonlight wreathing her form and causing her to cough blood as she flew through the air and crashed into the ground.

The woman lay sprawled among craters, wheezing and trying to conjure even a flicker of lunar flames to heal her internal wounds.

Ashlock was not so kind to let his foe recover.

Her eyes widened as a portal ripped itself into existence, and a black vine covered in thorns lashed out and impaled her to the ground. She gasped for breath as she reached up and tried to claw at the vine rammed through her chest. Such a wound would kill others, but the woman's flickering lunar Qi kept her alive long enough to experience a slow death.

The thorns drew blood from her hands that dyed her pristine white robes a dark crimson. Since she was managing to hold onto life, Ashlock flooded her body with digestive fluids, liquifying her organs, and the embers of life faded from her eyes.

"That's another one down," Ashlock said without a hint of emotion as he dragged the corpse over to the Bastion with telekinesis and cast {Necroflora Sovereign}. As much as he wanted credits, those could be gathered later. Creating Ents was the most efficient path to victory.

The last Ent perished under the Lunarshade Elders' concentrated efforts, but they wasted a lot of Qi doing so, whereas creating the Ents cost nothing for Ashlock as he wasn't putting in any effort to customize them to his liking.

While the new Ent was being created, Ashlock cast his sights back to the battle at hand. Elysia had lessened her pressure on the area as the other Grand Elders took to the battle. The Lunarshade Elders were strong under the moonlight and worked well together, but they weren't the only ones stronger during the night.

Evelyn, much like her sister Nox, wielded shadow Qi. However, the difference between the two's capabilities was vast from a mere glance. Her Shadow Armor was more like a dress than full medieval plate armor conjured from shadows. The fiends she summoned were more annoyances than threats, and her bladework was vastly inferior. It was clear that Evelyn had lived the life of a noble daughter, while Nox fought tooth and nail in the outside world, as her techniques lacked that refined ruthlessness.

Because of this, the Frostveil Grand Elder had to send a few of his Elders to assist her while she fought. Ashlock was honestly impressed as the man was an absolute tank. He manifested walls of ice to block crescent slashes and went toe-to-toe with a Lunarshade Elder in an airborne boxing match.

Ashlock also saw the Mystshroud family joining Elysia in the air. Abominations birthed from their imaginations manifested from their mystic Qi, and how they differed from Pluto was obvious. Their creations had more ethereal forms, like illusions, rather than physical bodies.

"After my talk with them, it looks like they are also going with an eye and tree theme, much like Pluto," Ashlock mused. He had gone all out earlier with {Abyssal Whispers} to flood their minds with visions to inspire them.

The Mystshroud Grand Elder commanded an ethereal giant hand made from black wood floating in the air. In its palm was a glowing red eye that seemed to carry a hint of Ashlock's demonic eye powers, capable of inducing madness in the Lunarshade Elders as they tried to flee its grasp.

That just left one group out of the fight. Ashlock looked back at the ground beyond the Bastion's shield and saw the Blightbane family gathered around the Lunarshade Elder's corpse and praying to it. Their bodies were withered and rotting and their eyes a liquid black.

"Bringer of death, heed our prayers," they chanted. *"Purge the*

lingering regrets from this nonbeliever and envelop us in your blessing."

Ashlock was curious about what death affinity cultivators were capable of, and he had no reason to refuse their pleas as it was simply a side effect of the skill and not something he was doing on purpose.

"I hear your prayers," Ashlock spoke into their minds, **"so have your reward."**

He didn't really know what to say to their misplaced prayers, but anything that would make them revere him more and boost his divine energy was a plus in his book.

The black root went down the corpse's throat and deposited the seed. All the Blightbane cultivators stood and clasped their hands before their chests as they waited for their god's blessing. Death Qi miasma exploded as the corpse twisted upward and took on its new wooden form, much like the last two.

The Blightbane family absorbed the death Qi and cried to the heavens as their skin melted off their bones, revealing the ivory color beneath. It was one of the most gruesome sights Ashlock had witnessed in this world and was made all the worse because they seemed to be *enjoying* it. Their cultivation soared the closer to death they came.

"Have they become undead? The Grand Elder almost resembles a lich at this point," Ashlock muttered to himself in disbelief.

With death miasma leaking from their mouths like bad breath, the half-dead-looking members of the Blightbane family finally joined the war after a brief celebration of Ashlock's god-like capabilities. The Grand Elder, whose black cloak flapped in the winds, barely concealed his skeleton body as he took to the sky and faced off the oldest-looking Lunarshade Elder.

"The scent of death around you is sickening." The man grimaced as he brandished his silver sword, burning with white flames. *"You are a plague on this realm that should be purified in the moonlight,"*

Grand Elder Blightbane answered with a crooked grin, *"I will be the judge of that."* He raised his finger and gathered Qi toward it before saying, with an almost inhuman voice reverberating through the lands, **"Life-Death Equilibrium."**

The Lunarshade Elder tried to run, but Ashlock cast Spatial Lock on him. He staggered in the air as his beloved moonlight rejected his passage, and the bolt of death fired from the Blightbane Grand Elder's finger impacted him. It phased right through his lunar Qi and clothes as if they weren't there.

"What did you do to me?" the Lunarshade asked as he frantically patted his chest with wide eyes.

"Just wait and see," the Blightbane Grand Elder sneered. *"Oh look, it's started."*

"What has..."

Ashlock saw wrinkles spread across the man's flawless skin, and his eyes darkened. He went limp as what Ashlock assumed was the man's soul rose into the air as a dense burning ball of white flames, illuminating the night sky.

But he wasn't the only one to have his soul exposed. From Grand Elder Blightbane's chest, a sinister black sun floated forward. Even Ashlock felt a chill run down his bark looking at it from afar, and he wasn't the only one. Everyone paused their fights and turned to watch the spectacle unfolding.

"Under the heavens, our souls will now be weighed against one another," Grand Elder Blightbane explained. *"Your life force will be compared to my death Qi, and whoever is found lacking will have their soul forfeit, and the victor will claim the other."*

Ashlock now realized why the Grand Elder sought out the oldest member of the Lunarshade Elders. No matter his foe's cultivation level, if they were nearing the end of their lifespan, then their life force could be close to that of a mortal. Only those in the Nascent Soul Realm and above could escape the shackles of mortality by reincarnating into their infant souls.

A heavenly scale manifested in the sky constructed from golden light and began to weigh the two burning souls.

The old man, who could not move his limbs, shouted to his fellow Elders, "Lend me your life force! I only have a century of lifeforce remaining, so I won't be able to survive!"

"What are you saying, Elder of house Lunarshade?" Grand Elder Blightbane laughed. *"Life force is the most precious thing. Why would these fine Elders here waste their life force to save a blundering old fool like you who can't even use Lunar Step correctly?"*

"You silver-tongued snake." The Lunarshade Elder grimaced. *"You spew lies about my good name to sow discord among us. We are all*

worshipers of the moon's grace and will stop at nothing to purge disgusting vermin like you from our sacred lands. Isn't that right, my fellow Elders?"

An uncomfortable silence was shared among all present.

"Isn't that right?" he insisted and still received no reply as his fellow Elders exchanged glances.

"Much like the moon, there is always a dark side to life." Grand Elder Blightbane shook his head wistfully. *"Only when one stands at the gates of Hell do they learn the truth of life."*

"No...this can't be," the old man, visibly aging as his life force was consumed by the sinister death, muttered in horror. *"I still had time! My foundation was perfect, and my path to take over the spot at the top of the family was assured!"*

"Lofty ambitions held back by a lack of talent. Your death was inevitable either to the clutches of time or at the blade of your Grand Elder," Blightbane, who resembled a lich, uttered a death sentence for the man. *"A fact your fellow Elders have known for a while. But don't fear. Now, your strength will become mine, and I shall wield it to slay those who turned their backs on you. Surrender yourself to me, and I will take on your regrets and burning desire for revenge."*

Desperation and rage flashed across the dying man's face. The Blightbane Grand Elder's words seemed to bite deep and tempt the darkest depths of his soul to give in.

"Only if you promise that the Lunarshade Grand Elder will die in the worst way possible will I surrender my soul to you," the man hissed.

As if he were the reaper himself, Grand Elder Blightbane grinned. *"I accept this pact."*

"Then I concede."

Upon uttering those words, the heavenly scale tipped drastically in the Blightbane Grand Elder's favor. The Lunarshade's soul was stripped of its life force and flowed to the Grand Elder, reforming his skin and flesh.

Meanwhile, the old man's corpse fell to the ground as nothing but a sack of flesh and bones with a sickening crunch—the soul and Qi having been stripped and added to the Grand Elder's strength.

"That's another century of life force to stave off the death Qi. Always important to maintain a healthy balance." The Blightbane

Grand Elder chuckled as he reabsorbed his soul and wreathed himself in death Qi. *"Now who is next—"*

An explosion rumbled the land as something shot through the sky. The titan of moonlight in the distance, dancing with a silver cloud of ash, tumbled to the floor with a metal rod sticking through it.

"Was that Douglas?!" Ashlock was in disbelief as he saw Geb slowly close his mouth. The Lunarshade Elders seemed to panic and dispersed. Most headed to their fallen Grand Elder, while one flew straight at the defenseless Geb and teleported into the stone tower's control room before anyone could react.

46
MUDCLOAK ASCENSION

Elaine noticed a sudden crushing pressure in the room a moment before Douglas. Without thinking, she grabbed Douglas's broad arm with both hands and twisted her body to haul him to the side.

"What?" Douglas yelped in surprise. Their fall was accompanied by a shockwave filled with shards of glass that threw them further than intended, and Elaine was blinded by a flash of white.

"Ugh," Elaine groaned as she hit the floor *hard*. She hadn't done much body tempering as neither void nor illusion Qi was suited for it, and she had cushioned Douglas's fall.

As she blinked away the blinding light, vague shapes and outlines gradually sharpened until she could see clearly again. Frozen shards of glass once belonging to the control room's window coated the room like spikes. Close to the window, a Mudcloak stood as a statue of ice with its hand stretched out toward her as it had been caught in the path of the moonbeam.

Elaine followed the frozen path of the moonbeam and found it led to a set of feet poking out of pristine white robes wreathed in dancing white flames.

"It's one of them," Douglas hissed under his breath with a grim expression.

Oh no. Elaine felt her heart jump to her throat in fear as she hauled her body around the table to get a better look. Sure enough, one of the Lunarshade Elders stood there, glaring at them with pupilless eyes.

They were nothing but white, much like his robes and flames. He stood at an impressive height, towering over the shorter tables used by the Mudcloaks, and his entirely bald head almost scraped the ceiling.

"Protect the king!" The Mudcloak, who was most well-versed in speech, brandished a crude dagger from his cloak and charged toward the far superior cultivator. Murky-brown flames ignited its entire form and weapon.

Douglas stood up and shouted, "No! Stand down."

The Mudcloak briefly paused its charge before redeciding its allegiance. "Protect the queen!" it shouted as it resumed its one-man crusade.

"No, damn it—" Elaine gasped out in horror as the looming Lunarshade cultivator stared down at the approaching monster with an amused smirk.

"What a pathetic little creature." The Elder's Star Core pressure pulsed out, and Elaine felt her breath stolen from her lungs. The charging Mudcloak fared even worse. It stumbled at the last step and face-planted before the Elder's feet. Desperately, it tried to raise its head and sword, but its limbs trembled due to the pressure weighing down upon it.

Elaine was mortified as she saw the Elder raise his sword like an executioner.

She loved the little guys. *Move, dammit.* Elaine cursed her body and soul for trembling before a foe. *MOVE.* The void answered her prayers, tearing open and swallowing her whole. She was now floating in the in-between. No matter how carefully woven Heaven's reality was, there were slight gaps between the rivers of Qi as they shifted about. It was these gaps that void cultivators used to traverse great distances.

Now floating in the void and unaffected by the Elder's pressure, Elaine freely traversed the void to position herself behind the Elder.

You can do this, Elaine lied to herself to calm the raging nerves. Defeating someone from a higher realm was almost unheard of, as their mere presence alone was enough to make lesser cultivators kneel at their feet and await death.

Elaine wasn't a fighter. She spent years studying and researching alongside her uncle in Darklight City. After joining the Ashfallen Sect, she began to catch up, but compared to the others, she was still lacking.

No. Stop thinking logically. Elaine shook her head and pulled on her ninth-stage Soul Core to draw upon her illusion Qi and a pitiful amount of void Qi. If the logical outcome was to escape and let this Elder slaughter everyone, then she would rather take the stupid approach—fight till the bitter end. Translucent flames that shifted between various colors wreathed her hands as she narrowed her eyes.

*I can do it. No, I **have** to do it. I am not the same as before. I have been blessed by the help of Ashlock and Mars to further myself by unlocking and developing this second affinity.*

A mere second had passed, yet it felt too long. Elaine *emerged* silently from the void as the Elder's sword blurred, horizontally cutting the trembling Mudcloak in two. Blood flew through the air as the sword completed its arc, splattering the far wall and Douglas's horrified face.

The Elder seemed to notice the sudden person behind him as he turned, but Elaine threw herself onto his back. The burning chill of the lunar Qi bit deep into her bones. Unable to hold back, she screamed in agony as she reached up and clamped both her hands on either side of the Elder's head.

"Elaine?!" Douglas roared as he staggered forward despite the immense pressure bearing down on him. His face was a deep red due to the splattered blood of the executed Mudcloak and the veins bulging through his skin.

Elaine felt more confident seeing Douglas daring to resist the Elder's wrath alongside her. They were in this together, and if she failed, Douglas's head might even be the one flying next.

Instead of running or begging for his life, he is more concerned about me. Elaine smiled slightly through the burning cold as she merged her pitiful void Qi with her illusion Qi to pierce the Elder's mental defenses and went straight to his consciousness. Flooding his mind with her void and illusion Qi combo, she gave the man a suggestion inspired by her enduring agony.

*The moonlight **burns** you.*

"Agh!" The Elder staggered away from the broken window and deeper into the control room to escape the moonlight streaking in.

Mudcloaks trembled all around as his pressure pinned them to the ground.

Elaine desperately held on with her legs wrapped around the Elder's waist and one hand gripping his shoulder. With a flash of silver, she summoned a dagger to her free hand and coated it in all the void Qi she could muster.

Die, you bastard! Elaine rarely felt genuine rage, but seeing the dead Mudcloak, who had died trying to protect her, awakened an indescribable anger.

Bringing her hand up, she aimed for the Elder's neck and stabbed downward. Her body was thrown to the side by the Elder's aggressive movements. The blade instead bit deep into his shoulder. Most of the void Qi on the dagger was consumed to penetrate the layers of lunar Qi, and the man's body was tempered to the point it felt like she had struck marble rather than flesh. Yet, despite their gap in cultivation and body constitution, the dagger made it all the way in.

The Elder howled in even more agony and desperately reached over his shoulder. Grabbing her wrist that was still holding the dagger hilt, Elaine heard an audible crack as every bone in her hand was crushed to dust.

Elaine's body took a second to register the shocking pain, and once she did, her entire body seized up as she cried out in pain, and tears welled in her eyes. Perhaps someone like Douglas could keep fighting through the pain, but Elaine had long reached her limit as she was thrown off the Elder's back and tumbled to the floor.

I did my best, was all Elaine could think as she lay there on the floor, watching the Elder stumbling about the room like a raging drunk as he believed the moonlight was burning him alive.

A small smile appeared on Elaine's lips. Even she was surprised at how ruthless of a suggestion she had given the Elder, and because the illusion Qi had been merged with some void Qi, dispelling it would be more problematic.

But at the end of the day, it's just an illusion. The moonlight isn't really harming the Elder. If he could ignore it, he could keep fighting like normal. Also, it was a suggestion. It wouldn't have worked if it was something he deemed impossible.

"What did you do to me?!" The Elder collapsed to his knees and clutched his head. "The moonlight, why does it reject me? Why does it

burn me?" The white lunar flames dancing across his skin diminished as he returned to screaming.

"Because you killed one of my people." Douglas trudged over to the collapsed Elder. The pressure on the room had lessened considerably so he could move. He kneed the Elder in the face, sending the man sprawling onto his back, and before the Elder knew what was happening, Douglas rammed his earth Qi–wreathed walking stick into his heart.

The Elder's eyes widened, and he wheezed. "You think…such a wound…will kill me?"

"No," Douglas said simply as he put his entire weight onto the Elder by sitting on his chest and brutally ripped out the dagger embedded in his shoulder. "But this will." Douglas's earth Qi coated the blade as he swiftly cut the Elder's head off.

The Elder's hand briefly lifted before it fell limp. All at once, the pressure blanketing the room vanished, and Elaine was able to let out a nervous breath. It was over.

"Elaine, you were amazing." Douglas let out a sigh of relief as he looked to the ceiling, his shoulders drooping as the tension left. "Since when could you do that?"

"Um…" Elaine felt her face go red. "I practiced hard recently."

"I could tell. That was very impressive," Douglas said, rolling off the Lunarshade Elder's corpse and staggering to his feet. He was clearly exhausted as he gave the corpse a half-hearted kick. "That was for my chief commander," he muttered sadly as he glanced at the other much smaller and gruesome corpse.

A portal suddenly rippled into existence, and three thick black vines covered in thorns wielding swords surged through. They seemed to wave around in the middle of the room in confusion.

"He's already dead?" Ashlock's voice echoed in Elaine's mind. *"How…?"*

"Elaine—"

"We killed him together," Elaine interrupted Douglas, and they exchanged a knowing, weary grin.

"I see, though I still don't see how. You are both in the Soul Fire Realm and lacking combat experience. That was a seasoned Elder in the Star Core Realm… Whatever, I don't have time. Good shot, Douglas. You hit the Grand Elder."

"Thank you, boss." Douglas briefly bowed toward Willow in the distance.

The black vines picked up the Lunarshade corpse and carried him through the portal, likely to be turned into an Ent or devoured by the demonic tree.

"Boss, I know you are busy." Douglas picked up the two bloody halves of the dead Mudcloak. "But is there anything you can do about this one?"

"I can't revive the dead, but I can turn the Mudcloak into an Ent. Is that agreeable?"

Douglas nodded. "Please."

"Very well." Spatial Qi enveloped the Mudcloak as it rose via telekinesis and was taken away through the portal.

"To Heaven!" a Mudcloak cheered, and the others joined in.

"Saved the king!"

"Mudcloak ascension!"

"No, no, no." Douglas shook his head. "What he did was very stupid. This is bad, understand?"

The Mudcloaks gathered around their king and exchanged confused glances. Their glowing blue eyes peeked through their black cloaks, which Elaine had verified was part of their body and acted like skin.

"Ugh, whatever." Douglas sighed as he pinched the bridge of his nose. "If I tell you guys not to fight, listen to me in the future, okay? The king is strong. I don't need your help sometimes."

"The king doesn't need us?" one of the Mudcloaks muttered, sending the rest into a frenzy.

Douglas grumbled, "That's not what I said…"

"We will die for the king! Don't abandon us!" They grabbed onto his legs and begged as he tried to pry them off.

Elaine chuckled at the scene as she used the table to support herself as she got to her feet. *Ow, ow, ow. How many bones did I break?* She flopped her crushed hand and winced. *It would be better to ask how many bones remain in my poor hand.*

A new portal rippled into existence, and Elaine recognized Red Vine Peak through it. *Home.*

"You two leave and take the Mudcloaks with you," Ashlock told them. *"I'll have Geb return once the battle is over, but it isn't safe for*

you two here anymore, and I can't spend time protecting you myself."

It was a very kind way to say they were in the way. This fact saddened Elaine a little, but he wasn't wrong. They had *barely* managed to kill a single Lunarshade Elder by ambushing him, and Elaine was all out of void Qi.

Douglas managed to get the Mudcloaks off him and let Elaine lean on him as they walked through the portal. She gasped in pain with every step as the adrenaline faded and the repercussions of her almost suicidal attack set in.

Before they passed through, Elaine looked through the frozen window at the avatar of moonlight impaled by a pillar of metal. He was surrounded by the remaining Lunarshade Elders, and she could feel the Qi fluctuations of the fight happening over there despite the distance.

It looks like we're winning, Elaine thought as her ears popped and the cold winds of Red Vine Peak ruffled her hair. The portal snapped close behind her, and she hated to admit it, but it was nice to be back to safety.

Douglas ran his fingers through her hair and gently caressed her back.

Elaine answered his advances by leaning further into his embrace. "We survived," she whispered.

Douglas's chest rumbled slightly as he hummed in agreement. "That we did."

"I was so scared," Elaine admitted. Her heart still pounded in her ears, and her legs shook.

"Honestly...me, too." Douglas met her gaze. "That I would lose you."

Elaine clicked her tongue and winced as she pushed him off. "Classic earth cultivator. Always having to act tough."

Douglas chuckled and scratched the back of his neck. "Okay, okay, you caught me. I was fucking terrified, all right? Though isn't it crazy to think Stella is at a stage of cultivation beyond that guy?"

"That's true." Elaine nodded and glanced at the demonic tree that lorded over the peak. *And the Patriarch is at a level even higher than that. I have a lot to catch up to if I want to be useful to this sect.*

A low thumping sound drew Elaine's focus. Turning around, she saw the light Ent trudging toward them. It collapsed to one knee and offered her a healing wisp.

"Thank you," Elaine said, accepting the offering and shivering in ecstasy as the pain washed away and the bones in her crushed hand reformed. Douglas led the Mudcloaks back to the citadel, and she chose to collapse onto Stella's bench under the tree and just take it all in.

After such an experience, she had a *lot* to think over. A while passed, and as her gaze drifted across the mountain peak, she noticed something large emerge from the library atop the citadel.

"Kaida?" Elaine tilted her head as the Lyndwrym tasted the outside air with his tongue. "What is he doing out here?"

A rift appeared beside Kaida, and the snake shot her a look before he slithered through.

"Did Kaida just join the fight?" Elaine's eyes widened. What was the situation on the other side?

47
PHANTOM MOON'S HEIR

The Lunarshade Grand Elder groaned as he clasped a hand around the shaft of metal that was impaling his side. It had torn through his lunar avatar as if it were nothing but water and had taken out his left arm and lung.

It should be impossible for something this primitive to hurt him to this extent, but Qi was a type of spiritual force at the end of the day. A well-made physical projectile coated in runic formations designed to pierce Qi defenses was difficult to stop, no matter how dense his lunar Qi avatar was.

Such a primitive weapon would be a waste of resources in most fights, as I would teleport away before it grazed my fair skin. Yet a technique originating from that darn spirit tree protected by a shield prevents my passage through the moonlight.

"Dorian, are you alive?"

The Grand Elder glanced up at the group of Elders left and scowled at the one who had uttered his name. "Elder Elio, are you cursing me to die?" he wheezed out at the man as he only had one lung. "Or have you grown so bold to utter my name as you believe I will not strike you down before you have contributed to this battle?"

Elder Elio clasped his hands and bowed deeply. "My deepest apologies, Grand Elder. That was not my intention. I will repent to the moon for my unthoughtful words."

"Good, now help remove this rod."

Elder Elio floated down with the rest, and Dorian granted them passage through his avatar of moonlight. He wouldn't usually trust his Elders to this degree as he knew they all eyed the seat at the top of the Lunarshade family that he had spent centuries building up to be a position of prestige.

Especially Elder Elio. He thinks I am blind to the family's ongoings as I enjoy my moonlit baths surrounded by jade beauties, but little does he know they whisper rumors in my ears as we make passionate love. I know his branch has started aggressively buying up pills from the pavilion, and his branch's younger generation has been locked away in closed-door cultivation for months. They are clearly preparing for a takeover.

The Elders tried to pull the rod free, but it was firmly planted into the earth and had somehow fused to his skin.

It must have an earth core below the metal coating, and the earth's Qi keeps it rooted in place. What an interesting weapon these bastards have devised.

"Overload it with Qi. The runic formations can only take so much," Dorian instructed.

His Elders exchanged a reluctant look.

He flared his pressure to remind these bastards that they were currently inside his avatar, and crushing them like insects would be easy. They took the hint and quickly got to work.

I could use my Qi or strength to destroy this rod, but I need all I can muster to keep this ash spider from consuming me alive. The infant soul will decay to nothing at this rate, and the Qi I gathered for it over the last few centuries will be wasted.

Lunar Qi surged down the silver metal rod, which must have cost thousands of high-grade spirit stones to make. The formations glowed white, and cracks appeared. Elder Elio reeled back his fist, and with a well-placed punch, the metal casing shattered and fell aside, revealing a stone core hardened with glowing earth Qi, as Dorian had suspected.

Now free from the rod that had been sapping away his Qi, Dorian pushed lunar Qi to his wounds and watched as the soft moonlight began regrowing his flesh and limbs. Within seconds, he had undone the damage caused by the projectile.

Just how rich are these bastards to waste so many spirit stones on a one-time-use weapon that hardly did anything? Dorian shook his head as he expelled his Elders from his avatar and rose to his full height once again. *Whatever, let's regain control of this battle and remind these insects why I am known as the Phantom Moon's Heir.*

Raising his hands to the moon, which had reached its zenith, he said a prayer. This was a last resort for most, as calling upon a divine being's assistance never came cheap, whether the debt be paid in this life or the next. But he had already lost too much for this to go on. At this rate, he might even *lose* to the ash spider.

"Goddess of the moon, cleanse me of this filth that dares to cloud the skies and sully your everlasting beauty!" Dorian bellowed to the heavens, and he felt it answer his call. A price would be paid for this salvation in due time, but for now, he did not care. This creature that dared to eat him alive needed to perish.

The heavens took interest, and the moon answered his prayer. The celestial object dominating the sky took on a sinister glow, and Dorian's face fell as he felt the price of his request. Strength left his body as life force was torn from his soul and gifted to the moon.

Such a steep price. Dorian couldn't believe it. A tribute of Qi, or perhaps a bottleneck, was to be expected, but life force? *Did I ask the heavens to strike down a fellow divine or something?*

It was unexpected but not the worst outcome. *So long as I can recover my infant soul before my lifespan is up, I can reincarnate into a new body and continue living.*

Having taken its tribute, the moon rapidly expanded in size as if trying to snuff out the stars and dominate the entire sky. Dorian could feel its pitiful gaze upon him as it honored his pathetic request.

The world went white as a moonbeam of unfathomable power bathed him in its cleansing wrath. The ash spider that had been devouring him barely managed to disperse in time through a hastily summoned portal, but most of it was disintegrated by the moonlight.

A moment passed, and the spider did not return.

It's a tall price to pay, but at least the main threat has been dealt with.

"Let's end this war... Wait, where are the rest of you?" the Grand Elder asked his remaining Elders. At least four were missing. Had they died in the moonlight blast, too? Had the moon goddess deemed them unworthy of her cold love?

"They were slain in a dishonorable battle, and then the bastards that dared to invade your sacred lands defiled their honorable corpses by turning them into twisted monstrosities and were made to fight against us," the very helpful Elder Elio informed him while pointing at humanoid-looking white trees near the spirit tree.

Dorian followed his Elder's finger, and sure enough, there were three lunar-wreathed abominations that strangely resembled his Elders despite their new monstrous forms. They stood in formation around the spirit tree as if guarding it. Many prominent Grand Elders of the other major families in Nightshade City were floating before the shield on swords, and they weren't the only ones. He could detect others, such as Magnus Redclaw, fighting off a wave of incoming bounty hunters in the distance.

"Elders, go and attack the ones fighting the bounty hunters from behind," Dorian instructed his Elders. They all teleported away to fulfill his order. He wasn't sure if the bounty hunters were on his side or not, as the Celestial Warden was likely involved, and that man's motives were never clear.

Friend or foe, my Elders should keep them busy. Now, let's deal with these pests one by one.

Dorian raised his hand. While he had the moon's attention, his Star Core pulsed as he called upon a Nascent Soul–level moonbeam from the heavens and aimed at the tortoise monster in the distance.

The heavens delivered, and the world went white. The head of that giant red wood mountain in the distance blew up. Since it was stationary and posed the most threat, he chose to eliminate it first as it was the thing that could shoot projectiles capable of killing him. In comparison, everyone else here was a weakling hardly worth his attention except for one other major threat.

Dorian's eyes narrowed at the creature from the beyond. Mystic Qi coated its wriggling tendrils and giant green eye, giving it a purple glow, but this monster felt *real*, unlike the other illusionary creations from the Mystshroud family. How such a young girl could order around a beast from the void was beyond Dorian, but the fact that it was a threat that needed to be eliminated didn't change.

There's a reason I never dare to dally in the beyond, Dorian thought as he looked into the girl's eyes. They were crazed to the degree that unnerved anyone as if she knew things no human should know and could break your mind by merely uttering these truths.

Lunar affinity was of a higher order than most, which was why he could shift between reality and the void and also had control over the spatial plane. Naturally, mastering it to the level he had required an unfathomable amount of time and dedication. Something his now-slain heir had shown promise of.

"You fuckers will pay for what you have done." Dorian clenched his avatar's fist. "And you will be the first."

The Mystshroud girl grinned wildly. "You dare defy my god's grace?"

"Defy?! I outright reject anything that isn't the lunar goddess's light!" Dorian dashed forward as teleportation was blocked and planted his avatar's lunar Qi–wreathed fist into the void monster. The mystic Qi coating its body evaporated in a wave, exposing the monster's body to reality. It let out an otherworldly scream of pain that shook Dorian's consciousness.

Killing a void monster is near impossible without me expending all the Qi I have, but to send it back to where it came from is easy enough. Without the mystic Qi protecting it, Heaven will expel it from its carefully woven reality for me, as creatures from the beyond aren't welcome here.

"What did you do?!" the Mystshroud girl shrieked as the void monster reentered her third eye carved into her forehead and vanished.

Dorian had no interest in educating a brat who relied on borrowed power. He twisted his body and slapped away the many illusionary creations coming at him from the other Mystshroud members. If not for the vast difference in cultivation, these would be harder to deal with than the void monster, as he couldn't simply get rid of the outer layer and would have to destroy them outright or somehow disrupt the Mystshroud's imagination with mental attacks so they lost focus.

"Enough of this nonsense," Dorian hissed in annoyance. As a Nascent Soul Realm cultivator, he could fly around unassisted by a sword, so he simply floated toward the Grand Elders and unleashed his pressure upon them.

Rifts opened around Dorian, and black vines coated in thorns surged toward him. Some even wielded swords coated in spatial Qi, and to his surprise, they could strike from seemingly impossible angles and tear into his avatar.

Luckily, like the void monster coated in mystic Qi, there was a simple solution. Dorian didn't even bother trying to cut or freeze the vines. He sent out a crescent slash from his sword and severed the portals instead. The popping sounds and rush of air accompanied the thuds of the thick black vines and the clattering of swords falling to the ground.

Their coordination is terrible, and they rely on too many proxy attacks. Only the ash spider dared to attack me head-on with his body. It's impossible to defeat a stronger opponent with such safe attacks from afar. My regeneration is unbeatable, and so long as the moon is at its zenith, I can call upon its wrath.

A yawn almost escaped Dorian's mouth as a wall of ice erupted from the ground.

"Are you trying to prevent my passage with ice? Do you know who I am?" Dorian sneered at the Frostviel Grand Elder as he snapped his fingers, and the wall crumbled into a sad lake of water in the mud.

The monstrosities birthed from his fallen Elders guarding the spirit tree began to move toward him. "My Elders feared and obeyed me in life. What do you think they could do to me in death?" Dorian opened his palm and reversed gravity on the Ents.

They groaned, and the sound of snapping wood filled the air. They were uprooted and pulled toward him. Once they collapsed below him in a pile, he floated down and greedily drew the moonlight from their souls into his avatar.

Dorian grinned at the refreshing feeling as the Ents withered as he drank on their souls. *Even in death, my Elders serve me.* Annoyingly, he couldn't recover his life force through this technique. For that, he would have to reincarnate via his infant soul or conduct a complicated sacrificial ritual with his own children.

With the Ents dealt with, Dorian floated up and sneered.

"Your attacks are all weak and pathetic. That ash spider was an interesting opponent, but I really have to wonder who gave you all the gall to slaughter my son? My Elders alone outnumber you all, and only the Celestial Warden has the strength to harm me. Did you truly think this fight would end any other way?" Dorian questioned the Grand Elders as they desperately tried to remain airborne under his crushing pressure. The weaker Elders of their family had already crashed into the ground below, sending up dust clouds.

When he received no reply, Dorian's patience began to waver.

"I was content in letting you insects live alongside me so long as Evelyn Duskwalker pleasured my son and kept you all in line." Dorian glared at Evelyn Duskwalker. "It seems my son's lust led to his downfall as he was enchanted by a vixen such as yourself. I knew you were bad news, always coming to my family and requesting funds in such a pitiful manner."

Evelyn glared at him with hatred. "It's not my fault you and your son are such fools and ugly bastards that were begging for death. If not by my hands, someone was bound to end your tyranny one day."

Dorian blinked in disbelief at Evelyn's words. She was supposed to be a weak kitten who would kneel and beg at his feet for scraps like an animal. To think it had all been an act, and she had been a tigress all along, waiting for the perfect opportunity to kill his dear son when he had his guard down!

"You finally show your true colors." Dorian floated toward her and opened his palm. "I will keep you as a statue to serve as a reminder to future generations to stay wary of two-faced bitches like you."

He called on the dark side of the moon, and the air around him crystallized into hail as ice Qi gathered in his palm. He used reverse gravity to pull her toward him and was about to encase her in ice when a rift tore open between them, swallowing Evelyn and transporting her somewhere else.

A vein popped in Dorian's forehead as he ground his teeth. Spatial cultivators were among the most troublesome to deal with. Usually, he could call on his comprehension of the spatial plane, which came with his lunar affinity, to block them. Yet, despite being in a lower realm, the amount of Qi this spatial cultivator had to blanket the entire city was monstrous. It was impossible to wrestle away control from them.

Dorian glared at the spirit tree aflame with spatial Qi under the shield. Ignoring the pathetic attacks from the weaklings, he floated closer, and raising his hand, he slammed down on the shield. It rippled, and he noticed the spirit tree's flames flare even more aggressively

A wide grin appeared on his face. He could feel its **fear**. This was how it should be. The weak should bow and cower before the strong like him. Sometimes, in eras of peace, people forgot who the true hidden dragons of this realm were. Dorian had no problem being given a chance to personally dish out that reminder.

Placing both palms on the spatial shield, he pulled deeply on both of his Star Cores and began squeezing the shield like an egg while burning it with lunar Qi. It only lasted a dozen seconds before it perished.

"Got you," Dorian said, grabbing the tree trunk and ripping it free from the black rock. He held it overhead and easily tore it in half. The pressure that had shrouded the entire battlefield since the beginning faded, and the spatial flames enshrouding the tree and its canopy were snuffed out. Just to be sure he eliminated all traces of this spatial cultivator, he threw the pieces of the tree to the side and crushed the black rock with his foot.

The technique that had been locking him out from the moonlight vanished, which should have been good news, but Dorian shook his foot in concern. "What is this?" A strange black liquid with the viscosity of blood was rapidly spreading through his avatar.

He shook his foot and stumbled backward from the black rock, noticing many severed roots leaking the same black liquid.

That same presence from before bloomed in his mind, and a demonic spirit tree appeared in his consciousness. Despite his efforts, he could not purge it from his mind this time, and he felt its roots sprawl out through his soul and join up with the black blood corrupting him.

"Grand Elder Lunarshade," a chorus of a hundred voices echoed creepily through his mind. ***"Have you ever wondered how nice it would be to bathe under the moonlight as a tree?"***

48

FEAST UNDER THE MOONLIGHT

Stella blinked in and out of the spatial plane as fast as the spatial Qi could flow through her spirit roots. Her mind was tranquil and calm due to her bloodline, but her body was struggling to keep up. Her Star Core burned fiercely in her chest, and her Qi-enhanced muscles ached as she deflected a needle of silver from piercing her brain with her sword in a shower of sparks and a terrible scraping sound that howled in her ear.

If not for Ash drowning the whole city in spatial Qi, I would have run out and likely died by now. There's just no end to these bounty hunters.

"Girl, you sure are good at running away." The silver-haired man wearing a jade mask clicked his tongue as he casually redirected the needle of silver to chase her. He was one of the jade sentinels sent to fight with them, and so far, he had been the most motivated. Stella wasn't sure how to describe it, but until now, every bounty hunter had held back as if trying to contribute the bare minimum to the battle and preserve their Qi.

Once they got slightly injured, they ran away instead of fighting to the death like normal cultivators. This was bizarre and confusing because if they had combined their strength, Stella, Diana, and the Redclaws would have been long overrun. There were simply too many of them.

What the hell is their goal? Stella wondered as she vanished into the spatial plane and did a longer-range teleport to reappear above Diana. Her ears popped as a wave of wind hit her, and she saw what appeared to be a cloaked person soaring toward the ground like a meteor. Once the person ate the dirt below, throwing up a plume of dust, a portal opened overhead, and black vines dragged the body elsewhere.

"There goes...another...one," Diana panted as she lowered the fist that had just sent the person flying. Blood dripped from her claws, and war scars painted her once-beautiful feathered wings.

Diana looked a mess, and she wasn't the only one.

The Redclaw family fiercely fighting in the distance wasn't much better off, and Stella was nursing a few deep cuts and torn clothes herself. This battle had been so brutal for all of them that Stella believed it was a genuine miracle that nobody had died yet.

Seeing Diana's condition, Stella hated asking for help, but the squirrel sleeping on her head had offered little assistance thus far. "Diana, could you help me out with a metal cultivator?"

Diana flapped her ruined wings to ascend to Stella's height. "The Jade Sentinel over there?" She tilted her head. "Why do they look familiar?"

"Mhm, I know what you mean. The silver hair and metal affinity remind me of the Silverspires, but I don't believe it's one of Ryker's siblings. They were sent to cities within the Blood Lotus Sect to begin the mutiny against the Patriarch, so they shouldn't be here in the Tainted Cloud Sect," Stella mused while using Qi to mask her voice. "But the Silverspire family has connections to the Eternal Pursuit Pavilion despite the pavilion being banned from the Blood Lotus Sect, so there's a decent chance that person could be from the Silverspire family."

Diana hummed in thought as she pushed her demonic mist Qi into the surroundings to obscure them. "Should we do something about it?" she suggested as they took a moment to rest and eat Ash's fruits. "We have close ties with the family, and they might not appreciate us killing one of their people in another sect."

Stella shrugged. "Food for Tree is food for Tree. I don't care what family he is from or his reasons. He almost killed me a moment ago, and he dares to try and get past us to hurt Ash, so he deserves what's coming."

"Right." Diana sighed, clearly too exhausted to argue. "Open a portal near him, and I will follow you—" She twisted her body as a moonbeam tore through her demonic mist, creating a tunnel through the fog that allowed Stella to see the source. A group of Lunarshade Elders had suddenly appeared behind them.

What in the nine realms is going on? I thought Ashlock was dealing with these guys. Stella gripped her sword tightly and bit her lip. *This isn't good. The bounty hunters were already bad enough, but all of these Elders are as strong as me and are radiating far more killing intent. Unlike the bounty hunters, these guys are here to kill.*

Stella suddenly had a sinking feeling in her stomach. If these Elders were here, that could only mean one thing. Narrowing her eyes, she looked past the floating Lunarshade Elders, who stood arrogantly on their swords and were bathed in moonlight, to confirm her fears.

"Willow?" Stella uttered in horror as she saw the titan of moonlight rip the spirit tree from the Bastion and hold it overhead. A sickening crunch was heard throughout the land as the tree was torn in half and its soul flames extinguished. With it, Ashlock's blanketing presence faded, and Stella felt the dense spatial Qi in the air begin to disperse.

Stella's mouth opened and closed several times as she failed to articulate what she had just witnessed. Eventually, all she managed to mutter in disbelief was, "Tree lost?"

Logically, she knew Willow was one of Ash's many offspring, so the tree dying didn't mean Ash had lost, but emotionally, she was shaken. Whether it be Ash or his offspring, the fading of Ash's presence on the battlefield broke her spirit, and she felt her bloodline retract and her calmness wash away, replaced with terror and confusion.

"Don't." Diana grabbed her arm.

"But we need to—"

"Get a hold of yourself." Diana shook her. "What will rushing over there do other than get yourself killed? Do you think these Lunarshade Elders will simply let you pass?"

"No, but…"

"Even if they did, that man is in the Nascent Soul Realm. He can squash you like a bug even with your bloodline."

Stella ground her teeth. Diana was right; it was suicidal to try to save Willow and restore Ash's presence on the battlefield, but what was she supposed to do now? *Without my bloodline and Ash's spatial Qi, I am crippled.*

It was looking bad. Really bad. Larry was missing, and the Bastion and Willow were destroyed, as was Geb in the distance. The families under Duskwalker, including the cult of the All-Seeing Eye, were being suppressed by a single cultivator. Stella couldn't even rush over and help if she wanted to because enemies surrounded them on all fronts.

"Tree…" Stella whispered as her heart pounded in her chest. "What should I do? How can we win?"

A warming presence bloomed in her mind. *"Are you losing faith in me?"*

Stella's eyes widened. How could she have lost faith in Ash? He had always been her firmly rooted tree in this life and rarely let her down. Why should she doubt him now?

"I would never." Stella controlled her breathing and brought her turbulent emotions under control. She had relied too heavily on her bloodline to keep her calm in situations like this, and from her bloodline, she knew how important keeping a cool head was.

"Good. Believe it or not, I have everything under control," Ash reassured her. *"Leave everything to me."*

Stella looked at the tree that had bloomed in her consciousness. That unwavering confidence made the tree in her mind take on a more impressive form as he loomed overhead and protected her from the heavens under his vast canopy.

I am safe under him, Stella thought and smiled.

"What did you have in mind?" Diana quickly asked as the Lunarshade Elders began preparing to attack again. If not for the demonic mist protecting them, the Elders likely would have teleported right next to them and cut off their heads.

Ashlock had a reason for his confidence. His attention was split between many things, and his vision constantly blurred as he shifted between Red Vine Peak and different locations on the battlefield, so unlike Stella, he had a better view of the overall state of the battle.

Although most of his Ents, and now his Bastion, had perished, leaving him with fewer chess pieces to work with, not all hope was lost. The Lunarshade side had also taken heavy losses, with multiple Elders dead and Albis Lunarshade's corpse piled up with many others on Red Vine Peak waiting to be devoured. No matter what, he intended to avenge his fallen offspring and Ents, but now wasn't the time to get emotional.

"I just need to find a way to deal with the Lunarshade Grand Elder, and then everything else will fall into place," Ashlock mused as he focused on securing a victory.

Luckily, the Lunarshade Grand Elder had become infected with his cursed blood.

His mutations, such as his cursed blood and demonic eye, weren't transferred to his offspring, but when the Lunarshade Grand Elder stomped on the Bastion, he destroyed Ashlock's roots wrapped around the Bastion's core, which caused his cursed blood to seep into the man's avatar.

Ashlock had expected the Grand Elder to quickly purge the cursed blood, but that had not happened so far. Instead, the man seemed profoundly concerned by the blood spreading through his avatar and stumbled about while shaking his foot.

"The only thing that has changed since the last time my cursed blood infected someone is that I formed a Chaos Nebula in my soul and became recognized as a divine being by the heavens. Does that mean my cursed blood is now divine as well?" Ashlock wondered but didn't have time to investigate it further. Every moment in this battle counted, and his sect members' lives were at risk.

It would be difficult, but as long as he played to his strengths as a spatial cultivator capable of fighting proxy battles, he saw a path to victory.

"Diana, you trust me, right?" Ashlock asked the demoness in response to her question.

She nodded. *"I do."*

"There's no time to explain, but bait the Elders into your demonic mist."

Diana grimaced at the suggestion, as it was the one thing keeping them alive. But against all logic, she complied and began widening the tunnel the moonbeam had carved out.

Ashlock's view shifted back to Red Vine Peak, where he had evacuated the wounded. Elaine was sitting under a bench, enjoying Sol's healing light. It was so peaceful here compared to the chaos occurring many miles away in Nightshade City. Well, if one were to ignore the giant blazing tree shaking the mountain. But what was he supposed to do about that?

"Ready to feast, Larry?" Ashlock asked his Nascent Soul Realm summon that he had barely managed to save from being incinerated by that moonbeam.

The ash spider was a tenth of his size at the start of the battle, but through decay, he could quickly regain his strength.

"I would be honored to fight again, Master," Larry replied gruffly. *"And I must protect Mistress Stella."*

"Good, act fast while the Lunarshade Grand Elder is distracted by my cursed blood," Ashlock said as he created a portal. He wasn't sure how long the Grand Elder would be distracted by the cursed blood and the random ominous sentences and visions he was spewing into the man's mind.

Larry gave the best bow he could muster before floating through the portal. His silver-ashen body shimmered under the moonlight, and his glowing red eyes made him seem like a celestial grim reaper as he descended upon the Lunarshade Elders who had teleported inside Diana's demonic mist.

"Without moonlight, how do you plan to teleport away from Larry?" Ashlock sneered at these fools as the tunnel through the demonic mist closed up, leaving them trapped inside with a very hungry spider.

Stella gasped as she used both hands on her sword hilt to block an overhead swing from one of the Lunarshade Elders. The sheer force of the attack made her already exhausted arms quiver and knocked the wind out of her lungs. She plummeted through the demonic mist that burned her skin and reacted violently with her flickering Qi.

Diana followed a moment later, spiraling downward with her tattered wings wrapped around her body as if she had used them to shield herself from an attack. Blood mixed with demonic mist trailed her as she fell, and her face was twisted in pain.

Stella's heart twisted at the sight of her friend being so heavily injured. *This whole war started because of me. It's all my fault—* Seeing something glint in the moonlight heading straight for Diana, Stella surged her spatial Qi and hopped through the spatial plane. Barely making it in time, she blocked a flurry of silver needles from impaling Diana with her bare hand.

Diana spread out her wings and caught herself from falling any further. "Are you all right?" she asked with concern as she glided over and eyed her up and down.

"Sort of." Stella winced in pain as she looked down at three silver spikes emerging from the back of her hand. She gripped them tightly and could feel their connection to someone else. Following the direction of the Qi, she saw the silver-haired man flying toward them, and he had a few other Jade Sentinels in tow.

"Are you from the Silverspire family?" Stella said casually as she hid her injured hand behind her back. She had to buy some time, as neither of them was in good enough condition to face off against five Jade Sentinels at peak condition, especially without her bloodline and Ash's presence.

The man paused, and so did the others. "So what if I am?"

"We work closely with the Silverspire family." Stella gestured to herself and Diana. "Fighting here is not in your family's best interests."

The man scoffed. "You are members of the Ashfallen Sect, isn't that right? I would know if we had dealings with a sect with such a name, but I have never heard of you—"

"Are you not participating in the mutiny?" Stella said causally, tilting her head.

The Silverspire man went deathly silent for a moment. "How much do you know?"

"Enough," Stella replied with as much confidence as she could muster. In her mind, she was begging Ash to hurry up with his plan. "If you lay a finger on me, your Grand Elder will have your head once he emerges from closed-door cultivation."

Once again, the man fell silent. A stream of silver spiraled around his body, and its constantly shifting speed and direction mirrored the man's turbulent internal thoughts.

"Who is your main contact within the family?" the man eventually asked.

I can't say it's Ryker or Sebastian, and I don't know anyone else in the family. Stella's eyes darted between the Jade Sentinels present. "Do you trust these people enough for me to openly disclose such information?"

"No…"

"Then come closer." Stella began gathering all the Qi she had left toward her hand behind her back, impaled by the silver spikes. The metal Qi helped mask the gathering of spatial Qi to her finger. "I have no Qi left to mask my voice from so far."

The man seemed to eye her suspiciously through his mask as the silver flowing around his body retracted and began to flow more defensively. "Fine." He floated closer until he was within strike range. His hand rested on the pommel of a sheathed sword, and he clearly had his guard up. "Now tell me, who is it?"

Ryker has six siblings, so there should be at least three branch families, right?

"The third Elder," Stella replied.

"Really?" The man seemed surprised.

"Yeah…?" Stella had no idea what she was saying.

"What's the third Elder's name?"

Stella bit her lip behind her mask. "He's a very secretive man when it comes to outsiders, so he used a clearly fake name when speaking with us."

The man nodded. "That's true. Third Elder had always been a sly old man. Though he should have given you a seal so we can recognize each other."

Chance!

"Oh! How could I have forgotten about it?" Stella reached forward and showed her palm. "But first, could you remove these spikes? They are interfering with my spatial rings, so I can't take out the seal."

"Sure." The man reached forward to take the spikes out of her hand—

Stella rammed her finger into his chest and used an inferior version of the Supreme Nirvana Finger technique that she pieced together from her fading memories of it.

In an explosion of spatial Qi that made reality ripple, the Silverspire man was thrown backward. Some of his flowing silver was consumed to block the attack, but he was otherwise unharmed.

"You bitch," the man roared out. "I don't know how you came across that information, but you dare lie to me." His flowing silver condensed into thousands of needles, and the other Jade Sentinels floating at his side decided to join the fight.

"Um, Tree..." Stella looked up at the demonic mist cloud above. "A little help?"

I have tried my best to buy time. Surely Ash doesn't expect me to fight off these people, too?

"Mistress, sorry I am late," a voice thundered from above. The demonic fog parted to reveal an ashen maw of silver large enough to devour an entire pavilion and glowing red eyes like miniature suns. The crown of horns atop his head radiated divinity, and the halo of ash orbiting it carried an immense presence that descended upon everyone as Larry dove down.

"Larry!" Stella shouted with glee. She had never been so happy to see her father's guardian.

The storm of silver ash surged down and rushed around Stella as Larry used his body to protect her and Diana from the barrage of silver needles heading her way. He then went after the Jade Sentinels, catching two of them in his maw. As they crumbled into silver dust, his body and pressure grew.

Stella looked up and saw a lack of Lunarshade Elders.

"Looks like Larry had a feast," Diana said with a sigh of relief and wrapped her hand around Stella's shoulder.

Stella helped hold up her wounded friend and returned a smile. "Sure looks like it."

"You two can head back now," Tree said, and a rift appeared leading back to Red Vine Peak. **"You both did great."**

"It's over?" Stella asked in confusion.

"No, but Larry and Kaida can handle the rest alongside the Redclaws. Even if we win or lose, the fact you two are safe is more important to me."

Stella felt warmth in her heart and was surprised at Ash's words. "Kaida is joining the fight? I thought that lazy snake did nothing but read and hiss at people."

"Yeah, the Grand Elder won't know what hit him. Kaida has been working with Quill to incorporate dozens of techniques into his

scales. He should have enough firepower to nuke the Grand Elder out of existence."

Stella wasn't sure what a nuke was, but it sounded powerful. She headed through the portal while shouldering Diana, who was limping. They both blinked in surprise when the Silverspire man's body fell at their feet through another portal with one of Ashlock's swords rammed through his chest.

49
SELFISH DEMISE

Dorian Lunarshade furrowed his brows in concern. The accursed blood invading his avatar continued to spread despite his best efforts to suppress it, and the demonic tree spreading its roots in his consciousness continued to taunt him with words and hallucinations.

"Mhm, such nice weather today, right? Clear skies and a pleasant breeze. It's almost a shame we are fighting on such a fine night as this."

The white fog encircling the edge of Dorian's consciousness flashed red as it transformed into a raging storm. A sudden gale howled through his mind, rustling the demonic tree's leaves and bringing in the storm until it entirely clouded his mind.

"I need to... What?" Dorian frowned in confusion. His trails of thought were getting lost in the chaos.

A thousand voices laughed at him. *"Are you getting senile in your old age, Grand Elder? Even my grandpa was more coherent on his deathbed than you."*

Dorian felt shivers down his spine as the storm took on a darker shade, and the wind became bone-chilling.

"Get out of my head!" Dorian raged as he cycled his Qi to fight back. None of this made any sense. He had purged this tree from his mind without difficulty earlier, yet now it felt like an immovable force that had dug its roots deep. Even more bizarre was that the storm and winds didn't feel like illusions, as wind Qi was invading his mind.

How could this person's presence carry wind affinity? Wasn't the cultivator using these trees as proxies for their techniques supposed to be a spatial cultivator? Could such a powerful, unknown Dual-Core cultivator really exist?

"It's impossible! You shouldn't exist!" Dorian gritted his teeth. "Such a being would have dominated the war era and become a title holder known to all who walked the realm. This is either a trick or the work of a divine being."

Unfortunately, he was becoming more convinced that he had somehow earned the ire of the latter from a higher realm. If the ash spider wasn't enough evidence, the cursed blood infecting his avatar was resistant to being cleansed by the moonlight, which meant it had to carry at least a hint of divinity.

Even if I can't cleanse it with moonlight, I should... What... I can expel it...right? Dorian massaged his temples as he tried to form a coherent trail of thought. *What a vile use of wind Qi—to invade my mind and blow away my thoughts and memories. What kind of ruthless being could come up with such a technique?*

Dorian flooded his consciousness with lunar Qi to try and get a hold of himself. Sitting on the ground in a crossed-legged pose, he breathed deeply and pulled on the moonlight. "Elders, I need to cultivate to rid myself of this foul blood. Protect me..."

Silence greeted his request.

"Feeling lonely under the moonlight, Grand Elder?" the chorus of voices said wistfully. **"It's often on nights such as these that one contemplates the deeper things in life. Have you ever sat in silence with nothing but the rustling leaves to accompany you?"**

"Do you ever shut up?" Dorian hissed through his clenched teeth. Not only did this person keep sprouting nonsense, but every word they uttered came with another wave of illusions that tormented him. Also, the many overlapping voices made focusing on anything it said an absolute chore.

"Elders! Come back. Stop fighting the bounty hunters!" Dorian roared to the heavens with Qi-empowered words.

Still nothing.

Confused, he spread out his spiritual sense, and to his horror, he couldn't feel the presence of a single one of his Elders. *Did those bastards flee?* No, that was an impossibility. They all knew that if they disobeyed his orders, their entire family branch would be wiped out for the next nine generations.

Which meant there was only one other possibility. The Lunarshade Elders had all been killed within the last few minutes. Dorian stood up in a hurry and resorted to cycling his Qi for now to try and suppress the spreading blood that was slowly turning his lunar avatar into wood.

Not only are my Elders missing, but so is everyone else. Dorian frowned. He was the only one here besides some bounty hunters fleeing to the pavilion. The Duskwalker, Frostveil, Mystshroud, and Blightbane families that had been protecting the spirit tree were nowhere to be seen. Even the giant turtle of red wood that had launched the projectile at him was missing.

"Eerie, isn't it?" The voices laughed. *"Just you and me."*

Dorian was *confused.* Never before had the battlefield just vanished in its entirety when he wasn't looking. He clenched his fist before letting it hang loosely at his side. Who was he supposed to throw his fist at if nobody was here? Even the pieces of the spirit tree and the black rock ship were gone.

"What is your goal?" Dorian asked the sky. "Is this a joke to you? How can someone of your status run like this after murdering my son?"

"What strange wording. Who said I ran?"

"Then what would you call this?" Dorian gestured to the silent battlefield. Despite the craters and bloodstains, not a single corpse had been left behind. Blazing fires dotted the landscape like candle flames, and there were piles of melting ice. The Qi in the air was thick and chaotic, with many competing types at war to reclaim control over the environment.

Evidence of a fierce battle between dozens of high-realm cultivators was everywhere. So where were the people?

"All I see is an upcoming construction project," the voice said with a hint of amusement. *"Your dungeon of sin appears to have not survived under the wrath of your big feet."*

Dorian looked around, and the voice was right. This area of the city had been thoroughly destroyed, including his gambling house.

"Ashfallen Sect, right? Just you wait: I will find your hiding hole soon enough and pull you out kicking and screaming with my bare hands and make you pay for those you have killed," Dorian said spitefully.

"I'm sure we will see each other soon, and to be honest, I would be very surprised if you could make me kick or scream."

Dorian huffed in annoyance as illusionary screams carried by wind Qi filled his mind due to the voice's words. Talking with it seemed pointless, so he ignored the taunting and gathered himself.

This bastard can flee all he wants, but I will end the Ashfallen Sect. I put my name and title on it as the Grand Elder of the Lunarshade family. I will not rest or falter until this spatial cultivator is dead.

Dorian pulled on the moonlight to teleport to his family's residence. His ears popped as he reappeared in a serene moonlit courtyard.

But first, I need to rid myself of this cursed blood and restore my cultivation base. Tracking down the Ashfallen Sect, even with the help of the pavilion, may take days, if not weeks, so I should recover until then— Wait, what's that?

A slab of black rock about the size of a person floated above his residence, and Dorian could feel spatial Qi surrounding it. Someone was floating it there with telekinesis. Dorian narrowed his eyes and saw the shadow of something moving on top of it.

"Who's there?" Dorian called out as he flexed his cultivation. "Show yourself."

The shadow paused before it poked its head over the edge of the floating rock. A large snake with golden eyes peered down at him curiously. Its scales seemed to shimmer in the moonlight as if they were doused in ink, and strange ancient runic engravings covered every inch of its body.

"Who are you?" Dorian asked in confusion. What would such a mythical-looking snake be doing floating over his family's residence? He stepped backward and almost tripped over something. *Huh, what is this? A tree root?* Glancing around, he noticed his residence had become overrun with black roots as if this place had been abandoned for years.

"Wait, where are all the maids? Why can't I feel the presence of anyone here? And the runic formations...they are all destroyed." Dorian glared at the floating snake. "Did you do this?"

The snake looked down at him with what could only be described as contempt as if he had bothered its evening somehow.

Did I anger another divine being? Dorian wondered.

"**Welcome home! You killed my Ents, destroyed my Bastion, and hurt my people,**" a thousand voices that had sounded amused before thundered in his mind. "**So I returned the favor. Everyone who held the Lunarshade name has been slaughtered, and your residence has been overtaken. Branch families fell, the maids were dragged off kicking and screaming, and every heir, whether young or old, was devoured. You alone remain as the sole survivor of your bloodline. Everything you have ever cared for is gone.**"

Dorian felt his heart sink as the reality of the cultivator's words set in. The residence could be replaced, and the maids were expendable, but his carefully nurtured Elders were missing, and branch families took time to raise. Generations—*centuries* of effort—gone in a single night. Spreading out his spiritual sense, he confirmed the cultivator's words. There were signs of a fight here, with far more lunar Qi than normal floating about alongside pockets of spatial Qi, likely from the opening and closing of rifts.

"How is this possible?" Dorian muttered. Where had it gone wrong?

"**Your selfishness was your own downfall,**" the voices mocked him. "**You summoned every Elder to your side, leaving the weaker ones with nothing but runic formations to defend them. All I had to do was break inside, and the rest is history—just like your bloodline is about to be.**"

Dorian ground his teeth in rage. "How can you utter such nonsense to my face? Does the title Phantom Moon's Heir mean nothing to you? I have dominated the realm for centuries, a title holder from the war era! Does my presence not shake your soul to its core—"

"**No, it does not. After experiencing multiple life cycles and fighting off cultivators from all the nine realms, someone like you is nothing but an annoyance that's in the way of my ascension.**"

Dorian clung to every word, and things began to fall into place.

"I knew it! You are the reincarnation of a divine being from the higher realms! As a title holder, I wouldn't lose to anyone in the Nascent Soul Realm in such a shameful way." Dorian weirdly felt relief. Even if he were to fall here, he would not curse the heavens in death. Losing to someone weaker would be shameful, but if a divine being wanted him dead? What was he, as a mere mortal in comparison stuck down here on the lowest realm of creation, supposed to do against that?

He controlled multiple affinities and was able to command divine beasts. My lunar Qi cannot suppress his blood or presence, and his words carry the wrath of wind Qi. Even his Qi reserves seem unfathomable, blanketing an entire city despite being far away. Such a cultivator should not exist, as they would have dominated the war era.

"To think the heavens have taken such offense to my exploits that they have sent one of their heralds to punish me." Dorian smiled wearily. "But if you think I will go without a fight, then you are sorely mistaken."

"Fight or not, the outcome will be the same," the chorus of voices declared. **"By sunrise, the Lunarshade bloodline will have ceased to exist."**

A sudden and familiar weight bore down on him. It was the technique used by the spirit tree that had prevented his passage through the moonlight earlier.

"Did you think I would try to run?" Dorian grinned at the snake, looking down at him as if he were a lesser being. One of the scales near its cheek had vanished, exposing its liquid ink body beneath.

"If you think this snake is enough to defeat me, then you are quite short-sighted for a divine being—" Dorian's eyes widened as the snake leaped into the air, and every single one of his scales flashed with golden light before being consumed.

Reality shuddered as Qi from heaven knew where gathered to form hundreds of techniques of varying affinities. The sky lit up with a myriad of colors. Blazing crimson flames, raging balls of clear blue water, howling gales filled with razor-sharp leaves... There were too many.

"What the fu—" Dorian raised his arms in terror as it felt like the combined wrath of reality slammed into him. His lunar Qi glowed as he greedily drew on both his Star Cores to try and resist the onslaught. Layers of lunar Qi he had spent countless nights interloping under the moonlight to acquire were purged in an instant, and he found himself thrown back.

He slammed through the wall of his residence's courtyard and groaned in pain. His arms were destroyed, reduced to bloodied messes of flesh and bone. His lunar Qi weakly flowed through the mess, trying to repair the damage.

"Ugh," Dorian groaned as he blinked away the dizziness. The once-serene courtyard was frozen over, on fire, and covered in water and leaves. Large gashes also scarred the floor, likely from spatial attacks.

The now-scaleless ink snake sneered at him before slithering away through a portal. The piece of rock it had been perched on unceremoniously crashed to the ground, cracking the ice.

Dorian looked up to the sky full of stars. *Is this the last time I will see this beautiful sight? There's no way they would just let me go, right?* A shadow loomed over him, and a spider of ashen silver and many red eyes looked down at him. *Ah, the reaper has somehow recovered and come for me.*

Its maw descended on him, and to his surprise, instead of turning him to ash, it picked him up as if he were a big bone and carried him across the courtyard. A rift rippled into existence, and Dorian groaned as his ears popped. The pressure changed again as he was taken through.

Thrown onto the ground, Dorian's face ate a mouthful of dirt and purple grass. Groaning again, he looked up and saw the greatest demonic tree he had ever seen. Its charcoal black trunk rose to the heavens, and its canopy of scarlet leaves blocked the night sky. The whole spirit tree blazed with wrathful spatial flames, and a godly pressure with a hint of divinity bore down on him.

The trunk began to crack down its length before slowly splitting open to reveal an eye that contained otherworldly insight as if gazing straight into his soul. It made the remnants of his infant soul flicker and his Star Core quake.

So this is the divine being behind my family's eradication. I have heard of the world tree but never a demonic spirit tree with divinity...

A bubble of pure light Qi suddenly expanded out from the tree, blinding Dorian and snuffing out the remnants of the lunar Qi he had protecting his ruined body.

"Any last words, Grand Elder Lunarshade, the Phantom Moon's Heir?"

Dorian had many questions, but the one burning in his mind was, "What are you?"

"*Just a tree doing his best to protect those he cares for,*" the divine being replied.

"Do you have a name?"

"*They call me Ashlock.*"

"Ashlock, eh?" Dorian grinned as he started going supernova. "Well, Ashlock, I always hated trees. They grow where they aren't wanted and dare to block the lunar goddess's loving light."

Lunar flames poured out his mouth as his Soul Core began to break down. If he was going to die here, he would take this spirit tree and everything it cared about with him by blowing up this entire region.

"*You cultivators are all the same,*" Ashlock said.

Dorian felt his breath leave his lungs as something impaled him. Looking down, he saw a void tendril buried deep in his chest. Strength left his body, and he fell on his face. The light realm burning him retracted, and he was back on the mountain peak. Turning his head to the side with all the strength he could muster, he came face to face with his son's corpse, staring at him with wide but soulless eyes.

"Albis…" Dorian wheezed out as soul flames leaked out his eyes and ears. His son's corpse did not answer his call.

In a pile behind his son were his Elders and all his family, though the many mortal maids he had employed were missing. Seeing his centuries of work laid out for him like this made him grimace.

The divine being had not lied. Dorian Lunarshade's bloodline really was wiped out in a single night before sunrise. Something he had thought impossible had been done so easily.

Black vines emerged from the ground below and wrapped around his body. The thorns impaled his skin, and he felt sticky fluid begin to dissolve him alive. The pain was unlike anything he had experienced in all his life as his body was dissolved and his soul broke down.

He howled as he was dying in both body and spirit.

"*Goodbye, house Lunarshade,*" Ashlock said, colder than the moon's dark side as a void tendril appeared between him and his son and rammed into his face. "*You will not be missed.*"

"Celestial Warden, Grand Elder Lunarshade has likely perished to the Ashfallen Sect."

Tiberius frowned at his Sage Advisor's words. "This is concerning on many levels. I intended to watch quietly from the sidelines and use Dorian to gauge this Ashfallen Sect's strength, but to think he would actually lose…"

"Are you not glad that old fool is dead, though?"

Tiberius eyed the newest of his disciples sitting across from him in the room. It seemed that the young man was still clueless about the world.

"Why would I be? Dorian Lunarshade was a good puppet and kept the city in order when I left on business. Now, if I leave the city, who will protect it from Vincent Nightrose if he chooses to attack?"

A wave of murmurs spread through the room.

"Then what should we do about this upstart sect, Celestial Warden?" one of the more senior Sage Advisors asked while stroking his white beard, which ran down to his waist.

Tiberius stood from his seat, the scraping of his chair on the floor drawing everyone's attention. "Dorian seemed convinced the leader of the Ashfallen Sect was the reincarnation of a divine being from the higher realms before he was dragged off by the spider. Angering such a person would be unwise. Increase the threat level of the Ashfallen Sect in our records to that of a divine and treat any members from that sect with the utmost hospitality."

"But Master—"

Tiberius flexed his cultivation, and everyone fell silent.

"This Ashfallen Sect is potentially powerful beyond measure. They wiped out an old family from the war era without their leader even stepping foot in the city. We will keep them at arm's length until we understand the extent of their capabilities. Do I make myself clear?"

"Is that possible, though?" a Sage Advisor sitting in the corner of the room spoke up. "They seemed antagonistic, and our bounty hunters interfered in their battle."

Tiberius hummed in thought. "I believe they only unleashed their wrath upon the Lunarshades when that girl called Stella got injured. She was wearing the outfit of a bounty hunter and seemed after Albis's bounty, so she is likely to understand we are not at fault for the acts of the bounty hunters."

"We should bump up that girl's priority level within the pavilion," the Sage Advisor mused.

"I agree." Tiberius nodded. "For now, we play nice until we figure out if we truly face a divine being or not."

A wave of agreeable murmurs spread through the room.

"Meeting adjourned," Tiberius announced, and the room was vacated. In the silence, he strode to a window and looked over Nightshade City.

"It would seem a new era may be upon us," Tiberius muttered, looking at the overgrown and destroyed Lunarshade residence on a far mountain peak. A family that had dominated the war era, commerce, and the Tainted Cloud Sect for centuries was wiped out in a single night.

All over a single girl's life being threatened. Tiberius frowned. Such actions were truly those of a divine being. *When Stella inevitably returns to hand in Albis's bounty, I should have a pleasant chat with her. After all, she is the one who cursed my dear Nox.*

50
LOOTING THE DEAD

Ashlock now understood why cultivators were so eager to go supernova upon dying. Or at least it made perfect sense for a Nascent Soul Realm cultivator like Grand Elder Lunarshade.

[+3143 Sc]

Despite the juicy notification confirming that he had devoured the Lunarshade Grand Elder's corpse in its entirety before he could go supernova and destroy everything, Ashlock found himself staring down at the Lunarshade Grand Elder who was standing over where his corpse had been, and only tattered bits of bloodstained white robe remained.

His body was ethereal, made entirely out of flickering moonlight, so faint that it looked like a sudden gust of wind would snuff it out. His appearance—a towering, fat, bald man with empty eyes—made it all the more creepy.

"So this is what an infant soul looks like. I can feel the strength of a Nascent Soul coming from it, but it's so weak that it's barely holding itself together," Ashlock mused as the ghostly man wordlessly floated over to Albis Lunarshade's corpse. "Trying to take over your own son's corpse? I'd expect nothing less from you…"

Ashlock used telekinesis and floated Albis's corpse away. The

Lunarshade Grand Elder's fading infant soul desperately went toward it like a cat chasing a laser pointer on a wall.

"No wonder Nascent Soul cultivators can usually live forever. If I hadn't used {Dimensional Overlap} to reduce his infant soul that he was using as spiritual armor to such a pathetic state, I would be facing another Nascent Soul cultivator right now. And that's on top of me being lucky that I can devour his body before going supernova."

Honestly, if not for his vast array of system abilities that let him do many impossible things, thinking he could defeat the Lunarshade Grand Elder would have been nothing but hubris.

"If not for Larry and his divine upgrade to become a herald of ash and ruler of decay, the Grand Elder would have never had a reason to use his infant soul as armor in the first place. Even void attacks struggled to penetrate his defenses."

"Tree, can you kill that creepy thing?" Stella begged as she sat beside Elaine and Diana on the bench under his canopy, looking deeply disturbed at the floating fat man.

"Sorry, I got lost in thought." Ashlock chuckled as he directed roots to surge up and devour the infant soul.

[+489 Sc]

"Almost five hundred credits for a ghost. Not bad." Ashlock brought up his system and checked on his progress in forming his Inner World and reaching the Nascent Soul Realm.

[Requirements to turn Chaos Nebula into an Inner World:
7143 / 10000 Sacrificial Credits
0 / 1 Absorbed Fire Star Cores
0 / 1 Absorbed Water Star Cores
0 / 1 Absorbed Earth Star Cores
1 / 1 Absorbed Wind Star Cores
0 / 1 Absorbed Metal Star Cores]

Ashlock had never seen so many credits. He had to admit there was a faint yearning to say fuck it and sign in for an insane draw, but he knew anything he could get from his system was unlikely to be as valuable as reaching Nascent Soul Realm.

Cultivation level aside, the system rewards were nothing to scoff at.

> [Rewards upon formation of the Inner World:
> You will ascend to the Nascent Soul Realm.
> The System will be upgraded with new features.
> {Transpiration of Heaven and Chaos [B]} will be upgraded.
> Your attacks will carry the weight of your Inner World behind them, and your rate of cultivation will increase the more you develop your Inner World.]

Ashlock was unsure how the system would upgrade. Still, his cultivation technique upgrading was easy enough to understand, as was the other reward. In the fight against the Grand Elder, he had already gotten a hint at what attacks carrying the weight of his inner world entailed with the wind Qi boosting the effectiveness of his {Abyssal Whispers} skill.

"That just leaves me sorting through these corpses and deciding what to do with them." Ashlock gazed over the mountain peak with his Demonic Eye. For some reason, seeing the piles of corpses under the moonlight really set in his victory in this war. He had won despite the odds.

But there had been losses on his side, which was evident in the overall mood on the mountain peak. No cheers or celebrations were occurring. Rather, everyone seemed exhausted as they sat in groups, leaning against his offspring surrounding the peak and having Sol tend to their wounds with whisps of healing light.

The Redclaws looked terrible, especially Amber, who hugged her knees and rocked back and forth. The Star Core prodigy of the Redclaw family was reduced to a terrified mess by the horrors of war. The scent of death on the peak likely wasn't helping, either, as her eyes were screwed shut, and sweat glistened on her forehead in the moonlight.

Elder Margret, who didn't look much better, tried to offer the young woman consoling words, but her voice shook too much for them to sound as reassuring as Ashlock assumed they were in her head.

Magnus Redclaw and Elder Mo sat together in silence on opposite sides of one of Ashlock's fire affinity offspring—their clothes were shredded in places, and the grim air of seasoned war veterans matched their serious expressions as they looked to the stars for comfort.

As none of them had been seriously injured, Ashlock sent the cultivators of Nightshade City back to the Duskwalker residence alongside all the mortal maids he had kidnapped from the Lunarshade residence before slaughtering all the cultivators there. He would let Evelyn decide what to do with them as he was sure a lot of the maids likely despised working for the Lunarshades, so killing them would have been too cruel of a fate.

"To think we actually won," Stella said, drawing Ashlock's attention as he shifted his Demonic Eye to look down at his adopted daughter. She was crouching beside Albis Lunarshade and pulling free his spatial rings. Despite Sol's healing energies, her every movement carried the weight of exhaustion. She huffed and sighed as she went about her work, looting the son of one of the strongest men in the realm.

"Yeah...we won," Ashlock replied, unsure of what else to say. With the battle over and the cold night breeze rustling his leaves, the desire to sleep and face this all tomorrow was hard to resist.

"Don't sleep yet, Tree. We have a lot to do." Stella wreathed her hand in spatial flames and, with a simple chop, decapitated Albis. Picking up the head, she dumped it into a cloth bag and stowed it away in her spatial ring in a flash of silver.

"I know! I'm not even sleepy," Ashlock replied, ignoring the effortless brutality Stella had just committed.

"Uh-huh, whatever. It may have gotten a little out of hand, but that's the bounty secured," Stella muttered with a weary smile. *"Ten thousand Yinxi Coins and one more step toward becoming a Crimson Tracker."*

"You're still planning to cash in that bounty?" Diana asked as she walked over from the bench. Her wings and claws were retracted, so her fangs were the only evidence of her being a demoness.

Stella shrugged. *"I don't have a choice. The Eternal Pursuit Pavilion is the only place to learn more about my father."*

"You don't have to be the one to go. If you give me Albis's head to cash in the bounty, I can ask for you."

"What difference does it make who goes?" Stella said as she held up the spatial ring she had ripped from Albis's cold finger to inspect

under the moonlight. *"We fought a battle on the pavilion's doorstep, and someone even sent bounty hunters to mess with the battle. Being covert is rather pointless now, don't you agree?"*

Diana hummed in agreement. *"You do have a point. Whether it be me, the Redclaws, or someone from the Duskwalker residence, it's obvious we are all working together since we took the same side against the Lunarshades."*

"Besides," Stella lowered the ring with a frown, *"I want to be the one to hear about my father, and advancing through the ranks in the pavilion is a nice side bonus."*

Diana covered her mouth as she suppressed a yawn. *"Yeah that makes sense. Heavens, I am exhausted. I can't remember the last time I fought until the bitter end like that."*

"What about our duel?" Stella raised a brow.

"Nah." Diana shook her head. *"Even though I lost myself, I still knew it was a duel in the back of my mind. Today...I was fighting for not only myself but for the Ashfallen Sect as well. There was so much on the line that anything less than my absolute best would not be enough."* Diana's shoulders sank. *"I used up so much Qi that I fear I will make little progress in the next Mystic Realm."*

Stella patted Diana on the shoulder. *"You and me both."* She leaned in closer, and her voice dropped to a whisper. *"But don't complain too loudly."*

"Why not?"

Stella winced. *"Did you see what happened to Kaida?"*

Diana's eyes closed with a sigh. *"Yeah...the poor guy looked like a wet noodle rather than a divine beast after using all his scales."*

Ashlock looked to the floor with his Demonic Eye in shame. Kaida was his ultimate trump card, and he didn't want to force his summon to expend all of his Qi in a single attack to help them win. It would take months for Kaida to regrow and inscribe his ink scales, and he doubted the Lindwyrm would be very eager to create heavenly contracts in the meantime.

Stella glanced around. *"Speaking of, where is Larry?"*

"I am here, Mistress." A cloud of silver ash descended from Ashlock's canopy and reformed into a spider. He was certainly less dense than before the battle, but the system's promise that he would

become an immortal being that could always reform so long as some ash remained turned out to be true.

Stella patted the giant ash spider on the head. *"You did a great job keeping the Grand Elder from killing us all during the battle. Thank you,"* she said, her small face turning to a frown. *"Actually, did we lose anyone?"*

"The Grand Elder destroyed Khaos and Zeus, but the Voidmind and Skyrend families are at war on our doorstep, so I can easily replace them. Same deal with the Lunarshade Ents that I raised, which were also wiped out," Ashlock said as his gaze drifted to a large mountain of wood of various colors ranging from red to black on the side of the mountain. **"Geb lost his head, and Titus lost his arms, but I should be able to repair them with time. That just leaves…"**

Stella followed his gaze, and her eyes widened. She teleported over to Douglas, who had dug a large hole in the stone and tried re-planting the splinters of Willow. Stella collapsed to her knees and placed an ear against Willow's bark as if listening for a heartbeat.

Despite the immense damage, Willow was still alive. It would take more than being split in half to kill a tree, and Ashlock had sacrificed his soul shard, which had resided in Willow, to take the brunt of the damage to try and keep him alive.

A potentially shortsighted move as the Bastion was utterly destroyed as the Bastion Core had crumbled to dust under the Lunarshade Grand Elder's foot, and soul damage was not something to take lightly. Still, so long as he slept under the nine moons, he would slowly regain what he lost, and he felt that it was a worthwhile sacrifice to keep one of his favorite trees around.

Yes, he played favorites with his children. Didn't every parent?

Stella sighed with relief. *"Whew, he's still alive but badly hurt."* She patted the bark with a serious expression. *"Don't worry, Willow. I will try to find a way to help you recover."*

"Yes, please do. I can't turn Willow back into a Bastion until he fully recovers." Ashlock had tried targeting Willow with his {Skyborne Bastion} skill, but it didn't recognize him as a qualified target in his current state. He should heal with nutrients and water over time, but there wasn't much else Ashlock could do for the tree besides supply Qi.

Stella stood up and put her hands on her hips as she surveyed the piles of corpses littering the mountain peak. Her usually bright blond hair had taken on a darker shade as it was mixed with dirt, blood, and sweat. Her casual white clothes she liked to wear had suffered a similar fate, with them barely working to maintain her dignity, much like the others who had returned from the battle.

Everyone needed a night's rest and a chance to freshen up.

"Stella, tell everyone to go and rest. I can deal with things here."

"Really?" Stella held up the silver ring she had looted. *"Because I am pretty sure you forgot to secure the spatial rings from the Lunarshade Grand Elder before you devoured him."*

"Erm…"

To be fair, the man had been about to go supernova and kill them all, so a shiny ring on his finger hadn't been his top priority.

"I know you want us all to leave you to this grand feast, but these people have spatial rings, jade masks, and artifact clothing we can take." Stella walked over to a nearby corpse and pulled off its cloak. Giving it a quick sniff and patting it down, she threw it over her shoulders to hide her tattered clothes and grinned. *"See? Free clothes!"*

Ashlock had to admit the scent of death was making him terribly hungry. He was also itching to reach Nascent Soul Realm and was super excited to see what would happen, but Stella was right. A lot of wealth was wrapping the corpses like pigs in blankets on a Christmas morning. It would be a terrible waste to devour *everything*.

"Okay, fine. But I want a portion of the loot to go to the Duskwalker, Frostveil, Mystshroud, and Blightbane families, as they contributed greatly to the battle. Especially Elysia and the Blightbane Grand Elder. The Redclaws should also naturally get a share."

Stella grumbled, *"I suppose it's only fair. But I will need some help. I don't want to be doing this alone until sunrise."*

"Don't worry. I can help with that." Douglas grinned as he tapped the stone crown on his head. *"A thousand helpers are at your command."*

Mudcloaks began to pour out of the Citadel beside them, wielding daggers and cheering.

"Loot!"

"Strip the humans!"

"Mwahaha!"

Ashlock did a double take at the one doing an evil laugh and saw a Mudcloak falling on his back after trying to wear one of the jade masks.

"Oh…" Stella blinked. *"I somehow forgot about these enthusiastic guys. Tell them to take everything and pile it up near Tree. I don't have enough Qi left to try and break open this many spatial rings, so Tree will have to do it."*

There was something deeply disturbing about a wave of knife-wielding midgets passing over the mountain and stripping the corpses of dozens of cultivators that had likely been prodigies or Elders of their various families to nothing but their birthday suits. It somehow felt even more disrespectful than killing them, and he was worried some of the corpses would reanimate merely out of terrible shame.

It didn't help that he had to shift through the piles with telekinesis and look deeply with his Demonic Eye at each corpse to find the ones with Star Cores he needed for his Inner World.

"Nope, nope, still nope—" Ashlock chucked the unneeded corpses into a "soon to be devoured for credits" pile, most of which were bounty hunters. "Ah! Here we go." Floating in the air like a rag doll was a silver-haired man.

[Absorb Metal Star Core for Inner World? If so, you will gain no Sacrificial Credits.]

"Yes. I should devour him before Ryker or Sebastian notice," Ashlock thought as vines erupted from the ground and cocooned the corpse. He hadn't seen another corpse with a metal core in the piles and wasn't sure if the strength of the chosen core would affect the strength of his Inner World, so he just went for it.

Stella casually walked past the corpse that was being dissolved, stretching her arms over her head and letting out a loud yawn. *"I'm going to go and take a bath and sleep. If you need me for anything, let me know, Tree."*

"I should have everything under control up here."

"Okay." Stella sleepily rubbed her eyes. *"You coming, Diana?"*

she asked the demoness after clicking her fingers to manifest a rift to the alchemy lab down below, which had a stream running through it.

Diana ran a hand through her now-long black hair, which was tinted blue—despite the battle, she had kept it silky smooth with her demonic mist. *"I can if you want? Though I don't really need a bath or anything."*

"Oh, right. Well, see you tomorrow, then." Stella vanished through the portal, which snapped close with a pop of air.

Diana shook her head with an amused smirk. *"I'll go check on Kaida."* Her wings spread out, and she flew over to the library, Ashlock's only remaining Bastion.

Meanwhile, Ashlock saw Douglas lead Elaine away from the terrible sight of the Mudcloaks looting the corpses. They held hands as they wandered down the mountain path off toward the illusion grove. Both were grinning and chatting about something under the moonlight.

"Magnus, you can take your family and return home, too," Ashlock told the remaining cultivators.

"Thank you, Patriarch." Magnus gave a deep bow. *"And congratulations on defeating a title holder from the war era. Such a feat will spread throughout the realm and make the Ashfallen Sect a feared name to all who hear it."*

"Right…" Ashlock suppressed a groan. He had almost forgotten how they had conducted a war right before the Eternal Pursuit Pavilion and *won*. There was no way their battle wouldn't become realm-wide knowledge by the morning.

"All the more reason to ascend to Nascent Soul Realm as soon as possible. The quiet days of remaining low-key are long over." Ashlock sighed as he watched the streaks of crimson soar through the sky toward White Stone Peak.

He was now all alone with a thousand Mudcloaks and piles of naked corpses.

"My life is really weird, isn't it?" Ashlock mused as he shifted through the corpses and found the others he needed while trying to avoid accidentally picking up a Mudcloak. Accepting the system prompts, he devoured them all and retreated into his soul to see how they affected his Chaos Nebula.

Metal Qi flowed down his roots and condensed into shards before joining the roaring ball of wind Qi that floated within his soul. Then came the fire, water, and earth Qi, which had been easy enough to gather as there were quite a few cultivators from the bounty hunters of each type. So that nothing went wrong, he picked out the ones with the strongest cultivation just in case the quality of the Qi mattered.

The swirling ball of wind and metal shards glowed red hot as the fire Qi was added, and then steam began to rise as the water flowed in. Finally, large slabs of rock that looked like continents drifted on the surface, kept in place by the steam and moved around by the wind.

"Wow…" Ashlock could feel the power emanating from this creation in his soul. It wasn't quite coherent like a world was and undoubtedly still deserved the name "Chaos Nebula," but he could see the shadows of how his Inner World would look once formed.

"Now I just need to gather the Sacrificial Credits necessary to complete the system's requirements." Ashlock returned to the mountain peak and spent the rest of the night indulging in a historical feast as he devoured many corpses. Only as the sun crested the horizon a while later did he get the notification he had been waiting for.

[Requirements to turn Chaos Nebula into an Inner World have been met!]
[10187 / 10000 Sacrificial Credits
1 / 1 Absorbed Fire Star Cores
1 / 1 Absorbed Water Star Cores
1 / 1 Absorbed Earth Star Cores
1 / 1 Absorbed Wind Star Cores
1 / 1 Absorbed Metal Star Cores]

[Do you wish to form your Inner World and begin the ascension process to Nascent Soul Realm?]

51
ROOTS OF THE WORLD

Ashlock didn't even have a chance to agree to begin his ascension before multiple system messages abruptly appeared.

[WARNING: Formation of Inner World and ascension to Nascent Soul Realm will shake the realm. The host is advised to take defensive measures as the process will take a week and there is a recovery time.]
[WARNING: Soul damage (32%?) detected. Formation of Inner World is ill-advised due to potential corruption.]
[WARNING: Qi reserves at low levels (27%?)]
[Generating solutions…]

Ashlock stared at the system message and let out a long sigh. As the sun crested the horizon and the gentle morning breeze rustled his canopy, he realized he was rushing things and calmed down.

His once-blazing Star Core was a flickering flame as his Qi flowed back into the root network to pay back the offspring he had drained, and his allies were off recovering. The mountain peak was desolate, covered in splatters of dried blood and dissolved human gunk, along with a few piles of corpses, including the Lunarshade Elders, with which he hadn't done anything yet.

Willow was still out of commission, and he was missing two of his strongest Ents. Meanwhile, Titus and Geb were slowly healing as he fed them Qi. Larry was in fighting condition, but Kaida was about as helpful in a fight as the Mudcloaks without his scales.

Ashlock realized that ascending now was almost suicidal. Even if the process took only minutes, there was no way he wouldn't earn the attention of the Blood Lotus Sect's Patriarch Vincent Nightrose, who was apparently strong enough to defend the Blood Lotus Sect until now by himself.

"If I started ascending and he showed up, that would be the end. But I can't hold my ascension off for long, as news of my existence is likely to reach the higher-ups of the Blood Lotus Sect within the next few days." Ashlock cursed his fate and hoped his system could generate some suitable solutions.

[Solutions found:
Activate the skill {Nocturnal Genesis} for three continuous days and nights. Result: Soul Damage reduced to acceptable levels.
Reduce Ethereal Root expansion toward the north and focus on growing down to meet the ley line. Result: Immense Qi regeneration from the ley line.]

Ashlock was surprised at how helpful his system was for once. It had even called him "host" earlier and seemed hellbent on ensuring his ascension went as smoothly as possible. Maybe it was really eager to upgrade?

"Mhm, three days and nights seems rather risky, too, but there's no helping it if the soul damage I incurred while saving Willow will corrupt my Inner World," Ashlock mused. "Meanwhile, reducing my expansion toward the spiritual spring to hit the ley line earlier seems like a good idea. That leaves the problem of defending myself for the next few days and during my ascension."

Ashlock's spiritual gaze drifted to the Lunarshade Elder corpses. Having been stripped of their spotless white robes, which had exuded arrogance and reduced to nothing but a pile of hairless men and women with empty eyes, they were an unsettling sight, to say the least.

"I suppose I could make them into lunar affinity Star Core Ents to guard me during the nights." Ashlock hummed in thought as he floated the corpses with telekinesis and began to line them up. "Actually, now that I think about it, shouldn't I eat some corpses before my ascension to maximize the number of credits I get from them? I will get a few hundred credits for each of these corpses, but after reaching Nascent Soul Realm, I might only get a hundred at most."

After some debating, Ashlock decided to turn four corpses into Ents and devour the rest for credits alongside any other bounty hunter corpses he had lying around. He could have turned them into Ents, but any Star Core–level threat shouldn't be able to get through his sect members once they had recovered, and no number of Star Core Ents would be able to defeat Vincent Nightrose if he showed up.

Idletree Daily Sign-In System
Day: 3606
Daily Credit: 43
Sacrifice Credit: 13743
[Sign in?]

Having finished his hearty breakfast, Ashlock stared at a very big number.

"You know they say 'what is war good for,' and it turns out the answer is a shit load of sacrificial credits." Ashlock whistled in awe. "Though I do wonder if the system is trying to get me killed. It rewards me for killing things that are stronger than me... Wait, is that so I am incentivized to keep my sect members stronger than me?"

Ashlock grew more suspicious of his system with every passing day. He was sure the dreams of the past world tree or perhaps the nine moons would one day lead to answers regarding its origin, but for now, he could only trust and rely on it to help him survive.

While lost in thought, four explosions of death Qi washed over the deserted mountain peak as the final four Lunarshade corpses rose to the sky as twisted abominations of white wood. They all had a similar appearance to the other Lunarshade Ents he had raised, except they had functioning legs instead of needing to use roots to shift around. Rivaling Titus's size at twenty meters each, the white wood Ents' empty eye sockets ignited with white flames, and the black flowers running down their backs glowed with power.

"**Protect me,**" Ashlock instructed his newly made Ents, and the monsters shook the peak as they trudged to their positions. Feeling a little safer being surrounded by Star Core Ents, Ashlock then spoke to

Quill, whose job was to handle the defenses of Red Vine Peak from the ink affinity Bastion.

"**Quill, I will be sleeping for three days and nights. If anything bad happens, shock me awake with as much Qi as you can muster. Otherwise, I leave the defense of the peak in your capable branches.**"

The tree wrote, 'Okay, Dad,' in ink on its bark.

Hoping everything would be fine, Ashlock returned to his trunk.

"Are you going to be sleeping?" Stella asked, appearing from thin air on her bench beneath his canopy.

"**Yes...how did you know?**"

"My brother told me."

"**Brother?**"

"Yep." Stella gestured to the library. *"Quill told me."*

"**How did he even... You know what? Never mind. Yes, I will be asleep. Look after the peak in my absence, okay?**"

Stella gave him a cheeky salute and smile. *"I'd do it even if you didn't ask."*

"**That's why I didn't bother to inform you.**" Ashlock chuckled as he brought up the system's suggestions to accept them. "**Good night.**"

"Night? It's morning, Tree. But have a pleasant sleep! You earned it." Stella grinned and patted his bark—though, despite her upbeat mood, there was concern in her eyes.

Ashlock hadn't told her the reason he needed to sleep for so long, but historically, he only slept like this when he was severely injured and needed to heal quickly. So her unsaid concern made sense.

"**Thank you, Stella, and don't worry. I will recover soon,**" Ashlock said as the world flickered and he was forcefully dragged into the dreamscape. As usual, the nine moons dominated the sky, and he felt their healing energies caress his fractured soul.

Before succumbing to sleep, he traversed the dreamscape and found Nox in a field of jasmine flowers.

"**We won. The Lunarshades are no more, and your sister is finally free.**"

Looking around in confusion, the shadow dryad under Nox's canopy glanced toward Red Vine Peak. *"That's a relief."* The dryad cupped her hands before her chest and seemed to say a silent prayer.

"Evelyn is finally free from the life I forced on her. That makes me happy."

"I'm sure you will meet her soon enough."

"I hope so," Nox agreed, and Ashlock felt his consciousness drift off to sleep.

[Time remaining: 00:00]

Ashlock jolted awake to a system notification. His body felt... refreshed. His Star Core was blazing like a godly furnace and glowing with divine energy. Just like that, he had fallen asleep, and three days had passed.

**Idletree Daily Sign-In System
Day: 3609
Daily Credit: 46
Sacrifice Credit: 13743
[Sign in?]**

The temptation to sign in was indeed tremendous, but he resisted.

"System, what is my soul damage now?" Ashlock asked in the darkness of his mind. He had already noticed that many memories had returned, and it was honestly terrifying how he felt no different despite missing a third of what made him...him.

[Soul Damage: 0%]

"That's a relief." Ashlock sighed as he cast his spiritual gaze beyond his trunk to see if his mountain had been destroyed during his slumber. To his pleasant surprise, it was almost as he had left it, except the blood stains had been cleaned up, and there were people.

As if feeling his attention, Stella glanced over her shoulder. *"Oh, Tree! You're awake."*

"I am," Ashlock replied. **"What are you two up to?"**

Beside Stella was a blob of green hair with a cute white flower nestled behind her ear. It was Stella's beloved disciple, Jasmine. The little girl had her hands on Willow's trunk, and her eyes were closed as Qi wreathed her hands.

Stella grinned. *"I am teaching Jasmine how to speak to a tree."*

"You can teach such a thing? I thought you could speak to trees because of your bloodline?"

Stella shrugged. *"Who knows? I thought that because Jasmine has nature affinity, she might be able to talk to Willow and even help him heal with her Qi."*

"I see. And how are the others?"

"Everyone has recovered by now. Though I heard Amber is still rather shaken by the whole thing, and Kaida has retreated into his ink lake—refusing to see anyone despite Diana's best efforts."

"I see the scars of war continue to haunt us despite our victory." Ashlock sighed. "And what about Albis's bounty? Have you handed it in yet?"

Stella shook her head. *"No, I was waiting until you awakened before doing something likely to cause issues."*

"Well, you will need to wait a little longer."

"Why?" Stella tilted her head in confusion. *"Are you still hurt?"*

"Quite the opposite, actually. I am finally ready to begin my ascension to Nascent Soul Realm, and we don't have much time. News of our battle with the Lunarshades has likely spread and soon—"

Ashlock was cut off as a notification flashed in his mind, and he felt a tingling sensation rise from below.

[Assimilating with ley line…]

"Go gather everyone quickly," Ashlock said before his vision shifted. The rock and dirt blurred as he plummeted through the realm, eventually arriving at the tips of his deepest roots. There, he found something he hadn't been expecting.

At first, he thought it was a massive layer of gold glowing with untamed Qi that rushed across its surface, but as he looked closer, he saw the texture and indents in the gold were rather familiar.

"Is that a…root? A giant golden root?" Ashlock muttered in awe as he saw his own roots, which were thick enough to allow people to use them as tunnels, look like strands of mycelium compared to this tree root, which had to be many miles thick.

"Hold on, the Celestial Empire *happens* to be built on the intersection of the three largest ley lines known to the cultivators. I thought it was a coincidence, but what if those three giant ley lines aren't the world's spiritual veins but rather the world tree's roots?"

Ashlock was stunned as many things began to fall into place. The Celestial Empire wasn't "lucky" that the Beast Tides rarely hit them. The World Tree decided the path the beasts took as it casually led the monsters around by their noses with its own Qi.

His roots met with the rushing river of untamed Qi that wreathed the seemingly endless surface of the golden root, and Ashlock saw arcs of Qi manifest between their roots like two live wires getting too close.

"System, are you sure this is a good idea?" Ashlock asked with concern but received no response except for a status report.

[Ley line assimilation at 42%]

Qi rushed up his roots, and moments later, he felt his Star Core being flooded. Unable to convert all this untamed Qi into spatial Qi, he redirected it into his root network toward his forests of trees spread throughout the realm. Red Vine Peak also began to undergo changes as whisps of untamed Qi leaked from gaps in the rock.

Ashlock panicked. He had no idea if this was a good thing or not. On the one hand, if he didn't link up with a ley line, his progress through the stages of the Nascent Soul Realm would take far too long, but surely leaching Qi from the World Tree was a bad idea.

"Maybe she will forgive me because I raised her daughter…" Ashlock chuckled nervously. Seeing a single root that was likely a hundred miles wide, so deep underground and overflowing with enough Qi that a light touch was enough to make his Star Core become overwhelmed, really hammered home the difference between himself and a Monarch Realm existence that stood at the pinnacle of this realm.

[Ley line assimilation at 74%]

He was nothing but a peak Star Core tree atop a mountain out in the wilderness, while the World Tree was the strongest being in the realm.

"What is happening?!?" Stella shouted from below his canopy.

Rifts she had created surrounded her, and people of the Ashfallen Sect poured through. Some were even wielding their swords or resting their hands on their pommels as they glanced around nervously.

"It would appear I am meeting your mother sooner than I had hoped," Ashlock replied. "I dug my roots down far enough to hit the ley line, and it turns out to likely be a root of the World Tree."

Stella's eyes widened as she looked to the floor. *"Mom is down there?"*

[Ley line assimilation at 100%]

Ashlock went to look and saw his ethereal roots had phased through the world tree's bark and dipped into the rivers of golden sap that flowed through the roots alongside divine Qi.

"This really is the World Tree… It's just like in those dreams," Ashlock muttered and slowly retracted his view, but he dared not take any of the divine aura or golden sap. The last thing he wanted was to earn the ire of a realm-spanning entity. "Let's just leave real slow. Nothing to see here, just a little shrub trying to siphon a smidge of Qi."

Returning to the surface, Ashlock waited a moment to see if there were any signs of the World Tree noticing.

"It seems I am in the clear—"

[A Monarch Realm entity has taken notice of you.]

52
A MONARCH'S AGONY

Ashlock felt a tingling sensation like pins and needles rising up through his roots, enveloping his entire land-spanning body. If the cries of concern echoing through the root network were anything to go by, his offspring suffered a similar fate.

"Is this what it feels like to earn the attention of the World Tree?" Ashlock shuddered, causing his bark to creak and his leaves to rustle violently as his Star Core quivered. It was an almost impossible sensation to describe, and it was made all the more concerning because he couldn't exactly flee from it.

"Agh!" Ashlock groaned as an incredibly low rumbling sound started reverberating through his consciousness, threatening to tear his very sense of being apart.

[Skill {Basic Mental Resistance [F]} Learned!]

A system notification he hadn't seen in a very long time barely managed to distract him from the rumbling getting worse.

[Upgraded {Basic Mental Resistance [F]} -> {Mental Resistance [E]}]

If his consciousness had been a serene lake before, it was now a choppy ocean as the low rumbling squeezed and pulled on his mind.

[Upgraded {Mental Resistance [E]} -> {Greater Mental Resistance [D]}]

The terrible pain of his consciousness being messed with subsided slightly, but it was not enough to stop him from screaming in terror.

[Upgraded {Greater Mental Resistance [D]} -> {Superior Mental Resistance [C]}]

Ashlock could feel his system's desperation to keep him alive as the system notifications practically overlaid one another, and his new mental resistance skill rapidly leveled up.

[Upgraded {Superior Mental Resistance [C]} -> {Mental Protection [B]}]

Like a shield, a bubble manifested around his consciousness, protecting him from the terrible rumbling. The tingling sensation and terror throughout his root network was still there, but at least he could think straight for a moment.

"Tree? Are you okay?" He could hear Stella's voice as she drummed her balled fists on his bark.

"No," Ashlock answered honestly. If not for the system's timely assistance and willingness to help him in self-preservation, he wouldn't have lasted another minute. He was not okay. That had been frightening, and he had no idea how long his new Mental Protection skill would hold out.

"What happened? Did Mom attack you?"

It took Ashlock a moment to realize Stella was talking about the World Tree when she spoke about her mom. He was still out of it and trying to pull himself together.

"Yeah...something like that. I'm not even sure if it was an attack, but I definitely earned her attention."

Stella turned around and sat with her back pressed against his bark. Closing her eyes, she controlled her breathing and rested her head.

Everyone watched in silence, including the Redclaws and Jasmine, as they let the Princess of Ashfallen figure out the best thing to do. Meanwhile, Ashlock poured as much Qi as possible into his mental defenses. Worst case, he would pull his roots back toward the surface and accept that he couldn't tap into the untamed Qi of the ley line.

A while passed until Stella eventually frowned and opened her eyes.

"**What is it?**" Ashlock asked.

"She's in pain."

"**Pain?**" Ashlock asked in confusion. "**Am I causing her pain?**"

Stella shook her head. *"I don't think so, as I can't see how you could cause such deep pain to such a powerful being."*

Ashlock thought back to his dreams and could still recall the phantom pain he experienced as the past World Trees, as he was harvested alive by those cultivators for eons.

"The Celestial Empire…" Ashlock mused to himself. "What if it's not a safe haven for the World Tree but rather a prison? We thought she was the protector of the Celestial Empire and was the reason the city had stood the test of time, unlike the demonic sects that had to keep moving. Once I learned that the World Tree's roots are the ley lines, I thought she was maliciously controlling the monsters to cause beast tides. But what if she's trying to create a beast tide big enough to free herself from the Celestial Empire by wiping it out instead?"

Stella looked to the floor, and she balled her fists. Feeling the World Tree's pain seemed to be a lot for her.

Ashlock slowly lowered his mental protection and listened more closely to the rumbling noise, which was reminiscent of a blue whale calling out through the ocean, just at the strength of a dying god. Sure enough, it didn't feel directed at him. It was just an overwhelming wave of a single emotion: agony.

"**You poor thing.**" Ashlock spoke through his roots with raw emotions, the same way he communicated with his offspring. Senior Lee had mentioned that the World Tree was capable of rudimentary conversation through emotions, but she seemed to ignore him as the waves of agony continued. "**Can you hear me? I can help you…**"

Ashlock tried his best to get a response, but nothing he said seemed to reach the miserable tree. Whatever pain she was suffering was simply too unbearable to even give him a sliver of her attention.

"Mom needs our help, Tree," Stella said into her knees as she rocked back and forth on one of his exposed roots. She looked up at his

canopy with tears in the corners of her eyes. *"She's suffering. Isn't there anything we can do?"*

Ashlock glanced at everyone on the mountain peak with his Demonic Eye, and nobody avoided his gaze. They were all members of Ashfallen—dependable allies that he had gathered in fear of suffering the fate of the World Tree from those terrible nightmares. Meanwhile, the World Tree was likely all alone, fated for a lifetime of suffering.

"Sorry, I seem to be missing something," Elder Margret said. *"Stella's mother is suffering somewhere?"*

Stella hesitantly nodded. *"Something like that...though I'm not totally sure if she is my mom."* Stella then whispered into Ashlock's mind, *"But even if she isn't my mom, feeling a tree in such pain makes me want to scream. Trees are such gentle and caring beings. To inflict misery to that level on one is something I can't understand."*

"There is one thing we can do," Ashlock said to all present, his voice echoing in their minds much like the World Trees did in his own. **"We have to get stronger to save her. That is the only way."**

Stella's face fell. *"We have to get stronger... Mom is in pain right now—she doesn't have time to wait for us. Is that really the only option?"*

"Always has been," Magnus Redclaw said. *"Since the day the first mortal gained the favor of the heavens and wielded Qi, it's been a race to the top. To the mortals, we are gods, and to the strong, we are ants."*

"The race to the top is exhausting, and I am sick of it," Stella snapped back and stood. Her hands trembled, and tears flowed down her cheeks. *"All my life, I have done nothing but endlessly pursue power, yet there seems to always be a higher mountain—a greater peak to reach. I am never enough and always on the back foot. When someone is suffering...I can't save them. I am a pathetic weakling when it matters."*

Magnus closed his eyes and let out a sigh. An aura of someone who had seen too many things and experienced all there was to experience swirled around him. *"To come to such a realization at such a young age,"* Magnus slowly opened his eyes, and he seemed genuinely sad for Stella, *"to realize it will **never** be enough. Not until the heavens fall, and you alone stand at the peak. This is a realization all cultivators reach at some point along their immortal journey. We call it the 'realization of the endless path,' and it's where many falter and become* *consumed by their heart demons. To finally stop charging endlessly ahead in the pursuit of power and stop to look up at the supposed destination...the realization of the journey ahead crushes the spirit of most."*

"I don't blame them." Stella planted a weak fist into Ashlock's bark and ranted at the floor. *"If even my mother, a Monarch Realm being at the peak of creation, has to endure so much suffering, is there any point in getting stronger!?"*

"All you can do is your best and strive to improve," Magnus replied seriously.

Stella ground her teeth. *"Is that really enough? Will doing my best save my mom from this overwhelming misery?"*

Ashlock noticed that Stella seemed overwhelmed because she was putting too big a task on her shoulders. Until now, they had mostly strived to simply survive day to day, fighting off local threats. But now? Stella wanted to help a Monarch Realm being, which was at the center of the strongest empire in the realm. Such a feat was impossible for their current selves...

Before Ashlock could console Stella, Magnus continued his lecture.

"Strength, no matter how much you wield, is pointless if you stagnate. The Lunarshade Grand Elder is a good example. Since the War Era, his cultivation hadn't improved much as he lost motivation and fell into a life ruled by sin. Now he's dead, despite having been one of the 'strongest' people that walked this realm." Magnus grinned. *"Meanwhile, here we all stand, alive, thanks to the Immortal's guidance in helping us improve. Don't give up. We can save your mother. It will just take time."*

Ashlock agreed with Magnus's words and was unsurprised to learn of cultivators realizing that the path to immortality was essentially a fruitless endeavor and deciding to give up and enjoy living out their hundreds if not thousands of years of life instead of spending it all sitting in a cave alone and meditating on the heavens' whispers for decades at a time.

"I can cheat because trees are quite well suited for cultivation. But these humans must conquer their heart demons and sit silently for *decades* in closed-door meditation. That's enough to drive even the hardest-headed cultivators insane once they learn it never ends. A son of Heaven will always stand upon a higher peak that can smite them down and eradicate their centuries of efforts and sacrifice in an instant."

The question was would they falter at the bottom of the cliff when faced with the impossible climb to their goal or defy the heavens and crawl their way up one root or foot at a time?

Ashlock had his answer, and it seemed Stella also had hers.

"Fine, let's do it." Stella patted his trunk and wiped her tears with her other arm. *"Let's all get stronger and kill all the bastards hurting Mom. One step at a time, no matter how many years it takes."*

Ashlock knew his heart would be aching if he had one right now. Stella, having grown up without any warmth from a family, finally got to "talk" to her supposed mom, and all she learned was that she was in intense agony.

"If we are to save her, as the Patriarch of this sect, allow me to lead the charge by ascending to Nascent Soul Realm. The coming days won't be easy. The Blood Lotus Sect is unlikely to let me ascend without interference, and the Eternal Pursuit Pavilion has its eyes on us. Are you all ready to stand with me and fight?"

Ashlock wasn't sure why, but the air seemed to subtly glow with divine light at his words. His sect members all exchanged a quick glance.

"If I said no, I fear Elder Mo would kill me in my sleep." Magnus chuckled as he stepped forward and promptly dropped to one knee. His Elders followed suit a step behind as they fell in line. *"Jokes aside, the Redclaws were founded on war and will stand with you until death. In fact, even in death, feel free to use our corpses to create Ents so we may serve you once more."*

A rather grim declaration coming from a living person's mouth, but Ashlock could see the fierce loyalty blazing in their eyes. This type of loyalty couldn't be bought or bullied out of someone with fear. It was genuine and wrathful.

Diana stepped forward with a fang-filled smile. "You know our answer." She gestured to Douglas and Elaine, who were lovingly holding hands to the side. A Mudcloak awkwardly stood under their clasped hands, giving an enthusiastic wave when pointed at.

"Then I will do two last gestures before I initiate my ascension. Since we will attract Heaven's wrath anyway, now is a good time to

make Bastions." Ashlock selected Willow and was glad the system interface recognized him as an offspring after Jasmine's efforts and three days under the nine moons in the dreamscape.

[Do you wish to activate the Skyborne Bastion? The cost is 1000 sacrificial credits and the required materials to form a Bastion Core.]

"Yes," Ashlock told his system. Clouds began to gather in the sky, and thunder roared over the mountain peak as the process started. Ignoring the system messages notifying him of Heaven's incoming wrath due to Willow's damaged cultivation, his vision blurred as he went to make a brand new Bastion.

Finding Nox in her usual field of white flowers, she was looking up at the gathering storm with interest.

"Nox, after careful consideration and observation of your change of heart and turning over a new leaf, you have been chosen as the next one to join the noble ranks of the Bastions, the current highest honor for any tree under the Ashfallen Sect. Do you accept this new role as the guardian and Bastion of Ashfallen City?"

The shadow dryad cupped her hands and respectfully bowed toward Red Vine Peak. *"It would be an honor. I always wanted to be a flying tree."*

"You...did?"

"Honestly? No. But a floating shadow tree emerging from the darkness sounds rather ominous, doesn't it? Better than sitting here all day, at least! Nobody even visits me..."

Ashlock wanted to point out that a scary shadow lady hanging around an already offputting-looking tree wouldn't attract curious visitors, but he refrained. He was glad as long as Nox was happy with becoming a floating island outfitted with shields and weapons to protect him while he ascended.

[Do you wish to activate the Skyborne Bastion? The cost is 1000 sacrificial credits and the required materials to form a Bastion Core.]

"Yes, I do," Ashlock told the system.

Another thousand credits vanished from his vision as he saw something begin to eat away at the rock below Nox.

[Forming Bastion Core…]
[Bastion's operator has been successfully designated as {Nox Duskwalker}]
[Bastion's affinity type set to Onyx (Shadow)]

Waves of dark power rippled out across the mountain around Nox as she began her transformation. The storm overhead suddenly expanded outward to the horizon and went from gray to an obsidian black. Thunder roared so loud that it shook every tree on the mountain, and the sky flashed as lightning gathered.

[Bastion {Nox Duskwalker}'s cultivation is unstable…initiating tribulation.]

An ungodly amount of lightning descended upon Nox, but she seemed to relish the onslaught as liquid shadow wreathed her bark, and she greedily absorbed the heavenly punishment.

"Looks like I will have a Nascent Soul Bastion real soon," Ashlock mused as he returned to Red Vine Peak to join the "fun." Who didn't love getting struck by lightning?

Once again, and hopefully for the last time, he pulled up his system to begin his ascension.

[Requirements to turn Chaos Nebula into an Inner World have been met!]
[11743 / 10000 Sacrificial Credits
1 / 1 Absorbed Fire Star Cores
1 / 1 Absorbed Water Star Cores
1 / 1 Absorbed Earth Star Cores
1 / 1 Absorbed Wind Star Cores
1 / 1 Absorbed Metal Star Cores]
[Do you wish to form your Inner World and begin the ascension process to Nascent Soul Realm?]

"Yes."

With that simple word, reality began to shake as his soul slowly rose out of his trunk, past his branches and canopy, to float as a literal sun of spatial Qi above him.

|Expanding Inner World...|

"Huh?" Ashlock said as his Star Core floating overhead suddenly began to balloon in size until it completely dwarfed the entire mountain range, illuminating everything in a lilac hue under the dark, cloudy sky. Through the lilac haze of his soul, he could see the Chaos Nebula being crushed under immense Qi pressure from a mixture of random Qis into an actual planet.

"That's ridiculous!" Magnus said over the roaring thunder as he pointed to the sky, his finger trembling. *"A Star Core of such size and to have the ego to rip it out and challenge the very heavens with nothing but your soul is...is...the act of a true immortal unfazed by Heaven's puny might!"*

Ashlock didn't want to admit this was the system's doing, as he had no idea how to handle an ascension.

|Beginning ascension to Nascent Soul Realm...|

The heavens answered his challenge by tearing the sky apart, and thousands of lightning bolts of every color and Qi imaginable struck his Star Core and, in turn, his forming Inner World. Some lightning bolts also went and targeted his offspring.

"You dare strike my children?" Ashlock now realized why his system had wanted him to link up with the ley line. He pulled deeply on as much Qi as possible and blanketed every one of his offspring in his Qi to protect them. He wouldn't let them become collateral damage like the mortals of Slymere had.

|Ascension to Nascent Soul Realm at 1% (estimated time of tribulation: 7 days)...|

Ashlock coated himself in his {Lightning Qi Barrier [A]} and hunkered down for the long haul. His past ascension to Star Core had been quick, but it seemed the inclusion of the Inner World and becoming a demi-divine being had upped the difficulty of the tribulation to hell level.

"I just hope the Blood Lotus Sect stays quiet—"

Vincent Nightrose's eyes snapped open.

"Too soon," he muttered as he stared at the stone ceiling. He could still smell and feel the vicious blood of the bloodline holder he was bathing in. There was still plenty to absorb before the ritual was complete, and he added their bloodline to his arsenal.

Vincent's eyes narrowed. "Why am I awake?"

Something felt wrong. *Terribly wrong.*

Raising his pale hand that dripped with blood, he gripped the edge of the stone coffin he was using to bathe in blood and hauled his naked body out. His skin was sunken, gripping his bones like a layer of paint, and his claw-like toenails scraped against the stone floor as he walked.

He sniffed the air, uninterested in the musky scent of death as he crushed the skull of the person's blood he had been bathing in. Instead, he used his bloodline-hunting ability and picked up on a *delectable* distant smell.

"Ripe already?" Vincent smirked as he licked the blood and dirt from between his spindly fingers with his pointed tongue but then paused. Something else was tainting the smell—something he hated.

A powerful infant soul was being born. Someone was ascending to Nascent Soul Realm on *his land.*

"Oh, this won't do at all." Vincent shuffled toward the door of his cultivation chamber.

It would seem someone had forgotten who ruled this place.

The story will continue in Reborn as a Demonic Tree 5!

THANK YOU FOR READING REBORN AS A DEMONIC TREE 4

We hope you enjoyed it as much as we enjoyed bringing it to you. We just wanted to take a moment to encourage you to review the book. Follow this link: Reborn as a Demonic Tree 4 to be directed to the book's Amazon product page to leave your review.

Every review helps further the author's reach and, ultimately, helps them continue writing fantastic books for us all to enjoy.

Also in series:

Also in series:
Reborn as a Demonic Tree
Reborn as a Demonic Tree 2
Reborn as a Demonic Tree 3
Reborn as a Demonic Tree 4
Reborn as a Demonic Tree 5

Check out the entire series here! (Tap or scan)

Want to discuss our books with other readers and even the authors? Join our Discord server today and be a part of the Aethon community.

Facebook | Instagram | Twitter | Website

You can also join our non-spam mailing list by visiting www.subscribepage.com/AethonReadersGroup and never miss out on future releases. You'll also receive three full books completely Free as our thanks to you.

Looking for more great LitRPG?

Check out our new releases!

He thought he was ready for the apocalypse. Then it happened... A Secret Service operative and dedicated survivalist, Special Agent Del Roosevelt had a plan for every world-ending scenario, and regularly trained for them all. But all that training, all those rations, all that prepping? Useless for the apocalypse that actually played out. Del wakes up half buried in a giant trash pile, missing his thumbs. And, um, covered in red fur. He's stuck in a world of fuzzy monsters, senseless violence, and cult-like crusaders. He knows he's got to get to the top of the tower he's in to find the wizard who presumably turned him into a living toy. Will the help of an academic rat and an exiled little dinosaur get him there? Doubtful. But in all his failing, Del starts to realize how ridiculous his life as a prepper actually was. After all, what's the point in surviving if you have no one to live for? **Master of Puppets is the first book in an all-new LitRPG Adventure by Eric Ugland, bestselling author of The Good Guys. Strap in for an immersive adventure full of quests, powerful magic, tower climbing, leveling up, wise-cracking landlords, and murderous cookies.**

Get Master of Puppets Now!

Order Now!

(Tap or Scan)

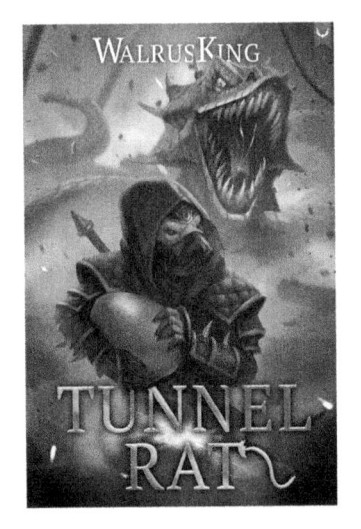

The secrets buried below can make him a Hero above... if he can find them.
Milo lives in a steel cave within a man-made mountain of steel and concrete. He spends his days repairing the machinery that keeps the habitat livable and tinkering with the prosthetics that help his twisted body move about through the small tunnels and air shafts that are his world. He's as much a piece of discarded machinery as the equipment he keeps running. An escaped lab experiment living in a hole. Given a chance at being someone different, will he become a hero and live in the sunlight? The light beckons, but there are secrets buried in the ground. Ancient mysteries left by races that delved deep and stayed below. Maybe only a tunnel rat can discover them... **Don't miss the start of this unique spin on LitRPG featuring an unusual MC you can't help but root for. Featuring plenty of humor, action, thievery, ninja abilities, a detailed world and System, science skills, magic tinkering, item invention, and more originality than you can shake a rat tail at!*

Get Tunnel Rat Now!

Order Now!

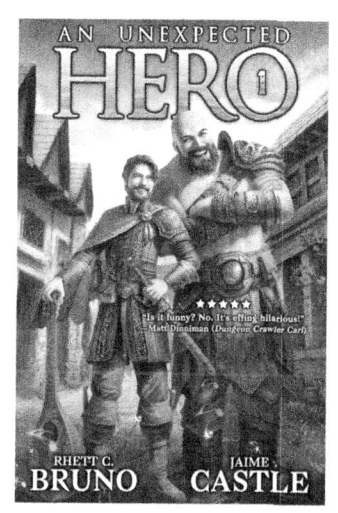

(Tap or Scan)

A magical new world. An ancient power. A chance to be a Hero. Danny Kendrick was a down-on-his luck performer who always struggled to find his place. He certainly never wanted to be a hero. He just hoped to earn a living doing what he loved. That all changes when he pisses off the wrong guy and gets transported to another world. Stuck in a fantasy realm straight out of a Renaissance Fair, Danny quickly discovers that there's more to life. Like magic, axe-wielding brutes, super hot elf assassins, and a talking screen that won't leave him alone. He'll need to adapt fast, turn on the charm, and get stronger if he hopes to survive this dangerous new world. But he has a knack for trouble. Gifted what seems like an innocent ancient lute after making a questionable deal with a Hag, Danny becomes the target of mysterious factions who seek to claim its power. It's up to him, Screenie, and his new barbaric friend, Curr, to uncover the truth and become the heroes nobody knew they needed. And maybe, just maybe, Danny will finally find a place where he belongs. **Don't miss the start of this isekai LitRPG Adventure filled with epic fantasy action, unforgettable characters, loveable companions, unlikely heroes, a detailed System, power progression, and plenty of laughs.** *From the minds of USA Today bestselling and Award-winning duo Rhett C Bruno & Jaime Castle,* An Expected Hero *is perfect for fans of* Dungeon Crawler Carl, Kings of the Wyld, *and* This Trilogy is Broken!

Get An Unexpected Hero now!

For all our LitRPG books, visit our website.

FROM THE AUTHOR

Thank you so much for reading *Reborn as a Demonic Tree*.
Reviews are greatly appreciated and make the word gods happy! We are only just getting started on a very long series, so spreading the word helps a lot.
If you wish to read ahead of official publication you can check out:
https://www.patreon.com/xkarnation

Otherwise, don't forget to pre-order Book 4!